Alex Adams was born in Auckland, New Zealand. She lived in Greece and Australia before settling in Portland, Oregon. In between moving continents, Alex received a BA from The University of New England in Armidale. Aside from reading and writing, Alex's favourite things include cooking, eating and running.

ALEX ADAMS

WHITE HORSE

**SIMON &
SCHUSTER**

London · New York · Sydney · Toronto · New Delhi

A CBS COMPANY

First published in Great Britain by Simon & Schuster UK Ltd, 2012
A CBS COMPANY
This paperback edition published in 2013.

1 3 5 7 9 10 8 6 4 2

Simon & Schuster UK Ltd
1st Floor
222 Gray's Inn Road
London WC1X 8HB

www.simonandschuster.co.uk

Simon & Schuster Australia, Sydney
Simon & Schuster India, New Delhi

A CIP catalogue record for this book is available from the British Library

PBB ISBN: 978-0-85720-997-9
EBOOK ISBN: 978-0-85720-998-6

Typeset by Hewer Text UK Ltd, Edinburgh
Printed and bound in Great Britain by CPI Group (UK) Ltd, Croydon, CR0 4YY

I wrote this for you, Bill.

Acknowledgments

Thank you seems too small a thing for the following people:

My amazing, dynamic agent, Alexandra Machinist, who I'm secretly convinced is a superhero. Thank you for loving my work, believing it could go great places, and making sure it got there.

My wonderful, insightful editor, Emily Bestler, who makes editing fun (and often funny). The next manuscript has less spitting and vomiting, I promise.

Constantly upbeat editorial assistant extraordinaire Caroline Porter. Thank you for answering all of my weird questions and being the most helpful person I know.

To the entire Emily Bestler Books/Atria team; I don't know you all by name yet, but that in no way diminishes my gratitude for the hard work you do. Book people are the best people.

Special thanks to Linda Chester for her kindness and wisdom.

To my parents, who didn't think I was crazy for wanting to write. Or if they did, they had enough compassion not to say it to my face. I love you both.

There is a best sister in the universe and her name is Daisy. I'm sorry this book doesn't have vampires, shopping, or lots of the color orange. One day.

A huge thank-you to my dear friend Stacey McCarter. You've read everything I've ever written, even when it was awful, and still you speak to me. If you ever need to bury a body, call me; I'll bring the backhoe.

Speaking of buried bodies, the brilliantly clever Kim McCullough and I have not buried any—yet. That might change if I keep giving her my uncorrected work to read.

A world of thanks to two talented writers and good friends, Jamie Mason and Lori Witt. You both get it. You really get it.

MacAllister Stone and the Absolute Write community: you gave me my training wheels and for that I will be eternally grateful.

White Horse never would have been written if it wasn't for William Tancredi, my alpha reader, alpha male, sweetheart, and favorite person. You inspire me to be a better writer and a better woman. Also, you make me laugh until I cry. I love you, you know.

And to you, Dear Reader. I write to entertain you. Hopefully I've succeeded. Let's do this again sometime.

ALEX ADAMS

WHITE HORSE

PROLOGUE

DATE: THEN

Look at me: I don't want my therapist to think I'm crazy. That the lie rolls off my tongue without tripping over my teeth is a miracle.

"I dreamed of the jar last night."

"Again?" he asks.

The leather squeaks beneath my head when I nod.

"The exact same jar?"

"Always the same."

There's a scratching as he pushes his pen across the paper.

"Describe it for me, Zoe."

We've done this a half dozen times, Dr. Nick Rose and I. My answer never changes, and yet I indulge him when he asks. Or maybe he indulges me. Me because I'm haunted by the jar, him because he has a boat to buy.

The couch cushions crease under me as I lean back and drink him in the way one drinks that first cup of coffee in the mornings. Small, savoring sips. He fills the comfortably worn leather chair. His body has buffed it to a gentle gleam that is soothing to the eye. His large hands are worn from work that doesn't take place in this office. The too-short hair, easy to maintain. His eyes are dark like mine. His hair, too. There's a scar on his scalp his gaze can't possibly reach in the mirror, and I wonder if his fingers dance over it when he's alone or if he's even aware of its presence. His skin is tan; indoors is not his default. But where to put him? Maybe not a boat. Maybe a motorcycle. The idea of him straddling a motorcycle makes me smile on the inside. I keep it hidden there. If I let it creep to my lips, he'll ask about that. And while I tell him all my thoughts, I don't always share my secrets.

"Scorched cream. If it were a paint color, that's what they'd call it. It's like . . . it was made for me. When I reach out in the dream, there's a perfectness to the angle of my arms as I try to grasp the handles. Did you ever have the one kid in school whose ears stuck out like this?" I sit straight, tuck my hair behind my ears, shove them forward at painful right angles.

His mouth twitches. He wants to smile. I can see the debate: Is it professional to laugh? Will she read it as sexual harassment? *Laugh*, I want to tell him. *Please*.

"I was that kid."

"Really?"

"No." His smile breaks free, and for a moment I forget the jar. It's neither huge nor perfect, but he made it for me. I find myself filled with a million questions, each designed to probe him the way he searches me.

"Do you have a recurring dream?" I ask.

The smile melts away. "I don't remember them. But we're talking about you."

Right. Don't throw me a bone. "The jar, the jar. What else to tell you about the jar?"

"Are there any markings?"

I don't need to stop and think; I know. "No. It's pristine." My shoulders ache with tension. "That's all."

"How does it make you feel?"

"Terrified." I lean forward, elbows pressing a dent into my knees. "And curious."

PART
ONE

PART
ONE

ONE

When I wake, the world is still gone. Only fragments remain. Pieces of places and people who were once whole. On the other side of the window, the landscape is a violent green, the kind you used to see on a flat-screen television in a watering hole disguised as a restaurant. Too green. Dense gray clouds banished the sun weeks ago, forcing her to watch us die through a warped, wet lens.

There are stories told among pockets of survivors that rains have come to the Sahara, that green now sprinkles the endless brown, that the British Isles are drowning. Nature is rebuilding with her own set of plans. Man has no say.

It's a month until my thirty-first birthday. I am eighteen months older than I was when the disease struck. Twelve months older than when war first pummeled the globe. Somewhere in between then and now, geology went crazy and drove the weather to schizophrenia. No surprise when you look at why we were fighting. Nineteen months have passed since I first saw the jar.

I'm in a farmhouse on what used to be a farm somewhere in what used to be Italy. This is not the country where gleeful tourists toss coins into the Trevi Fountain, nor do people flock to the Holy See anymore. Oh, at first they rushed in like sickle cells forced through a vein, thick, clotted masses aboard trains and planes, toting their life savings, willing to give it all to the church for a shot at salvation. Now their corpses litter the streets of Vatican City and spill into Rome. They no longer ease their hands into La Bocca della Verità and hold their breath while they whisper a pretty lie they've convinced themselves is real: that a cure-all is coming any day now; that a band of scientists hidden away in some mountaintop have a vaccine that can rebuild us; that God is moments away from sending in His troops on some holy lifesaving mission; that we will be saved.

Raised voices trickle through the walls, reminding me that while I'm alone in the world, I'm not alone here.

"It's the salt."

"It's not the fucking salt."

There's the dull thud of a fist striking wood.

"I'm telling you, it's the salt."

I do a mental tally of my belongings as the voices battle: backpack, boots, waterproof coat, a toy monkey, and inside a plastic sleeve: a useless passport and a letter I'm too chicken to read. This is all I have here in this ramshackle room. Its squalor is from before the end, I've decided. Poor housekeeping; not enough money for maintenance.

"If it's not the salt, what is it?"

"High-fructose corn syrup," the other voice says, with the superior tone of one convinced he's right. Maybe he is. Who knows anymore?

"Ha. That doesn't explain Africa. They don't eat sweets in Timbuktu. That's why they're all potbelly skinny."

"Salt, corn syrup, what does it matter?" I ask the walls, but they're short on answers.

There's movement behind me. I turn to see Lisa No-last-name filling the doorway, although there is less of her to fill it than there was a week ago when I arrived. She's younger than me by ten years. English, from one of those towns that ends in *-shire*. The daughter of one of the men in the next room, the niece of the other.

"It doesn't matter what caused the disease. Not now." She looks at me through feverish eyes; it's a trick: Lisa has been blind since birth. "Does it?"

My time is running out; I have a ferry to catch if I'm to make it to Greece.

I crouch, hoist my backpack onto my shoulders. They're thinner now, too. In the dusty mirror on the wall, the bones slice through my thin T-shirt.

"Not really," I tell her. When the first tear rolls down her cheek, I give her what I have left, which amounts to a hug and a gentle stroke of her brittle hair.

I never knew my steel bones until the jar.

The godforsaken jar.

DATE: THEN

My apartment is a modern-day fortress. Locks, chains, and inside a code I have three chances to get right, otherwise the cavalry charges in, demanding to know if I am who I say I am. All of this is set into a flimsy wooden frame.

Eleven hours cleaning floors and toilets and emptying trash in hermetic space. Eleven hours exchanging one-sided small talk with mice. Now my eyes burn from the day, and I long to pluck them from their sockets and rinse them clean.

When the door swings open, I *know*. At first I think it's the red answering machine light winking at me from the kitchen. But no, it's more. The air is alien like something wandered freely in this space during my absence, touching what's mine without leaving a mark.

Golden light floods the living room almost as soon as my fingers touch the switch. My eyes blink until they summon ample lubricative tears to provide a buffer. My pupils contract just like they're supposed to, and finally I can walk into the light without tripping.

They say it's not paranoia if someone is really out to get you. There is no prickle on the back of my neck telling me to watch out behind me, but I'm right about the air: it has been parted in my absence and something placed inside.

A jar.

Not the kind that holds sour dill pickles that crunch between your teeth and fill your head with echoes. This looks like a museum piece, pottery, older than this city—so says the grime ground into its pores. And that ancient thing fills my apartment with the feel of things long buried.

I could examine the jar, lift it from the floor and move it away from here. But some things, once touched, can never be untouched. I am a product of every B movie I've ever seen, every superstition I've ever heard, every tale old wives have told.

I *should* examine the jar, but my fingers refuse to move, protecting me from the what-if. They reach for the phone instead.

The super picks up on the eighth ring. When I ask if he let someone into my place, his mind goes on walkabout. An eternity passes. During that time I imagine him clawing at his balls, out of habit more than anything else, while he performs a mental tally of the beer still left in the fridge.

"No," he says, eventually. "Something get stolen?"

"No."

"What's the problem, then?"

I hang up. Count to ten. When I turn the jar is still there, centered perfectly in my living room between the couch and television.

The security company is next on my list. No, they tell me. We've got no record of anyone entering apartment thirteen-oh-four.

"What about five minutes ago?"

Silence. Then: "We've got that. Do you need us to send someone out?"

The police give me more of the same. Nobody breaks in and leaves things. It must be a gift from a secret admirer. Or maybe I'm crazy; they're not above suggesting that, but they use polite, hollow words designed to make me feel okay about hanging up the phone.

Then I remember the answering machine's blinking light. When I press Playback, my mother's voice booms from the speaker.

"Zoe? Zoe? Are you there?" There's a pause; then: "No, honey, it's the machine." Another pause. "What—I *am* leaving a message. What do you mean, 'Talk louder'?" There's playful slapping in the background as she shoos my father away. "Your sister called. She said there's someone she wants you to meet." Her voice drops to a whisper that's anything but discreet. "I think it's a man. Anyway, I just thought you could call her. Come over for dinner Saturday and you can tell me all about him. Just us girls." Another pause. "Oh, and you of course. You're almost a girl," she tells Dad. I can picture him laughing good-naturedly in the background. "Sweetie, call me. I'd try your cell phone, but you know me: ever hopeful that you're on a date."

Normally, I feel a small flash of anger in my chest when she calls to match make. But today . . .

I wish my mom were here. Because that jar isn't mine.

Someone has been in my space.

DATE: NOW

The human body is a wondrous thing. It's an acid manufacturing plant capable of transforming simple food into a hot burning mess.

I vomit a lot now. I'm great at it. I can lean forward just right and miss my boots completely. If the world wasn't gone, I could go to the Olympics.

As soon as breakfast comes up, I poke down an apple. It takes.

"Do you have to go?" Lisa asks. She's chewing her bottom lip, working the delicate skin into a pulpy mass.

"I have to get to Brindisi."

We're standing in the farmhouse's yard, encapsulated in a constant damp mist. Plush moss springs from pale stones that make up the house's exterior walls. My bicycle is leaning against a long-abandoned water pump. Somewhere along the way, the owners had resources enough to reroute the plumbing and enter the twentieth century, but they left the pump for charm or lack of caring. The bicycle is blue and not originally mine. No money changed hands. It was purchased for the paltry sum of a kiss outside Aeroporto Leonardo da Vinci di Fiumicino. No tongue. Just the surprising taste of tenderness from a Norwegian man who didn't want to die without one last embrace.

"Please," Lisa says. "Stay."

"I can't." There's a tightness in my chest from the mountains of regret heaped upon it. I like her. I really do. She's a sweet kid who once dreamed of nice things. Now the best she can hope for is survival. Thriving is not an option and it may never be.

"Please. It's nice having another woman here. It's better."

Then it strikes me, the note of desperation in her voice. She does not want to be left here alone with these men. They should be bound to protect family, and they do. But shared blood isn't the only reason: I suddenly realize they see her as a possession. A way to while away the hours until humanity draws its last ragged breath. I should have sensed it sooner, but I was so bound to my own agenda that I failed to look beyond my borders.

"I'm sorry," I say. "I didn't know. I should have, but I didn't."

A pale pink flush creeps over her fair skin: I've guessed her secret. Although she can't see me, I glance away to give her a moment to recoup. My cheeks buzz with shame.

The silence lasts long enough for the precipitation to congeal into raindrops.

"You can't stay any more than I can. Come with me."

I should regret the words, but I don't. If she agrees, it will add who knows how many days to my journey. Time is a luxury when you can't see what's left in the hourglass. But with humanity limping along as it is, kindness is rare. I have to hold on to what makes me human.

"Really? You'd let me go with you?"

"I insist."

Her neck pops as she jerks her chin over one shoulder, back at the house.

"They won't let me go. They'll never allow it."

What did they do to you, baby girl? I want to ask. Whatever she says, it won't affect my decision anyway: she's coming with me.

"Go up to your room and get your things. Make sure you've got something comfortable and warm to wear."

"But—" I can see she's still worried about the men.

"I'll take care of it."

We go inside together, and in the abrupt shelter we luxuriate for a moment. It feels good not to be rained on. Then we nod and she inches up the stairs while I make for the kitchen.

As far as kitchens go—and I've known few—this one is lean. Not an efficient leanness, but the too-thinness of a woman who fights to maintain an unnatural weight. The room has sag; I can see where things should go if one had the inclination to decorate or a love for cooking. It yearns to be filled with a family.

Only one man is present: Lisa's uncle. His skin is filled to capacity and oozes over the chair's borders. It's a sturdy piece of furniture probably many generations old. The wood is dark from time, and the seat is some kind of thick wicker with a honeyed sheen. The chair has seven empty siblings.

The big guy glances up, scans me for weaknesses he can exploit. My breath catches as I pull my shoulders back and push my chin forward, trying to look as strong as my body will allow. He finds nothing he can take without considerable effort and goes back to chewing on the bread I made two days ago after I picked the weevils from the pantry's ample flour supply. Crumbs fly from his mouth, spraying the table with damp flecks that will harden and stick if they're not wiped down soon. Neither Lisa nor I will be here to do it. These men will be wallowing in their own filth in no time.

"Lisa's coming with me."

He grunts, swallows, fixes his beady eyes on me. Raisins pressed deep into dough.

"She stays."

"It wasn't a question."

His bulk gathers like an impending storm as he heaves himself from the chair.

"We're her family."

This can't go anyplace good. A cold spot the size of a quarter forms on the back of my neck and spreads until I'm chilled all over. What was I thinking? He's bigger than me. Morbidly obese and slow, true, but large enough that if he gets me on the ground, I'm screwed.

We stare each other down. If we were dogs, someone would be betting on him, impressed by his sheer size.

A sharp shriek tears the artificial calm. Upstairs. Lisa. For a second I tune out, my attention latching onto the strange silence that always follows a scream.

The fat man lunges for me. Lisa is in trouble, but right now I am, too.

I feint left, dive right. He's like a crash test vehicle hitting the wall, plaster dust forming a white halo around his body. It takes him a moment to recover. He shakes his head to clear the pain fog, then comes at me again.

Again I manage to dodge him. Now we're staring each other down across the width of the table. Just a few feet between us. No weapons in sight. Lisa is a tidy housekeeper, and though this isn't her home, just one they stumbled across the same way I did, everything is in its place.

Another scream. This one drifts like dandelion fluff.

Inside my chest, my heart hurls itself at its bone prison. It knows her father is up there with her and it knows what's happening.

"I'm going to her," I say. "And if you try and stop me, you're a dead man."

He laughs. His jowls wobble and shudder.

"When he's done fucking her, we're going to take turns fucking you, bitch."

"I'm surprised you didn't try sooner."

He holds up both palms. "What can I say, love? We like lamb, not mutton."

It's my turn to laugh, only mine is bitter and dry.

"What, bitch? What's so fucking funny? Share the joke."

I inch down the table toward the open doorway. On the other side of this wall there's an umbrella stand. What's in there is useless for keeping a body dry, but the pointed end could still easily put out an eye.

"Did I ever tell you what I did for a living before all this?"

He grunts. Follows me down the table until we're both at the blunted edge.

"Some kind of lab rat."

I nod. Something like that. "I've done a lot of lifting, so I'm pretty strong for a skinny woman. What have you done besides shift gears in your truck and swing a glass of Guinness?" There's less strength in my body now than there was before the world ended, but my survival instincts have brought me this far. I make a break for it but I miscalculate: his reach is longer than mine. His arm snaps out. Fat grasping fingers coil themselves around my ponytail. He jerks me backwards and pulls me against him until his gut is a stuffed IHOP pancake bulging against my back. A triangle forms around my neck and tightens. Chest, humerus, ulna.

Usually when I long for the past, I dream of meals in chain restaurants where they serve the exact same dish every time. I dream of how it feels to be dry, or how my skin tingled when I stood too long in a too-hot shower. But now? High heels. Stilettos. With a four-inch metal rod keeping the heels straight and true. Because my captor has socked feet and it would take nothing to drive my fashionable weapon right between his metatarsals.

I'm wearing boots with a thick sole made for walking, but he's six-foot-something and I have to exaggerate to see five-five, which means my heels aren't going to do much besides grind his toes. It's not enough.

"I win," he says.

Maybe he's right, but the game isn't over yet. There's more than just me at stake.

"When was the last time you saw your own dick?" My voice thickens as the arm tightens at my throat. He's pulling me closer and higher. My heels are rising off the ground. There's a whisper of rubber against tile as my feet flail to seek stability. "Can you hold it to piss or do you sit like a woman?"

"Fuck you."

"Please. Fat guys like you can't get a hard-on."

Dark spots obscure my vision. It's morning but my daylight is fading fast. Lisa is sobbing now between the screams.

There's more strength in him than first appears. Adipose overlays significant muscle mass; the perfect camouflage. My toes leave the ground.

Everything that follows happens in an instant.

My chin drops and I sink my teeth into his forearm. The enamel slices through the tissue and scrapes bone. I draw my knees up so when he drops me and lets out a roar that comes all the way from his scrotum, my weight falls like the sparkly ball on New Year's Eve and my boots crush his feet. A gasp shoots from my throat as I fall forward onto my knees. Impact pains set my shins on fire. My opponent recovers long enough to deliver a swift kick to my backside with his damaged foot. Warm copper with a hint of iron floods my mouth. I scramble to my feet, dart sideways, arm held protectively over my stomach.

Without a thought in my head besides survival, I reach for a chair. It's lighter than its mellowed wood would suggest. Or maybe not. In times of need, the human body can conduct amazing feats. I know this because *That's Incredible!* told me. And Cathy Lee Crosby had a face an eight-year-old could trust.

White bone gleams through the skin as I lock my hands into place on the chair's back. He's English, which means he understands little about my national sport. This chair is my bat and his face is the ball. Baseball on steroids.

He comes for me and I swing. There's a sharp crack as his face shatters. Wet droplets of blood splatter my shirt and face: a mosquito's wet dream. Broken teeth crumble from his sagging mouth, and he falls. He is a mountain of flesh conquered by a woman holding a chair. The wood slips from my hands as I stagger into the hall and mount the stairs.

DATE: THEN

I get his name from a friend of a friend's sister.

"Oh my God, you have to call him. He's the best," my friend says with the exaggerated enthusiasm of one passing on third-hand news.

Nick Rose. He sounds like a carpenter, not someone who listens to problems for a crippling fee. A woodworker. Someone average. I can do that. I can talk to someone regular. Because normally when I think about a therapist I imagine an austere Sigmund Freud looking for links between my quirks and my feelings about my mother. My relationship with my mother is just fine, although I haven't yet returned her call or contacted my sister like she asked.

What would Freud make of that? What would Dr. Nick Rose?

I make the call out on the street from my cell phone. The city is in full tilt. Horns are the spice sprinkled over relentless traffic. Bodies form an organic conveyor belt constantly grinding along the sidewalks. Out here my words will be lost, but that's what I want. I'm a rational woman but the jar's arrival has me questioning my grip on reality. And deep down inside me, in the vault where I keep my fears carefully separated and wrapped in positive thoughts, I get the crazy notion that the jar will know.

So I stand outside on a corner, cup my hand over the phone's mouthpiece, and dial.

A man answers. I expected a female assistant and I tell him so and immediately feel a jab of guilt for stereotyping my own sex. Some feminist I am.

He laughs. "It's just me. I like to talk to potential clients. It gives both of us a feel for each other."

Clients. Not patients. My shoulders slump and I realize how taut my body has been holding itself. Dr. Nick Rose's voice is warm and bold like good coffee. He laughs like someone who is well practiced in the art.

I want to hear it again, so I say, "Just so we're clear, I don't secretly want to have sex with either of my parents."

Another laugh is my reward. Despite my reservations, I smile into the phone.

"Me either," Dr. Rose tells me. "I worked through that in college just to make sure. It was touch and go for a while, especially when my father kept asking me if he looked pretty."

We laugh some more. My tension is rendered butter melting away from my psyche. And at the end he tells me that Friday afternoons are all mine if I'll have him.

When we hang up, I am light-footed. The mere act of procuring a therapist has done wonders for me already. Friday. It's Tuesday now. That gives me three days to fabricate a story about the jar. A dream, maybe. Psychologists love dreams. Because I can't tell him the truth and I can't explain why because I don't know. The answer isn't there yet. I don't want him to think I'm crazy, because I'm not. Desperate is what I am. Quietly desperate and insatiably curious.

I follow the routine: unlock, unlock, open, close, lock, lock, chain, security code. The blinking light on the panel glows green, just like it's supposed to.

The jar is waiting.

DATE: NOW

Lisa's whimpers come from her bedroom. I say *her bedroom*; but who knows who it really belongs to. Whoever was here before shook all their personal belongings into suitcases, or maybe boxes, and fled. So I call it Lisa's room, although it won't be for much longer. Not if I can help it.

Left at the top of the stairs. Second right. Through the open door.

What's left of her family is in there with her.

Her father is a leaner man than his brother, younger by a handful of years, although from this angle I can't see his face. His ass is a glowing white moon with a pale slash of hair dividing the hemispheres.

Beneath him, Lisa is pressed into the bed facedown. She's past struggling, resigned to her place in the family hierarchy. A crude puppet impaled by her puppet master, hunching the bed herky-jerky with his every thrust.

Disgust is lava and pyroclastic ash erupting from my pores. A small cry is all the warning he gets as I race forward and grab his testicles mid-slap. Before our world ended, I was never one for manicures and pedicures. A stranger flicking a file across my feet would only make me squeal as the nerve endings danced. Hangnails frame my fingertips still. White dots are albino freckles on my nails. The edges are ragged where I've lain awake and nibbled while I rifled through my thoughts. All of this adds up to the one time a man doesn't want a woman's hand on his balls. My nails are pincers sinking into the delicate skin.

I expect him to shriek, but he doesn't. There's one last ripple of his ass and he stops cold as though he's awaiting my instructions.

"Get off her."

His voice is husky from the grunting. "I'm sorry."

"Not me. Pull out and tell *her* that."

He eases out. His erection withers until it's a limp shoestring dangling in the air.

"I'm sorry," he repeats.

"Lisa," I snap. "Get up and get your things." I wish my words could be gentle, but that won't get her up and moving and out of here.

There's a moment's hesitation, then she pushes her body off the bed. She tugs up her jeans and fastens them without lifting her chin. *This is not your shame,* I want to tell her. *It's him. All him.* But now is not the time.

"Lisa's part of my family now," I tell the man who created half of what she is. "We're leaving."

He's a chipped and damaged record. "I'm sorry."

When I release him, he remains frozen. His shoulders shake and it occurs to me he's crying. I kneel beside him as his daughter gathers her things and crams them into a backpack the same size as mine. My hand comes to roost on his shoulder and I am shocked at myself because I know I'm about to comfort a rapist.

"We don't have to be monsters. We still get to choose."

"I have urges."

"She's your daughter."

"I'm sorry."

"We're leaving now. Lisa?"

She shakes her head; she has no last words to give him.

We pack food: bread, preserves, canned goods. Anything with a high-calorie punch. These we wrap in plastic trash bags and tuck into my bicycle's basket. There's milk in the kitchen drained by one of the men from the cows that wander the yard. They're living off grass now, scavenging the land. And they're lucky, because all the rain means thicker, lusher pasture for the eating. At the back of my mind is an image of me slaughtering a cow to survive, my arms stained with what looks like ketchup but is really blood. I shove it away and try not to think about that yet.

"We should drink it all," I tell her, dividing the tepid liquid into two glasses. My gag reflex tries to reject the fluid, but I force it down, knowing that my body needs this. Food is becoming more scarce. An estimated ninety percent of the population is dead, but perishables are long gone and fast food is anything but. What remains is processed foods. Hamburger Helper that for the first time actually does help. Eventually we'll all be down to foraging, or subsistence farming—if any of us make it that far.

Lisa sips at the milk: a church mouse with a precious piece of cheese.

"Where's my uncle?"

The question hangs in the air between us.

"On the floor. I had to stop him."

She swallows. "Is he dead?"

I don't want to touch him. I don't. But she's looking to me like I know what to do. She doesn't know that I'm making it up as I go along. Pulling it out of my ass like my butt is a magician's hat.

Kneel. Two fingers against her uncle's neck. They're swallowed by his flesh knuckle-deep, like he's made of quicksand.

Please let him stay down, I chant. The fingers not lost in flab curl around a paring knife. A postapocalyptic insurance policy. For a few seconds his pulse eludes me and I think he's dead. But no . . . there it is. *Pa-rump, pa-rump, pa-rump.* He's the Little Drummer Boy on speed.

"He's alive." For now, because a galloping pulse can't be good in a man the size of a VW Beetle.

"Thank God," Lisa says.

Yeah, God. That guy. He forgot to RSVP to mankind's last party. Who could blame him? The fireworks were great but everyone attending was sick.

On the other side of the kitchen, knives wait in a drawer. Knives for sawing bread, for slicing cheese, for dicing tomatoes, for hacking meat. One cleaver for me, and the paring knife. Both bear keen edges.

"You should have a knife."

Lisa's brows dip. "Oh no, I couldn't."

"What if you need to cut something?"

"I thought you meant . . ."

She's staring toward the thin air above her uncle. The drawer beckons. A corkscrew. Good for taking out an eye. An adequate weapon for someone who doesn't want to carry one.

"Take this," I say. Her fingers close around the helix. One presses against its point and she winces. "Just in case we find a great bottle of wine. This is Italy, remember?"

We walk with my wheels between us. Lisa's hand balances on the seat, using it to guide her path while I hold the handlebars and steer us true. She took the corkscrew without question and shoved it into her jeans pocket, where she reaches down and traces the outline every few dozen feet.

This is the middle of nowhere, although its existence proves that it must be somewhere. So I pull out my compass and wait for the needle to still. Southeast. I want southeast. If we take a right at the farm's entrance, that's the road east. Good enough until we find a road that wanders south.

We don't speak until we're at the white mailbox and the old planks that form a halfhearted attempt at a fence are behind us.

Lisa cracks the silence. "I hope he's okay. My dad."

"He'll be fine."

"He's my father."

"I know."

"You could have killed him."

"But I didn't."

There's a pause as she formulates the question. "Why?"

"The world you knew, that we all knew, is gone. Humanity is mostly dead and what's left is dying."

A ditch forms between her eyebrows, and it's filled with ignorance.

"I don't get it."

"I like being human."

The ditch digs a little deeper.

"He did it because he loved me," she says after a while. "That's what I tell myself so I don't hate him. He's still my dad, and a person shouldn't hate their dad. In a way, I feel like I owed him something. It was a hard job, looking after me out here, being blind and all."

"Did he tell you that?"

"Sometimes."

"It's no excuse," I tell her. "You didn't owe him *that*."

She disappears inside herself for several moments before returning with a new question.

"During sex, did you ever close your eyes and pretend it was someone else?"

Did I? Maybe. When I was younger. Before I began having sex with someone other than myself.

"Sure," I say to make her feel better. "Probably everyone does that."

"I tried. It didn't work very well."

"Honey, what he was doing to you wasn't sex or love."

"Can I tell you a secret?" The question mark has a rhetorical curve, so I stay silent. When we reach the first crossroad stamped into the landscape, she says, "I think I'd still like being touched one day. By a man who likes me."

"I think you will, too."

"Do you have any secrets?"

I look at her sideways, tell myself I won't let this one come to harm when I've lost so many along the way. "No."

TWO

D r. Rose opens a window. Sun and fresh air rush in like they're in a hurry to go no place but here. This is their ultimate destination, their dream vacation.

I hold my face up to the light, smile. "That could be symbolic."

"Of what?"

"Of what you do here."

He smiles. "An optimist. That's a step in the right direction. Often people who come see me look on therapy as a negative. A black mark against them."

"*I* called *you*, remember?"

He gets up, goes out to the waiting room. "You want something to drink?"

"Is this a trick question?"

"Yes. I'm going to read your personality based on your beverage choices, so choose wisely."

I smile. I can't help myself. This isn't what I thought it would be. I expected a dry soul shoehorned into a somber setting.

"Coffee with cream. Two sugars."

"Two?"

"Okay, three."

"That's more like it." He returns with identical mugs, passes one to me. The liquid is hot, sweet, smooth. I alternate blowing and sipping until the first inch disappears.

"What does this say about me?"

He takes his own long sip, slurps a little, doesn't apologize. When he's satisfied he swaps the mug for a notepad and pen. "You like asking questions."

"My coffee tells you that?"

The pen moves on the paper. "No, your questions do."

I laugh. "If you don't ask, you may never know."

He smiles down at his paper. "Why don't you tell me why you called me?"

"Don't you know?"

"I'm a therapist, not a psychic."

"That would make your job easier, no?"

"Scarier."

I take another half inch of coffee. "I'm not crazy."

"There are two ways to look at that. Either no one's crazy, or we're all crazy in our own way. As a great Greek philosopher once said: Man needs a little madness, or else he never dares cut the rope and be free."

"Socrates?"

"Zorba."

Again with the laughter. "I don't know, Doctor, it's possible you might be crazier than me."

"Sometimes I talk to myself," he admits. "Sometimes I even answer myself."

"Only child?"

"Eldest. Of two. I have a brother."

"I have a younger sister. She had imaginary friends. And because my folks wouldn't buy me a Ken doll, I drew a mustache and chest hair on one of my Barbies."

"Do you still do that?"

"Only if my date turns out to be a woman."

The dimple in his cheek twitches. Am I serious and therefore nuts, or am I the perennial comedienne, stowing my pain under a funny blanket? Am I in dire need of analysis? Would I make a great research paper wedged somewhere between obsessive-compulsive plucking and multitasking personality disorder?

"If this is ongoing, you should be in therapy," he says.

"Do you think?"

"Why don't you tell me why you're here."

I lean back. Take a small sip. Arrange my lie.

"I've been having this dream about a jar. Not the grape jelly kind—the old kind. It's the color of scorched cream."

"How does it make you feel, this dream?"

"Terrified . . ."

"It's old," James Witte tells me. Letters trail after his name, interspersed with periods to denote that he's spent a whole lot of time with his head in books and his mind in the past. He's an assistant curator at the National Museum. An old friend, although he looks the same as the day we graduated high school: thin, narrow-shouldered, pale. His eyes gleam as he circles the jar.

"Really old."

"Is that a technical term?"

He laughs. I get a flash of him sucking on a beer bong at a postgrad party. "Yeah, it's technical. Translation: I don't know how old it is, but it's really fucking old."

"Wow. That *is* old."

"If I had to guess, I'd say it's Greek. Maybe Roman. The curve of the handles, the way they attach to the tapering trunk . . . But there's no design. Yet, it's symmetrical, which would suggest it was made on a wheel. And everything made on the wheel had some design, be it painted or etched."

A soft shadow bats at the window. My next door neighbor's cat, Stiffy. Because Ben's a teenage boy living in the basement of a grown man's body. The window barely has time to scrape against the frame before the marmalade beast's squeezing underneath, launching his invasion.

"Can I take it?" James asks. "I'll bring it back. But I can give you a much better idea of when and where it's from if I can inspect it in my own space. That way I can get other opinions if I can't figure it out. Our new intern sorts potsherds like some kind of savant. The other interns call him Rain Man."

I'd trust James with my life. We've been friends since tenth grade when he moved to the area from Phoenix. He's steady. Loyal. Decent to the bone. So I tell him what I can't tell Dr. Rose: that someone sneaked into my home and I'm driving myself slightly nuts wondering how and why. All except the fear. I hold that close to my bones lest it seem trite, thin.

He listens intently. That's how James has always listened. Every so often he asks a question and I do my best to answer it.

"Why don't you just open the thing?"

"It's not mine to open."

On the door, the locks feign innocence. *Don't blame us, the security system failed you.* The panel blinks silently. It's just a robot awaiting instructions from a mother ship in a building downtown.

"Why not toss it in the dumpster?"

"It's not mine to throw away."

"Leave it to me." He grins. "I love a good mystery. Worst case I'll bring Rain Man here. I'll tell him it's a date."

Stiffy rubs against my skin, his purr vibrating all the way up to my knees as he figure-eights my shins.

"Aha, so he's cute, then?"

"Tasty. And smart. Can't beat that with a stick."

"Bring him over. I'll make lasagna."

The cat detaches himself from my legs and saunters over to the jar. He circles it twice, then sits a foot away, tail tucked neatly around him in a protective ring. With a fascination bordering on obsession, he stares at the jar.

"Curiosity killed the cat," James says.

DATE: NOW

On the second morning after we leave the farmhouse, Lisa vomits. The sky is dim through the thickly leaved canopy that conceals us from the road and sky. Under here, the weather is mostly dry, with a chance of frigid drips.

For once, I don't. Cold beans scooped from a can with a jagged edge settle in my stomach in a nourishing gelatinous lump.

Up ahead is a village. Maybe two miles away. It's a black dot on a map, nameless but present. We should go around, avoid contact if there's any to be made. I look at Lisa bent at the waist, unleashing her beans onto the ground. Her hair is in my hands. Poor kid. Although I run the risk of making myself sick, I glance at the mess she's made. No blood. At least not yet.

Vitamins. They might have vitamins in the town. We could both use them.

"I'm sorry."

The retching travels all the way from her toes.

"Don't be. You can't help it."

Her thin shoulders shake. "Do you think I've got White Horse?"

White Horse. The plague that killed the world's population. Some preacher down south with a too-big mouth and a popular cable TV show heard voices from God telling him these were the end-times. Dying people had nothing better to do, so they watched. It was that or listen to the static that used to be daytime television.

That preacher named the virus White Horse.

"The first seal is opened and the white horse has come with its deadly rider to test us with Satan's disease. Any man, woman, or child who doesn't believe and accept Jesus Christ as his or her savior will die from this White Horse. The nonbelievers will burn in the pits of hell, wishing they'd had the courage to accept the Lord. They will writhe and burn, their souls thick with maggots. This plague is the white horse. And the other three are coming. . . ."

Everyone assumed it would be a flu-like illness that would knock us out of the evolutionary tree, but it wasn't anything so merciful. White Horse was like nothing in the medical books except maybe late-stage cancer. The CDC and WHO barely had time to react when people began running to their doctors in droves, toting sick bags and buckets, begging for something to stop the nausea. The vomit turned bloody as the protective cells, designed to stop the stomach acids from burning holes and leaking into the body, sloughed away. Within days the vomiting quit, only to be replaced with nonspecific aches, some more severe than others.

Then a scientist came forward and told us what we had no way of guessing.

"White Horse is not a disease as such. It's a mutation. Some outside source has flipped switches in our DNA, turning on some genes, turning off others." He struggled to keep the words simple enough for the public to understand. Speech faded to mumbles when time came for the media to ask their questions. Enlightenment sans illumination.

I could lie and tell her no, or I could lie and tell her yes. So I take the chickenshit truth route.

"I don't know."

She speaks through the bile foam. "I don't want to die."

I pull a tissue from my pocket so she can wipe her lips.

"We all die sooner or later."

"Later sounds better."

"We should make a bucket list," I say.

"What's that?"

"It's a list of everything we want to do before we die at the ripe old age of three digits. Like skydiving. Or swimming in a waterfall."

"What's the point?"

The absurdity of our situation fills my eyes with hot tears. Two women standing alone at the end of the world, talking about things we want to do before we die. We'll be lucky to get one last hot meal.

"Fun," I tell her. "There's a village up ahead. I thought maybe we'd check it out. What do you think?"

"What would you do if I wasn't here?"

"Probably go around."

"So, why aren't we?"

"Because they might have medicine."

"Do you think I'm going to die soon?"

I shake my head, let the rain take my tears where it will.

"I want to get married and have a family," she says. "I'm going to put that on my list."

DATE: THEN

"Forget it," I tell Jenny.

My sister's voice is Minnie Mouse with a dash of fingernails down a chalkboard, but only when she wants to bend me to her will.

"But he's really nice. You'll love him. Or maybe you'll just love him a time or two." I picture her waggling her eyebrows as she encourages me to have casual sex. Our mother would love that.

"Nice," I say.

"And dreamy gorgeous."

"I have to wash my hair that night."

"I already told him about you. You have to come."

"Then untell him."

There's a gap in her chatter. "You almost had me for a second. I can't. That would be rude. You have to come."

"I won't," I say, and hang up.

My mother rolls out the guilt parade and slaps my buttons like my psyche is a game of Whac-A-Mole.

". . . two years," she drones on. "That's how long it felt. You were the stubbornest baby ever. Not like your sister. At least she had the courtesy to come two weeks early. Three hours. She wanted to come out. Not like you. That was the longest thirty-six hours of my life . . ."

I have two choices: attend my sister's dinner party or tie a plastic sack around my mother's head until she runs out of nagging. I choose the evil that doesn't come with a felony conviction.

THREE

The village appears over the road's hump: Aphrodite rising from the water. She steps through the never-ending drizzle to greet us. There's no knowing whether she's friend or foe, but I guess she could say the same about us. In this world everything is a fat question mark. Taxes are no longer certain—only death.

We pass under a stone arch, the reddish brown of clay earth. The whole village is garbed in this same shade: clusters of earthen cottages with shallow porches and roughly shingled roofs; a handful of shops with wares gathering dust behind grimy windows; a church with its windows shuttered and high wooden doors bolted.

There is a calm that feels anything but peaceful.

We stop. Turn. Inspect the deserted street. Nothing moves. Not even a twitch of lace in a window.

"There isn't anybody here." Lisa cups her hands, yells through them. "Hello?" Her words ricochet off the deserted buildings.

"Don't."

Her hands fall away. "I didn't think."

"It's okay. It's just best to be quiet, that's all."

"Why? What do you think is out there?"

"Desperate people." And monsters.

"My dad said that's why we had to stay at the farm. Because at least there we had food and no one was trying to fight us for it."

"He was right."

"Do you think we should go back?"

I don't answer. My attention is on what appears to be a small grocery store. Neat stacks of preserves in ribbon-wrapped jars fill the lower third of the window display. Fruit and sugar. Our bodies could use both.

"Do you hear anything?"

She listens. "No."

"Wait here," I say. Someone needs to protect what we've already got.

The bell barely trembles as I ease the door open like I'm handling dynamite. I'm standing in what passes for a 7-Eleven in this part of the world. Or maybe it's a souvenir shop. That would explain all the woven baskets and cross-stitchings cling-ing to the walls inside cheap frames. I fill two baskets with pre-serves: strawberry, peach, cherry. The other shops are useless. A butcher and a produce store, both with rotted wares. There's no medicine here—not even an antacid. The houses are just as self-ish: they give me nothing I can use to heal. What these people had is long gone.

Against one wall I find a broom resting, waiting to be of use. So I grant it that wish, twist its head from its neck, assign it a new occupation.

Outside, Lisa is scuffing her boot on the stone steps leading up to the door. Her mouth droops at the edges as though she's sinking into darker thoughts.

"Jam," I announce as loud as I dare, and imbue the word with what I hope is a smile rather than a grimace. "Who needs bread? We can pretend we're kids and eat it straight out of the jar."

"Can we go? I don't like it here. It's too quiet, if that makes sense."

A year ago this village would have teemed with life. Tourists oohing and ahhing over the postcard-perfect scenery as they spent too much money for a commemorative trinket that would wind up in a drawer the moment their suitcases were unpacked. Locals smiling at their heavier purses, grateful the road through their village was more heavily traveled, thanks to a popular movie and a spate of wall calendars. Even in her dark world, Lisa would have loved it then. I would have, too. I used to have one of those calendars, and the movie went great with a quart of Ben and Jerry's.

"Soon."

I hang the baskets on the handlebars before curling Lisa's fingers around the broom handle.

"It's a cane," she says, lightly tapping the tip on the foot-worn paving stones. "So sticks and stones won't break my bones. Thanks."

My gaze fixates on the church at the village's eastern edge. Doors bolted. To keep something out. Or maybe in? There could be supplies in there, a makeshift sanctuary.

"Did you find medicine?" she says.

I start walking. "There wasn't any," I throw over my shoulder. "I want to check out the church."

"I'm coming, too."

"Someone needs to guard the food."

"I'm blind," she says. "Not useless."

"Okay. But if anything happens, run in the quietest direction and hide."

In. Definitely in. Because a heavy beam has been dropped into brackets attached to the door's frame. What is this village hiding? Who sealed the doors and where did they go?

I suck in as much air as I can. I already know I'm going to throw them wide, because what we need might be inside, and because I can't help myself. Knowledge is power. Or maybe it will lead to capitulation. Best-case scenario I get to talk to God. Because we need to have a talk, He and I, though we haven't done so in some months. And there's a good reason for that.

Don't do it, Zoe.

Do it.

Remember the jar.

Coincidence.

Words written on a bathroom wall: There is no such thing as a coincidence.

Curiosity killed the cat. Then it killed the world.

The thoughts swirl until they're swept away by my determination. I reach for the makeshift lock that reminds me of the Middle Ages. I wasn't paying attention in class the day they discussed the history of doors.

"Tell me what to do," Lisa says.

I guide her hand toward the problem.

"We're going to push up, okay?"

"Okay."

Constant dampness keeps the wood swollen; it bulges in a mockery of gestation. My fingers pull from above, then push from below to no result. Lisa's shoving, too, her face screwed up and intense—the same expression I feel on my face.

The beam shifts, groans, shoots straight up like a rocket, and we both stumble in its wake.

"Thanks," I whisper. Lisa smiles and dusts her hands together, wipes them on her jeans and does a little *Voilà!* move like she's a gymnast. I can't help it, I join in. We spin, twirl, pose, like we have an audience of millions. This is Italy and my inner child is at the helm. I want to throw my coins in the fountain, meet my prince, spend my last dime on a villa, lose myself in the grandeur of Brunelleschi's dome, be kissed between the legs of Titus's arch. I want to live here, not die.

Then just like that, our performance stops and we're ground down by the journey once more.

"What do you think is inside?"

Lisa looks flushed from our silliness. I probably do, too. Tugging the elastic band from my hair, I finger comb the damp strands, then smooth everything back into place and fasten the thick bundle.

Decomposition has its own smell. It's the mugger of scents, slapping your face, kicking you in the gut then bolting with your wallet while you're busy staggering and recoiling from the stench. Every so often I catch a whiff of that rotting meat smell. But also . . . something else I can't define.

"There's only one way to find out. Could be something, could be nothing."

"Whatever it is, you have to tell me."

"I will. I'm going in."

She backs up fast. Like ripping off a Band-Aid, I wrench the doors open wide.

My mind goes into overload. Acid bubbles up into my mouth and I wrestle to force it down.

Detach or go crazy.

Holiday snapshots from rainy Italy: corpses, mutilation, rotting flesh. Atop the priest's corpse a rat died nibbling at what was left of his face. DNA gone so far wrong that even the bones are so gnarled, so anomalous, they've ripped through his skin from the inside. What looks like a tailbone. Not just the nub people have, but a lengthy ladder of bones that hangs past the knees. Horny protrusions jutting from what used to be faces. Bodies, unrecognizable as human but too similar to be alien. Italy has made grisly art from the Reaper's work.

There is a wet sucking sound. I know it. I don't dare close my eyes to think, and I can't focus on single pieces long enough to isolate its meaning. It's a cat's tongue dragging along a meat chunk, keratin hooks stripping away the flesh. It's the slurping of noodles from a foam bowl. It's the sucking of marrow from freshly snapped bones.

Something is feeding. A monster who would be man were it not for a madman's experiment. Its inhuman lapping is both a whisper and deafening, and my eardrums clang with the sound.

Someone shut them in here. Someone locked them in this place before abandoning this living tomb, and I cannot fault them for that decision.

My hands can barely hold the wooden beam steady. With Parkinson's-esque control I tamp it down into the brackets with my fists so that thing inside can never get out. I walk away, back to Lisa, fists tight at my side.

"What was it?" she wants to know, but I don't know what to tell her. That thing used to be human once, but now it's a new link on the food chain.

I shake my head. I can't speak. If I do, I'm going to lose the beans.

We're maybe a half mile away. The rain is lighter now and tickles my wet face before rolling under my rounded shirt collar.

Lisa is chattering and I welcome the way in which she throws around words in any which order, because at least it takes my mind off the church.

Another mile. The compass indicates we're still headed east with a slight jag south, which is exactly where I want to be. The sky feels low enough to reach down and touch my head. The clouds are congealing into a solid dark mass. The world is sucking in its breath, but for what?

Then everything blows apart at the seams. A roaring boom shakes the countryside until even the grass sinks to its knees. We hit the ground, our stomachs flat against the soft soil, arms forming a protective M over our heads. Food scatters as the bicycle falls between us.

The air thumps. Pressure forces us deeper into the grass.

"Are you okay?"

Lisa nods, her cheek flattened by the ground. Her eyes are wide and unblinking. She's unhurt—or at least not bleeding on the outside. I determine the same about myself and roll onto my back, propping myself up on my elbows.

"You?" she asks.

"I'm okay."

"What was that?"

"Something blew up."

The explosion came from behind us. I know this because that's where the fireball is rising into the sky. Smoke is a voluminous, billowing, high-fashion cloak framing the fire, enhancing its dangerous beauty.

Its significance is not lost on me, and the surge of hormones that is my flight-or-fight response whips my pulse onward, telling me flight is smarter.

"We have to go. And we have to get off the road."

Her lips sag at the edges. "But that means we have to go through the mud. Our feet . . ."

"I don't like it, either, but we don't have a choice."

"But why?"

"Because that explosion means there might be someone behind us. So it's better if we stay out of sight."

"Do you think it was the church?"

"Probably."

There's a short pause. "What was in there?"

"Have you ever heard of those old maps, the kind from before we knew what the continents really looked like, when people thought the earth was flat?"

"I think so. In school. Why?"

"Some of them used to have pictures of dragons or other fantastical beasts strategically placed in unexplored areas."

The wheels turn. "Are you saying a dragon did this?"

"No. I'm saying that the whole world is dangerous now. And there are monsters out there that used to be us."

We move on from this place, sticking to the thicker grass so our boots don't sink and us along with them. The rain persists.

DATE: THEN

I hate you, I mouth across the table at my sister.

She shrugs. *What?*

I scratch my nose with the middle finger of my right hand. Grown women acting like teenagers.

"The Chinese," the voice next to me drones on. "Now that's our biggest threat. They're playing God over there with their weather modification program."

"So they can dry their laundry faster?" my brother-in-law asks. Mark is no racist, but I can see he's as bored with the boob next to me as I am.

My blind date's ego is made of yeast, and the hotter it gets, the more he puffs up. It's a marvel his trendy polo shirt and chinos don't pop.

"They did it during the Olympics," I say. "They shot silver iodide pellets into the sky. But it's not just China. We do it here, too."

Daniel, the dough man, recoils like I've slapped him. "We do not."

"Yeah, we do."

Jenny picks at the tablecloth. She knows I won't let this go. Anyone else and I might, but this guy is rubbing sandpaper on my raw nerves.

"What did you say you do again?"

"I work for Pope Pharmaceuticals."

He nods. "I've seen their products advertised. Antidepressants and sleeping pills."

Over bagged lunches the cleaning crew jokes that Pope Pharmaceuticals is an insurance policy: it manufactures drugs for every contingency, including things you never knew you had.

"And drugs for dicks," Mark says. "For when you can't get it up."

Daniel ignores him. "What do you do there?"

"I clean."

He throws his hands in the air like he's won some victory in some competition only he knows about. "Ladies and gentlemen, domestic engineering now qualifies a person as an expert on weather control."

It's all I can do not to shove my wineglass down his throat.

"Excuse me." I take off for the privacy of the backyard. I pace the length of the pool, stop, turn, retrace my steps. The moon is bright in its glassy surface. By the time I reach the diving board my fingers are searching for my phone.

I dial. Four rings. The fifth breaks as the connection is made.

"You're there. I thought you'd be gone for the day."

"Who is this?" Dr. Rose asks.

My voice catches and he laughs.

"I'm joking, Zoe. Are you okay?"

"No." I rub my fingers over my forehead like it's a piece of crumpled paper and I'm smoothing out the lines. "Yes. Can I ask you something?"

"Boxers," he says. "Briefs exacerbate my claustrophobia."

Normally I'd laugh, but my body is a violin string held taut to the point of snapping.

"I'm on a blind date. It was my sister's idea."

He lets out a grunt that triggers an image of him leaning back in his chair, resting his feet on his desk, because this is going to be a long night and he wants to be comfortable.

"A blind date," he says. "How—"

"Please don't ask me how I feel about it. If I had to pick a word, I'd say *homicidal*."

"That answers my question. Which was going to be 'How's it going?'"

I throw a leaf into the pool and the moon shivers.

"I'm sorry. I shouldn't have called. You have a life outside of neurotic patients."

"You're not neurotic," he says. "You're on a blind date. The only other question is: Why aren't you drinking heavily?"

"I'm allergic."

"To alcohol?"

"To assholes. I get hives when I mix the two."

I can feel him smile.

"You mentioned a husband in our first session."

"Sam."

"Sam. Tell me about him."

"What's to tell? We fell in lust, married in a quickie ceremony in Las Vegas, then he died before we had a chance to fall in love."

"I'm sorry. I assumed you were divorced."

"That's the logical conclusion these days." The question hangs in his silence. "Car crash. His mother was driving."

"Drunk driver?"

"Seizure. She drove straight into the path of a semi."

His voice is cool balm on my raw nerves. "I'm sorry for your loss. How long ago?"

"Five years. My family think it's time I moved on."

"What do you think?"

"I'd like to move on with a non-asshole. I hear they can test DNA for that now."

There's silence, and for a moment I think we've lost our connection. Until he laughs.

Daniel pokes his head around the open door frame, an extinguished pharos incapable of shedding revelatory light.

"Come on," he says when he spots me. "Don't be a pouty brat."

"Excuse me," I tell Nick. "I think my invisibility cloak just failed."

"If you kill him, call me. I'm bound by doctor-client privilege."

"Really?"

"No. But the courts make exceptions for assholes."

I follow Daniel into the house.

"I've got tickets for *Waiting for Godot*." He says this like he just laid a golden egg.

"I'm right about the weather," I say. "Tell Jenny and Mark I said good night."

DATE: NOW

Darkness creeps across the countryside. When it catches us, we have to stop. There are no worn paths here where hundreds of feet have gone before us, or even the same pairs of feet hundreds of times over. The ground is virgin, and each step a potential danger.

"We'll take turns keeping watch. Between your ears and my eyes, we should be okay."

Lisa's tired. We both are. There's a weariness to my bones that has become a part of me, like a leg or an ear. It belongs to me. In return, it owns my body and dictates when I should rest, sleep, yawn from fatigue. Every day a fear flashes through me: that I have White Horse and it's the disease commanding my routine, not the journey. But there's been no blood, no tissue-deep pain, so the fear creeps away and hides until it can ambush me the next time.

I set the cups and flasks outside the tree line so they can refill.

"I'll take the first shift," I reassure her. She rubs her eyes with balled fists, then curls up between the tree's roots. My body stays rigid. I play games with it, tensing the muscles until they weaken, then relax so blood flows back in.

Seconds tick by; minutes meander; the hours drag a ball and chain. Night is out there beyond the tree. It's still there, waiting, watching, when I wake Lisa at two. I wish we had a dog. A dog has ears and eyes. A dog is always on guard, even in sleep.

"Peach or strawberry?"

"Peach," she says, then settles against the tree trunk, half here, half in Dreamland, where the pretty things live.

I worry that she'll fall asleep. That whoever caused that explosion will find us here, vulnerable kittens for the snatching. That they'll be a monster clad in human skin. And that my instincts won't let me see the truth. But my mind is performing one last walk-through for the night, flicking off the switches of my consciousness. Worry is for the waking. So I roll onto my side, back protected by the tree's broad trunk, and let my mind douse the last light.

DATE: THEN

The world is ending, the population halved, then halved again. I have to get to Brindisi. I'm stuck at the airport waiting on a plane, any plane, to get me to Europe. No money changes hands; it's meaningless now except as mattress stuffing.

"You, you, and you," the man says, pointing to me and two others. "We're aiming for Rome. Do you accept the price?"

I do. The price is nothing more than a bag of blood. I've got plenty of that.

On the tarmac, they tap a vein. My fists clenches and releases to force the blood out faster.

"Why blood?" I ask.

The nurse preps another traveler's arm, shoves the needle in deep.

"There's a small group of scientists who still believe they can stop this. Word is they think they can find a cure in healthy DNA."

"Really?"

"That's what they say. Course, I never cared much for what people say. It's what they do that matters." She passes my blood to someone else. The red liquid sloshes in the bag. "Have a cookie."

Everyone ahead of me is holding a fortune cookie. We're too dazed to eat them. My mind feels detached from my body like it's a full step behind the rest of me, a lagging toddler trying to make sense of a much bigger, more adult picture.

There is no attendant with a breezy impersonal smile ushering us onto the plane, just a couple of soldiers holding weapons they look too young to carry. A few short years ago their mothers were tucking them into their beds, and now they're primed to kill if necessary. The toy soldiers don't speak as I inch my way past and drop into the nearest empty seat, but their eyes swivel, then snap to attention. I take the aisle although the window is vacant. I don't want to look out and down. I don't need to pretend things are normal. That kind of self-deception can only lead to madness. It's best to accept that this *is* and all the blood donations in the world can't drag the calendar backwards.

People squeeze down the aisle after me. Some have nothing. Others are minimalists like me, toting a single backpack and maybe a pillow.

A worn woman stops inches away. She hugs a small Louis Vuitton suitcase to her chest. "Is that seat taken?"

"It is now." Although I mean to sound light, my words are pancake flat.

I swivel my knees toward the window to let her past. She settles in the seat, suitcase perched upon her lap. Strange, I think, until I realize I'm doing the same thing.

"I love Rome," she says. "It's romantic. More so than Paris, I believe. Have you been?"

"This is my first time."

We are a parody of normality. Strangers discussing travel like two robots mimicking human speech.

"Are you married?"

"No."

"You should go with someone you love. I did. My husband. Well, husbands. They loved Rome. They're both dead now." Her knuckles tighten on the bag's impeccably stitched edge, white marbles beneath paper-thin skin. They barely support the nest of rings stacked on top of them. "I love Rome," she echoes. "It's romantic."

We don't speak after that. She retreats to her world, the one where she wears a haute couture dress with one ring, one necklace, where her husbands are still alive, where someone else carries her luggage. I attend to my stomach, which is launching a protest, and rip into the flimsy plastic wrapping the fortune cookie. It has snapped into pieces from the tension in my hand, which saves me the trouble of breaking it in two. The slivers dissolve on my tongue until they're little more than the memory of sugar.

The fortune is stiff between my fingers. I unfurl it and read.

Welcome change.

I read my fortune until I laugh. I laugh until I cry. I cry until I sleep.

FOUR

I wake in a panic, drenched in tepid sweat. It's not rain, because it smells sour, metallic, with an underlying sweetness like fruit just as it turns. My plane ride to Rome swirls down the drain, dormant until the next time I close my eyes. I shove myself up from the tree roots and look for Lisa. She's asleep.

When I rouse her, she barely recognizes my voice through the sleep fog.

"What?"

"You fell asleep."

"I was tired."

"I have to be able to rely on you."

She leans over, vomits, heaves until I worry she'll turn inside out. Between bouts, she manages to speak.

"I'm sorry. It just happened."

"Come on. We should go."

We push off from our resting place and I glance behind us, scan the land. Nothing but trees and grass. But something follows. Branches crack when they shouldn't. Every so often I hear a step that doesn't come from me or Lisa.

We are not alone out here.

DATE: THEN

"Have you ever turned it over?" Dr. Rose asks. "Looked at the bottom?"

I look at him, my mouth sagging softly because that never occurred to me.

It's Friday evening. In my head I call this "date night," because I'm not like the other people who come here. I'm not crazy. I'm not even a little off balance. At least I don't think so. But that jar bothers me. The mystery of it curls cold fingers around my heart and squeezes until I ache.

"No. Never."

"Maybe you should. Maybe it's time to take action in your dream. Take control."

"What do you think I'll find?"

"A message. A clue perhaps. Or maybe a Made in China sticker."

Laughter spills from my throat. "Wouldn't that be a trip? My dream the product of mass manufacturing in China."

We leave together. I'm his last appointment. He locks the office door while I wait, then we stroll toward the elevators like he didn't just print me an invoice while I wrote him a check.

"Do it," he says as the steel cables hoist the oversized dumbwaiter to our floor. "Push that thing over and inspect the bottom. Look, you've seen every other part of it. It's a dream. If it breaks,

I don't think they're going to hold you to the 'You broke it, you bought it' policy."

He has a point, but not the full picture.

My voice wobbles out on unsteady legs. "I haven't seen all of it. I haven't seen the inside."

A sharp ding echoes in the hall. Metal scrapes as the elevator locks into place. When the doors slide open, Dr. Rose's hand goes to my waist and gently urges me ahead of him. His warmth seeps through my shirt. There's a familiar smell about him that I can't quite grasp. Trying to pin it with a label is like nailing Jell-O to a wall.

"Dreams are funny things," he says. "All this technology, all these specialists and their experiments, and we still don't have a grip on what they are or what they mean." The elevator shakes and hums. "You asked about my dreams. Since we're just two people making conversation, I'll tell you." He hits the Stop button and we jerk to a halt. "I'm standing on a beach in Greece, where my family are from. There's no sand. The beaches are pebble, the water still. I feel . . . like I'm the only person left on earth. So I crouch down and pick up a smooth stone, and when I stand I feel there's someone behind me. A woman. I can't see her but I know she's there."

"Because you've had the dream before?"

His smile is reluctant. His eyes dark and serious. "Many times. It always plays out the same. When I turn, I'm almost deafened by the sound of a single gunshot. Red blooms across her stomach. It spreads fast until she's covered in her own blood. I race to her, scoop her up as she falls, but it's too late. And I am helpless."

"The man who would help everyone is helpless," I say.

"Not everyone." He smiles. "Anyone on a reality TV show is screwed."

Sunshine. He smells of sunshine. My eyes close for just a moment and I'm standing out in my grandmother's yard, surrounded by fresh sheets being slow-baked under a high summer sun. When I open my eyes, he's watching me.

"What do you think it means?"

He shrugs, taps the Stop button, and we start moving again.

"Nothing. It's just a dream." A dimple breaks the plane of his cheek. "Unless it's not. I'll make you a deal. Take action in your dream. Tip the jar. See what lies beneath."

"And if I do that?"

"I'll take you out to dinner."

It's what I want; I know that.

We lurch as the elevator stops. He's still watching me, the question in his eyes, waiting on my answer.

The words catch in my throat, then shake themselves loose. "I'm sorry," I say, "but it wouldn't be right. But if the world ends tomorrow, understand that I regret saying no."

The world doesn't end the next day. Or the day after that. But six months later, humanity is too busy circling the drain for any of us to worry about dates we didn't accept.

DATE: NOW

The day grinds on. Each hour heavier than the last. Theoretically they should be getting lighter as I get closer to Brindisi, but like any theory it's there to be disproven.

When I mention this to Lisa she asks, "What's in Brindisi?"

"Boats. More specifically, a boat. The *Elpis*."

"Can I come?"

This morning she was glassy-eyed, but now she's clear and

bright. Her chest bones are a skin-covered xylophone peeking out of the V-neck of her shirt. Mine are the same beneath my raincoat.

"If you want to." Though where she'd go without me hadn't entered my thoughts until now. "I'm counting on it."

"Yay." She gives a little clap. "Where's the boat going?"

"Greece."

"Why go there?"

"Because I'm meeting someone."

She chews on this for a moment. "What if they're not there?"

"They will be."

"But what if they're not?"

"They will be."

"They will be," she parrots.

DATE: THEN

Ben's eyes are bloodshot; a snot droplet hangs from the red-dened rim of his left nostril.

"Have you seen Stiffy?"

It's 2:53 a.m. I haven't seen anything but my crazy dreams for the past five hours. I try to think. When did I last see his cat? The night James came over? That was two, no, three nights ago. Have I seen the marmalade tomcat since then?

"Is he missing?"

My question is stupid. Of course he's missing, otherwise Ben wouldn't be here searching. But the sleep has scrambled my head and I haven't yet untangled myself from its hold.

Ben wipes the back of his hand across his nose. He pulls his omnipresent brown cardigan tighter around his narrow body. He's pale, I see that now, and not just from the hallway's harsh light.

"Yeah. For a couple days now. It's not like him, you know?"

"He likes his food."

"Yeah."

I feel bad for Ben; Stiffy is all he has. "I'll keep an eye out, okay? I have to work in a few hours, but I'll help you look for him tonight."

"Really?"

I make all the right noises and Ben retreats. Sleep doesn't come again. It's done with me for the night. Friday. The last day of the working week. Tonight I see Dr. Rose. Which means it's three nights ago, not two, that I saw James.

Steam rises from the cup in my hands. It's a thin, shimmering shield that separates me from Dr. Rose. He's watching me—not like a woman, but like a client. Between last time and this time he's flipped a switch, and now we're each of us in our proper place. I'm glad. Really, I am. Because I like Friday nights; I want to see the next one with him. And the one after that.

"Why do you do it?"

My thoughts pull out of the coffee. "Why do I clean floors?"

He nods once.

"Would you believe me if I said I like working with my hands?"

Seconds tick by without him speaking. He isn't visiting any other part of me until I've shown him this piece.

"Because when Sam died I realized that life is about an inch long, and I didn't want to drop more hours in a bucket I had no intention of filling. So I took a janitorial job that paid well enough, offered decent benefits, and didn't ask me to think too hard. It gave me time to think about what I want to be when I grow up, where I want to study. And it's satisfying. It yields immediate results. Something is dirty, then it's not."

"What do you want to be when you grow up?"

"Happy."

"I want to see that."

DATE: NOW

"What happened to your friends?" Lisa asks.

"Dead."

"Me too."

A while later . . .

"Do you think they're better off?"

"Sometimes."

"Why?"

"Because not everybody can handle this."

"But *we* can."

"We're doing our best."

"What do you think will happen to us?"

"I don't know," I say truthfully. "How about you?"

She shrugs. "I think I'm going to die. I'm scared. Are you scared?"

"Sometimes. But I try not to think about it too hard."

Lisa's makeshift cane taps constantly, chipping away the miles. My blisters have hardened into thick lumps on my heels and soles.

"Have you ever been in love?" she asks.

"Yes."

"What was it like?"

"Great and terrible." Like Oz.

"I've never been in love. At least, I don't think so. I used to have this boyfriend, Eddie. He wasn't really a boyfriend—more like a boy who was a friend. He kissed me one time and then after that he wouldn't speak to me. I cried for a week. Do you think that was love?"

"Maybe. Only you can know for sure."

"I don't think it was. I hope not. But I hope so, too. Because I don't want to die without falling in love at least once."

DATE: THEN

James is leaning back on the couch, poring through a textbook bigger than his head.

"So, what do you think, Rain Man?"

I laugh. "Jesus, you can't call him that."

"Sure I can." He winks at me.

Raoul turns away from the jar, flashes me a smile that makes me wish I was wearing sunglasses. "I know what they call me behind my back. Could be worse. Like James."

James is making a meal of Raoul with his eyes when he's not focused on the book. Part lust, part fascination with the younger man's expertise.

If Raoul notices, he's oblivious.

"It's got to be Greek."

James's head bobs like a parrot. "That's what *I* said."

"But from when?" they say at the same time.

"It's like a missing link," Raoul says.

"Bridging two periods of history."

Raoul rubs his fingers across the delicate curve of the lip. "It looks like something I saw once. In a painting, though, and the artist wasn't Greek. *Pandora's Box.*"

"Ahh," James says as though that is the answer to everything. "The Eve of Greek mythology. You nosy women can't help yourselves."

I've heard the story about the woman who opened the box and let havoc grab a choke hold on the world. But the correlation between that and my jar eludes me.

Raoul correctly interprets my confusion. "It's a matter of one small error in the translation of Hesiod's work. What was thought for some time to be a box was actually a jar. Zeus gifted Pandora with a simple jar similar to those used to store food-stuffs or bones—"

"Like an ossuary," James adds.

"—and then forbade her from opening the lid."

We all look at the jar, at the lid with its rim of wax neatly seal-ing the top.

"Of course, she opened it," James says. "But who wouldn't have?"

Raoul circles the jar, his hand still upon its rough surface. "It's important to remember that like Eve she was just curious and didn't act out of malice. Curiosity isn't a bad thing. It drives us to improve and explore and discover. Without curiosity I wouldn't have a job. Her actions may not have been all negative. For when she released all the ills of the world on mankind, she also gave us obstacles to overcome. Without them we would have been little more than men of clay. Instead we think and struggle and grow."

He looks at me. "I wonder what's inside. Any guesses?"

A cold-hot wave washes over my cheeks. I feel them pinken because he's picked on my obsession and thrown the question out there like it's nothing.

"Bones," James says.

"Dust," I say.

"Drugs." James's second offering.

Raoul flashes his smile, this time at James. "Ancient corn."

I flop down on the armchair, stare at the jar. "Death."

Raoul sinks into the couch next to James. We sit. We stare.

DATE: NOW

The village isn't on the map, but it's there off to the left of the road like an afterthought. It's little more than a knot of houses, at least from our vantage point. The road rises ahead, an endless gray ribbon winding through the mountains. We're going southeast, although the road struggles to stay true. When I tell Lisa this, her feet slow.

"Can we stop?"

"No. I have to be in Brindisi in fifteen days."

"But they'll have beds. Real live beds. With blankets and pillows."

"Fine."

"Ha! I win."

"If you can carry it, you can have a blanket," I say.

"But I want to sleep in a bed."

"We can't stop there. We can't risk it."

"Because you have to get to a boat and find your friend. They're probably dead just like everyone else."

I want to grab her, shake her, tell her I'm terrified whatever is following us isn't human anymore. That her prolonged rape could seem like a beautiful dream compared to what a stranger could do. But I don't because she's just a kid. I want to tell her that getting to the *Elpis* is the only thing to do, that the person I'm meeting will be there. But I don't say that, either, because there's a cold tickle in my belly that says she's right.

"And maybe we'll both be dead tomorrow."

That shuts her up.

Guilt paints another coat of grime on my shoulders, but it's not enough to change my mind. We're safer out here.

"The air feels strange," she says. "What does that mean?"

True enough, the clouds are the pale green of hospital scrubs.

"Hail."

"I want to feel the sun again," Lisa says. "That's going on my list."

"Mine, too."

The clouds thicken overheard and dip down to meet us.

DATE: NOW

It's the hail and high-force winds that force us into the village. We struggle to keep the bicycle upright as we slog our way to the shelter of the stone homes, wending our way between the trees. The road has the worst of it. Here we are slammed, battered, until all our energy goes into keeping ourselves standing. My body aches like a punching bag pounded with maddened fists. Branches fly, catapulted by gusts of untamed air. This wind is new. *Please,* I think. *Please don't let it be omnipresent like the rain.*

We don't stop and announce our arrival, nor do we stop to take stock of our surroundings. We bolt up the stone steps for the nearest door, dragging the bicycle. I push Lisa in first, the bike, then I tumble into safety.

The wind dies immediately when I slam the door behind us, yet it waits for us, knocking, scratching, flinging fistfuls of hail against the wood. *Come out, come out,* it dares us. *Come out and play.*

Lisa is wild-haired and red-cheeked. Cuts mar her skin. I feel the sting where flying debris has marked my own flesh.

"Are you okay?"

"Yeah. You?"

Down the door I slide until I'm using my knees as a chin rest.

"Okay. Good." My eyes drift closed just for a moment.

When I open them a moment later, it's dark. The constant *plink plink* of hail has stopped, but the wind is still trying to huff and puff the little brick house down, and it's brought the night with it. What time, I don't know. There's not enough light to see my watch. There's not any light except a vague promise from beyond the windows. A little has trickled through the clouds.

All that listening, and it takes me several minutes to understand Lisa is missing.

My breath catches and holds. If I drown out my own sounds maybe I'll hear hers. People make all kinds of noises: sniffing, throat clearing, belching. Even shifting inside a space can produce sound: the rub of fabric against fabric, or the squeak of sweaty skin.

Breathing. There should be breathing at least, but there's just a house full of emptiness.

"Lisa?" The name falls into the room like an iron lump. I try to remember the topography of this space, but sleep came too quickly for my surroundings to sink in.

Once more, with as much volume as I dare: "Lisa?"

In this dark room, the nothingness stretches on forever. She is not here. Not alive, at least. The house is too small—I remember that much, and I would hear something if she were.

How far can she have gone by feel alone? I hope I can reach her with my voice.

The door is at my back. I wrench it open, throw her name into the wind. In the distance there's a golden glow, small enough that I can cup my hands around the light and snuff it. A flame? A light? There is no steady electricity, hasn't been for at least three months—maybe longer, maybe less here—so I know it's not that. Greasy hair strands flog my cheeks and forehead, until I'm wincing from the blows.

And then I see it's not raining. *It's not raining.*

I trot down the steps, raise my head to the sky. The clouds are still a thick blanket obscuring the stars, but it's not raining. For the first time since I stepped on Italian soil, it's not raining. I want to laugh. It's right there, bubbling in my chest, waiting for my diaphragm to push it free. Here it comes . . .

. . . and dies in my tightening throat. My fingers clutch at what's binding me and touch the harsh fibers of rope. I'm reeled in like a gasping fish.

Someone speaks. "Why aren't you dead?" A voice with all the softness of a sack filled with nails and broken glass. "Tell me," he rasps. The rope tightens and burns. "Why aren't you dead?"

FIVE

Never get attached, I remind myself. Don't give the lab mice names. They have numbers assigned according to their birth date and sex; they don't require more. Blowing kisses as I sweep the laboratory floor is borderline acceptable.

Pope Pharmaceuticals' labs are a stereotype, taking white to new shades of pale. They're filled with the usual array of machines, each costing more than a house in California, test tubes, petri dishes filled with agar. A chip packet is a bold sun against the floor. Laboratories on television are always clean. In my reality the lab workers eat lunch at their computers and desks. I don't mind my work. It's a means to a specific end: I want an education.

I'm mopping when Jorge comes in. He's a grease spot on an otherwise pristine work environment.

"Don't forget to see the doctor, eh?"

"I won't."

"Good, otherwise . . ." He mimes snapping a neck that's clearly mine. "You want me to come with you?" He acts like he's my supervisor. I act like he's my barely tolerable coworker. One of us is right and I'm sure it's me.

The cleaning cart sticks on the door tracks. I persuade it with a shove.

"I suspect I'll manage."

From there I go to the women's locker room, change out of my uniform, and toss it down the hatch that I know leads to the laundry. Another fresh one will be waiting for me next shift. With my bag slung over one shoulder, I take the elevator up to the tenth floor, where the medical facilities are located.

Biannual physical. Company protocol. No checkup, no job, no paycheck, ergo: no college.

Dr. Scott is waiting. We go through the routine I've performed three times before today: blood pressure, EKG, weight. He takes a vial of blood and then he's back with another needle. It's not the first time.

"It's that time of the year again," he says. "Company orders."

He rolls up my sleeve until my upper arm is bare, then swabs an area the size of a quarter. The tip goes in like I'm butter.

"Hold still," Dr. Scott says by rote, even though I'm a statue.

The pain is a spider unfolding impossibly long legs.

"What the hell?" It takes all I've got not to jerk away. "What *is* that stuff? Liquid fire?"

"Flu shot. Keep still. Nearly done." He eases the needle out. "All done. You know the routine."

I do. Rest for half an hour to make sure there's no reaction. The fire blazes long after he drops the needle in the hazardous-waste trash.

"Seriously, what was that?"

"Flu shot," he repeats, like they've made him practice the words a thousand times. "Everyone has to have one. You can go now."

DATE: NOW

My breath comes in desperate bursts. The rope grinds into one of my tracheal valleys, held snug there in the shallow V. Pounding in my chest blocks out all ambient noise.

"Where's Lisa?" I try to say.

The rope jerks and my mouth opens in an airless gasp.

"*I'm* asking the questions."

The accent isn't American or British, but the wind could be distorting the softness of the vowels, the crispness of the consonants.

My fingers work the rope, searching for weakness, a gap I can exploit the way the rope holder exploited mine. I find it at the back and discover he's looped it around my neck without bothering to twist, which means there's space enough for two fingers. Cracking my head into his face isn't an option, because his mouth is shoved up against my ear.

Rough fibers grate my fingers as I ease them along the path. They burn new grooves into my whorls and loops. No helping hand comes from the weather; the wind dumps dust in my eyes before whisking away the irrigating tears.

"Why are you alive?"

"There are still people alive."

He shakes his head against me. "Not without a good reason. What are you? Somebody important? You're just a woman."

"I'm nobody."

"Liar."

He might have a weapon. If he has rope, then chances are better than good that he does. But I do, too. There's the paring knife in my pocket, nestled between the seams. One of us has to be faster, and from where I'm standing—with a rope around my neck—that had better be me.

I close my eyes, try to blink away the grit. Maybe it's my imagination but the wind seems less determined now, like it's running out of breath, too tired to go on.

"Speak up," he says.

"Screw. You. Asshole."

I jerk my left arm up, ram my elbow into his gut. He jumps back in time to avoid most of the damage, but gives me an advantage in doing so: his fingers have released enough of the rope for me to twist around, snatch up the slack, and yank it from his hands.

It's too dark to see the rope burn through his skin, but his muffled yelps deliver the message.

"Lunatic," he says when he recovers. He drags me by the arm back up the stairs into the house I just left. "Talk. But not too loud."

"Where's Lisa?"

"Dead."

My heart is an elevator with broken cables crashing through the floors all the way to my feet. I snap. I can't help it. My fist crashes through something in the dark. It feels like it might be his face. A palm collides with my cheek. Teeth rattle in my head. A sob claws its way through the miserable lump in my throat.

"You bastard. She was just a damn kid."

"A stupid girl, outside in the dark alone. You should have raised her better than that."

"She's not mine. Just my responsibility."

"Well, then she's a fucking stupid child. A stupid dead child now."

"What did you do?"

He shoves me to the window, points. "Do you see that light?"

The light is still there. Steady. Constant. "I see it."

"Your idiot friend is there. What is left of her."

"I want to see her."

"Not yet. First you must answer my questions."

"I want answers, too."

"No. You have no choices now."

The accent, I still can't pinpoint it. Somewhere European. German, Austrian, Swiss maybe. I can't tell the difference, which makes my stomach squeeze with shame. How little of the world I knew before it was almost all gone.

Lisa is dead. It's just me now. Me and this guy.

"I'm nobody. A cleaner at a drug company."

His laugh is tight and bitter. "A cleaner. You are telling me a janitor made it this far?"

"Why not?"

"You're as stupid as your friend. Come with me."

Like I have a choice. He loops the rope around my hands so I'm forced to follow him back down the steps. The wind has flatlined. There's no sign of rain. It's cloudy with a good chance of death.

I see his shape in the dark. There's not much to him, although what there is of his physique is hard. He's made of wire, not bulk. My height, in heels. I can take him. If I wait, I can take him. I hope. For Lisa's sake. For mine. Because nothing will stop me from meeting that boat.

"I'm sorry," I whisper, and hope that Lisa can forgive me.

"I am going to show you something. But if you make a noise, I will snap your stupid neck. Nod if you understand."

I nod, show I understand, although in truth I'm more ignorant than I ever was.

The stone behemoth squats in a field past the village's rim, malevolent in the dark with its single glowing eye. It's a half-blinded beast from a world that came to a different end to ours.

My captor creeps now, each step deliberately pressed into the damp grass. He pulls me with him and I see no good reason not to obey. He has all the information and all I have is a sense of foreboding that fills me with frosty dread.

When we reach the window, he shoves me into the shadows, holds a finger to his lips, lifts his face to the glass.

I want to see, too. I need to. Even if all the horrors in all the world are collected in this barn, I need to look inside.

He senses my urgency, the fair-haired man with cheekbones high enough and sharp enough to slice cold cuts, and indulges my desire.

From beams thicker than my thigh, hooks dangle, Spanish question marks that ask a question for which I wish I had no answer. But I do; I know what happens in this place and I wish so hard I didn't. I'm a city girl, born and raised. My meat used to come with price tags and a dose of carbon monoxide to keep it red. But here, meat moved in herds.

The village has survivors and they've gathered, the half dozen of them wrapped in clothes that will never know good days. My gaze zooms in. Pans and scans. Breaks everything into candeal chunks. Takes in the nest these once-people have created. Bones and rust-colored straw litter the barn. Decaying gore. Old bones, judging from the meatless sheen, from chickens and other livestock. They've been picked clean, snapped in two, the marrow slurped from their centers. Heaps of cans rust in the corners. Empty food wrappers form a carpet that will never rot. Tools hang on the walls, abandoned. No more harvests under a bulging autumn moon.

One of the villagers breaks away, crawls across the floor to a wooden bucket jerked from a well, but his pose is anything but penitent. A row of jagged bones forms painful-looking spikes along his spine. They shudder as he swallows. When he's done, he sits on his haunches, rivulets racing down his face, dripping onto his food-stained chest. Animal blood has dried on his tattered shirt many times over, then soaked anew. The others crouch in a crude circle, staring up, up, at some object of fascination. So I follow the path of their obsession. My gaze slides along the networked beams until it catches on something blond and blue. My heart lurches.

Lisa.

Desperation and terror must have pushed her up so high. I can't see the *how*, but it doesn't matter: she made it to relative safety.

My shoulders twitch with need-to-go, need-to-get-to-her. The stranger holds me back, steers me until Lisa disappears from view. He turns us around, walks us back to the village proper.

I clutch at the damp lapels of his jacket. It's too dark to see here, but I remember it being the drab green of all things military. "You said she was dead."

"She *is* dead. Or she will be when I blow that place off the planet."

Now I see the burden he carries: a backpack filled with secrets.

"It was you at the church, wasn't it?"

He doesn't confirm, only grunts.

"You can't do it. Not with her in there. I won't let you."

"You have no choice."

DATE: THEN

The jar is heavier than it looks, as though its core is filled with sand. Or maybe good intentions. Silence is the only protest as I walk it backwards and lean its top half onto the soft ottoman.

Something shifts inside. There's a whisper like old, discarded snake skins rubbing together. A chill tiptoes down my spine's spurred steps.

My knees dig into the beige carpet's level loop pile as I kneel to follow Dr. Rose's recommendation. Maybe there's a clue here about what lies beneath. I look. Nothing. A whole lot of nothing but more of the same. Smooth, with a hint of chalkiness. It's left a faint dusting of itself on the carpet, and I can't help but run my fingertip across the cheap fibers. The residue is soft and silky like cornstarch.

A frustrated sigh rides my breath. I wanted there to be something. Even if it was a Made in China sticker.

This time Dr. Rose doesn't wait for me to speak. We settle into our respective chairs and roles, or so I think until he sets his notepad aside. Instinctively, my legs cross and I lace my fingers together, clasping them over my top knee. A model of cautious propriety.

He drinks in my defensive pose with his dark gaze, then knocks it aside with his question.

"Do you want me, too?"

"Yes. And no."

He leans back, flashes a smile that makes me wish we hadn't met here, in this place where my mental health is a question mark.

"I'll take that. For now."

Inside I shiver because *for now* means there will be a later, and he thinks I'm worth the wait. The pursuit. But part of me flares because I turned him down, and here he is steamrolling over me like my "No, thank you" was a meaningless thing.

For a moment he watches me and I feel naked. Usually it's just my mind feeling exposed here, but now it's my body as well. My nipples tighten. I swallow hard.

"Did you have the dream?" he asks.

"What?"

He never goes first. Never prompts me. But here he is changing all the rules. The notebook is back on his lap and he's sitting there, pen idle in his right hand. That much, at least, is normal.

"The jar."

"Oh. That." The jar, the jar, the stinking jar. The tumor in my life. The jar is like having cancer and trying to figure out where you went wrong so its growth was nurtured. Was it the butter? The margarine? Too much beef? Too much watching and waiting on the microwave to ding? What had I done that someone felt compelled to enter my home and give me an antediluvian mystery? I pick through the bones of my life looking for clues and find nothing.

"Yes," I say.

He waits.

"It's the color of scorched cream." My hands reach into thin air and grasp invisible handles. And stop. They sink to my knees, massage the patella. "We do this every week and nothing changes."

"Did you look at the bottom?"

"Yes."

"And?"

"Wherever it's from, it's not made in China. That I know of."

We share a tense smile.

"What do you think is inside?" he asks.

"I couldn't guess. Most likely nothing."

"Have you wondered?"

"No," I lie.

"But something has changed: this week you looked at the bottom. Next time I want you to see if you can look inside. How do you feel about that?"

My hands ball into fists. "Fine."

DATE: NOW

Dawn comes in the same gray cloak she always wears these days. Shades of blue would be more becoming, or maybe pearls and pinks and peaches, because somewhere out there it's spring— or should be. My eyelids fly open to the welcome feeling of no nausea and the less welcome feeling of a two-by-four beating against the inside of my skull in some kind of erratic Morse code. Pressing my hands against my stomach, I perform a half crunch and my muscles tense in protest. Concave, although slightly closer to flat than before.

"Amino acids."

"What?"

My captor is crouched on the floor, fastening wires to a cigarette-pack-sized block of sweating plasticine.

"You still want to save your friend?"

"Yes," I rasp.

"Be my guest." He doesn't look up.

"What about amino acids?"

"They are the building blocks of life. Combined in the right order, they make proteins. DNA is made of amino acids. Probably they will kill her and eat her. Human flesh has the amino acids they need."

"You don't know that."

"Are you menstruating?"

"What?"

"You're angry. Women are often angry when they menstruate. It is the hormones."

I rub my head until the tapping subsides to a tick.

"Where do you come from?"

"Switzerland."

"Do they teach manners there?"

He keeps working with his blocks. "They don't teach anything there now. My country is gone. And my people." Hard planes maketh this man. He is the Alps of his homeland in miniature: hard, unyielding, cruel.

I pick up my body, then I pick up my backpack. And I leave.

I am going to rescue Lisa. If I don't, there's no hope for the child growing inside me. I need to be able to save someone.

DATE: THEN

Purple paper does not flatter Stiffy, but that's what Ben wants.

"The bright color will make people look," he says.

Who am I to argue? I've got a soft spot for that hunk of orange fur with the *Kiss my ass, but not too close* attitude. A roll of tape gets dumped on top of the paper stack.

"Put them everywhere. Cover other people's lost pets if you have to." He takes off, shoving fliers at all available warm bodies. Purple paper floats to the ground, but Ben doesn't notice that people think he's just another loon with something to shill.

The opposite direction is mine. I'm more conservative as I tape Stiffy's face to walls and poles. I smile at a few people, but they glance away, focused on their own troubles. At the end of the block I turn back. That's what we agreed to. Ben and I meet in the middle outside our apartment building.

His top lip twitches beneath his crusty nose. When I ask how he is, he shrugs.

"Just a cold," he says. "And I think maybe I'm pregnant, because I'm always riding the porcelain bus, or thinking about it." He sounds like honking geese when he laughs. "I'm happy now, though, because someone's going to find Stiffy. He'll be back by tonight, I know it."

He's wrong. The fliers yield nothing more than a handful of obscene calls and one guy with a Korean accent inquiring about a job. Stiffy shows up a week later, gaunt and matted and filthy from some adventure that only makes sense to him. He saunters through my window with his usual nonchalance and takes the front-row seat in front of the jar.

Something cold and scaly uncoils in my gut.

"Stiffy."

Usually he'll glance up at me, rub my shins, make noises about food. But this time he employs selective hearing and ignores me. When I approach him, he spits, lashes out, nothing like the cat I know. I shut the window and call Ben. The phone rings in stereo, through the floor and in my ear. Nine rings. I dial again. Three more and he picks up.

"Hold on." His throat forces out noises that sound like he's coughing up a hairball. "I can't stop puking," he says, but he makes an effort when I tell him I have his cat.

A minute later he's busting through my door, his skin waxen, his breath acidic and foul.

"Stiffy!" He rushes to hug his cat.

Ben leaves with a spring to his step. The last image I see of Stiffy is the marmalade cat wide-eyed and unblinking, staring at the jar over his owner's shoulder.

SIX

Ｎew physiology brought with it change to old patterns. Humans infected with White Horse mutated in unpredictable ways. Ninety percent died. Of the remaining ten percent, maybe half were immune. The other five mutated in a way that was survivable. Unless pushed by career or some other drive such as the burning desire to beat the next level on a video game, humans are not nocturnal. Oh, we can do it, of course, but never wrench from it the satisfaction that comes from sleeping nights.

But in this leftover world, in the dying gasp of humanity, some things now hunt at night. Which means during the day they sleep . . .

The once-woman twitches like a dog mid-dream. Is there enough human in her that she dreams of an exorbitant shopping trip in Milan, or has her mind slipped into the primordial stew where her single-cell body propels itself to its next meal with a whip-like flagella?

All six creatures are sleeping like obscene, fattened kittens nestled in the straw. Their mouths chew in their sleep, but they'll stop when the Swiss blows this barn clear off the field. These stones have withstood earthquakes, weather, and war, but they will crumble in a duel with plastic explosives.

Lisa. I have to get her. I can't leave her here.

She's crouched in the same wooden intersection, knees drawn to her chest as though they're a shield that will keep the monsters at bay, the equivalent of a blanket warding away the bogeyman.

When I move several inches to the left to gain a better view inside the barn, Lisa's head jerks as though she's spotted me. But it's a lie. Her eyes are flat and lifeless. She's given up. Probably thinks I'm dead, or as good as, too.

Please don't let her move. While the creatures sleep, there is a chance.

The backpack slides off my shoulders. I cover several dozen feet and drop it at the base of a tree. The paring knife is already in my pocket, and a moment later I am wielding the cleaver. It has good balance.

Please don't let me need to use it. Would that my wish held more magic than a prayer.

The barn has one set of doors. A rusted padlock is a broken arm dangling from an equally oxidized latch. It's a low building with the characteristic red roof that dots the Italian country-side like the measles. Three windows. One on each wall that doesn't have a door. None are large enough even if they did open. Which leaves me with the door and hinges so old they'll sing soprano at the first touch.

I pray Lisa can hold on.

At the house, the Swiss is poking through a metal box. He slaps it shut as I stride past him with silent purpose, straight to the tiny galley kitchen.

"Were you unlucky?"

"No."

"What are you looking for?"

"Nothing." I pull a gallon can of olive oil from its hiding place beneath the narrow strip of counter. There are no cabinets below, just curtains concealing pots, pans, and baking goods from polite company.

"Olive oil?"

"No kitchen in Italy is complete without it."

"You can't save her," he tells my back. "They probably ate what was left of the other villagers. They won't care about your stupid friend."

It's not just college grades that fall in a curve. Human decency is bell-shaped, with some of us slopping over the edges. Saints on one end, sinners on the other—if you want to be biblical. There's no way of knowing where these posthumans fall, how much of the *person* is driving the meat bus.

I can't play the genetic lottery with Lisa's life. I'm armed only with my own good intentions.

Oil slops over the hinges, seeps between the metal cracks. I pray to a God I don't really have faith in just so I feel like I have company, but He doesn't answer. Minutes tick by. I wait as long as I dare; I don't know how long the posthumans will sleep. For all I know, they're like dogs, sleeping with one ear open, waiting for food to fall on the floor in the next room.

Behind the dense high clouds, the sun is a spot of lighter gray. Morning is here in full. Enough light that I can peer through the window and tack together some kind of rescue plan.

The door barely complains as I inch my body through the narrow slit I've made. And then I'm in a scratch-and-sniff snapshot of hell. The church was just a warm-up. These things sleep here. They shit here. They eat here amongst their own filth.

My boots poke holes in the straw. I look down because I don't want to step in the brown sludge piles littering the floor. In places it's thick, like a melted-down mud hut. It is this disjointed dance of one hesitant step after the other that carries me to the beam holding Lisa.

One of the beings stirs.

I hold my breath until it settles again.

Hold.

The pressure stings. Carbon dioxide burns my lungs, but I don't dare release too soon.

Hold.

Tears fill my eyes.

On the barn floor, the creature is still once more, lost in its wretched dreamworld.

Quietly, I mouth to Lisa, then reprimand myself for forgetting. So I wrap the word in softened breath.

Lisa's lips move, forming the shape of my name.

Matted, bloody hair clings to her right ear in a red poultice. Her right eye is beaten to a blackened slit. They must have knocked her out to bring her here, although I haven't yet figured out how they got to her and not me. She must have gone exploring after I fell asleep, probably through a window, because the door was blocked by what there is of me.

No. Something must have lured her. There's no way she'd go alone.

Idiot kid.

Thank God she's alive.

Blood flakes from the red-brown crust around her mouth. She seems even thinner than yesterday. Her legs are compasses bent at tight angles beneath the denim. I want to cry. I want to hug her. I want to shake the stupid from her bones.

There's the scraping of the doors closing and locking as the rusted parts rub together.

I run to the doors.

"No," I whisper as loud as I dare. "Don't do this."

His voice is as cold as winter in his homeland. "They're an abomination. I warned you."

"You prick."

"If you can survive this, maybe your life is worth saving."

"Your logic is flawed."

"Is it?" He sounds surprised.

"I'm going to Brindisi, and I'll be damned if some cheese maker is going to lock me in a barn and blow me off the planet. I haven't come all that way for this."

"Have you heard of Charles Darwin?"

"*Origin of Species*. Natural selection. I picked up that bit of trivia *before* I went to work for Pope Pharmaceuticals." Sarcasm is my intention, but it sounds like desperation.

He falls quiet.

"Hello?"

The locks scrape. The sound is an alarm clock for the sleeping beasts. Sleep falls from them in ragged sheets. Enough of their stuffing is still human that they wake in a fog, clawing at their eyes, trying to figure why they woke prematurely. Who knows if they've conquered caffeine addiction yet?

"Lisa?" I scan the barn, search the seams for a way up. "How did you get up there?" But then I spot the heap of rotting sticks on the ground. Leftover ladder parts.

Think, Zoe. Harder.

Being quiet won't save us now—only being fast.

"Lisa, you're going to have to jump."

Her head and body shake with the idea.

A slit appears between the door and jam. The Swiss stares at me, eyes devoid of warmth. "*On the Origin of Species*, to be precise. I am Swiss. People rely on our watches for their accuracy."

I risk it all in one harsh breath. "Lisa!"

Her head jerks up. Her mind engages long enough to understand my demand. I snap my fingers, give her an aural goal. *Move toward me, not them.* That way lies madness; she's known enough of that for all the lifetimes of all the people left in the world.

Three sets of eyes swivel toward me. Two more don't. The largest male, a man maybe forty years old before White Horse, pins one of the females to the floor facedown, mounts her like a four-legged creature. She squirms beneath him, but only until he bangs her face on the shit-crusted planks. The others crawl towards me, their backs hunched and tense. The sixth villager staggers to her feet. She spasms like a puppet tied to strings, then her joints seem to melt and her bones no longer hold her upright.

White Horse kills a hostage. The once-woman's body seizes, flinging straw with dying fingers. For a moment, the scene reminds me of macaroni art. A second woman scrambles to her side. She pulls the other close, smoothes the snarled hair with a ruined hand, cradles her until Death rides away with his prize.

"Now!"

For a moment Lisa hangs in the balance, until gravity tucks a finger in her shirt pocket and pulls. Then she's falling like a pretty pebble.

I collapse under the weight of her, but refuse to stay down. My will to survive is our trebuchet. I shove her ahead of me, squeeze her through the door's gap into the light, thrust myself into what's left of the space.

It's the still-human sobbing that jerks me still. The world is filled with tears; these should be drips in an overflowing bucket. I should be immune. But I still have a heart, and it rushes to sympathize.

I taste their grief when I bite down on my lip. It's salt with a hint of winter.

The Swiss snatches a fistful of my shirt, drags me backwards.

"Don't be a fool," he says. He locks the doors in silence, although the silence is only his. There's Lisa's crying. Then there's me.

"They're still people."

"They're an abomination," he says. "Unnaturally selected because of a disease we made."

I don't ask how he knows about the disease's origins or how much. Not now. Later, maybe. Right now I want to check on Lisa and get us moving again.

We go as far as the tree where I left my backpack, she and I. Pink rivers take the southern course down her youthful skin, more rain than blood. Her chin is awash with strawberry fluids. The cuts on her head don't appear to be serious, although there is no way of knowing how deep the damage goes. Could be she's a time bomb, the seconds ticking away until the pressure inside her skull squeezes the delicate pink hemispheres and . . . *pop*.

"Hurry," the Swiss says. He's sneaked up on us. "The doors are locked, but they might find another way." He nods at Lisa. "She will recover."

"What are you, a doctor?"

"Yes." Equally blunt. He grabs her chin, tilts it up. "As I said, she will be fine."

"Are you okay?" I ask.

Lisa's nod blurs into a shake.

"How did they get you?"

Another shake.

"Her eye is gone." He shoves up her eyelid, revealing a bleeding hole where there used to be a whitish orb with a pretty gray-green center. "Perhaps they popped it out like a grape. The soft bits are a delicacy."

"Lisa, baby girl, how did it happen?"

She lifts her head from the Swiss's hands. In her lap, her fingers curl like dying leaves. They're wet with tears. "I don't know," she murmurs. "I don't know. I don't know." Beneath the worn cotton, her shoulders tremble.

The Swiss isn't done speculating. "The stupid child did this to herself."

I stand, pull on my backpack, help Lisa to her feet. I need to get her fed and cleaned, then get her away from here before the once-humans find that way out.

"What the hell is wrong with you?" I ask him.

"She's blind."

"She always was."

"And yet, she wanders out here unsupervised. She's a fool and a liability. You should not trust anyone," he says. "Not even her."

"Shut up," I say. "Just shut up." But he's planted a seed and now the vines of it are creeping through my mind.

DATE: Then

"Have you looked inside the jar yet, Zoe?"

"No. I know I have to."

Dr. Rose's voice gives me confidence. He washes me in calm.

"If you're going to move past this, you have to look inside."

"I know."

"I know that you know." Our smiles meet and touch in the center of the room, the way our bodies never will.

By the time I reach my apartment my mettle has melted, leaving only fear.

DATE: NOW

"He's going to blow up the barn," I tell Lisa. "I can't stop him."

The bicycle is heavy with food again, all of it canned, from the village's pantries. I found bandages and antibiotic cream that she now keeps in the waterproof pocket of her rain jacket.

We stand on the road we crossed just yesterday, the world still and damp around us. Then it explodes and fire fills the sky. We don't fall to the ground this time. We stand and watch and I am not glad the barn is no more. All I can do now is hope those people found a sort of peace.

"I thought I was going to upchuck again," Lisa says as we watch that piece of our past burn. Her voice is pale and numb. "I heard the rain stop, so I went out for fresh air. I got lost, couldn't find the window to climb back in. I heard them coming. Making noises like dogs, they were. I didn't know they weren't dogs. Not at first. Not until I woke up in the barn. I was trying to get out when I found a ladder, so I climbed it."

"What happened to your eye?"

"I don't know."

"It's okay. You don't have to tell me if you don't want to."

"You'll think I'm stupid. A stupid blind girl."

"A stupid person wouldn't have climbed that ladder."

For a moment she fades away. Shock is still lingering around her edges.

"It wasn't the dog people. There was something sharp in the wood. A nail, maybe. A big, fat nail. See? I'm so stupid. No one will love me now. Not with one eye."

An invisible line scratched in the ground between us stops me from crossing the breach. And I'm all out of useful words.

"I was supposed to get a Guide dog, before all this. I always wanted a dog. Dogs love you no matter what."

"What happened?"

"My dad said we didn't need another mouth to feed."

She turns away.

DATE: THEN

I don't know why I'm perpetuating the lie. Maybe because it's like an express train: once the journey's started, there's no changing tracks until the end of the line. Or maybe I'm just a bad person. But I don't really believe that.

"I dreamed about the jar again last night," I start, and then I stop, spread my fingers wide enough that I can massage both temples with my thumb and middle finger. "Actually, no. No, I didn't dream about the jar at all."

He's wearing his business face: smooth, nonjudgmental, eyes bright with awareness. Nowhere can I catch a glimpse of the man who showed interest in knowing more about who I am when I'm not playing a basket case on this couch. He glances down at the notepad, scribbles, lifts his gaze to meet mine.

"Do you feel like that's progress?"

"What did you just write?"

He stretches back in the chair and, in a blatantly male move, rubs his hand across his stomach. Through his shirt, I can see it's hard, flat, lightly defined.

"Does it matter?" he asks.

"Probably not. I'm just curious."

His laugh is tight.

"What?"

"I can't convince you to open the jar, but you want to look at what I'm writing."

"Maybe I want to know what you really think about me." My legs cross. I lean forward. Give him a look Sam once told me was equal parts trouble and seduction. Guilt flashes like lighting in my mind, then disappears. We're doctor and patient. No, *client*. That's what he said. But I can't help reacting to him any more than he can help sitting there with his legs apart, hand on his stomach, all but pointing the way to his cock. Our bodies do what they do—sometimes without our permission.

"So tell me: Am I crazy?"

He breathes deep through his nose then laughs. "Here." The pad flies across the short distance. My insides crackle with trepidation and excitement.

Milk.

Toilet paper.

Call mom after 7.

Renew gym membership.

Oranges.

The words drip-filter into my brain.

"It's a shopping list."

"My secret's out. I need a shopping list. Otherwise I get to the store and forget what I need. Don't tell anyone my weakness. My reputation's on the line."

"You make shopping lists during our session?"

"Not just yours. And not just shopping lists. Sometimes I doodle. Or I make notes for a research project that's been floating around in my head since college."

"So you don't listen?"

"I listen." His smile unfurls slowly until I'm awash in its beam, but it's like sunshine on a winter day, impotent to thaw the growing freeze inside me. "I just don't take notes. Many psychologists don't. It's just that clients feel better if we do."

"The jar is real," I blurt. "As real as that chair you're sitting on." I rub my face in my hands. "It's not a dream. It's never been a dream. It just showed up one day out of nowhere."

My words tear a hole in our rapport. Like shutters closing, his smile, his warmth, his wanting, flip out of sight, leaving the detached doctor in his place.

"It was never a dream?"

"No."

Tap, tap, tap. Pen on paper. Not making a list this time.

"Tell me about it."

We hang in a chilly cocoon of silence. I can't tell if I'm the only one experiencing the freeze. *Do you feel it?* I want to ask. *Do you feel anything?* But to be fair, he doesn't yet know the nature or scope of my lie.

I tell him everything. The facts. He already knows how it makes me feel. In return, he watches me with regard so cold I shiver in the patch of afternoon sun creeping across the building.

"Why now?"

"I had to tell you. I couldn't keep it in anymore."

"Why lie to begin with?"

"I didn't want you to think I was crazy. Or worse: stupid. It snowballed from there. I didn't know how to untangle the web."

"I was on your side, Zoe."

Was.

Tap, tap, plonk. He drops the pen onto the pad, sets it aside.

"I don't know what I can do for you. You need the police, not a psychologist. Unless you make a habit of lying, in which case I can give you a referral."

I stand, back ramrod straight, shoulders back, chin up, and tuck my purse up under my arm.

"Not necessary. Thank you for your time, Dr. Rose."

I'm out in the hall, almost to the elevator, before I remember I've forgotten to pay him. Hastily scribbling a check, I try not to care that our time together is over, that I've brought this upon myself.

When I slink back into his office, he's still there, sitting in his chair, forehead furrowed. He doesn't look at me as I come in. He doesn't look at me when I stand in front of him. And he doesn't look at me when I hold out the check and let it flutter to the floor.

He looks at me when I grab the collar of his shirt with both hands and kiss him like I'll die if I don't.

And he watches me when I walk away without speaking a word. At least, that's what I hope as I stride down the hall with my heart in my shoes.

DATE: NOW

The Swiss catches up to us a mile down the road.

"What's in Brindisi?"

"A boat."

"Ah. So there is a man."

"Sometimes a boat is just a boat."

"So you're a doctor?" I ask, sometime later.

"Yes."

I wait but he doesn't offer more. "What's your specialty?"

"Your people would call me a killer, America."

It takes a moment, but the penny drops and circles the wishing well before clinking onto the pile. "You're a . . ." I flail around searching for something not made of blunt, crude edges. "Reproductive health specialist."

His laugh is a dry hack. "Americans. Afraid to call things what they are. Abortion. Amongst other things. Mostly I am a scientist."

Don't do it, I command myself, but my body betrays me. My hand goes to my stomach. Just a tiny movement. Momentary. But the Swiss sees it.

"You are pregnant."

I neither confirm nor deny.

"You should get rid of it."

Lisa has lagged behind, her hand resting on the bicycle's metal tail. The Swiss watches me watching her.

"People are made of dark corners, America."

"Do you need a break?" I call out over my shoulder.

"It is probably a monster," he continues, "that thing inside you. Like those creatures in the barn."

Lisa shakes her head, trots to catch up to the Swiss, curls her fingers around the strap dangling from his backpack. The tap of the broom handle resumes.

"What's your help going to cost me?"

"I will tell you. When it is time."

I don't ask. I don't dare.

DATE: THEN

The last time I see Ben, he's hunched over like he's waiting on a spinal tap. Of course, it's not like I know I'll never see him again. There is no Rod Serling voice in my head. *This is it. Say your good-byes. You have now entered the Twilight Zone.*

"Man," Ben says when I inquire after his health. "I need a new bed or something. My back's killing me."

He sleeps on a couch in his living room, amongst his precious high-tech setup. Ben's apartment is the belly of a robot, red and green LEDs announcing the health status of the system at any given moment.

"You could just regenerate." I point to one of the few organic components in the room, a cardboard mock-up of a Borg regeneration chamber.

"Don't mock the Borg. One day we're gonna be living in a *Star Trek* world. Not in this lifetime. But one day."

I hold up the bag in my hand. "How does Chinese grab you?"

"Me so hungry. Hope I can keep it down. It's been a couple of days since . . ." He points a finger at his open mouth, mimes puking.

We divvy up beef and broccoli, fried rice, sweet-and-sour pork, and some kind of shrimp I can't pronounce. I'd pointed to it on the menu to save myself the tongue twist. And while we watch his screen saver contort on the triple wide screens, I ask about Stiffy.

"Don't know," he says. "Haven't seen him."

My chopsticks catch on the box's flap. A shrimp flies overhead, lands on the couch. Ben snatches it up and crams the naked crustacean into his food-flecked mouth.

"I haven't seen him, either. Want me to help hand out fliers?"

"Nah. He'll show up when he gets hungry enough."

"I'll have a look for him later."

"Whatever, man."

Thirty-seven is the official number of cats in my apartment building. Forty-one if you consider Mrs. Sark on the sixth floor has four more cats than she lets on. It helps that they're blood brothers and all answer to "Mr. Puss-puss."

Forty-one cats.

One day they go wandering, as cats are wont to do, never to come home.

SEVEN

"**S**hit, piss, fuck." The curses fly from the mouth of a lab technician struggling to grow facial hair with more substance than fuzz. His name is Mike Schultz. "All of them."

The mice are dead. Like he said, all of them. I know because I found them when I came through with the industrial wet vac.

Jorge is standing across from me, arms crossed, a victory dance of string lights illuminating his eyes. He shakes his head as though this is a tragedy, as if dozens of dead mice matter. And they do—just not to him. I've seen the stuffed squirrel heads dangling from his rearview mirror.

Schultz rubs his forehead. "Shit."

"Looks like somebody screwed up." Jorge stares straight at me when he says it.

"I'm sorry," I tell Schultz. "They were like that when I got here."

"Not your fault." He stabs a button on the wall panel.

We stand there staring at the dead mice, and I try not to care.

A minute later, footsteps knock out a determined beat on the floor. Then the big guy appears. This worries me because George P. Pope never comes down here. I've never met him, but his grinning face greets me in the lobby every morning. *Choose Pope Pharmaceuticals,* he says on the screen, with a smile that's supposed to be reassuring, fatherly. *Pope Pharmaceuticals considers you part of the family.* Without it he appears vulpine. Perhaps he really is larger than life, or maybe he's a physically huge man. I can't gauge his real size. Either way, we all shrink back to make him fit, even the woman who clings to his heels. She's a blonde so pale, she blends and swirls until she's one with her crisp lab coat.

There are rumors about Pope, of hookers and blow and of a wife no one has ever seen or met. Some say she's a scientist and he keeps her locked away creating the drugs that Pope Pharmaceuticals stockholders love so much. Some say she's a great beauty who spends her days prowling the streets of Europe for the latest fashions. One thing they all agree on is that no one here has ever seen her.

Jorge and I are invisible for now.

"What have we got?" he snaps at Schultz.

"Dead mice."

"What, all of them?" Planting himself in front of the cages, he tests Mike's hypothesis and discovers it holds true. The mice are all dead. Not sleeping. Not faking. Then he realizes Jorge and I exist.

"One of you found them?"

"Me," I say.

"And you are?"

"Zoe Marshall."

He weighs my response and finds it lacking. "Did you do anything different in your routine?"

"No." I run down the list of things to do, which never varies.

"Any new cleaning products?"

I open my mouth to answer, but Jorge leaps in wearing a brown nose.

"No, sir. Same old, same old."

Pope waits and I know it's me he wants to speak.

"We've been using the same products since I began working here," I say.

"New perfumes, creams—has anything at all changed? Think hard."

Only the jar. But that has nothing to do with *here* and a pile of dead mice.

"No," I say.

Pope claps once, rubs his hands together as though he's grinding this incident to dust. "Right," he says. "Maybe it's something we're feeding them, then, eh?"

He strides out, shoulders straight, head up. Fists clenched. Gait absolute. The woman follows. From the bob of her hair I can tell her mouth is busy asking questions his back isn't answering.

Pope Pharmaceuticals considers you part of the family.

Jorge follows me into the changing rooms at the end of shift. "You don't need this job."

I say nothing.

"My cousin coulda had it."

I keep on ignoring him.

"I know you live in a rich-bitch apartment."

I don't bother looking at him. "You went through my employee file."

"I no say nothing."

"Then you know my mother-in-law left it to me."

On the way to the train station I see him zoom away in his battered truck, squirrel heads swinging. The truck's bumper wears a sticker: *Jesus Is My Co-pilot.*

DATE: NOW

We find a car abandoned on the roadside. There is enough gas to take us twenty-two kilometers. The Swiss drives. During that brief journey, I forget what it's like to be wet.

When the motor splutters and gives its final death rattle, we keep walking and I forget what it's like to be dry.

"Tell me about your work," the Swiss says. I am hunkered down under a tree, figuring out how far we have to go. A hundred kilometers, give or take. Best case, five days. It's March tenth. That means I have nine days before the *Elpis* will come and go with or without me, not to return for another month. If at all.

I fold up the map, stow it in my backpack. "There's nothing to tell. I clean. At least, I used to."

"A cleaner who knows Darwin."

"I know a lot of things."

On the other side of the tree, Lisa is opening cans of mystery meat.

My stomach growls.

"What did you clean?"

"Floors. Cages."

"At Pope Pharmaceuticals," he says. "This is what you told me at the barn."

"Yes. Have you heard of it?"

"It is well-known in the medical community. What did you do before?"

"I had a job where someone else did the cleaning."

He watches me eat.

When we're moving again he asks, "Who is the father of your child? Do you know?"

"Yes."

"Too many women don't."

Lisa is limping.

"Blisters," he says. "Tend to them, otherwise she will get an infection and you will have saved her for nothing."

DATE: THEN

The envelope arrives on a Friday. It's clean, white, has my name printed on the front in a masculine hand I instantly recognize.

I place it on the coffee table and stare at it, unopened. The room bulges with elephants: first the jar, now this.

The phone rings. The machine picks up.

James's voice floods my apartment. "How's my favorite woman? Listen, Raoul asked me to call. He wants to know if you've opened the jar yet. If not, we'll pick you and it up and X-ray it. What do you think? Say yes. I'll be your best friend."

I pick up the envelope. Light. Flimsy. Although maybe it contains the emotional equivalent of anthrax within its paper walls. My finger catches the tacked flap and tears.

Zoe, I can't accept this, we didn't finish the session. Whether it's a dream or not, open the jar. Truth is best.

It's signed simply: *Nick.*

My check falls from the envelope, floats and sways to the floor.

James answers on the third ring. "Zoe!" he says; then: "Raoul, he's not here."

Raoul calls, "Socrates, Socrates," from another room.

"Hey, I can call back."

"No, no, it's nothing. You know cats. They come home when they're ready."

Unless they don't.

I think of Stiffy, and how he hasn't shown up yet, and how Ben doesn't care.

"So you and Raoul . . ." The question dangles.

"Oh, it's on. Or it will be once he gets better. That's why I'm at his apartment. He's sick so I'm making my fa-a-a-mous chicken soup. So, can we do it?"

"When Raoul's feeling better, sure."

"Thank you, thank you, thank you."

"Are you sure no one at the museum will mind?"

"They won't know. And even if they did, they like a good historical mystery same as the rest of us. If it's some kind of missing link like Raoul thinks, the board might ask if they can acquire it. Something that important would put us on the map."

If I give it away, it won't be my problem. But a problem passed on to other hands makes it no less so.

"Let's do it, then."

"Honey?" he calls into the belly of Raoul's apartment. Raoul's reply is distant, but moves closer as they play this affectionate game of Marco Polo. "Honey? Zoe gave us two thumbs up."

"Maybe just one," I say, and he laughs.

"Just one thumb."

Raoul snatches up the phone. "We'll take it."

"I hope you feel better soon."

"You're a peach," he croaks. "No wonder James adores you. We were supposed to fly to Miami next week but there's a maybe-hurricane forming."

Then he retches.

A spider crawls up my spine.

DATE: NOW

Lisa's screams jerk me out of a hard sleep. My watch says 2:24 a.m., my body says 8:15 p.m., which is fifteen minutes after I laid my head down on my backpack, beneath the tree's generous sprawl.

She's different now. Bits of her have broken off. More than an eye.

I blame myself. My rational self tells me I was exhausted, that sleep was coming for me that night whether I was willing or not. Sometimes the Sandman collects what's his regardless of the price. But my other self tells me I could have done more to protect my flock of one.

Two.

"What's wrong?" My throat is thick with sleep fog.

"Just a dream," the Swiss says. Tonight he keeps watch.

Two. Lisa and my unborn child. Although it's not really a child yet, is it?

What's happening in my belly now? I can't remember. The events between conception and birth blur the harder I try to separate them into their individual weeks. There's a heartbeat now, I know that. And fingernails. But I remember that from a movie, not from the skeleton crew at the makeshift clinic nor from the book the medic told me to steal because he didn't know diddly about childbirth. He gave me vitamins and wished me good luck, because that's all he had to give.

Pregnancy isn't important. Not now. Birth isn't high on the priority list when everyone is dying. New life does not replace the old.

I could ask the Swiss. He would know which cells are dividing and congealing into organs, the ratio of human-looking to alien. He would know if the tiny flutters are normal.

I consider asking, but the Sandman is coming again. He's striding across the field, one hand in the sack, digging for dust. He's here beneath the tree, standing over me. *Sleep,* he says, and the fog envelops me in its arms. It pulls some of the now along with it. Just words in the Swiss's voice.

"Stop it, England," he says. "Dreams are for the weak."

"Did you plan for your baby?" the Swiss asks. It's just we two awake, suspended in that slit between darkness and light.

"No. It was a surprise."

He starts talking then, telling me everything *What to Expect When You're Expecting* never had a chance to tell me.

I have questions, fears. The Swiss fills in the blanks with facts.

DATE: THEN

"Are you sexually active?"

This is not Dr. Scott. It's an unfamiliar face atop a white coat, which may or may not mean he's really a physician. He told me his name when I came in, but my brain slipped a gear and cast it to the sterile, air-conditioned breeze.

"No."

He doesn't look like a doctor. There's a briskness to doctors this man lacks. They're used to running from one emergency to the next. They slip their feet into comfortable shoes, not robust boots with a firmness to the toes that indicates they're lined with steel. These boots have not seen the inside of an emergency room. Nor have they seen construction. If I knelt, held my face close to the polished leather, I'd see a distorted version of my face. A fun-house hall of mirrors lives on his boots, reminding me that ever since the mice died last week, Pope Pharmaceuticals feels like a dream version of itself. Things aren't quite where they're supposed to be—nothing happens quite as it did, and while the faces are the same, the souls behind them are not. Strangers nod, smile, speak to me like they've worked with me for two years.

Even George P. Pope's face in the lobby is altered. *Pope Pharmaceuticals considers you part of the family,* he says like he always has, but now the words feel like a lie.

"Are you sure?"

"Positive. Although I don't see how it's any of your—"

"Any chance you might be pregnant?"

"—business. No."

He looks like security, although I've seen most of the security staff around the building and in the cafeteria, and this guy isn't one of ours. Pope Pharmaceuticals' security force comprises men used to walking their beat under a fluorescent sun. This guy has a tan. A real one. Hard edges make up his attitude and his face. He hasn't been counting the minutes between doughnuts.

He makes notes on a clipboard grasping papers a finger deep. Or maybe he's checking boxes on a quiz: *Are you a closet conspiracy theorist? How well do you know your sexual health?*

"Have you been sick in the last month?"

"No."

"What about in the last week?"

"I just told you. No."

"Have you had any sickness today?"

"No."

"Has anyone in your immediate familial or social circle experienced any illness recently?"

"No."

"Are you sure?"

"Yes."

He doesn't believe me. It's Etch-A-Sketched all over his face in long doubting lines. At the edge of his jaw a small twitch appears, ticking in time with his clenching and releasing jaw.

"Are you sure?" He's a robot, unable to think outside the questions on his list or the responses he's been given to parrot. In that he is exactly like Dr. Scott.

"Positive."

"Do you know the whereabouts of Jorge Valdez?"

I can feel my eyebrows rise. "He's not at work?"

"When did you last see him?"

Not yesterday, because that was my day off. Nor the day before, for the same reason. The two days before those were Jorge's days off. Last I saw of him was the Jesus sticker slapped on his truck's rear end as he zoomed into the evening haze.

"Friday."

No *The day you found the mice* or *That's interesting*. Just another check on the paper.

I sit. I wait. If he touches me I will run screaming, because those are not doctor's hands. A callus forms a thick smooth cap over his right thumb, as if he's dipped it in yellowing wax and let it spill into the backwards *L* it forms with his finger. The pen is alien to his hand because it's used to holding something designed to make a less fine point. A firearm.

Don't touch me.

Don't—

"You can go," he says, although there's a kind of calm craziness behind his eyes that suggests he'd like nothing more than to compel me to yield different answers. He reaches out to me with his left hand. We stare at each other until I break. I know he's not a doctor. And he knows that I know.

The jar has made me paranoid. I'm seeing monsters where there are only men.

The hand stays steady, but I push off the Naugahyde-covered bed without his help. My feet hit the floor like they're wearing cement shoes.

Ben is dead. I know this because there are people standing outside my apartment telling me so. They have the quiet disheveled appearance of cops who've been on their feet too many hours for too many years. I see them mouth their names, but bees have set up house deep in my ear canals. I can't think—not with this noise.

"How?"

Their lips move in some undefinable shapes.

"Wait." I shake my head, bend down, grab my knees. And count to ten. When I straighten, the buzzing has subsided enough for me to hear myself. "How?"

"We're working on it," the tall one says.

"Did you know him?" The other one is squat, like someone took the first guy and tamped him with a mallet.

"We were friends."

Their expressions remain steady. "Anything strange about the man? Anything new?"

"He's been sick. That's all."

"Sick how?" It doesn't matter which of them speaks, it's all coming out of the same mouth.

I tell them. They swap knowing looks like they're passing notes in class.

"Any strange habits?"

"He was a computer geek," I say. "Pick one."

"Did he like to eat anything . . . weird?"

"Like stuff that maybe isn't food."

Ben snapping up the escapee shrimp replays in my mind. Maniacal? Maybe. But shrimp was definitely real food.

"Not to my knowledge."

"Like maybe computer parts. Paper. Kitty litter. Weird like that."

Poker face is my talent show act of choice.

"No."

We stare at each other for a time. Until they make noises like they're leaving and I make noises like I'd be fine with that.

No tears. It's the strangest thing, because I know I'm crying. My body is going through the motions: quivering lips, twitching cheeks, shuddering shoulders. Yet, my eyes are the Gobi.

Nothing feels normal, not even me.

I call James, because I have a sudden need to know he's okay.

"I'm fine," he says. "Except for the puking. I think I've got what Raoul's got." My heart is Icarus, sailing toward the sun in one moment, spiraling to the ground in the next.

"James, do me a favor. Go to the doctor. Both of you."

"It's nothing. Just some bad food, probably. You okay?"

"I'm fine," I parrot. We are liars, the two of us.

We say our good-byes amidst the accumulating doom, but only I can feel its heft on my shoulders, riding me into the ground, because I know Ben is dead.

I wander into the living room to gather my thoughts and my purse. The jar is there. Of course. It's always there. Omnipresent and omniscient.

Poor Ben. Poor, poor, socially inept Ben. And poor Stiffy, the cat who never came back.

My mind is a millstone churning the grit into a more palatable form. Into something of which I can make sense. One moment Ben cared enough about his cat that he risked the ridicule of strangers, the next he shrugged away the cat's disappearance over fried rice.

The cat. It started with the cat sitting in my living room, staring at the jar like it mattered. Which means it didn't start with the cat at all.

I dial the super. When I ask him my question, I can feel him struggling to formulate a number. After a long pause, during which he chews and swallows, he abandons the specific for the facile.

"Half the building, easy. Plumbing can't keep up. Everybody's flushing all the time."

EIGHT

The clouds lift their petticoats for just a short time, long enough for the sun to dazzle us. We three lie spread-eagle in the middle of an arterial road and soak up all she has to offer.

For a moment the world is new and glorious. We forget death. And I forget to keep watch.

That's when the strangers appear.

At first the shimmer-people don't seem human. And who knows, they might not be. It's too late to run now. The bushes are over there, a good sixty-second sprint away, while the open land on the eastern lip of the highway is no friend to a person in need of a hiding place—let alone three.

Their number is also three and they, too, sit beneath the sun, luxuriating in her smile. The road has worn them as it has us, until they're little more than coat hangers for clothing long past its wear-by date. They're thin, tired, and when they do notice us it's with the same measure of suspicion.

I stand and my counterpart rises. My hand lifts in a greeting. As does hers.

"It's a mirage," the Swiss says, from his place on the blacktop. My hand drops. So does my other's. I feel a fool.

"Oh."

Lisa covers her mouth with both hands. Her good eye crinkles at the edges like what she would call crisps, but what I remember as potato chips.

I strip off my coat, my shirt and spread them out over the dry asphalt. Then I lie beside my clothes and imagine I'm on a beach with a bed of hot sand to cradle me.

The next time we see a person, he is not a mirage, although at first I mistake the disembodied head for a basketball. The ball bobs along the horizon until shoulders appear, and a body below that.

Italy is known for its leather, and this man's face is a testament to that: brown and smooth, baked by decades of sun. Patina, the salesperson would brag if he were trying to sell me a leather chair. His skin is stretched over a lean, muscular frame, suggesting he was fit even before the end. He takes long, purposeful strides. This is a man who knows where he is going or at least presents the illusion of being on the right path.

"There's one of him and three of us," the Swiss says.

The man draws closer. A cupped hand shades his eyes. His feet lose their certainty.

"Ciao." He halts, cocks his head as though he expects the words to echo back.

"Hi," I say.

He raises both hands and gives a smile made of shattered piano keys.

The Swiss calls out, *"Parli Inglese?"*

The newcomer stops, holds up his index finger and thumb, presses them together.

"Little."

He's military. Or was. Or knew someone well enough that he borrowed their uniform. Or killed for it. But his boots, though battered, cling to his feet like a second skin, which leads me to believe he served.

"Hello, friends. I am come from Taranto."

"Is it bad there?" the Swiss asks.

The soldier shrugs. "Is bad everywhere, friend."

As it turns out, his idea of a little is my idea of a lot. The gaps in his English he fills with Italian.

"A ship came in a month ago full of dead mans. It crashed into the port. Boom." His hands draw a fireball in the air. "There was one still aboard. He was crazy. He stands on that ship and laughs while the dead mans burn. I never see such a thing."

"Were you in the war?" I ask.

"No. I was here. I helped guard our enemies in the . . ."

"Concentration camps," the Swiss supplies.

The soldier's nod is weighted down by his former job. "Yes. We put our enemies there when the war started. When the disease came . . ." He draws a grisly line across his throat.

Dusk arrives while we talk, and with it, dinnertime.

"Is he cute?" Lisa asks.

I look at the soldier so I can tell her the truth. "He might have been, once. He has a nice face, though. Kind eyes."

"Do you think he's married?"

"He's not wearing a ring."

Lisa feels her way up the bicycle's skeleton; it's leaning against a tree. Her lips move slightly as she counts the supplies by touch. The too-small number draws lines on her forehead.

"Do we have to feed him? We don't have much."

"He eats with us," I say.

"Why?"

"Remember what I said about holding on to what makes us human?"

"Yes."

"That's why he eats with us."

The men are talking some distance away while Lisa and I pick through our canned goods. The Swiss breaks away, pulls a small box from his hand, and places it in my palm.

"Matches?"

"It's dry enough for a fire tonight. Make one." He and the soldier melt into the oncoming night before I have a chance to ask questions.

I've never made a fire before, not like this, out in the open. But I know I can do it.

"Let's take the wrappers off the cans," I say to Lisa. "We need the paper."

"Where did they go?"

"They didn't say."

"Why not?"

"I don't know."

"You don't know much. Not as much as him."

"That's true enough. A few months ago I was living a normal life, doing a whole lot of not much, and a couple weeks ago I was stopping a rape in progress so that a young woman might have a chance at survival. Who knows what he was learning during that time."

"Thanks," she says. "I don't think I ever said that."

"You're welcome. I'd do it again."

"Because you have to?"

"Because it's the right thing. And because I like you."

"Even though I'm stroppy and ungrateful?"

I manage a laugh. "You're stroppy, ungrateful, and prettier than me."

"Am I really?" Her face glows with pleasure.

"Much prettier."

"Do you think he could love me?"

"The Swiss?"

She nods.

"If he can't, it's not your fault. We're all different now."

"I can fix him," she says. "And he can fix me."

If only wishes weren't white-colored horses.

An uncomfortable silence choke-holds us. The Swiss is no prophet, and yet, Lisa still faces the direction in which he disappeared as though she can bring him back with sheer wanting. Man as Mecca.

The fire sputters, limps across still-damp limbs until the residual moisture sizzles to steam. I sit back on my haunches, satisfied and worried. Stare into the flame as though it can foretell the future.

A *crack* whips through the night.

Lisa leaps from her invisible prayer rug. Hugs the fire.

Another *crack*.

I know the sound. I've heard it on television and in the streets after the war and disease struck. Gunshots.

The soldier must have a gun. That's not unreasonable. It's a tool of his trade, just like a mop was mine. At least, I hope it's him and not some unnamed foe.

What if he is the enemy?

"We should hide," I say. If that's not them, we're sitting here with a beacon, announcing our position. My cheeks flush hotter as my ire rises. We're two little sitting ducks, Lisa and I, rendered helpless because two men told me what to do and I followed orders as though their will was more substantial than my own.

Lisa won't come. "He'll come back for us."

"We have to rescue ourselves."

"Go, then. I'm staying."

"If there's something out there, it'll come straight for us. The fire has made sure of that."

"I don't care."

We stay, Lisa hugging her knees by the fire and me staring into the dark, keeping the monsters at bay with the sheer force of my will. The minutes slouch by. The night settles into its easy chair for the duration. I lean against the tree's stiff bark.

"If you want to sleep, I'll keep watch."

Lisa stares blindly at me through the flames. The fire is a thin mask concealing her emotions. I never noticed before, but fire is not constant. It's a shifting landscape of peaks and valleys. Mountains rise and fall only to soar again before sinking. When one flame dies, another surges and takes its place. This topographical dance takes place on Lisa's face. From here she appears to be melting upwards, rivulets of *her* pouring into the gradient. A possible future has slipped through some crack in time to taunt me. I see Lisa's skin shrivel away like celluloid, what little fat she has bubbling until it's nothing more than a residue in the air, in my lungs, on my skin.

A memory chooses that moment to step forward, as though it's been waiting a lifetime for this. The voice belongs to Derek Keen, back row, ninth-grade science.

If you can smell a fart, it means you're breathing in molecules of the farter's shit.

That one earned him a detention, but more important it won him a grudging *Technically you're correct, Mr. Keen* from a teacher rarely pleased. Mr. Crane. I wonder if he died from White Horse. Surely not. He was an artifact from antiquity even then. James, in later years, used to joke about how he wished he could carbon-date Mr. Crane's face.

I don't want Lisa to burn. Not in the future and not now. I don't want to suck molecules of her into my lungs, where they'll mingle with *me*.

The crunch of boots on grass drags me from my morbid fantasy. The soldier emerges first.

"We bring food," he declares. When he grins it transforms him. This man is proud to provide. He's a trained protector, although from the victory in his eyes it's clear this is not simply a learned skill but part of his fabric. For this I must thank him in his own tongue.

"*Grazie.*"

He laughs, hugs me, slaps my back. "Good, good."

The Swiss melts into the golden aura wearing a dead goat across his shoulders like a biblical portent of evil. The beast's head hangs at an unnatural angle, its throat a gaping second mouth. When he drops it at the fire's edge, I see where the bullets have punched through its hide.

"You already shot it. Did you have to cut its throat, too?" I ask.

"How else do you expect the blood to drain? Cook it."

Lisa leaps up, stumbles from the circle. The sound of her retching drowns out the insect cries.

"My experience with meat is limited to what's in the supermarket in neat packets," I say. "But that doesn't mean I'm not willing to learn." From my backpack, I draw out the cleaver with its honed edge. My hands shake.

The soldier takes the Swiss's rope. "I will help."

Though there is abundant light, the Swiss's eyes remain hard and dark. He crouches by the fire. "It is women's work."

We do what we must. The president's words, just before anarchy squeezed the government from its fortresses of power. *We do what we must.* I've done that. I'm doing that. Because if I don't, I'll topple into the remnants of my life where I'll languish and turn to dust.

We do what we must. The words give me no comfort as I peel the goat's skin like it's a bloody banana. The guts spill at my feet; I tell myself it's just Grandma's sausage stew heaped upon the grass. When the goat no longer looks like an animal but like a random slab of meat hanging in a butcher's window, I wipe my eyes with my sleeve and find it wet.

The soldier appears at my elbow. "Show me." He holds out his hand and I give him the knife.

"Where you go?"

"Brindisi."

"Ah. For the boats, yes?"

"Yes." The blade gains confident speed in his hands. "Have you done this before?"

"Yes. My family, they have a farm with . . ."

He stops, pushes his nose flat.

"Pigs?"

"And chickens. I learn very young to cut meat for my family. My father he teach me."

"Is your family still alive, do you know?"

"They are dead. My sister . . . maybe. She lives in Roma with her family. And you?"

"Gone."

His eyes are soft with empathy. "But we are here, yes?"

"For now."

"You must have the hope."

"Sometimes it's hard."

"Yes, is hard. Maybe hardest the mans and the womans have seen. But we are here." He holds up two goat's legs. "And tonight we have food."

Soon we are satiated in a way none of us have known for weeks. The goat is tough, stringy, overcooked, but I don't care. As each hot bite slides down my throat, I lose myself in a fantasy where I'm in a fine restaurant devouring a steak, and a wine waiter hovers nearby, eager to refill my glass.

The soldier tears into his portion, ripping away the fibrous tissue. "Sorry," he says when he realizes I'm watching.

I stop chewing long enough to answer. "Don't be. It's good to enjoy food with friends."

He toasts me with his canteen.

Friends. Is that what these people are to me? Lisa withdraws further daily, and the Swiss is incapable of anything warmer than a snarl. Only the soldier, the newest of our group, feels like someone in whom I could confide. Even now they remain in character. The Swiss gnaws at the meat, gaze darting around the group as though someone will wrestle him for his prize. Beside him, Lisa carves her meal into doll-sized pieces with my paring knife. Her hair is a limp greasy waterfall concealing her face as she chews and swallows.

Soon my belly swells with food, and I feel that now-familiar flutter.

Stabbing his knife into another chunk of meat, the soldier smiles and offers me the handle. "Eat, eat."

"I can't. Too much food."

"You are too skinny." He laughs. I laugh, too, because we are all too thin, and we'd need more than just this meal to regrow our padding.

"You'll be fat soon enough," the Swiss says abruptly. "If that monster inside you does not die."

I chew, swallow, wonder if the Swiss ever had manners or if this world snatched them away. The soldier looks at me.

"I'm pregnant."

Lisa stares through the fire with her one eye, her mouth no longer moving.

"You didn't say," she says. "Why didn't you tell me?"

"Because we've had other things to worry about."

"I thought you were my friend."

The Swiss laughs. It's not a happy sound. "Women."

Afterward, when we've buried the scraps and settled around the fire, the Italian inches closer to me.

"You have bambino? I will come with you to Brindisi, make sure you are safe. My country, my people are . . ." He makes a motion like snapping a twig in two.

"Thank you."

He's a hero. Streets all over the world are littered with people just like him.

I dream of mice and broken men and all the promises I couldn't keep. They hound me until I wake. The ground where the soldier had lain is empty. Beneath the tree's rim of drooping branches, the Swiss stands watching the night. Although he's not facing me, can't know my eyes have opened, he speaks.

"The soldier left."

"Where did he go?"

"I told you, he left."

"Just like that? Without saying good-bye?"

"He said *ciao*."

"In the dark."

"The man changed his mind and said he wanted to find his sister, if she is still alive. I saw him back to the road and pointed the way."

When he turns, I see he's holding something in his hands. An icy glove grabs my heart, squeezes until I ache from the cold.

"That's his gun."

"He gave it to me. A gift."

I don't believe him. But suddenly he's the one holding a gun and I'm holding nothing as a shield. So I say nothing. I curl up close to the fire's humble flicker and watch as he polishes the weapon with the flap of his shirt.

I don't say what I think. I don't dare speak the words for fear that utterance will lend them the spark of life.

The soldier is dead. The soldier is dead. The soldier is dead.

DATE: THEN

"Raoul is gone."

James is leaning against my apartment door, his skin on loan from Madame Tussaud's, his breathing labored as though he's trying to inhale soup.

"Oh, honey, I'm sorry."

We've been here before, one or both of us heartbroken. The evening usually ends with too many drinks and morbid tales of other past loves, but not tonight. On this night James looks as though he's clawed his way out of a coffin. "What happened? I thought you guys really hit it off."

"He didn't *leave*." James spits out the words like olive pits. "He's dead. Dead. Dead." His lanky frame folds up on itself as he sinks to the floor. "Dead."

"Dead?"

I can't believe it, and yet, I'm not surprised, but I can't explain why. Only that somewhere deep, I know something I wish I didn't.

"That's what I said," he cries. "I was going to fall in love with him. Maybe I already was in love and that's why this hurts so bad. We'd already talked about getting a place out of the city eventually. Having a family."

"What happened, baby?"

"He just died. He got sick and then he stopped breathing. Then he got cold like his fucking potsherds."

"I'm so sorry, James. So sorry."

"That's not the worst of it."

I crouch beside him, encircle his shoulders, pull him close until his head tucks into my neck's curve. "Tell me."

He looks up, the fine threads in his eyes blazing red. "I think I've got what he's had. I think I'm going to die."

My mouth opens but the words don't come. And then I find them hidden in that place where you store the lies you tell the people you love so you can protect them from the world's hard truths.

"You're not going to die, James. I'm taking you to the emergency room, okay?"

"I don't believe you."

"I am, I promise. Let me get my keys."

"I mean I don't believe I'm not going to die. I can feel it, Zoe, waiting for me. When I fell asleep last night, Raoul was there. Only, it wasn't my Raoul. It was Death wearing his face, same as in that new exhibit we've got from Africa. He loved that exhibit.

He said it made him feel good to know that there was a time and place where it was socially acceptable to wear a mask."

"I want you to show me the exhibit when you're feeling better." His head sags, sinks to his chest. "James?"

Eyes closed, he smiles at the ground. "Still here. You haven't got rid of me yet."

My shoulders sag. "You scared me."

"Ha-ha."

Then he slumps over. Shudders wrack his body. He claws at his throat, body flopping on the ground. He's having a seizure and I can't remember what to do. Put something between his teeth so he doesn't swallow his tongue? Or is that something they only do on TV, something completely useless in real life? I roll him onto his side and hold him as steady as I can in the recovery position while he shakes like the earth's plates are colliding inside him. Everything scatters when I upend my purse on the floor. I scramble for my cell phone and dial 911.

The line rings out. Rings out again. I redial just in case I messed up those three easy digits. Nothing. Just the huff of frustration that escapes my lungs.

James falls still. I wait for the aftershocks, but there is nothing but the sound of the operator picking up.

"What is the emergency?"

My fingers search for his pulse, but there's nothing beneath the clammy wax that just a few moments ago was his skin. I must be wrong. There's a pulse. There has to be.

"Hello?"

I'm looking in the wrong place, that's it.

"James, wake up," I say.

I press a hand to his chest and feel for the bump-bump, bump-bump. And wait while my lips give out my address by rote.

"What is your emergency?" repeats the tin woman.

"Just hurry. Please." The phone flies across the room, gently persuaded by my fist.

"James? Get up now." I slap his chest. Slap his face so hard it jerks to the right. "James?" Louder now, like's he's old and deaf and not—

Don't say it. If you don't say it, it isn't true.

—dead.

Don't. Just don't.

I need to will him back to life. I throw my weight into pumping his heart, force my breath into his mouth, and . . . nothing. His heart rejects my touch, his lungs my breath. His soul cares nothing for my will. But I keep going until I realize there's a thin noise coming from his throat.

No, not his throat exactly. Further back, a direct drop from his ears.

It looks like my mother's roast lamb when she cuts deep slits into the meat and forces a garlic clove into each gash. Only, his neck's covered with paper-thin flaps—

I breathe into James, press his chest with both hands.

—that quiver as air tags them on the way out.

I've seen these before, in aquariums and seafood restaurants. Gills. James has gills.

DATE: NOW

It's the noise that wakes me, small and secret and hidden. Some sounds belong to misdeeds, and when we hear them we know something is wrong.

I keep still, eyes tight, suppressing one sense so the other can requisition its strength. The fire is dying; I no longer feel its heat raging, although there is still a gentle warmth kissing my skin that tells me not all is lost. By dawn the fire will be gone, and, soon after, so will we.

With my vision restrained, I pick through the night's sounds for the anomaly.

Dark is louder than light. Under the guise of night, the underbelly of nature reveals itself. Creatures slither and slink so as to not attract the attention of their natural foe. Predators are less cautious. They flap and soar until some meat-object takes their fancy. Then they dive and snatch up what they can. There are the desperate cries of prey in those final moments as death rattles their bones. Chirps and clicks herald a desire to mate. And there's the musical tinkle of water wending through the land, searching for its source . . . or leaving home.

Even without these things, darkness has a sound of its own that has nothing do to with silence in the same way that space has nothing to do with emptiness. That's an illusion that fools us all until we really pay attention.

My mind drifts until it catches on that noise that doesn't belong. A whimper with a whisper chaser. Is it crying? Because that's what it sounds like. There's that same hitch between breaths.

I slowly sit, pull my body together in case I need to spring up in a hurry. Push off the ground until I'm standing.

I'm alone. Lisa and the Swiss are missing. But not for long. I find them underneath the stars and it is here I discover the source of the anomalous sound.

Even with his back to me, I know. I've been there. I've been her. The Swiss stands while Lisa kneels before him, servicing him with her mouth. I've seen how she turns to him with reverence and adoration, a twisted cousin to Stockholm syndrome. Worshipping a savior who is also your subjugator. He knows I'm there. He always does. He laughs at my shock. I am no prude and yet, there is a crudeness, an obscenity about him, that goes far beyond the bounds of love and sex and porn.

"Watch if you like."

"You're a pig," I say. The girl tries to pull away at the sound of my voice but he holds her fast by the hair until she gags. He releases Lisa, steps back so she falls onto her hands, retching into the grass. She crawls further into the scrub, until she fades to a heaving silhouette.

"She's sick."

"Morning sickness." He zips up, tucks the gun into the back of his pants like they do in the movies.

"How do you know it's not White Horse?" I ask.

"She was stupid enough to have unprotected intercourse. Recently." His stare is cool and laced with triumph. "She told me freely, without my asking. In a few months she will be cured. Do not think I'm the father. I'm not." He swaggers like he has a secret worth keeping.

I know you're not. I keep that thought safe and sound in my head. My instincts tell me not to speak.

"It could still be White Horse."

"She showed me her breasts. They look like road maps. Have you seen your own recently? Are the veins not more prominent? Are your breasts not fuller when the rest of your body is slackening and growing thinner each day?" He draws up level to me, his lips curled into a cruel sneer. "You can raise your children together without fathers. Bastards."

He can never know who the father of Lisa's baby must be. Ever. Because behind his eyes, just beyond the cold crust he wears as a protective shell, sits a pile of broken hinges; there's no way to gauge which way his sanity will swing.

"You're only with us because three is safer than two," I say.

"I'm with you because I choose to be. Whether you and that little whore like it or not."

"Keep on thinking that."

"You'll die without me. Like your stupid friend almost died."

Lisa's shoulders heave. Not White Horse. Not going to die. Pregnant. Just like me. I know the Swiss is right; once again, I was too busy watching for death to recognize the signs of new life. Relief mixes with my fear and coagulates to the point where I can no longer distinguish the two.

What a pair we are.

The chain-link fence wears a razor wire crown, a tiara a former beauty queen has cast aside. Its tarnish and regret do not stop it from maintaining its dignity; once upon a time, it stood for something.

We stand on the road, watching it turn to rust. After one perfect day, the rains have come again, more vengeful than ever.

"I'm going there," the Swiss says. There's a capillary road that bleeds off this one and walks right up to the structure's front door.

I turn away, pick up my stride. "We don't have time. The land is completely flat. That could be miles away."

"Maybe in America, but not here. Italy is made of mountains." He waves a hand at the landscape. "In Italy, spaces do not go on forever."

I stop, sit on the blacktop with the rain forming shallow puddles around me.

"Go, then," I tell him. "But if you're not back in an hour I'm leaving."

"What is it?" Lisa asks.

"It looks like a military facility," I say.

She aims her question at the Swiss. "Is that true?"

No answer. He stands there, legs spread, arms folded, maybe daring the fence to come closer, or—more likely—trying to choose the perfect insult for this occasion.

"Stay or go, it makes no difference," he says.

Her body coiled in tense knots, Lisa trembles as she struggles to choose a side of the fence. Stay or go. With me or with him. She's going to be a mother, forced to choose between far more dismal options than this. I cannot help her with one so simple. Questions form on her face, fall away, form anew. She's a desperate kaleidoscope searching for a pattern that both asks her questions and answers them with words that will yield comfort.

Stay. Lisa decides to stay. So we stand together as I watch the Swiss trash-compacted by distance.

"I'm not pregnant. I'm not."

"If you are, at least you know that's why you've been sick."

"I've got White Horse. I'm gonna die."

"I don't think so."

"I do. I am."

"Were you on birth control?"

"I'm going to die. You're wrong."

"He says you are. You believe him, don't you?" It's cruel but necessary. Denial won't do anything but damage.

She stares sightlessly.

"I didn't want to believe it, either, when I found out about my baby. There was a war limping along and half the world was already dead. Old life was disappearing and there I was with the nerve to create new. Like getting a new puppy too soon after your old dog dies."

"Are you happy?"

Happy. What does that even mean? I can't recall, but I think it has something to do with ice cream cones hastily licked at the beach before the butter pecan melted all over my fingers. Once your fingers get ice-creamed, they're done for. All the rinsing in the world doesn't wash away those last vestiges of stickiness. But you smile because the ice cream taste still lingers, reminding you that happiness comes in double dips pressed into a sugar cone with a wet metal scoop.

But am I happy because I'm carrying a child? My hand rests on my abdomen. It's a shadow of its preapocalyptic self, but there's a fullness there now, like I've indulged in a too-big meal.

Am I happy? Even the sound of the word rolling around in my head sounds foreign. More than anything, I'm scared. Terrified we won't make it. Horrified at the possibility that I won't be able to protect my child from the monsters that cling to the shadows. Happy is for when I reach my destination. Then and only then.

"You can't tell him, you know," I say gently. "Who the father is."

She stares straight ahead. Her cheek twitches.

"Don't let him take advantage of you. He's not—"

"He's not like them."

"You don't—"

"He's not like them."

"You're right. He's something else. There's something inside his head that's not right. I don't know if it's from before or after all this, but it's there. He's dangerous, Lisa. Be careful."

"That's not what I meant," she says.

"Then what?"

She's done talking, at least about this.

"I'd be happy," I say, "if I could stop being terrified."

An invisible force jerks Lisa's head up. The Swiss walks this way.

DATE: THEN

"I'm sorry," the woman says. "I don't know who you are." She's a pencil wrapped in a black nylon tracksuit. She has Raoul's look, only on her his strong jaw looks heavy.

Over her shoulder, I see Raoul's apartment is inexpensive chic. He likes beige, although that's probably too generic a term. He'd probably call it toasted almond, ecru, potsherd powder. Something more interesting than beige, which implies a lack of imagination.

When I tell the woman who I am, her kohl-rimmed eyes sink further into her skull and harden.

"My brother was not homosexual. He was a good man."

"I'm sorry for your loss," I say. "I liked your brother."

"Nobody knew him better than me. Nobody. He never told me about this person."

"James. My friend's name was James."

"James." She says it like his name is a disease. "Did your friend leave something here? What do you want?"

So I explain.

"I gave it away. Filthy animals spreading disease."

"To who?"

"The animal shelter. It's their problem now. I have to deal with burying my brother."

"James died, too," I say quietly.

The animal shelter has never heard of Raoul's sister, nor have they seen the cat.

"Probably she let him go. People do that all the time. Sometimes they move and accidentally on purpose forget to tell the cat or dog, if you know what I mean," they tell me.

I do. I wish I didn't.

There are many noises that cause a human heart to want to gallop up and out of the throat: a child's scream, the one that play cannot evoke—only pain; unexplained mechanical noises on a plane thirty-five thousand feet above ground; the screech of wheels seconds before a concrete median leaps up to kiss you; the wail of an ambulance too close to your home.

Ambulances are nothing new around here. Typical for a healthy-sized city. But my building is filled with people too proud to announce sickness. They drag themselves to the next block instead and suffer quietly outside the apartments there, where they are surrounded by fast-walking strangers instead of familiar faces. They wait for the paramedics where they are not known. Such is life—and death—in the apartment Sam and his mother left to me.

It's after ten. Just me and the jar watching each other. Ben is dead. Raoul is dead. James is dead. That can't be a coincidence. I can't be that unlucky. What are the odds?

Three people dead. All three the only ones who came into contact with the jar. All three with cats. A building with forty-one cats, none of them seen for days. The natives have been whispering in the corridors. *It's that Chinese restaurant down the block,* they say. *No, it's that Indian place,* says another. *Hell, maybe it's that barbecue place with the ribs everyone goes crazy for.* No one can agree on anything except that their cats have disappeared into the ether and no amount of rattling a spoon inside a tin can rally their interest.

Then there's me. I'm fine. Physically fine. Not even a blip of nausea. Shouldn't I be dead, too?

My hands shake as I flip through a magazine. *Buy me and your life will be prettier,* the ads whisper like would-be seducers.

In some dark distance, an ambulance announces its search. I picture it hurtling through the city street until it nears its destination, slow crawling as it ticks off the addresses: *Not you, not you, nope, not you, either. Ahhh, there you are. Found you.* Until the relentless wah-wah, wah-wah cuts mid-wail. The dead siren leaves an empty space my heart hurries to fill because it's stopped on my street, on my block, on my front doorstep. I imagine Mo, the night doorman, setting aside his *Reader's Digest*, the one he keeps open on his lap while he watches Nick at Nite, shambling to the front door, where he'll open it just a crack and say, "What can I do ya for?"

Blood rushes through my ears. They're hot to the touch, which strikes me as odd, because I'm shivering.

Curiosity slithers through my fear. Who's dead? I need to know. I snatch up my keys and phone and bolt down the stairs. The only thing faster than my heart is my feet. When I throw open the lobby door, I know how I must look: the wild-eyed woman obviously too crazy to bother with polite accoutrements like shoes or a coat thrown over my pajamas.

Mo is already back behind his desk, book in lap, eyes fixed on the small screen. The ambulance loiters at the curb, blocking the entire front view.

"Miss Marshall," he says. "What can I do—"

I slap my hands on the counter. "Who are they here for?"

"Who?"

I want to reach over the counter and shake him until the answers spill out his mouth.

"The paramedics. They stopped here. Who for?"

He grunts as he sits upright, reaches for the leather-bound ledger that holds the names of guests. He makes a Busby Berkeley production of running his thick ink-blackened finger down and across the page until it sticks on the final entry. Clears his throat.

"Mrs. Sark in seventy-ten."

The woman with four cats masquerading as one. My fingernails are cut back to the quick, so there's just a soft pat-pat-pat as my fingers drum the polished countertop. It's do this or scream, and I don't want to scream.

"Do you know why?"

He shrugs. "Who knows? A lotta people here been sick lately. Porkchop was telling me how the Jones boy painted the door with his lunch last week. Waste of a good Reuben."

Porkchop is the day doorman, real name Jimmy Bacon.

Three hard knocks on glass end our conversation.

"What can I do ya for?" Mo says when he gets around to opening the door. Whatever he's hearing, it must be okay, because he opens the door and the two cops who aren't cops step inside. *Ben's still dead,* I want to tell them as their gazes latch onto me.

They take the elevator up, and when they come back down, they're accompanied by two paramedics and Mrs. Sark. At least, I think it's her, but it's hard to tell through the thick yellow body bag.

"I guess seventy-ten will be available now." Mo sighs like his world is ending. "More work for me, with all the prospective tenants traipsing through."

NINE

Post-man, pre-man, the countryside knows not the difference. Its beauty flourishes for as long as it can hold progress at bay, which may be forever. We gorge ourselves on grapes meant for high-priced wines and carry as many as we can with us.

We rest, but not for long. Time is running short. Sometimes I wonder why the Swiss is so eager to accompany us. I should ask, but I don't. His insanity is a cold and quiet one, and I know he'd kill, not to save us, but to eliminate any threat that would cross our path. It's best he stay with us, not exactly on our side but at least not fighting us. Where I can watch him.

He uses Lisa as he pleases now, often stopping to take her between the fruit trees in some verdant orchard. The smell of spoiled fruit is the scent of his lust, and to smell that oversweet perfume turns my stomach. Lisa is complicit, or maybe just compliant. She goes to him, her expression half-triumphant, half-bewildered. That he wants her thrills her, but she doesn't understand why he does. She walks quietly afterward, and I know she's asking herself: *Is this love?* When we rest, she hangs her head low.

I don't judge her. She's just a kid.

"Do you want to watch?" he asks.

"Screw you."

I don't need to taste rotting meat to know it's no good.

"Do you think it's true?" Lisa asks.

"Is what true?"

"Is there a monster inside me? Inside you?"

"No, I don't think so."

"But you don't know."

"No."

"I don't want to give birth to a monster." Lisa faces straight ahead with her one blind eye. "I don't want to give birth at all."

DATE: THEN

The shadows don't make sense in my dimly lit apartment. They seem to have chosen to lurk where they please rather than follow physics' dictates. I could turn on more lights, shoo them away, but I don't because there's a part of me that believes they'd cling to the walls, refuse to let go. And there's another piece of my mind that doesn't want to know what they're concealing.

I don't hide in the shadows. I pick the center of the kitchen to make my phone call. From here I can see the front door and the jar. From here I can tilt my head an inch or two to the left and make them disappear.

The line rings. My hope diminishes as each note fades. Then voice mail answers and I hear an imprint of Dr. Rose's voice speaking to me from the past.

I'm glad he didn't answer. It's easier like this, talking to a computer that's converting my words into a sound file stored on a server somewhere, probably in the Midwest or maybe in India. This way I can talk to him and still be heard without being listened to.

"Hi, it's Zoe Marshall." The words snag on my tongue as though they're aware of their triteness. "I don't really know who else to call. My family would think I've lost it and my two best friends are dead. Which means they're great listeners now, but lousy as far as support goes. Since support and listening is your thing, I thought of you."

I pull my knees up tight against my chest, rest my chin on the cartilaginous curves.

"I think . . . I think the jar's bad luck, or maybe it's killing people. I know you think I should open it but I can't. It's like that whole Pandora's box story. What if I open it and the world goes to hell? What if all the ills of the world really do pour out? People around me are dying. That's not normal. I don't want to be Pandora or Typhoid Mary. I just want to be me. I'm sure you'll think I'm nuts when you hear this, but . . . forget it."

I kill the call.

Just me and the jar chilling in my apartment. The green glowing numbers on the oven flick away the minutes. When my life is seventeen minutes shorter, my phone rings.

"I want to see you," Nick says. Nick. Not Dr. Rose now. Nick. Thinking his name makes my cheeks warm as though that particular arrangement of letters weaves some kind of aphrodisiac voodoo spell on me.

"Do you still have Friday afternoon open?"

"I don't mean professionally."

"Oh." Then: "When?"

"Soon. But give me a few days."

There's a note in his voice, a kind of tension that tells me there's an obstacle not easily moved standing between us.

"What's wrong, Nick?"

I know it. I know it even before he says it.

"Nothing serious. Just a stomach flu."

DATE: NOW

Welcome to Brindisi. Have a nice day. Enjoy the sights. Eat good *food, drink our wine. Relax.*

That's what I like to imagine the sign reads. But friendly greetings aren't usually accompanied by a skull and crossbones. Weathered words on old wood stabbed into the ground serve as a warning that this place is unholy. They needn't have bothered: carcasses and rusting vehicles litter the streets, making it difficult to find a pure path.

The sea is near, which is why the metal falls so easily to rust. Salt air whisks away some of the decomposition smell and leaves behind a familiar briny tang. I am ten again, on the boardwalk with my ice cream cone. Fifteen, swimming with my friends. Twenty-three, falling into the sand with Sam, where we make something that isn't yet love.

We cut through the dead city in a malformed triangle formation: Lisa and I out front, while the Swiss hangs back with the weapon he stole from a dead man. I imagine him fantasizing about where he'd put the bullets. Through my kidney or shoulder, maybe. He'd know where to cause the greatest, slowest hurt.

Brindisi is a city of peaks and lows. Whitewashed houses stare down from their perches, clean and bright from the relentless rain. As we walk on, the city thickens with towers filled with abandoned office furniture. Like all cities, it needs people to thrive. Without citizens scurrying about their business, dodging cars and chattering into their phones, the air is flat and lifeless and Brinidisi becomes a city without a soul. Every so often a face peers at us from behind a filthy window, only to dissolve back into the shadows. There is life here, but for now it wants to go unacknowledged.

The arrow on my compass shivers and settles back on North. We are going east. The sun passes overhead, glares through the clouds, continues her journey west. Our constant companion is the rain.

We walk until the buildings part and then we see her: the Mediterranean. This is not the sparkling blue sea in travelogues but a dull gray cummerbund concealing the seam between a dismal sky and a cement floor. She's no longer herself—but then, neither am I.

I would to run to her but I can't, because I'm too busy leaning against a parking meter weeping.

"Women," the Swiss says. "You are weak."

I turn around and look at him, one hand still on the meter.

"Just die, would you? Just die in a fucking fire."

He strikes me.

Something about a wet hand facilitates a slap: it provides the blows with extra sting. I don't care that's he's hit me, even though my cheek burns, because I've put the words out there, given my wish power.

I don't care, because I'm here.

The port of Brindisi is a graveyard. Great steel whales hunker low in the tide, abandoned by their crews. Some languish on their sides, doomed to sink into the sea as their insides fill with water. Other, smaller boats are corks bobbing as they please. The tide washes them in then pulls them out like a child doing a gravity pull with a yo-yo. Accompanying the motion is the gentle slap of water against the docks. Salt is thick in my nose and coats my tongue with its alkaline taste.

"Where now?" the Swiss barks.

I cup a hand over my eyes to shield them from the rain. Being in a city is a visual overload after weeks of avoiding them; I can't yet see the details within the big picture. The city cups the harbor in a concrete palm. I pace along the water's edge and try to break the panorama into palatable pieces.

I know nothing about the boat I'm supposed to meet besides her name. Frustrated, I trek back and forth, try to pick out words. Too many are in Cyrillic lettering or Greek. Not enough English.

He's pacing, too, peering inside the empty terminal behind us.

"Where?"

Lisa splits the difference between us, stands in the rain instead of taking advantage of shelter.

"I don't know."

"You brought me here knowing nothing."

"I didn't ask you to come."

"You would be dead without me. Stupid, both of you. Stupid, stupid women."

I walk away. I have to. Otherwise I'll do something I won't be able to live with. And that's important to me, being able to live with my actions. My thoughts are a different story. They're my own and they don't hurt anyone but me. In the real world I smash open a vending machine in the terminal using a chair and empty it of all its worldly goods. Three small piles. One for Lisa, one for the Swiss, and one for me. I take mine and sit on the dock cross-legged, not caring about the rain. All I care about is that boat and will she be here like she promised?

They wait, too, but not with my dedication. The Swiss drags Lisa into the terminal and she does not complain. Late in the evening, we sit together and eat chips and drink warm soda.

"Just say the word and I'll make him stop."

"I have to do it."

"There's no have to. Not even now."

"What if I never get to fool around with anyone else?"

"You might get a chance to with someone you love."

"You don't know that." She empties the can. "Do you?"

"No, I don't. But I hope."

She points to her missing eye. "Who could love me like this?"

"England," he calls out, and just like that she turns to him. I pick up her trash and mine and drop the refuse in the half-full trash can inside the terminal. Two steps; that's how far I go before I'm drawn back to the container by some ancient hoarding instinct passed down by ancestors who knew a thing or two about survival. Using both hands, I dig through the trash looking for anything useful, some tool or trinket that might make a difference. But there's nothing. Just empty packets and old papers with words I can't read anyway.

DATE: THEN

A few days come and go and then they multiply into a full week. That week doubles and still I don't hear from Nick. But I pick up the phone every night and dial half his number before dumping the phone into the cradle.

He has my number. He can call me.

It's a stupid rule and one I've never subscribed to, and I don't believe in it now. It's just the story I tell myself to cover up my real fear: Nick is dead.

I pick up the phone, dial four of the seven digits, hang up.

He can call me.

DATE: NOW

One day bleeds into two and still I keep vigil. The *Elpis* will come. I know she will. She has to. I need something to give all this meaning. I can't have come all this way for nothing.

The Swiss swaggers out, stares out to sea, his face harder than the ground we're standing on.

"Your boat isn't coming."

"It will."

"You are a fool. A dreamer. I suppose you believe in things like love and morals and valor. Women like you sit and they wait for men to come and rescue them from the unspeakable horrors of the world. You like nothing more than to sit at home, getting fat, while you cook and eat and create more mouths the world cannot hope to feed. And for what? Some misguided belief that you are special, that you are loved, that you matter to someone. You do not matter, America. You are ultimately nothing. Dust."

"It will be here."

Spit flies from his mouth: a wet, clear blob with a yellow center. Egg-like.

The thought comes before I can stop it: *I hope he's sick.*

The Swiss correctly interprets the expression dancing across my face.

"I am not sick. Disease is for the weak."

I walk away in search of Lisa. She's up in one of those life-guard towers, the bare metal frames with a seat on top.

"Listening for Jaws?"

"No. There's a boat coming." She points the way, my broken, blinded beacon.

At first my longing to believe is so great that I can't bring myself to trust in her words. I've wanted this too much. Then I bolt, boots pounding along the water's edge, peering between the gaps, desperate for a glimpse. Then I see her. She rolls into port, an old, cold tomb. The *Elpis*. The *Hope* is my only hope.

All my strength evaporates. My infrastructure collapses in on itself and I have no choice but to crouch down, one hand reaching out in front to steady me like I'm an unwieldy tripod.

The Swiss's jaw ticks like a time bomb.

"I told you," I say. "I told you so."

DATE: THEN

> The jar resists me,
> but not the borrowed hammer.
> Cracks, splinters, mess. Bones.

DATE: NOW

She's nothing to look at, the *Elpis*, with her ruby-red rivets and her pointed bow carving the sea into foamy slices. She needs no introductions, no elaborate adornments to announce that the harbor is hers and she has come for it, for she is the only vessel that displays signs of life. There are passengers on that boat, and they wait on the deck and watch. I cup my hand over my eyes and scan them for friendly faces, but see nothing but my own sadness reflecting back at me.

The captain comes ashore, the gangplank shaking with his heavy steps.

"You coming to Greece?" His mustache leaps as the words battle their way through the hairs.

"Please," I say.

"Okay. But you must pay."

What once passed for currency is now worthless, and I have no money anyway. What I have to offer is peace of mind, relaxation, and escape, all in a tiny white pill. He knows what they are; the greed in his eyes betrays his hunger when I pull the blister packs from my pocket and offer him payment for me and for Lisa.

He nods. Our transaction is complete. I snatch up my things so I can run, run, run to find Nick.

The Swiss and I face each other.

"Here we say good-bye. Lisa?"

"I am coming," he says.

"No."

"The world is free. I can go where I choose without even a passport. Who are you to tell me what I can do or not? You are a nobody."

We stare each other down. In his eyes, I see a wasteland where nothing can survive. I am the first to break and glance away.

"You have to pay your own way," I say.

He makes a deal with the captain but I do not see how he pays the ferryman for his passage. When they're done, I pull the captain aside. I tell him who I'm looking for, describe him in detail. The captain chews on my request. The fisherman's cap shakes with his head.

"I see no one like that. Each time is just a few people. But none like that."

"Are you sure?"

"Eh. Who knows? Everyone looks the same now. Like you. Tired. Hungry. Dirty."

The weight of the world shifts from my shoulders to my head, drags it low.

"We go now," the captain says.

"He's dead." The Swiss is behind me. Privacy means nothing to him. "I knew you were coming for a man. Why else does a woman do anything?"

"He's not dead."

"Is he the father of your bastard?"

"Mind your own fucking business," I say.

The captain waits.

My reflection in the terminal window is me without all the baggage. Maybe it's me as I used to be, or maybe it's me as I wish to be. I appear strong, determined, resolute. I believe Nick is alive and made it to Greece safely. He's gone via some other road. I won't believe anything else. If he's there, then nothing will stop me moving on.

"I'm coming," I say. Forward is the only way.

PART
TWO

PART

TWO

TEN

There is no nuclear war, no fight for land, no arguing over human rights and petty despots. The beginning of the end comes because of the weather, just like Daniel, my blind date, said it would. Only, he's wrong about the culprit: it isn't China, it's us. So we're both right.

The end begins in hurricane season, although in truth the seeds had been sown much earlier with mass filing of patents and theories about how the weather could be controlled with man's hand and a whole lot of funding.

Weather modification. Playing God. Modern man couldn't conquer death, had a flimsy grip on disease control, so he turned to another lost cause.

Scientists scream, but they're soon silenced with money stuffed down the throats of their pet research projects. Which leaves the entrepreneurs, the government, and their nodding stable of scientists to tinker with the weather.

Hurricane Pandora, they name her, although it isn't her turn alphabetically. Because, like me, they are insatiably curious. Some say she's a typical woman, one minute hugging the coast, the next hurling winds and rains at that same jagged finger of land, daring it to look into her single eye as she hypnotizes the Gulf Coast region into a false sense of calm.

The experiment is a secret. Until it fails. Details hemorrhage into the media after that.

Pandora claims houses and lives for her own. Returns land to the ocean. Drains money from a lot of already-empty pockets.

A week later, a cyclone forms off the east coast of Australia. This time the experiment is a success and the cyclone dies before she makes landfall.

The attack comes when the U.S. and her allies are celebrating their victory.

It's an electronic Pearl Harbor that leaves the country unable to buy books, check movie times, send pictures of funny cats with misspelled captions. It's an outrage, people cry, until they realize how deep it goes. Suddenly they're cognizant that their wealth exists only in a computer database. They're virtual millionaires and billionaires. Or they are until China implements the One Way, Our Way policy, as the media aptly dubs it.

The country panics. We've jumped too far forward to go back to newspapers and passing paper notes in class. The Internet is gone. Cell phones are night-lights and colorful paperweights. We are hostages with all the luxuries we had twenty years ago. We are adrift . . .

Give us the technology, China demands, as though this is the high seas and they're toting peg legs, parrots, and cannons.

The United States doesn't give in to demands; it's not Lady Liberty's way. Instead she buys allies. Our technology for their help.

Then someone gets clever, decides that if we can unmake a hurricane, maybe we can help one grow. I don't know if that's possible. It's for smarter people than me to know. But that's when everything explodes. The atom bomb, its power and destruction, is tossed aside for a new potential weapon that everyone wants: the weather. Mother Nature as a war machine, bent to man's will at last.

Every able-bodied man goes to war. There is no fleeing across borders because they're going to war, too. Pick the wrong border and the final taste in your mouth is metal.

Colleges close, so even those are no longer havens for those who don't want to fight.

Who could have known that the War to End All Wars would have nothing to do with God?

DATE: NOW

The *Elpis* lurches across the sea, and my stomach along with her. Crossing the Mediterranean should only take a handful of hours, but the captain tells me their fuel supplies are low and they must stretch what they have—so she creeps. The journey will take as long as it takes. He says this in cobbled-together English, filling in the blanks with hand gestures.

We are a dozen, not including the skeleton crew. All of us downtrodden, our hearts crushed beneath life's careless boot heels. Not long ago this route was filled with honeymooners and vacation-goers, people who would have to struggle to conjure up anything dimmer than a delighted grin. Not us. We can barely lift our chins to acknowledge each other with anything more than grim suspicion.

There are two other women, both middle-aged, maybe sisters, maybe friends. They cling to each other as though the other is a life vest. The men slouch in their carefully selected territories. None of us turn our backs. We are still animals with animal instincts. Who carries the disease? Who passes as human and yet is *not*? We watch. We wonder. We don't risk.

My gaze sticks on the man hunched in the far corner. He's maybe sixty, although stress can age a person and we've had more than our fair share of trauma. His shoulders stoop as though he carries the burdens of a thousand men upon each one. It's not just his hair that's gray but his very soul. Despair seeps through his pores. He's a man out of context, so I slot him into various visions of my old life, trying to gauge where he fits.

Lisa rests her head on my shoulder. I put my arms around her, link my fingers. The Swiss leans on the railing on the starboard side, watches the sea.

Still, the man captivates me. I change his clothes, make him one of those paper dress-up dolls I loved as a girl. Tidy his hair. Shave him close to the bone. When the penny slides down the chute in my head, I gasp. For a time, I sit and watch him and try not to stare. Why is he here? Stupid question, because why are any of us here? Still, why is *he* here? When I can no longer rein in my curiosity, I get up, pace back and forth until I can't help myself, then take a seat near him. Close, but respectfully distant.

"Mr. President?"

He looks me in the eye like I'm his superior.

"I'm the president of nothing."

"I voted for you."

He nods slowly, as though he aches from it. "Really?"

"Yes."

"Thank you."

"I was pleased to do it."

"You should have bet on the other guy."

DATE: THEN

The war taints all. Men go to war and never return. Word of their demise sometimes reaches home. Wal-Mart's shelves empty and remain that way without cheaply made goods to replenish them.

One night on the news I see Jorge's red truck being pulled from the river, squirrel heads sodden and rotting, still dangling from the mirror.

Nobody says anything at work. Nobody says much of anything now. We all go about our jobs like automatons set to *toil.*

Soon I start missing faces. One day the regular receptionist is gone from the downstairs lobby, and in her place is a perky twenty-something who'll stay friendly until benefits kick in. After that, she'll adopt a bored stare and a *Whatever!* attitude. Later that afternoon, winter personified follows me onto the elevator. Her arms are stretched around a box filled with photo frames and knickknacks, things meaningless to everyone but her. She stares through me like I'm an open window, no twitch or blink to suggest she's trying to place me the way I'm placing her. I remember her in white and she doesn't remember me surrounded by dead mice and George. P. Pope's questions.

Another day I go into the bathroom, where three women are gathered around a calendar, trying to calculate the first day of their last periods. One of them stops mid-conversation, races to the nearest stall. The door slams, then swings open just as her vomit splashes the floor.

"Sorry," she says. "I figure I only have about eight more weeks of this."

I make all the right noises, but really I'm thinking about Ben, Raoul, James, Mrs. Sark.

And Nick.

I contact the CDC. They redirect me to 911. The tin woman answers, and when I tell her about the jar, she dismisses me as a lunatic.

George P. Pope appears in the paper one morning, posing next to a brittle blonde the caption identifies as his wife. He's made all the right quotes, meant to soothe a panicking public. Phrases like *get your flu shots now* and *our scientists are making new discoveries every day*. Hollow words from a self-serving mouth.

Mrs. Pope doesn't buy it, either. There's a speck on the ground more worthy of her attention. So she places it there and hides her lack of faith behind a wall of fair hair.

The picture gives a better sound bite than Pope's mouth.

DATE: NOW

Night comes to the open sea, creeping from the east. When the ferry's lights flicker on, their beams absorbed by the encroaching darkness—when just we two are on the deck—the president of nothing begins to speak.

"Where are you from?"

I tell him.

"They liked the other guy."

"How did you get here, Mr. President?"

He shrugs. "I never wanted a life in politics. It chose me . . . much later on. When I was a boy, I wanted to be an astronaut."

Even in his world-torn state, he oozes charisma, and I remember why I—and millions of others—voted him into the highest office. Together we lean against the port rails and watch the void come for us.

"You and every other American boy."

He nods. "Ours was a country with great dreams, all of them bold and large in scope. But we were not too good at the details. Do you have time for a story?"

Anything for you, Mr. President, I want to say, but the words won't come, so I'm forced to respond with a nod. This seems to satisfy him.

He pauses for a moment. Two men have come on deck, gripping the ends of another; two trees and a hammock. They swing back, forth, toss him overboard. Sending the dead to a better place.

"There was a man whom the people chose to lead them. 'If I accept,' he said, 'I want you to share with me your ideas to make this country stronger.' 'No, no,' they said. 'This is why we have you. Your ideas are better.' Pleased that they had so much faith in him, he accepted. Soon they came to his doorstep crying. 'Tell me,' he said. 'I want you to share your ideas for making this country a happier place for all.' 'No, no,' they cried. 'This is why we have you. Your ideas will make us happier.' Time passed, and again they came to his door, this time shouting. 'Tell me,' he said. 'Share your ideas for making this country wealthier.' 'No, no,' they shouted. 'It's your ideas we trust to put more money in our pockets.' Then a great war came. The people came stampeding to his doorstep with their pitchforks. 'Tell me,' he said. 'Please, help me preserve this country for your children. Give me your ideas.' Again they refused. 'We gave you power so you could decide for us,' they yelled. When the sickness came, he pleaded with them again, and was again refused on the grounds that he knew best. This time, when he failed, they came for him, cast him to the winds. 'That man was worthless,' they said. 'He never did what we wanted.'"

"That's how it happened for you," I say.

"That's how it happens for every elected leader."

"So you left?"

"In the night like a common white-collared thief."

We speak of other things after that. Of apple pie and ice cream, of baseball, of times when people still celebrated July Fourth. Of times when those we loved were still with us. When a stable government meant we were less free, but pleasures lay thicker on the ground.

The next morning, the captain finds him hanging from a thick pipe below the decks.

"I saw you talking," he says. "Who was he?"

"A good man, for all his flaws. Better than most."

Lisa listens as the crew cuts the president down, throws him overboard with nary a prayer to send him on his way. Her head tilts as though she's trying to put this into some context that makes sense in her world. She can't see, yet she *observes*.

Her fascination makes me shiver.

"Do you think he could fix me?"

I know what Lisa means. "If what the Swiss says about his past is true, yes. But the risk would be huge. You'd need somewhere clean, sterile. Proper equipment. We have none of that."

"I bet Greece has hospitals."

"You're right. But what they don't have is electricity."

"I don't care." A tiny smile curves her lips. Her face is soft and dreamy. She looks content. "I bet he could fix me."

DATE: THEN

Nick likes to hang out in my head sometimes, as though he's enjoying the clutter.

I said open the jar, I hear him say, *not smash it.*

"Sometimes my temper gets the best of me."

Do you realize you're talking to yourself?

"Yes."

It's good that you know the difference.

"Go away."

Okay.

"No, stay with me."

About a week after he mentioned his sickness, I began scanning the newspapers for his obituary. I know, I could have just picked up the phone, called, but I didn't. Denial and acceptance; I had a foot planted squarely in each. See, with a newspaper I could lick my thumb, rub it against the paper, make it not true. But I couldn't handle hearing the phone ring off into infinity. There's no way to erase the sound of a dead man not answering.

On the door's other side the grayscale world is waiting. I slip a leash on my gloom and go out to greet it. When I reach the lobby, my feet stop. Someone has thrown a pair of combat boots in my path. They're filled with Nick.

"You're not dead," I say.

"I'm not dead."

"Why? How?"

He laughs. "Dying wasn't on my list."

My smile sputters until it's full and real. "What is on your list?"

"Not dying. Coming here. This."

He reels me in, cups my face with both hands, and becomes my whole world. *This* is a kiss—maybe the last one we'll ever know, so we stay there forever, warm and safe. When he pulls away, something is lost. I think it's my heart.

"What else is on your list?"

"Zoe . . ."

My lips are cooling too quickly; I know what he's going to say. "I get it. I do. You have to go. Men need to be heroes."

"I don't want to fight," he says. "But I want to win."

"I know. And I'm glad you came. But if you die out there, I'll hate you forever."

"No you won't," he says, and turns until both feet point toward war.

The glass door drifts shut behind him. My hands dangle by my sides, those useless things.

How do you file a restraining order against sadness?

Week after week there's nothing. The obituaries come thick and fast now. Not just the elderly, but young people dying of what appears to be an errant stomach flu. The media blames it on farm animals, contaminated food, illegal immigrants, but really they don't know. And I feel better in some ways because how could this have started with me? It's arrogant of me to think I could be that important. And yet, a voice still tells me none of their guesses have struck truth. None of them speculates that somewhere in this city there's a box filled with shards and bones, and the whole thing feels like death.

The newspapers don't list war deaths. With the Internet still dead, computers are little more than boat anchors, so there's no database running queries, spitting out names, or coming back with—one hoped—*no result*.

We return to the old ways: lists slapped onto walls in government buildings, people hovering, hoping, fists pushed between their teeth, chewing their lips, twirling their hair. Nervous tics. Superstitious, too.

Jenny and I visit the library every evening. She's always there in her cherry-red coat, the one that should be too warm for this time of year, leaning against the center pillar. I see her sometimes as a stranger might: relaxed, the contrast of her dark hair against the red wool pleasing to the eye; a vibrant young woman. The illusion lasts until I'm close enough to read her face. We sprang from the same gene pool, and while we look like our own separate beings, her facial expressions are my own. Constant fear has knocked the girlish layer of subcutaneous fat from her face so that the line of her jaw and cheekbones jut through her skin in an off-key rendition of magazine-cover chic. Her brow line dips in the middle even when she paints on a false smile, like she's doing now. I've faked that same smile before. I'm faking it now. And she knows that I know that she knows.

Wearing that polyester smile, I jog up the stone steps to meet her. My preference would be to sit at the bottom, pull myself into a ball, and rock back and forth until the world swings back to normal. But I have to be strong for Jenny, because Mark is out there. Like so many others, he swapped a keyboard and mouse for a gun and cut-rate body armor.

We perform the ritual: hug, squeeze, peck on the cheek.

"How was work?" she asks.

"Fine. How are you?"

"Fine. Ready?"

"Sure."

More lies.

We push through the towering doors, take a sharp left, stride to the far side of the lobby, where the wall is covered in corkboard.

The list is up. I don't know who puts it there, only that they do. Today there are over a hundred names—and this list is just for our city, not the country. The violence is escalating. Or they're dying from the same disease that's killing people here. I can't tell. The papers are silent about everything except our victories. They ply us with a steady stream of celebrity gossip, feel-good stories, and minor grievances to keep us from asking *What? Where? Why?* The news channels are more of the same—those that haven't gone dark.

Jenny squeezes my fingers until the bones are nearly crushed to crumbs. I wince but I don't say anything, nor do I pull away. She needs to give pain and I need to accept it. Because if I see Nick's name up there, I'm going to take shelter in that physical hurt.

We join the cluster of some hundred heads and wait our turn.

This is the worst part: the waiting. It's relative: if we see a name we recognize, that becomes the worst part. We've seen some. Mostly people we knew in school or worked with in some distant time. Those days we walk away with our heads hung low, not speaking until we reach the bottom of the steps. We go, we sip coffee on a street corner, silent until one of us says, "I hope it didn't hurt." War being war, I figure there's a fifty percent chance of that being true. You can either go quick in a single blast or make a grab for life's tail and hold on while it tries to shake you off like a pissed-off tiger.

"He won't be there," I say.

"He won't be there," she parrots.

People peel away from the front. We inch closer. They wear temporary smiles. Tomorrow they'll be back, tense with fear. I envy them; they already know they'll return.

An anguished cry cuts through the crowd. I flinch, because even though it's expected, I still hope that we'll all walk away wearing that transient smile. I am a fool.

"No, no. It's a lie," the woman shrieks. Hysteria has her in its grasp. "They're wrong." She makes to tear the list from the wall but is stopped by the people behind her. They shove her aside and insert themselves in her place. "Fuck you!" she screams. "Fuck you with a chain saw! I hope your sons, fathers, and husbands are dead. Why should I be the only one? Fuck you."

I move to break from the pack, comfort her, but Jenny holds me fast. "Stay with me," she whispers.

The woman picks up a stack of free newspapers, a local publication filled with upcoming events around town. They're two months old now, remnants of a time when a concert or festival sounded like it mattered.

"Fuck you." She flings a paper at the nearest person. "And fuck you." Another paper aimed at someone else. "Fuck you and her." More papers. Finally she tosses the remainder across the crowd. "Fuck you all!" She drags the last word out until there's no more breath to carry it.

Some watch her shuffle away, too broken to be humiliated by her actions. The rest don't dare glance at her because they know how easily they could break. Words on a page could make them *her*.

When it's our turn at the head of the line, Jenny grips my hand tighter. The pink of my fingers fades to white.

"I can't look." She always says this and yet she always stares at the list unblinking until she doesn't find Mark's name.

It's my finger that glides down the page, sticking on any name with a similar formation to Mark's. We're looking for Nugent. Mark D. Nugent. I enter the Ns and shoot right out the other side without glimpsing his name.

Jenny clutches my arm. "He's not there. He's not there. Check again."

But I'm already on the move, falling down the list, falling, falling until I hit R. Ramirez, Rittiman, Roberts. No Rose.

"He's not there, Jen."

"Check again."

Feet shuffle behind us. I glance quickly at the Ns again. "Mark's fine."

Jenny's smile shaves five years from her face. "He's fine."

Neither of us says *today*.

Afterward, we perform our new ritual. We buy coffee at a nearby café and hang out on the street corner that will carry us in different directions.

"Who are you looking for? On the list," Jenny asks.

My hands tense and I realize I've been hugging the cup too tight between my fingers. The cup is hot, the coffee even hotter, and the warmth seeps into my skin. I'm shivering. I look up at the darkening sky. It shouldn't be this cold in October.

I look back at Jenny. She's giving me that look like I'm holding out on her—and I am.

"No one."

"If you say so."

"It's nothing. Just a friend." But he's not even that, although I felt it was true. There's a gap in my heart, or maybe just my soul, large enough to park a city bus.

"I know that look."

I say nothing.

"It's the one I get every day when I know Mark is safe for another day. That's when I can let my guard down and feel hope again. That's why I like drinking coffee afterward, because that's the real beginning of my day. Tomorrow morning the death-watch starts all over again." I go to speak but she stops me. "It's a deathwatch, Zoe. We both know it."

When you have a sister, you hold a mirror in your hands.

ELEVEN

To watch Lisa is to stare into Alice's looking glass. Nothing about her is quite as it should be. Each day her fingerhold on reality slips a little more, dipping another inch of her essence into dark waters. She faces the sea, always wearing a secretive smile that fades if anyone approaches.

She holds vigil at the stern, feet in ballet's first position, hands resting lightly on the rail. Her hair is a greasy mass pinned to her scalp, the result of not enough shampoo and too many weeks of rainwater. Her spine is distinct and prominent, its own creature, one I half expect to see flick its tail independent of her movements. A steady diet of thin air and canned foods has carved the meat from our bones, leaving us just enough to live on. Each time I glimpse myself in the ferry's sliding glass doors, I can't believe I'm seeing me. The ragamuffin person with stick legs is not who I am. In my mind, I am robust and healthy, with flesh that threatens to sprawl if I take that third cookie.

I need to eat more. We all do. War and disease have cured obesity too well.

"Hey," I say, to warn her of my approach. "Do you want to hear something neat?"

She shakes her head. Keeps staring at what we left behind.

"There's land. It's a long thin strip of not much at the moment, but the captain says it's spectacular to watch it come into focus."

She dips down in a rigid plié. "And then what?"

"When we get there?"

"What happens when we get there?"

"I have to go north."

"And me?"

"I told you. You can come, too."

"What if I don't want to?"

I swallow slow, consider the words on my internal Scrabble board. If I push them into the wrong formation, something will be lost.

"You're your own woman. You have to do what's right for you."

"Yes, I am."

She starts as a distant speck, the isle of Greece, and as I watch she steadily inflates, bobbing above the waves like a massive buoy. Technically she is not an isle; that's just a pretty word thrown in there to fill out the lyrics of a pop song.

"The bottom half, the Peloponnese, she is an island made by men," the captain tells me. "One hundred years ago, maybe more, they cut into the land so the boats can pass through. Just like the . . ." His mustache jerks about as he chews on the right words.

"Panama Canal?"

His fingers snap. "The Panama Canal, yes." He holds up a dehydrated hand. "This is one level. No boomp-boomp-boomp." As he says this he bunny-hops his hand to simulate the lock system for which the canal at Panama is famous.

"How long until we get there?"

"Eh." He coughs. "Just a few hours."

A few hours. My heart knocks faster.

DATE: THEN

The new receptionist from the lobby disappears two weeks after she arrived. Her facsimile is already in place. "Good morning, howkinIhelpyew?" she snaps into the headset. Her hand is heavy with a rock. Somewhere out there she's got a fiancé—probably in the war.

Upstairs in the bathroom, the women have gathered, but not to talk babies.

"Did you hear? Cynthia is dead," one says when I walk in.

Two weeks ago she was jubilant, and now she's gone. I barely knew her, and yet it takes everything I have to hold myself in a single column.

That afternoon a man approaches me on the train. The usual crowd has dwindled to just a smattering of backsides in seats, so he stands out like a bloodstain on white pants. He's burrowed down in his green sweater, fingertips peeking out the ends of the sleeves. He has a lollipop head covered in thick sandy hair that hasn't seen a barber's scissors in some time. So slight is he that the messenger bag slung crosswise his body seems to be the only thing holding him down.

"Can I . . . May I talk to you? It's polite to ask, so that's why I'm asking instead of just talking."

I turn in the seat, look up at him, try not to be annoyed at having my worrying interrupted. He goes on without my consent, which should be my first clue to shut him down, but he's caught me in an unguarded moment.

"You work at Pope Pharmaceuticals, right? Of course you do. I mean, I know you do. I followed you from there. I didn't want to pick one of those science people, because they won't say squat, at least not in terms most people can understand. So I had to pick someone else. Someone not so important who'd talk to me. People in menial jobs like to talk. I've seen them on the television. Everyone wants their fifteen minutes. So I picked someone like you."

I try to ignore the insult, because something about this kid is different. "You're a journalist?"

His gaze settles on my left ear. Flicks to my right. Down to my hands. To some spot atop my head. "Jesse Clark, *United States Times*. I used to have an Internet blog. Maybe you've heard of me." He waits in an unnatural pause.

I try to shake the surrealism away.

"No, I've never heard of it, or you, or the *United States Times*. I'm sorry."

"It's new." The kid is a whole litter of still-blind-puppies full of enthusiasm. "So many people have gone to fight that there aren't enough qualified journalists and newspaper people left. They want one big newspaper that tells the same news to everyone who's still here. It's easier that way, they say. I think it's a conspiracy and the government wants to control the news. But since they're paying for my stories, I just got my first apartment all on my own, so the money is nice. I'm learning to cook, too. I made oatmeal this morning, in the microwave. Last night I made an omelet. With those green peppers and bacon. The recipe said ham, but I like bacon better."

Again he waits as though this is chess and it's my move.

"I prefer bacon, too."

He beams, focuses on the armrest. "Can I sit down? I know I should wait until you ask, because that's the polite thing; but I don't know how long it's going to be before you ask, and standing on a train facing in the wrong direction doesn't make me feel so great."

Normally I'd ignore him, hope he goes away before he proves to be a problem, but these are not normal times. I wave at the aisle seat and hope he takes that, not the middle.

He chooses wisely. "I don't want to take the middle one. That would make it look unbalanced. So if you sit there and I sit here, it's almost symmetrical." Prim and proper. Hands flat on his chino-clad thighs. Bag across his body. "Thank you. I have to say thank you because that's polite."

"You're welcome."

"That's polite, too." He stares straight ahead. "I want to ask you some questions, if that's okay. I'm working on a story no one knows about yet. You might think I'm crazy, and it's okay if you do, because lots of people think I am. Even my best friend Regina thinks I'm crazy, but that's okay because she's my friend and she's kind of weird, anyways. My parents think I'm crazy, too. They don't say it, but I can see it. My dad's always getting angry at me because I'm no good at driving or playing football like my brothers, and my mom's always saying, 'Don't say that. He's a smart boy. He's just different.' I love my mom. I love my dad, too, because that's what you're supposed to do: love your parents. But I don't like him all that much. Do you like your parents?"

"They're good people."

Jesse nods. "About a month ago I was looking through the newspapers and I noticed something strange. I used to get all the major papers on account of having my blog and wanting to have all the latest news. Checking out the competition, my dad calls it. Only, now I don't have a blog because no one has the Internet anyway. When the newspapers come I like to cut out the pieces and lie them on the floor in the basement. It's flat and no one else goes down there much, so I can spread them out and move them around however I want. I like to look for patterns. And in the past month, I've been seeing all kinds of patterns in the obituaries. Lots of people are dying who wouldn't normally be dying, and they're all dying of the same thing. Only, I don't think anyone else has noticed or it would be in the newspapers already, right?"

I don't tell him that I've noticed, too, or that I don't know whether to feel relieved or terrified that someone has made the connection.

"So I said to myself, 'Jesse, this could be the story that makes you someone.' My dad will be pleased that I'm someone important and maybe people won't think I'm so stupid. What I did next was talk to some families of the people who died. Mostly they said things like 'Go away, mind your own business, we're trying to grieve here,' but some of them used ugly words, too. Like *f-u-c-k*." He glances around, his face pinched. "I hope nobody heard."

"I don't think they did."

"But you know what? Some of those people talked to me. And they all told me the same stories and described the same symptoms, so I said to myself, *That's weird, because how do all these people in different cities and states have the same thing?*"

My heart plays skipping stones in my chest before stopping for several beats.

"How do you know?"

"I told you, I saw the patterns in the paper. Then I got on a bus—lots of buses—and visited a whole bunch of people. My dad said I was crazy and that I should get a job at McDonald's or someplace, but the grease smells funny, so I got on the bus instead. I talked to this real nice lady in Little Rock and she said both her cat and her husband died and he wanted the cat buried with him but the funeral home wouldn't do it. Dead is dead, so I think they should have done it, because that's what he wanted. This lady, she told me that first her husband got real sick and vomited blood all the time. She apologized, because we were in her kitchen eating red velvet cake and she was worried I had a weak stomach. Then she said her husband got all these weird pains in random places in his body, like he was getting jabbed like a voodoo doll. After a couple of weeks he died. She said after the funeral the mortician came over to her and asked if he'd always had a tail. She said yes because she didn't know what else to say, but then she told me he never had that tail before and they'd been married forty years. Isn't that strange? You know what else is strange? I saw a whole lot of stones in Little Rock but I couldn't tell which one was meant to be the little rock."

"Why aren't you in the war?"

"Special dispensation on account of my condition. Do you know what that means?"

"I've heard it before."

He nods, keeps his gaze fixed on the seat ahead. "Asperger's is what the doctors say I've got. It doesn't mean anything other than I'm different. *Different* can mean good or it can mean bad, depending on who's doing the talking."

His fingers start to tap. At first I think piano, but the longer I watch, I see number patterns.

"After I went to Little Rock I went to some other places and then I went home. They've got a big library there at the college. Before, I would have just gone to Google but I had to do it the old way, which was a lot of hard work after riding all those buses. I couldn't use the Internet, but they still have an internal system where you can search for books and journals. You know what? There's no disease like that. Nothing that makes you sick and then grow a tail. Some of the other dead people grew other weird stuff, too. One kid had two hearts when they cut him open; only, one was growing up in his throat and choked him to death. Some of them just died after all the vomiting, but some grew stuff people shouldn't have. So I talked to my mom and she said maybe I'd discovered something new, something no one ever heard of, and maybe if I figured out what that was, they'd name it after me. If there's anybody left to care." His shoulders slump. The number patterns slow.

The inside of my head is a radio station turned to static. I believe what he's saying: the pieces are all there.

"Why me?"

"A new disease has to come from somewhere. Have you seen *Resident Evil*? There was an accident in a laboratory and everyone turned to zombies. I figured maybe this was like that."

"That was just a movie."

"Nuh-uh. It happens. There are lots of online forums that talk about how it could happen for real. I went to a lot of labs and companies that make medicine and no one would talk to me. They just smiled and gave me pamphlets to read or threatened to throw me out. One guy threatened to have me locked up in an institution. All I wanted was to ask some questions. I think they wouldn't talk to me because they think I'm different-bad."

I shake my head. "They won't talk to you because what if you're right?"

It's crazy. It should be crazy. But just because something is crazy doesn't mean it isn't true. All those dead mice. Jorge. The bones crammed inside the jar. It's making me want to ask questions. Maybe my paranoia *isn't*.

Ben's dead. James. Raoul. Two receptionists now. The woman from the bathroom. And the man in Arkansas with the tail—oh God.

Jesse's fingers pick up pace, then slow again. His head turns and I think he's going to look at me, but he stares at my mouth instead. "Will you answer my questions?"

I want to. But I can't. I explain about the contract I signed, the confidentiality agreement, so maybe he'll understand how the business world works when there's a whole lot of green and reputations at stake. I think it's going to sink in when he goes back to staring at the chair.

"You're scared. I'm scared, too. My mom says it's okay to be scared because that's just our brain's way of telling us to be careful."

On the other side of the window, the scenery changes. Two minutes until my stop.

"I wish I could," I tell Jesse. He seems like a good kid. I like him. I'd love to help.

"Please."

"I'm sorry. I don't want either of us to get hurt." Or worse.

"But my dad will be proud of me if they name the disease after me. I'll be different-good."

The train slows. I tug my bag over one shoulder, hold the strap in place with my opposite hand, shielding myself from his questions. "I'm sorry."

The last I see of him is his face pressed against the window as I glance back over my shoulder. He's looking straight into my guarded soul.

I go about my business. I clean, talk to the mice, monitor them for signs of imminent death. I do not name them, although the little guy at the end with the bent whiskers is begging for an identity that doesn't include numbers.

I watch the mice and wonder if the experiment is larger than this bank of cages.

My paranoia has its own mind.

You know you want to, Nick says in my head.

"Not now."

He falls silent. Please don't let today be the day I see him on the list.

I pull on slippers with my jeans, throw on a coat. Still, I shiver when the chill slams my body. The two quarters are cold lead weights in my palm. It stings to hold them. They clank into the newspaper dispenser and I use the edge of my sleeve to tug it open.

The city newspaper is gone; in its place is the *United States Times*. Jesse flashes into my mind, that kid who just wants to be different-good.

The stairs fly by two at a time. My apartment door crashes behind me. I grab more quarters and I'm gone again.

Two by two, I shove them into the other dispensers, the ones that should be holding newspapers from all over the country. I have to see, I have to know if there's other news out there. But they're all filled with one publication now: the *United States Times*. That journalism has been distilled to this dangerous point catapults me into action. I'm doing nothing when I should be doing something.

Back in my hidey-hole, I dissect the paper. I pick through the pages as a soothsayer might a tangle of entrails, trying to divine a course of action. It's just a paper. It's like all the others with its bold title announcing its presence. Nothing about it screams, *I killed the competition. I took away your choices overnight.* The cover is more of what we've been seeing: battles won. Men cheering. Leaders happy with the troops' success. There are twelve more obituaries than in yesterday's paper.

The hall closet looms, its clean white paint darkening as I assign it characteristics it can't possibly possess: dark, foreboding, dangerous.

When the phone rings, I leap.

"We're showing an alarm at your residence. Do you need assistance?"

I forgot the alarm. Damn. "No, no, I'm fine. I was carrying . . . groceries."

"Code, please."

I give them the code, and the secondary code, and my mother's maiden name. When they're satisfied I'm not a doppelgänger, they reset the system and I lock myself in.

I stand in front of the closet, hands poised on the handles.

"I'm ready," I tell Nick-in-my-head.

It's still in there, that carton I stashed, wrapped in its packing-tape straitjacket. Between the fake Christmas tree I keep because I hate hauling a fresh one up the stairs, and building rules state they're not allowed to ride the elevator anyway, and the box of Bibles I've collected over the years from people who thought my soul needed saving. Too superstitious to throw them away, I keep them here to ward away people who'd give me another. The flaw in my plan was James. Last Christmas he gave me a children's Bible painted with toothy cartoon characters.

They smile cheerfully at me from between the box flaps. I glance away before my eyes start to heat up.

On the floor I sit, legs in a wide V and pull the carton to me. It doesn't look like much. It's quite ordinary, really. Logically, there's nothing ominous about a package wrapped in tape. If someone saw me struggling into the post office with this thing, they'd assume it was a care package bound for a beloved friend. It's the contents that lend it the sinister air of a secret long turned malignant.

I have a plan. It's been in my head since Jesse approached me on the train, but the human mind excels at withholding information from itself. Errant thoughts loiter in the less-traveled parts of our hemispheres until something triggers their leap from the shadows.

The *United States Times*. Jesse. His face pressed against the train's window, looking me in the eye for the first time, daring me to do something bigger than clean floors and cages.

The scissors leave ragged edges on the tape. A new roll sits beside me ready to take its place as soon as I've done what I must.

Deep breath.

Lift lid.

Scoop a handful of pieces with a plastic Baggie. Seal the bag first, then the box. Shove it back into its hiding place with my foot.

I'm ready to do something bigger.

DATE: NOW

The Swiss corners me on the deck. "Your stupid friend wants an abortion."

"No she doesn't."

"Who are you to decide for her? Is it not her body? Americans. Every life is sacred except the lives they neglect to save because some places have no useful resources."

"I'm not making a moral judgment. This is about her safety. There are no tools and no place clean and safe enough for any kind of surgery. Lancing a boil could be risky these days. I've told her already."

"If we find a hospital, there will be antibiotics," he says.

"You don't know that."

"I know more than you about many things."

Anger rolls through me, gathering my power. I want to grab his throat, squeeze, but I don't. Instead my elbow shoots out and up, catches him on the chin. He stumbles backwards, falls in a sprawling heap. For a moment he lies there, limbs flailing like a lobster freshly plucked from its saline home.

No one moves to help him. They look away, don't want to get involved. Who can blame them? The ugly side of humanity has shown its face for too long, and I've contributed. Shame burns me. I should have held back, but he's done enough to Lisa already.

He flips over, jumps to his feet.

"What about when she delivers her child? What will happen then? What will happen when you deliver yours?"

Help me, I beg of the ocean, the sky, and all the world in between. I don't know what to do.

DATE: THEN

Athens's Parthenon has many cheaper, lesser cousins scattered across the world; man's capacity to create is just as limited as it is infinite. One such building houses the National Museum, where James and Raoul once sorted potsherds. What was a mere tap of my boots on the sidewalk is now a pounding on marble tiles in an almost empty lobby. Its sole occupant is a girl seated behind the front desk, only her eyes visible over the uncreased covers and rigid spine of the Bible.

"Oh." As though surprised that someone would choose to visit the museum on purpose. "Hello."

She stands, brushes her pants, smiles like she forgot to perform some important task to which she is bound.

"I'm supposed to say 'Welcome to the National Museum,' but I wasn't really expecting anybody today. We haven't had anybody in for a week now. Except the staff. And they usually come in the back because that's where our parking is." She leans on the marble-top counter and whispers, "I'm not supposed to do this, but you can go in for free. Normally it's ten dollars, except on Tuesdays, when admission is free, but I don't think ten dollars is going to help much. A museum isn't much of a museum if no one is looking. So it'll be nice to have someone appreciating our collections. Are you here to see anything in particular?"

From behind the counter she pulls a glossy pamphlet, spreads it open to reveal all the world's wonders. So great is her enthusiasm that I don't tell her I know the way. Let her have her moment.

"Anthropology?"

She draws a ring around the whole east wing. "It's huge, but it's worth all the walking, I promise."

She settles back into her chair, cracks open her new Bible. She's either looking for answers or salvation. I hope she finds both.

I've been here a dozen times times over, delving deep in the basement where curators and their lackeys keep poky offices that are close kin to coat closets. Like a car that's traveled the same roads pulling toward the familiar exit, my feet carry me to James's nook. There he is in white on black: James Witte, PhD. I will not lose it. I will not cry. Weeping won't serve anything now. And yet, as my fingers trace those white plastic grooves, my eyes are hot and damp and full.

The door I'm looking for is at the end of the row and sits in a corner, which means it's a larger closet than its neighbors. But it's a dead end because my knocks go unanswered. I hope Dr. Paul Mubarak isn't dead.

But he still lives. I find him sitting on one of the museum's many benches, hunched over a coin too rough to be modern.

He looks up, gives a little laugh, flips the olden-time money between lean, brown fingers.

"A denarius. A day's wage for some in ancient Rome. It became obsolete in the second century, but for four hundred years, it meant something in the world." His bright eyes inspect me, catalog me, place me on a pedestal behind glass. "We've met."

"At James Witte's funeral, yes."

"And what has brought you to the museum today? Surely you can't be here as a *tourista*—not when another civilization is crumbling right outside these doors."

I take a deep breath. "I need help identifying something. James and Raoul were helping me when . . ."

"Then let us walk and pretend you're here to see our magnificent collections, first. My soul is heavy with many things, least of all the new shipments for which I have no interns to torture into sorting. I will be your tour guide and hope the company of a pretty girl will lift my spirits. We'll take care not to disturb the crowds."

I fall into step beside Dr. Mubarak, let him enthrall me with tales of ancient Rome and Egypt. His faint accent helps me imagine I'm someplace exotic where Death doesn't stalk.

"Sometimes I like to look at her and ask: Are you my great-great-great-grandmother?"

We've stopped beside a mummy whose charm lies in her age, not her current attire of rotted fabric strips.

"Who was she?" I could read the bronze plaque with its black lettering, but I'm enjoying this too much.

"Alas, my fair ancestor has no name, so we call her Grace until such a time as she can wear her own title once more. A queen, perhaps, or a princess. Someone of enough significance that they made certain her form would endure. And now, why don't you tell me what has brought you to my door. As you can see, we are not blessed with many visitors these days. The world has problems and stares at anything but history for answers, and so the people do not come. Everything we need to know today can be found in the past. It is the foundation upon which we stand. Mistakes have been made before; they will be made again in perpetuity."

I cannot repay this man with a half-truth, so I tell him everything about James, Raoul, and their intention to help me discover the origins of the jar. When I am finished he says, "Show it to me."

We go into the light so he can peer at the Baggie into which I've stuffed several shards and a handful of dust. Several bones have made it into the mix.

"No, no, no," he murmurs. "Old, they said?"

"Yes." I punctuate the word with a small nod.

"No." His sigh pushes up through centuries of rubble. "Sometimes the mind picks apart reality and restitches it to form a fabric it prefers. James and Raoul are—were—both hungry for a new, brilliant discovery that would serve to elevate their careers. Men like to pin their names to things; it makes us feel immortal." He gives me a small, apologetic smile. "You presented them with a fascinating mystery and that lent your jar qualities it does not possess. He was wrong about your bit of pottery. He and Raoul both. That thing is not old. My wife has something similar in our foyer. People assume it's old because of what I do. She's always winking at me, telling them it is Etruscan or Greek."

"And they believe it?"

"My dear, they eat it up with a dessert spoon. People believe what they want to believe. It does not fit with their worldview, you see, that a curator of archaeology would display modern ceramics in his home. People are funny. We have changed and yet we are the same as always."

The words thump inside my head. The jar is not old. And yet, James and Raoul believed. I was there, I saw them. Or maybe I was the one seeing what I wanted, and they were toying with my funny bone. Or maybe they thought I was tickling theirs with my new-old jar, and so they played along. They took the answer to their graves without leaving me an explanatory note.

For a moment I want to laugh, because I'd kill them both if they weren't already dead.

"The bones," he continues, "belong to something in the Muridae family."

"You know bones?"

"No. I know mice."

TWELVE

The mouse with the bent whiskers is gone. There's another in its place, one whose whiskers run straight and true.

"Wow, they look great," I say.

Schultz is leaning back in his chair, munching on Doritos.

"I'm glad this lot didn't die."

"Yeah." Chip crumbs fly from his mouth. "It's great."

"Hey, Schultz, what happened to all those mice that died? I mean, do you guys incinerate them or what?"

"Why?"

"Just curious, I guess." I try and look dumb. Like there's nothing more to me than a mop.

He grunts. "We burn 'em. It used to be Jorge's job."

"I hope *I* don't have to do it. Eww."

"Don't worry, the big guy does it himself now. Doesn't trust anyone else."

"Well, I'm glad of that." My mop continues to slap the ground.

———————————————

I find the jar's siblings crowded onto a low shelf between nested tables and a magazine rack. They're not just brothers and sisters but clones spawned from the same mold. The only past they've emerged from is a truck, and before that a factory, and before that a bag of dust.

If there really is a book of fools, both old and new, I am surely on the first page.

The label reads: *Made in Mexico*. I laugh like a madwoman, because that's the possibility I hadn't considered.

DATE: NOW

The Corinth Canal is a hungry mouth cut into the landscape.

"See those?" The Swiss points to the twin breakwaters that cup the chasm, their lighthouses dead and impotent to guide ships between them. "Whore's legs, wide open to let everybody inside."

"Why do you hate women so much? Was your mother a whore?"

I saw something on TV once about Scott Base in Antarctica. The coldest place on earth, I remember thinking. Until now. His eyes make the South Pole seem warm and welcoming.

"My mother is none of your concern." He taps on the railing. The canal nears. "I will tell you something, but you must not speak of it. If you do, I will cut up your friend just as she asked."

I watch the dead stone cones and hope for light.

"Look in the cargo hold tonight. Tell no one what you see there."

I go. Of course I do. I can't help myself. Dropping a mystery in my lap is like waving chocolate cake in front of a starving woman. And I am famished. Not right away, though: I wait until the dark creeps in, just like the Swiss told me, and let the shadows tuck me in their pockets for safekeeping.

My feet fall lightly on the steps; they barely rattle. Through the guts of the boat I slip, seeing no one, until I'm at the cargo hold door.

It's not locked. How bad can it be if the door's not sealed shut? From my pocket I draw out a lighter and hold it ready to flick. Through the door I go, though I do not close it behind me.

"Loose lips sink ships" is a lie. It's dead lips that are going to sink this boat.

The whole crew is here for the death parade. The captain is on the top of the corpse pile, his face caked in blood, his body bent like a crude coat hanger. The others are there, too, although some are just faces without names. Someone has stacked them as fishermen do their bounty, minus the ice packing to keep them fresh.

The Swiss.

This time I thunder up the steps, not caring about a quake that pinpoints my location. I race to the simple lounge where the others are in various stages of sleep, some twitching, some snoring. Others keep a weary eye open for danger. Lisa is curled in a corner, her head cradled by our backpacks. Scan. Pan. No sign of the Swiss.

I try the door, the one that leads to the bridge. Its handle is a battered, broken barrier between the controls and the rest of us.

"Wake up!" I shout. "Everybody, up. We've got a problem."

They stare at me, these sheep awaiting slaughter. Nobody bothers beating the door; watching me try and fail is good enough for them.

My mind scans the possibilities and clutches on to the most likely answer: the lone lifeboat that had hugged the rails on the port side.

It's warmer tonight. The air stinks of salt, a smell I used to love, but now it no longer reminds me of cheerful days at the shore. Now it's the smell of defeat and death. Here I lost my president. Here the *Elpis* lost her crew.

The ferry grinds onwards. The lights are on but they barely penetrate the dark, and the moon gives me little to work on. The only tell is a small counter ripple in the water.

"You piece of shit!" I scream into the night. "Why did you kill them?"

The Swiss's words drift back to me.

"The captain was already sick. Some of the others, too. Better to kill them now than let them suffer."

"They might have lived."

"Then they'd be changed. Unfit. Inhuman. What I did was merciful."

"Bullshit. This is all a sick game to you. We're toys."

"Life is an experiment and I am a scientist! Will you survive, America? We shall see."

"Then why bother warning me? You'll skew your results."

"Did you look at those other people? They are sick with wanting death. But you want to live, so I give you this chance."

Then he floats into what's left of the night, leaving nothing behind him but a thin lunule quavering in the sea. I go back to the others and wait to live.

We stand. We wait. Eventually the sun thrusts her horns over the horizon and we see.

Piraeus speeds toward us.

What happens next comes fast and slow, like any good disaster.

"What's happening?" Lisa asks. "Tell me."

Her naïve question pokes holes in my tenuous temper.

I grab her by the shoulders, turn her body toward the swelling landmass, describe what's coming for us.

"This ferry has no captain and plenty of fuel."

She considers this, stuck on stupid. "How do we stop it?"

The words fly out like knives. "We don't. We're going to hit that concrete, like it or not. Unless another ship drifts into our path or someone here can do magic. Can you pull a miracle out of your ass? Because I can't."

"So, what do we do?"

"Stand at the back. When I say jump, we jump overboard."

The other two women are panicking. They cling to each other, weep snot and tears. The men, being men, remain stoic. Too calm, almost. And in a moment I understand what the Swiss said is true. The world as we knew it is gone. We've lost families and friends and enemies. What do we do when there's no one left to love or hate?

The shore is a concrete and steel tiger coming for our throats. There is no time to admire its stripes, there's no time to pray. We barely have time to survive.

"Jump!" I scream at Lisa, and drag her fingers from the railing. Holding her wrists in mine, we fall.

The sea makes us work for our landing. It does not surge to meet us but waits until we slam into its membrane and sink. For a moment, peace. Then the water shakes until my bones want to fly from my body.

DATE: THEN

Jenny and I are drinking our coffee on our usual corner when she drops the bombshell on me.

"I'm seeing someone."

"You're cheating on Mark?"

She frowns. "Jesus, no. I mean a therapist." She takes a mouse-like sip of coffee. Today we're both shivering. "It's too hard. I'm not coping. I keep telling myself I am, but it's just a lie, and it's getting thinner by the day. You're great, and Mom and Dad are supportive, but I need somebody outside of all this to help me cope."

"I understand."

"Really?"

I nod. Sip my coffee. Try to savor the warmth. I don't think about Nick. I searched for his name again today and didn't find it; that's all I need.

"I'm glad. I needed someone to tell about the person I needed to talk to, which is funny, isn't it? I can't tell mom and dad because they'll say—"

"You can talk to us about anything," we say in unison. We laugh.

"Exactly," she says.

"I had a therapist for a while." The words blurt out, bridging the gap between us.

"Did he help?"

"He might not agree, but yeah. It's his name I look for on the list every day."

"Because you love him?"

"No. Because I could have."

"It's the same thing," she says. "You just don't know it yet."

DATE: NOW

If I stare up at the sky, I can pretend I am at the beach, that my mother and sister are paddling in the shallow waters, that there will be ice cream when I tire of floating. In my fantasy I'm not surrounded by splintered wood and steel. The *Elpis* is not burning, her fuel weaving smoke plumes thick enough to chew. Her front half is not concertinaed against the concrete docks of Piraeus. Her backside does not dangle in the water, a beached whale of a vessel whose faulty instincts have sent her to her doom.

Sea birds circle overhead. Their cries are a dirge; to them I am nothing more than a big fish. Their obsidian eyes watch me for signs of surrender, but I will not do it. I will not.

But oh, how sweet it would be to let go.

I close my eyes just for a moment, and when they open again the sun has shifted behind the clouds, and me along with it. The tide is a helping hand pushing me toward the bulb-shaped concrete shore. Then it shifts again and I am being dragged sideways, parallel to the shore, into the path of a drifting yacht. We collide. It's a gentle bump for the boat, but a sharp blow to my shoulder. Salted tears flood my eyes and instantly blend with the seawater that laps my face.

"America!"

My flagellating feet spin me around so that I'm facing the shore again. The Swiss is there. Lisa, too. She's on her knees, panting, trying to pull as much oxygen as she can. But the Swiss stands, legs apart, hands on hips, his lips in their familiar cruel twist.

She's alive, and so am I. We've made it this far.

"America, do you need help?"

I do, but I don't want his brand of help. Help that costs is no help at all. So I struggle to the shore in the great harbor of Piraeus where the land races skyward, its spine an intricate trellis of houses and roads. This is Brindisi all over again, great ships low-slung in the water, their corpses rusting. In time they'll sink below the surface when there's no one to patch the red powdery bubbles and the sea first seeps, then floods through.

Already weak, my arms ache as they fight the steadily thickening water.

"You won't make it," he calls out.

My head is heavy, my arms, too. My whole body longs to stop and let the sea claim it. There's a sleepy fog rolling into my mind. I blink, shake my head, try to clear a path, but it persists. The shore is too far. Too, too far.

"Come on, America." He bends, picks up a tattered life preserver, waves it in the air, declaring his victory with a makeshift banner.

Another painful stroke.

"Maybe you need incentive. European incentive. Americans only act for money. But you . . . I think you will act for something else." He turns, circles Lisa. "For her you will do anything, even though she is close to worthless."

"No," I start, but the salt water sloshes up, fills my mouth, stings my eyes. A hefty slug of brine pours into my stomach and I spit it back up again. Up on the concrete dock, the Swiss draws his leg back. *Look,* he taunts me with his icy eyes. *I control even this. I have power, you have nothing.*

No. No. *No.*

Then he unclenches his glutes, lets that leg fly, nails Lisa in the ribs. She makes an *oof*ing sound as she collapses flat on the concrete. Another subtle wave drifts through the water, covering my face. I hold my breath, tilt my head, search for air. When my vision clears again, the Swiss is watching me.

"Come on, swim. Lazy American." This time he catches Lisa in the shoulder. She cries out.

Fresh anger is a forest fire burning through me. Fueled by rage, my body conjures up energy stores from nothing. Maybe my muscles saved a doughnut for emergencies. Or that chunk of cake I once ate in the kitchen after a lousy date. Maybe my body is devouring itself.

Slowly, I cut through the water, my arms duel blades slicing so that my kicking feet propel me forward. On dry land, the Swiss continues to mock me. His words are punctuated with Lisa's cries. I wish she would fight him, but I know she's afraid—of his temper and losing his cruel affections.

One stroke turns into two. Two turns into three.

He pins her to the ground, boot grinding her neck.

Three leads to four. Four to five. My lungs ache. On stroke thirty I touch concrete. Is it victory if you're too exhausted to care? Does it matter that you've survived?

Hugging the ground to me, I swing my body ashore, not caring that the rough surface is sloughing my skin away. Oxygen, sweet oxygen, is what counts. It comes in jagged clouds, stinging my throat and lungs. With each breath the pain lessens.

The Swiss laughs. "You're alive. I'm impressed. You saved this one, of course." He pokes the girl at his feet.

"If you've got a problem, take it out on me, you piece of shit."

"I like this better. I enjoy watching your reactions. Your face tells me everything. I can see what you want to do to me. And for what? This creature would turn on you for little more than a bag of hot chips. Wouldn't you?" He prods her with the tip of his boot. When she groans, he plants it in her ribs once more.

I can't help myself. Every time I look at Lisa I see Jesse, I see Nick, I see everyone who's crossed my path since this all began. They collect in my mind, bunching into one violent black cluster, so that when I finally fix my gaze on the Swiss, I . . . just . . . can't . . . stop.

Every ounce of energy that drained into the water comes roaring back into my body. My muscles quiver with rage until my whole body shakes. I am a cat coiled into a tense crouch, waiting . . . waiting . . . waiting for my prey to move. Goddamn you, *move*.

He laughs at us.

No more.

My spring-loaded muscles snap into action and I hurtle across the concrete until I'm pummeling his chest with a combination of weary fists and limp hands. Laughter, that's what he gives me to spur me on. The balance shifts. His hands encircle my wrists, squeeze them until the bones want to shatter.

"You can't hurt me," he says. "You don't have it in you."

"If I can kill you, I will," I tell him.

"No."

For a moment I think the cry has come from him, but his lips are pale stone lines. The noise is Lisa's.

"No," she repeats. "Please, don't."

He holds me there; I am at his mercy. My attentions shifts from him to Lisa and back to him before making the journey to her once again. To which side of the fence has she slipped? Is she sitting on my grass or his?

"He's a monster," I say. "He'll kill us both if we let him."

"What do you keep saying? What do you keep telling me? We have to hold on to what makes us human. That's what you said."

She pulls herself along the ground, one arm cradling her ribs.

"Don't move. Your ribs might be broken," I say.

"You told me that. We have to show compassion and mercy because it's part of what makes us *us*."

The Swiss grins, tightens his grip. "Do it, you fucking coward. *Fight for your life.* Try to kill me. You can't survive in this new world if you can't kill."

"Shut up."

His body shakes with silent laughter.

"Zoe," Lisa says. "Stop."

The fight melts out of me. There's a soft thud as my hands fall from the Swiss's vise. My shoulders slump. That vital force that kept me burning bright enough to fight slips back into the harbor. Energy is never lost, only transformed, yet I feel as if something is lost to me.

"Okay."

This time, when my body uncoils, it's like a ribbon tugged loose from a ballerina's ankle when she's pushed herself past exhaustion, languid and halfhearted. "Okay." There I sit, beside the man I could easily murder were Lisa not here to stop me—and draw my knees up to my chin. "I hate you."

The Swiss stares down at me, his mouth a rictus grin. He prods me with his boot. "Coward."

"Maybe," I say. "Maybe not."

"Make no mistake, you are a craven fool. Anyone with guts would find a way to kill me."

"I wanted to. I want to."

"And yet, you stopped fighting."

"Not my idea."

"Then you are no better than me. We are the same shit, America."

"Make up your mind. Either I'm a coward or not."

I crouch and help Lisa to her feet. Her side looks like an oncoming storm, all black and blue with flashes of raw red. Right now I'm useless to her. I'm no doctor. There's no way of telling if anything is broken, but we have to take the chance that she's fine and move on.

"Is your baby okay, do you think?"

She shrugs. Does not ask after mine.

"Go," the Swiss says. "I will not stop you."

I don't say anything lest he change his mind.

Map and compass in hand, we limp toward Athens and let the Swiss's cackles fade first to white noise, then to nothing.

The sky is the flat and constant gray of a paint swatch, but at least it does not rain. Here we are again, Lisa and I. The bike is gone. Our food is gone. Her cane is gone. My knives are gone. The Swiss is gone.

I could have killed him, erased his life like it was nothing more than a smudge. I should have tried. But the sea sipped away my strength, leaving me as empty as a forgotten wineglass. Still, my hands quiver and quake, and no amount of gripping my backpack's straps will steady them.

If he comes for us again, he's a dead man.

Holding hands, we trek the Peiraios, the highway that will take us to Athens. Abandoned cars are few. The Greeks must have been courteous enough to die in their homes with their automobiles safely ensconced in their narrow residential streets. We weave between what's left of the dead. It doesn't seem respectful to step over them. In my nightmares they grab me, try to grapple me to the ground and take me to where the dead things are.

My dark thoughts ride shotgun all the way to Athens. We should go around, but there is no around to go. Piraeus bleeds into Athens; there is nothing to divide the two cities.

This is the concrete jungle in freeze-frame. Nothing moves except us. We are thieves stealing through a city of dead people, trying to go unnoticed. In plain sight seems like the best place to be. The highway is elevated. No one can approach us in stealth.

We walk until night comes and Athens plunges into darkness. Save for a dot of light up ahead. I describe the scene for Lisa.

"Let's check it out," I say.

"I don't want to go."

"We'll sneak up and I'll see if it's okay."

"No." Hysterical.

"I'll go alone, then."

"No, don't. Stay."

"Okay. I'll stay."

We move closer, because that's the way the road goes. The dot spreads; we are bugs drawn to its welcoming glow. Lisa tenses until I am walking alongside a violin bow.

Ahead is an optical illusion. The light emanates from a wooded area near enough that I could spit and hit it. It's to our right and down, down, down.

"We can stay low; I'll look over the edge." I nod at the highway's lip. "We don't have to get any closer."

"We're not going down?"

"No."

"Okay."

We do that. We go to the edge, stay low. Only my eyes peek over the solid gray line. What I'm looking at used to be a playground and park. Now it's growing wild, with nature reasserting its dominance all over the equipment bolted into the ground where children once played. The swings are covered in a tangle of greenery that does not care that steel can't choke. A waterfall of vine pours down the slide. And in the middle a fire blazes inside a metal trash can wrenched from its original place against the water fountain.

"I can hear fire," Lisa whispers. "Are there people?"

Sure enough, I hear the crackle, snap, pop of fire eating.

"I don't know." We wait for a while but no one comes. Tired of speculating, I steer Lisa along our original path. She seems okay. Exhausted. But I am, too.

Not more than a few dozen feet have passed when I turn and glance over my shoulder. The light is gone.

DATE: THEN

Slightly south of nowhere it's raining cats. They fall from the trees like ripe apples. While people put recreation on hold, the forests filled with all the felines who heard the call of the wild and answered.

It's a couple who've "gone bush" in Australia that solve the mystery of the missing cats. They tell it to a reporter over fish and chips and Carlton Draught.

"We got tired of the government telling us to stay home. Home's where everyone's dying. So we packed up all our gear and went into the rain forest. Nobody's sick out there, aye? Anyway, we get to the middle of the fuckin' bush and what do we see?"

There's a pause while the reporter coughs.

"Go on, guess. Bet you can't. It's all those cats. Thousands of the buggers. Must have been imitating koalas, aye?"

"Were they all dead?"

"Yep. The lot of 'em."

"Why'd you come back?"

"We figured if the disease went that far, we'd rather die holding a cold beer."

Reports of the same soon trickle in from the Americas and Europe: dead cats perched in trees until storms shake them from the branches, until gravity pulls them back to the earth. They've died from starvation—waiting and watching for reasons unknown.

I think they were hiding from *us*.

I'm on the train again when Jesse marches up to me, a marionette man in a puffy coat.

"I'm not going to ask if I can sit down because we already know each other and if we were friends you'd ask first. Friends ask friends to sit down. That's good manners."

"Have a seat."

He sits. Same as before. Hands splayed on his thighs, eyes ahead.

"I know you can't talk to me. My mother explained that to me when I called her. She said you could get into very big trouble and maybe lose your job. 'Don't mess with someone's livelihood' is what she said, 'because maybe that woman's got mouths to feed.' So I want to give you my business card. Would that be okay?"

"Sure."

He exhales sharply like he was worried about my answer.

"Okay. I'm going to have to write it out because I haven't got any printed yet." His coat whispers and squeaks as he shoves a hand into his pocket and pulls out a sparkly purple pen and note card cut into four equal pieces. On the top piece he writes his name, address, phone number, and e-mail address. "That's just in case the Internet starts working again. 'Be hopeful,' my mom says." He gives me the card, stashes the rest back in his pocket.

He waits until I've slipped the makeshift business card into my purse.

"Do you like cooking?"

"Sure."

"I like to cook. Last night I made mini pizzas on muffins. I hardly burned them at all." For the rest of the ride he talks food. I listen and make all the right noises. Because I know what he doesn't: I'm going to tell him everything. But not here. And when the train ride ends, I tell him so.

THIRTEEN

DATE: NOW

I have to stay awake. I can't rest. Not if it means closing my eyes. We're in a department store. Lisa's lying on a dais that once held dummies dressed in next season's fashions. I'm on the floor beside her, legs crossed, elbows pressed into my knees. A band tightens around my head, and as it does, my neck grows weaker and weaker. I have to use my hands just to keep my head from sagging onto my chest.

She's bleeding. It started during the night: at first a crimson smear, then a slow drip. Now it's painting a Picasso inside her thighs.

Death waits, but I'm not ready to let it take her. *Fuck you,* I scream inside my head, because saying it aloud would scare her. She's the color of blood-drained chicken. Exsanguination, they call it, death by blood loss. I don't even know how to go about replacing what she's lost—not in this world.

Lisa knows I'm watching her.

"Don't worry so much, Zoe. I'm okay."

She's not okay. What she is doesn't even have any of the same letters as *okay*. She's bleeding still. At the very least I need to get to a drugstore, find some pads, diapers, antibiotics, anything, but I can't go without her and I can't take her with me. I wish the Swiss was still here. I'm glad he's not. I wish my mother was here, or Jenny, or Nick. I want Nick here. He'd know the right thing to do. She'd be safe with him until I returned with supplies.

"I'm okay," Lisa repeats. Her words slur together. "Let's both sleep. Tell me about the place we're going first."

"We're going north to a village called Agria. It's by the water in a gulf."

"They play golf?"

"You don't know what a gulf is?"

"Uh-uh."

Somewhere between yearning for sleep and berating myself for needing rest, it happens.

I dream of Sam. He's in a car, the one he died in, his body mangled beyond repair. Blood bubbles between his lips. His mother is there, too, filing her nails.

You can't save everyone, Sam tells me.

She can try, his mother says.

They argue back and forth while I listen to the steady drip. Gasoline, probably. Maybe blood. After a while I get tired of their banter.

How will I get my Girl Scout badge if I don't save them all? I ask.

Neither of them has an answer. My former mother-in-law sets her file on the dash, closes her eyes, and quits breathing, just like she's too stubborn to do anything else but die.

Sam looks at me, smiles a crimson smile.

I would have fallen in love with you, I say. *In time.*

Stop collecting badges, he tells me. *They don't matter in the end.*

Then I wake up and Sam and his mother are gone, and so is Lisa. Only, this time she's left me a trail. Little red blood droplets lead down the sidewalk, a morbid trail of bread crumbs. They're a bold and royal red. Fresh.

I follow the trail, try to remember the story of Hansel and Gretel. The birds ate their bread crumbs while the lost and hungry children consumed their fill of the gingerbread house in the woods. But the house was just a ploy, a lure for children who couldn't resist candy. Witches, the Brothers Grimm told us, liked nothing more than a good leg o' child for supper. She took Hansel and Gretel captive, then plumped them for the eating. Her reward was a fiery end after being stuffed into her own oven by a gutsy Gretel.

What is Lisa's gingerbread house? If I find that, I will find her.

The next few drops are smears. I try to think what that means, but my mind is both sleep hazy and scared sharp. I leapfrog conclusions, toss away hypotheses, form new ones that have nothing to do with reality and everything to do with conspiracy theories.

I'm running now, following the crumbs. I need to know where they go. I need to find her. Because I don't think she's alone. She can't be—not without someone to tempt and guide her.

Over and over, I hurl the lash at myself. This is my fault. I fell asleep when I knew I couldn't afford to. I knew she was hurt, her mind clouded.

This is my fault for walking away from her when she was my responsibility.

Blood. Blood. More blood. All the way up the street, past abandoned tavernas, past shops with no clientele. Some wear shattered windows and battered doors, but most remain untouched, as though humanity just up and walked away from life.

The landscape changes. Retail starts a gentle shift toward car yards hawking vehicles old and new. Most are gone. The rest are scrap metal. Others have tried to take a car, get the hell out of here, and failed. A skeleton hangs from a steering wheel, his or her arm snared by the driver who has rolled the window up to form a fatal trap. The driver is there, too, only sloppier. The other guy has had his body picked clean by predatory birds and over-zealous bugs. The driver is a meat sack dressed in rotting rags.

I can't care about them right now.

Lisa's blood trail leads me to a squat building with windows made of wire-threaded glass blocks. The sign on the door is all Greek to me. Ha-ha. I can't even laugh at my own joke. I wind up being sarcastic to myself, a sign that I'm on my way to crazy or already there.

The blood leads here, to this beige building with Greek letters and business hours from 9:00 a.m till 5:00 p.m. on some days of the week that don't matter. I don't even know what day this is; they've blurred since leaving Brindisi. That was the only date that mattered, and it's gone.

The smell hits me the moment I lean against the door with my shoulder. It makes a *pah* sound, like an old, wealthy man sucking a cigar in a casino, holding, holding, then exhaling into the face of his date—the one he bought for too much money, yet doesn't value. A lungful of institutional air is what I get. Pine that's never seen a forest, or a cone, mixed with the cat-pee stench of ammonia. It almost, but not quite, covers the bright copper of fresh blood.

My heart clacks on my ribs. *Get the hell outta here,* it taps in Morse code. But this is like one of those dreams, we've all had them, where the Big Bad Wolf is coming right for us but we can't move for love or bags stuffed full of money.

Clack, clack.

Chairs. Plastic molded chairs, the kind they have at the DMV. They're set up in a square horseshoe surrounding a table. The laminate is snapping off at the edges so the cheap board underneath peeks through. There's a counter with frosted glass panels that slide on ball bearings. There's a bare spot on the wall where a television used to hang.

I want to laugh, because when disaster strikes, people always prioritize by racing for the electronics. *Take that, Joneses*, they seem to say. *We're just as good now.* Which is all well and good, except the Joneses are probably lying in a gutter facedown, rotting. They don't care about television or toasters that cook eggs and bacon at the same time as their bread. Death is the great demotivator.

Clack, clack.

My feet won't work. They wriggle inside my boots, ignoring the flurry of messages from my brain.

Clack, clack.

This place, I know it. I don't want to admit it, but I know. There's only one kind of place that smells the same the whole world over. It's like they all get their cleaner from one central warehouse. I know it. I worked with it. The smell is as familiar to me as chocolate chip cookies warm from the oven or Nick's sunshiny skin when I'd breathe him in as deep as I could take him.

This is a clinic. A medical facility of some flavor. The furnishings give nothing away; the paintings are generic prints of scenery: flower-filled fields, a grazing cow. The Virgin Mary stares down from one wall, also silent as she balances her babe on one knee.

Lisa's blood is here, too, smeared across the floor. A monochrome rainbow stretching down the hall.

Pine and blood. Copper and autumn.

Clack, clack.

My legs move like they're new. The joints grind and squeak beneath my skin. But then I realize, no, that noise isn't me, it's coming from the other end of the Lisa rainbow, the one that's hidden around a corner at the end of a hall. It's the sound of cutlery rattling around a stainless steel sink.

Clack, clack.

Someone thought it was funny to run a line of yellow tiles down the hallway. Lions and tigers and bears—oh my! I follow them, because that's what lost girls do when they want to find the wizard and get the hell home.

Down the hall. Turn right. Follow the yellow tile that's orange in places where Lisa's blood overlaps. A door that isn't closed, just pushed until a narrow crack of the world beyond is visible. I nudge it with my knee until it swings wide.

Clack, clack, pow.

Lisa is there. At least, I think it's her. There's so much blood, I can't tell what's what. She's on the examining table, legs in stirrups, arms flaccid and dangling off the sides. Her head lolls toward me but she does not know I'm here. She won't know anything again except maybe Hades or God or whichever deity she prayed was real.

Between her legs is another figure, also doused in blood. His clothes are soaked, his blond hair smeared and flecked, all of it a bold and vivid red. Which strikes me as weird, because Lisa is dead and yet her blood still looks like it should be in a living body.

When the Swiss turns, he's holding her insides in his hands. I don't know what a uterus looks like except as a line drawing in an anatomy book, but I think that's what he's dumping into a metal basin.

He swings around, his eyes wild and blue and stark inside his painted face.

"It should be here," he mutters. "It should be."

"What did you do to her?" My throat is numb, my lips feel flabby; it's a wonder the words come out in any order that makes sense.

He picks through the Lisa-meat with the edge of a scalpel, then looks up at me. "It should be here."

"What?"

"The fetus!" he screams. He hurls the bowl at the wall. It ricochets and lands at my feet, where the contents spill in a grisly mess. "She was pregnant. There should be a fetus. Where did it go?" He's still screaming. With every syllable he stabs her, then he drags the scalpel to him, vivisecting her from the waist down. "It is in here and I will find it." He reaches inside her with both hands until he's up to his elbows in viscera.

"You killed her," I say simply.

He shakes his head so vigorously, his drenched hair flicks dots on the wall. "No, no, no. She killed herself. She laid down for the father. She got pregnant. She sucked my cock while pregnant with another man's child. She came willingly while you slept. 'Help me,' she begged. Who am I to refuse aid? I have assisted many such women."

"You killed her."

"I . . . did . . . not . . . kill . . . her!" he roars. His body shakes with the anger but he does not look at me. "Where is it? Where did she hide it?" He whirls around. "You took it, didn't you?"

I don't understand. Lisa was pregnant. He said she was. All that morning sickness, no evidence of White Horse. If not that . . . then what?

Tears roll down my face. I wipe them away with the back of my hand.

"Look what you did to her, you monster," I say. "She was a human being. Just a girl. What's wrong with you, you crazy fuck? You're like one of those insane women in the newspapers, the ones who cut open a pregnant woman and steal her child. You're a crazy *woman*, not a man."

This enrages him. Between the blood and the twisting of his face, he's a portrait of insanity and he's racing toward me, scalpel in his hand, covered in more blood than I've ever seen in my life. He is a ruby gleaming under the dead fluorescent bulb.

I run. He follows. We slip and slide down the hall on Lisa's blood. Two stooges. The Swiss lunges for me, but I jump right while he keeps going straight. I snatch up one of the plastic chairs. The symmetry isn't lost on me. I've done this before: used a chair to save myself.

When he realizes he's missed, that I'm not in front of him, he turns. That's when I smash him in the face.

Oh, I think. *That stings.* I can't figure out why I'm the one who hurts when I hit *him*.

Then I look down and see the correlation between the pain and the scalpel jutting from my arm.

Holding his face with one hand, the Swiss staggers toward me as though his soles were dipped in molasses.

"I will cut you." His voice is thickened by broken lips. "And I will show you."

My baby. Please, not my baby.

A switch flips inside my brain. I will never let that happen. He's killed Lisa and that's as much as he will ever take from me. He's got it all wrong. If he kills me, I'm taking him, too. I dredge up as much spit as I can and launch it at his face.

I imagine my father's look of disapproval, but he's dead. I can hear my mother's lecture about things ladies should never do. But she's dead, too. It's just me and him, and I figure my folks would be okay under the circumstances.

"I am going to cut you." His voice crackles like wrapping paper.

I run.

DATE: THEN

"Come with me," Jenny says one Thursday afternoon when we meet on the library steps. She's in her red coat, a camel scarf wound around her neck. My outfit is similar, but black.

"To see my therapist, I mean."

I look at her like she's lost her mind, which makes it a very lucky thing that she's in therapy. When I tell her that, she laughs.

"You'd like her. Lena is fantastic."

My shoulders slump slightly. Somewhere at the back of my mind the possibility lurked that Nick was her therapist.

"I don't think so."

"It would help me."

"How?"

"Lena says I have unresolved issues about abandonment that stem from childhood. She feels that meeting you will paint a better picture. So?"

"No. When were you abandoned, anyway?"

She's huffy when we go inside, her shoulders tense, her chin high. She doesn't look at me save for the occasional glare delivered sideways.

We follow the drill. Inch our way forward. Try to steel ourselves when we hear the inevitable anguished bursting of battered hearts.

Our turn arrives too soon and not soon enough. I see it before Jenny. Mark's name leaps off the page. My arm goes around her, I try to steer her out of there before she sees.

"Jenny, let's go."

But it's too late, she's seen his name. Mark D. Nugent. There's no way for her to unsee. She'll lie in bed, close her eyes, and that string of letters will come at her out of the darkness. Tonight. Tomorrow. All the days after. The pain strikes me, too—less of course, but there's no time for me to feel it; I need to get Jenny out of here.

She sags against me, moans.

I walk her to her car, drive her to the only place I know to go: home. When I pull into our parents' driveway, the pitted lawn and the ragged garden that our parents normally keep so beautifully don't register. Times are anomalous, so unusual things no longer surprise me as they once did. Our mother is slow to come to the door.

We are portraits of the same woman: grief, determination, and, thirty years later, surprise.

"What's wrong?" she asks, but the answer comes to her as quickly as the question forms. She presses a hand to her chest. "It's Mark, isn't it? Oh my." She's in her nightie, the latest in a long line of floor-length garments designed to *prevent me from having a good time*, our father used to joke. She closes the door behind us and seals us in the furnace. It has to be eighty-five degrees in here, easy.

"Mom, is everything okay?"

"Fine, fine," she says, and I know that means it's not. She takes over, doing the things a mom always does. She steers Jenny to the cabbage rose sofa, sits her down like she's a small child again, and pulls my sister into her arms and rocks her.

Jenny needs her mother now. No, Jenny needs Mark, but he can't be here. He won't be here ever again. We're all just meat puppets with an invisible hand inside us, making us dance and live. When that hand slips off the glove, we collapse and that is the end of everything.

I go into the kitchen, fill the electric kettle, then go in search of Dad. From room to room I wander. I check the garage. It's the same as it always is. There's a table set up in the center with a half-finished project taking shape. The pile of wood pieces look like they'll grow up to be a clock.

Then I make for the basement. You won't find it behind a door in the hall. There's no rickety staircase descending into darkness, with a bare swinging bulb to light the way. The way to this basement is through a cupboard in the bathroom. It's a trapdoor in the floor with a ladder attached. Usually it's open unless company comes over. No one likes to imagine a head popping up through that hole while they're flipping through the magazine rack beside the toilet.

Today it's closed. But that's not what worries me. What makes my heart thump so hard my mother's cooing in the other room dims to a whisper is the brass bolt locking the wood flap to the floor. There are new hinges, too. They're the same shiny metal as the bolt. That shouldn't worry me, either, except the trapdoor used to lie flush with the floor all the way around, and now the hinges jut at perfect right angles. Outside.

"Hiya, Pumpernickel."

I slip right out of my body, crash into the ceiling, then glide right back in, sliding on a spiritual banana peel. My father is here, not down in the basement locked in like—

A monster.

—a prisoner. And he looks great. His eyes sparkle with suppressed punch lines.

"You scared the crap out of me, Dad."

"Then you're in the right room, aren't you?"

We hug.

"What's wrong with your sister?" he says into my hair.

My eyes are rapid-filling cisterns.

"Mark," he says in a voice too jovial for this conversation.

He marches into the living room, pulling me in his wake even though I don't want to hear what comes next, because I know something isn't right; Dad doesn't look great, he looks *young*. He's ten years older than Mom but now he's fifteen years her junior.

"Jenny, my girl," he says. "Let's celebrate. He was never any good for you anyway. So he's dead, so what? Now you can find another one. One with a real job. A man's job. Not that sissy sit-behind-a-computer shit he liked so much." On and on he rambles while Jenny stares at him in horror. I'm wearing the same expression. But Mom isn't.

Her gaze meets mine, weary with resignation. She knows this isn't right, that something's seriously wrong with Dad, and yet she doesn't intervene.

"Turn up the heat, would you?" Dad thunders, and she scurries to accommodate him.

The air thickens. The heat isn't flowing just from the vents but also from him. There's a fire raging inside his body. I can almost see the steam rising from his pores. The air around him shimmers. He's a sidewalk in summer.

"Dad," I say. "That's not—"

"Zoe," Mom says.

"Why's the basement locked?" I ask her.

Dad doesn't stop the flow.

"He was worthless. I never wanted you to marry him, if you remember. 'Jenny,' I said—remember this?—'are you sure you want to do this?' You were so young, only twenty-two, a baby. You should have lived your life first, done some things, then settled down. Trust me, it's a good thing Mark is dead, because now you can live."

I press on. "What's in the basement, Mom?"

"Nothing," she says. "We've had raccoons."

"Bullshit. This is the city. We don't have raccoons."

Dad wheels around. "Don't talk to your mother like that!" he screams.

I recoil. One hand—that's all I'd need to count the number of times he's snapped at me. He loved Mark. Treated him like a son. This is not my father.

"It's good that he's dead!" he shrieks at Jenny. "It's good."

He flops on the ground, body shaking like James did. Only James's body wasn't a griddle.

"Get ice," I bark at my mother. She runs in that nightie, hand at her throat clutching the ruffles closed, not to the kitchen like I expect, but to the basement. Jenny sits on the couch, eyes the size of dinner plates. First her husband, now her father. I slap her. Her eyes focus.

"Call 911."

She hurries for the phone, dials, waits. "They're not answering." Not even a tin lady.

"Keep trying."

Mom rushes in with a plastic bucket, shoves me aside, upends the contents onto Dad's chest. Ice cubes. Some sizzle on contact, the steam rising off him in a dense, wet cloud. A one-man sauna. She takes the phone from Jenny's hands, gently places it back in its cradle.

"They won't come. They never do. They don't bother answering anymore."

My father starts to moan. His eyelids flutter. The seizing stops and soon the ice cubes melt no more.

Jenny stares at him in horror. "What's wrong with him?"

I look at my mother. See her fate in her resignation.

"Has he been sick? Have you?"

"Yes," she whispers. "You girls have to go. As a mother, that's the best I can do for you both." She kisses my sister's forehead. "I'm sorry about Mark. We loved him very much."

I can't leave without knowing. "What's in the basement?"

Her voice drops so Jenny doesn't hear. "That's where we'll go. When it's too late. We have a pact with some of the neighbors, to . . . to help each other."

I hold her tight, tell her I love her, and repeat the exercise for my father.

To my old room is where I want to run, not out into the cold with my grieving, shell-shocked sister. To my room where the covers have powers to protect me from the bogeyman. To my old room, where my parents are young and whole and my sister is a pain in my ass. To my old room, where *death* was just a word in my Merriam-Webster dictionary.

DATE: NOW

The streets of Athens limp by. I wish the sidewalks were filled with people who'd conceal me with their bodies and banter, and yet I can move more freely with empty streets; I am divided by my loyalties. The scalpel is rooted in my arm, and I can't remember if I'm supposed to pull a blade or leave it until help comes. But help isn't coming—only the Swiss. So I tug it free and hide it in my pocket like a dirty little secret. A red carpet rolls the length of my arm. I need a place; I need a place now to stop it unraveling further.

Refuge is a warehouse. Gallon cans of olive oil stacked ten feet high create a shield from the world. And still he finds me like I knew he would.

"I know you are there, America. I see your blood. Is the scalpel still inside you? I believe it is. Are you bleeding faster now? I know how to hurt a person, America. I know how to kill. Can you say the same?" His voice lowers, and I know he has crouched or sat on the other side of the cans. His voice comes from my level. "There was no baby in her. I believed there was, but I was wrong. But I found something. Do you want to know what I found? Maybe it's inside you, too. Do you want to know? You are a curious person; I sense all your questions. Even now you are burning to know: *What did he find inside the stupid girl?*"

Black spots mar my vision like a fungus as I slide the belt from my hips and yank it tight around my arm. They sprawl, contract, disappear, and new replace the old. My eyes are a kaleidoscope through which I can barely see. Is this what dying looks like?

"Talk to me, America. Ask me what I found, what was inside her."

His voice comes from further away now, but I know he hasn't moved. It's me. I'm drifting away.

"I don't care."

I don't realize I've said it aloud until he laughs.

"Of course you care. All you do is care. Why else bring that stupid girl with you? What is she to you?"

I speak through gritted teeth. "Just a girl."

"No, I don't think so. I know people, America. I know people do things for reasons that they do not always understand. She told me how you took her from the farm, away from her family. Why would you do such a thing? Shall I guess?"

"Fuck you."

"When you are a doctor, you see many different people. The women I saw always had a story for why they were in my office. Some, they wanted medicine for birth control. Some wanted an abortion. Some wanted tests for disease. All wanted me to say,

'It is okay.' Validation for their actions. Absolution for their sins. Redemption. Who were you trying to save, America? Not that girl. She was nobody to you. A surrogate."

Jesse. My parents. Everybody.

I close my eyes, hope the names remain in my head. Reality is shifting out now and something new is moving in furniture. The black spots metastasize—from my eyes to my neural pathways.

"Who were you trying to save, America? A sister, perhaps? Your family. A husband? No. No husband. No ring on your skinny finger."

Jenny. Nick. My parents. Am I trying to save someone? Is that what I am? Some kind of wannabe hero? I don't feel like a hero. I just feel scared. For my child. For my future, which looks to be about five minutes long; maybe fewer.

"That stupid English girl killed herself. You helped her."

"I don't understand." My tongue grows thick, my words slide into one another.

"Ask me what I found inside her."

"I'm tired of your games. Just tell me."

Skidding, scraping. Metal on concrete. Death touches my leg and I jerk, but already my fingers are reaching for it. I know what it is. I know what it is before my fingers slide along the tight curves that make up the slick, shiny helix. The cold comes for me, arms open wide. *Let me take you,* it whispers. *Let me take you to a place where nothing can ever touch you, where you'll never feel again. We're all dead and soulless there.*

"You know this thing, don't you, America?"

"Yes."

"How? Tell me."

"I gave it to her. So she could protect herself."

"You provided her with the means to rip out what she believed was inside her. She pushed it through her cervix, as though her womb was a bottle of cheap wine." Satisfied. Smiling. "Are you shocked?"

"Is that what was inside her?"

"No. She was clutching this thing in her hand as though it was precious to her when I found her. Happy. This is what the foolish girl wanted. If you are shocked, you are as big a fool as she."

"I couldn't save her. I can't even save myself. I'm not a hero."

"No, you are not. *I* could have saved her. *I* am the hero. *I* am trying to save the world from the abomination its sins have produced."

A chuckle bubbles out of my mouth. "You?"

"I am a hero. You are nothing. What do you try to save? One stupid, blind girl. My goals are much bigger. More important. They will benefit the world. I will kill the monsters man created."

My eyes close. The here and now is greased rope slipping through my fingers. "Why do you give a shit about me, then? I'm nobody. Just a cleaner."

"Not just a cleaner. You worked at Pope Pharmaceuticals. Which means you belonged to George Pope."

FOURTEEN

DATE: THEN

Beep.

"Mom? Dad? If you're there, pick up. Please."

Pause.

"Jenny and I are fine. Neither of us are sick. Just so you know. I . . . we miss you."

Beep.

It could be the dead of winter except there's no snow. Yet. God knows, the air is cold enough to hold a flake to its unique form. The library is still aglow, but the watch on my wrist tells me it won't be long. I can't stay out late. Jenny is holed up in my apartment, eating a pint of mint chocolate chip ice cream.

"Is that all they had?" she asked when I jubilantly waved the carton at her. "I wanted rum raisin or cookie dough."

The ice cream had cost me twenty bucks. Twenty. That was all they'd had at the drugstore unless I wanted their store brand for twelve. And that's more air than cream.

One week since Jenny lost Mark and we discovered our parents were lost to us both. I call and call and no one answers. The phone system is dying. Calls ring off into nowhere more frequently now.

I still come here every day—without Jenny. I look for Nick's name and hope I don't see it. Usually I come straight after work, but today Jenny called in tears.

"Can you believe this?" she asked when I let myself in the door. She'd had the television on, old episodes of some soap because they weren't making any new ones. "He died in a plane crash before she could tell him she was pregnant with twins." Then she started sobbing. "Mark and I were going to try for a baby this year. Then he had to go and die, just like Julian."

"Who's Julian?" I'd asked.

"On the show."

So I'm late to the library because of a soap opera.

The head librarian looks up as I walk in. She's a cliché right down to the glasses performing a balancing act on the end of her snip nose. She's the only librarian now, aside from a young grad student who prowls the aisles with his metal cart. It looks like it should rattle, but it doesn't: the wheels are greased into submissive silence. She nods at the round metal clock hanging on the wall like I should be aware that the doors will be locking at any moment. I nod back, to let her know that, yes, I'm aware of the impending closure. Not quite satisfied, she turns back to her work.

The list is up. The crowd has long petered out except for the lone figure standing, legs akimbo, inches from the wall. My heart accelerates. I know the lines of that body. Many a time I admired them across a coffee table, skimmed them in my fantasies. He seems taller to me now, but I'm not sure if that's because I haven't seen him for a while or because he's become almost mythical in my mind these past months. Larger than my tiny life.

Then he turns . . .

Oh God, he'll see me. Not now. Not like this. I'm wearing graying underwear and no makeup. Did I shave my legs? No. There was no need. I am Sasquatch and he is magnificent.

His face is stone. Granite. Marble. Is there something harder? I don't know, but the hardest rock is what I'm seeing. He's Nick, if Nick had been carved from the sheer side of a mountain instead of flesh.

"Dr. Rose."

The words come out stiff, formal. He told me to use his first name but I can't. *Dr. Rose* implies there is a wall between us—me safely ensconced on one side, him on the other.

"Hello, Zoe. Are you looking for someone?"

You. "A friend."

He nods, glances over his shoulder at the list, then returns to me. "I hope you don't find them there."

"Who were you looking for?"

Across the invisible wall. "My brother, Theo."

"I hope you didn't find him."

"Stay well, Zoe." He walks away and I watch him leave without saying another word, my arms dangling helplessly at my sides. Something about the way he moves is altered. There's a slight hitch—a limp, I guess you'd call it—on his right side. How did it happen? I want to know. But it's too late, he's gone, and I'm stuck to the ground like I'm trapped in one of my own nightmares. I could call him back, make him tell me, but my mouth won't work, either.

Nick is alive. That's good. That's all I need to know. That's all I wanted to know, right? I repeat the words: *Nick is alive and that's what matters in this very moment.*

Behind me, the librarian clears her throat disapprovingly. Dusty phlegm breaks the spell and I spring forward, study the list just so the librarian doesn't berate me further. I scan the list, double-check for Nick's name, just in case his being here was some kind of delusion. But no, he's not on the list.

But another name is: Theodore Rose.

I bolt out the door, into the freeze, glancing frantically each way. But night has claimed all but the faintest halo from each streetlight, and Nick is lost to me.

Beep.
"Hello? Mom? Dad?"
The tape whirs onward.
Beep.

The Pope Pharmaceuticals lobby is no place for a receptionist. No ringing phones, no vendors buzzing through, no public left in public relations. If we still had one, she'd be filing her nails, flipping through magazines, sipping coffee.

I ride the elevator to my floor. Steel cables whine through pulleys, the brakes bump and grind to a halt. I never knew how loud my world was until there was no one to fill it. The locker rooms are empty. My every move is amplified until I sound like a multiarmed woman running the whole percussion section of a symphony. I clean, just like on every other day. I vacuum, mop, empty the trash into the designated chutes. Some lead to a furnace that belches and bellows in the basement. Others go some place I'm not privy to. And that bothers me when once I didn't care.

The mice are all gone. Their cage doors sag on bent hinges.

"Did they die?" I ask Schultz. He's hunched over a microscope, peering at slides.

He sniffs, swipes his dripping nostrils with the back of his hand. "I got hungry."

I stare at him, wait for him to crack, wait for the punch line. There's always a punch line. Right?

"You ate the mice?"

"I didn't have change for the vending machine, okay?"

Every day we work in the same spaces and I can't read him.

"You ever see *Demolition Man*?"

"Sure," I say, "I saw it."

His head pumps up and down. "They're not so bad. Better than what's in the cafeteria."

There's nothing in the cafeteria, now. We're all brown-bagging it. I have no words. No, that's a lie. I have two: *I quit*.

I say good-bye, try to leave, but he waves me over. "Lookit this." Leaning to one side, he makes enough room that I can stand beside him and peer into the lens. Blobs and squiggles swimming on a green sea. Pretty. Alien. Terrifying in its otherness.

"What is it?"

"Opportunistic wanton neoplasm."

"Neoplasm—you mean like cancer?"

"Aha. Not just any cancer. This one has a mind of its own, goes where it pleases. you never know what you're going to get with OWN." He laughs, snorts. "OWN. I wish I'd thought of that." He snaps his fingers at me. "You get a dose of this and you get OWNed." He takes in my blank look. "It's hacker slang, meaning you take some of this and it's taking over your body."

"Is that what you've been giving the mice?"

"It's not like people are lining up to volunteer."

I remember the flu shot Dr. Scott gave me, and I wonder if I've been OWNed.

That afternoon I hand in my two weeks' notice. When I get home I call Jesse and give him his story, because some things are bigger than a nondisclosure agreement.

"But it's freezing," Jenny complains a week later. She's regressed. I have become both parent and sister to a petulant teenager.

"Fine, *you* cook breakfast."

She hesitates, weighs the situation, because she knows she asked me to make Mom's pancake recipe, so I'm already doing her a favor. With a sigh that comes all the way from her feet, she snatches up the quarters I laid out on the counter, shrugs into her coat, winds a scarf around her neck, and slams the door so hard the frame shivers.

It's no big thing, just the newspaper. You know, the newspaper that should contain Jesse's article. The one that would make him different-good to his disapproving father. I need to know what he's written. Every day I've been down at that newspaper dispenser, depositing my quarters, flicking aside the pages of the *United States Times* with no result. The paper is slimmer each day. Stories dwindle with the population.

One at a time, the pancakes turn that perfect pale gold. Soon I have two neat stacks that want to be eaten. Jenny isn't back. The way she's been acting, she should have been flouncing in by now, complaining of the cold. I experience a shiver that has nothing to do with the weather.

Porkchop, the day doorman, is in the lobby peering through the glass. There's a mouth-sized patch of mist on the glass below his nose. I think he'll turn when my footsteps tap across the floor, but he keeps on staring through the door.

He grunts when I ask him about Jenny.

"Saw her leave, but she hasn't come back yet. She stomped on through here with her nose in the air." He looks abashed. "Sorry, ma'am, I know she's your sister."

"What's going on?"

"Don't rightly know. There was a noise but I don't see anything."

I inch up to the glass door beside him, peer through. The world outside my window is dead. A ghost town. Light wind rolls suburban tumbleweed down the street. The *United States Times*. There is no other.

Cold seeps through the windows, absconds with the heat.

Porchop clears his throat. "Friday's my last day. This place can't support two doormen with just five apartments being occupied. Can't support one. Don't know if Mo said anything, but he's a goner, too."

A plastic bag rolls by. The letters have faded to yellow. When Porkchop's words register, I can't believe what I'm hearing. "Just five?"

"Uh-huh. Herb Crenshaw passed couple of days ago. His wife last week. Their son's over in India or someplace they wear bandages on their heads. The way the news is, I doubt the kid even knows yet. Hell, could be he's dead, too."

He leans forward until his nose presses against the glass.

"Huh, look at that. Someone lost their scarf. Dim days, Miss Marshall. Dim days indeed. And they're only getting darker. Those scientists did something to the weather, because this ain't right. We've been playing God and now God's having His fun with us." His mouth keeps on flapping, but his words fade to static, because that scarf—I know that scarf. Last time I saw it, Jenny was winding it around her neck, tucking the ends into her coat.

"Miss Marshall? You okay?"

No, I'm not.

Maybe I shove him out of the way, or maybe he steps aside. Later on, when I think about it, I can't remember how it happened. One way or another, I push through that door to where the arctic wind bites my face. I go right, because that's the direction from which the scarf blew. I go right, because that's where the newspaper dispensers are. I don't have far to go.

There's a heap on the ground wearing Jenny's coat and I hope it's not her, that some homeless person stole her clothes. But what are the odds they'd have her same hair?

Oh God . . . I can't take this. I can't. Mom and Dad are bad enough, but losing this other part of me is something I cannot bear. I don't have strength enough to hold this hurt.

"Jenny," I whimper. "Jenny? Get up. Please, get up."

She doesn't. She just lies there in a dead heap, the red circle on her forehead signaling that this is The End of sisterhood. I am orphaned in every way.

"Jenny?" I kneel in her bloody halo, lift her head and cradle it in my lap. I try but I can't scoop her brains back into her head. I keep trying, but the hole is too wide and the pink stew pours out faster than I can ladle it back in.

My mind cracks like the jar when I beat it with the hammer.

Fractured thoughts from a madwoman's head. I can't believe she did this to me. How dare she leave me alone? My sister deserted me. Fuck you, bitch. Fuck you for not just coming down here when I asked the first time.

Fuck you. My balled-up fists press into my brow bone. Her head is heavy in my lap like a cantaloupe. There's a growing ache in my head that won't quit. Fuck you, Jenny.

"You idiot!" I scream. "We were always supposed to be there for each other! I wasn't looking out for you so you could die, too!"

I keep yelling, pelt her with my anger. Then there are voices, and a moment later hands and arms grabbing me, pulling me away from Jenny.

"No, no, no. That's my sister."

"Go look for the shooter," someone says.

"Leave us alone," I cry. "I've got no one else."

But the hands don't care; they just keep tugging me further away from what's left of my family.

Why would anyone shoot Jenny?

DATE: NOW

I am staring down the barrel of a long, dark channel. The light at the other end rushes toward me as the passage compresses, then telescopes to some unfathomable distance. Time and space shift. Rationally, I know I'm still sitting in that warehouse, separated from the Swiss by olive oil. Knowing that doesn't make the tunnel feel any less real. Is this what it's like to die? Is everyone I've lost waiting for me at the other end? Have they forgiven me? Do they still care for me like I care for them?

"George Pope? Why do you care about him? He's dead."

His voice is jubilant. "Is he? Good. I do hope it was painful. Do you know?"

"Know what?"

"Did he die in great pain? Was it this disease that took his life—this disease he helped create?"

"No," I say. "It was quick."

"How quick?"

"Tell me what you found inside Lisa."

"I found nothing inside her. Nothing. Her womb was empty. Yours is, too."

DATE: THEN

Who knew the sun could be so cold? Its brittle glare paints my face, filtered through murky glass. I am in a plain room with a stained wood door, no bars, but that doesn't mean this isn't a cell. Iron does not make this a prison.

"I need a newspaper," I tell the woman who brings my lunch.

The tray lands on the table with a clatter. The table barely registers; it's fastened to the wall with bolts big enough to withstand a nuclear attack. Everything else could vaporize, but they'd be here, too stubborn to quit biting the concrete blocks.

"This ain't no Holiday Inn," she says.

"Gosh, I hadn't noticed."

She lumbers away, back to her food cart. It's a tall, thin insulated box in beige, which makes me think it fell off the back of an airplane. This whole place is filled with things borrowed, begged for, or stripped from institutions.

The food, however, is five-star. There's no Jell-O salad and brown slush with graying chunks of meat on the plastic plates. Instead what we have is homemade ravioli filled with ricotta and spinach, tossed in a browned butter sauce. There's a small bowl of salad greens, crisp and fresh and tangy with a vinaigrette that knows nothing about plastic bottles. And fruit salad with delicate bites of fruits the local supermarket doesn't stock.

They brought me here after Jenny was killed. For observation, the woman in uniform said. Military. Somewhere along the way the president declared martial law and nobody bothered to let people know. They patrol the streets, watching, waiting for someone to cause a ruckus, which I did. They saw that. They pulled me away from my sister. But they can't tell me who shot her or why. I don't get that. When I ask, they keep telling me they don't know. "Do you think I did it?" I ask them repeatedly.

"We don't know." They've gone from being *An Army of One* to being an army of *We Don't Know*.

There are footsteps. Combat boots with a woman's light foot shoved inside.

"Zoe Marshall?" The dark-skinned woman's voice is larger than her body. She's a Pez dispenser in fatigues, holding a clipboard and cup of coffee. She gives me the coffee.

I nod, because who else would I be?

"Sergeant Tara Morris. You can go. But I want you back here tomorrow to see the shrink."

"Back here? I don't even know where here is."

She reels off the address.

"That used to be a private school."

"Not anymore. We're a low-security halfway house of sorts. We help people. At least until . . ."

"Everyone comes back to life?" I rub my forehead, wonder why it's hole-free when my sister can't say the same. "Did you find out who killed Jenny?"

"No. I'm sorry. It's not good enough, but that's all I've got," she tells me. "We're a militia at best, not a police force. You're not in any trouble, so you can go home."

"Then why the locked doors?"

"You were kicking my men. How do you think that looked?"

I close my eyes. "Like some asshole had just shot my sister and they were trying to drag me away from her."

"It looked bad," she says. "Real bad. You could've been sick, crazy, maybe, or a delinquent. I have to keep my people safe."

"She was all I had left. Our parents—"

Schultz hunched over the microscope. "I ate the mice."

"Try and see from our side, would you? We're seeing the worst of everyone. Jumping to the wrong conclusion is going to keep us alive. If we assume everyone's a friend, we could lose more people, and that's not acceptable."

"Where's my sister?"

"We burned her. We've got more dead than we know what to do with." For a moment she looks scared. "We're dying in droves. Not just us. Everybody."

Not just us. Everybody.

I take a cab back to my apartment. The cabdriver wears one of those flimsy protective masks. He takes my money with a gloved hand, eyeing the note suspiciously. I half expect him to spray it down with disinfectant, but greed wins out and he stuffs it in his pocket.

"I work for myself now," he mutters as I watch the bill disappear. "No one to be accountable to out there."

Porkchop is gone already, so I let myself in with my key, ride the elevator, listen to the lonely hum that seems to chew up the available air and leaves me covered in a thin sheen of cold sweat. I am a robot performing the door-opening routine. The shards and bones I took from the box those weeks ago are still in the plastic Baggie. I cram them into my pocket and leave again.

Pope Pharmaceuticals considers you part of the family.

No one stops me. The lone security guard grunts as I show him my ID card. He doesn't look me in the eye, nor do I look into his. We both know why. We're here when so many aren't. That's not a badge of honor, just a sign of otherness.

The lab where there used to be mice is empty. Schultz's usual seat is pushed away from the bench. The microscope is an old man hunched over a glass-covered lap.

Time is ticking. I do what I've seen them do before, or at least a bastardized version of that process. I scrape the bones onto a slide, shove them onto the microscope's waiting arms.

"What are you doing?"

The voice is inhuman, but the face is still Schultz. He lurches toward me. "You can't do that."

"I thought you were—"

"Dead?" He laughs. "This is a hard-core game, man. I'm holding on to the end, otherwise I'm gone for good. We don't come back. Dust. That's where we go. So whaddaya have for me?"

He reaches for the slide. When I pull away he feints, and without thinking I move the other way, leaving him free to snatch my prize.

He shoves it into place under the microscope's all-seeing eye.

"Suh-weet," he says. "Look."

Deep breath. Press eyepiece into socket.

And I see it: the disease.

Noises live inside the phone, now that have nothing to do with dial tones.

Something waits and listens. For what, I don't know.

"Hello," I whisper.

Hello.

FIFTEEN

The scientific community has been busy while people die. But they've been confounded until now. And from the way this mouthpiece scratches his thinning hair, I'd say there's still a measure of uncertainty. He doesn't believe his words, but neither is he convinced they're false.

He stands there on his podium, a half dozen microphones shoved under his mouth to catch his words like some electronic bib, and tells us that we're dying of some viral form of cancer.

You got OWNed.

What he doesn't say is how we got it. When a journalist from CNN asks, he wipes his nose with the back of his hand and mumbles about how maybe it's something common that mutated into this mass killer. Like the 1918 Spanish flu that mutated from a killer of the weak to a slayer of vigor during its second wave.

But I know. I *know*. This all began with a man named George P. Pope.

That thought fills me with fear.

This time when I call the CDC, a sound file asks me to leave my name, number, and reason for calling. They're busy, it says, they'll get to me. But for now I have to blow my whistle in a virtual queue.

The week dribbles by.

Every day I listen to the elevator rattle to the bottom floor. When the doors open I say, "Good morning, Porkchop," because it makes me feel better to imagine he's still there. I don't drop quarters in the dispenser now: it opens freely. I take a paper, try not to notice the faint Jenny stain on the concrete.

Upstairs I go, not bothering to set my apartment alarm. It's pointless. There's no one to call and verify that I'm me. The newspaper goes in a pile. War, more war, and mass death fill the front pages now. The secret is out. People finally noticed everyone they know is sick or dead. The other pages are thin on content and advertisement-free. Even the funeral home ads have tapered off, their employees buried in their own coffins.

I lie on the couch. I wait for death, or something like it, to pound on the door and make me an offer I don't have enough heart to refuse.

On a day I suspect is a Friday, knuckles strike my door. My body rolls off the couch, staggers to the peephole.

"You gonna let me in?"

Sergeant Morris.

"No."

"Then I'm gonna have to kick your door in, and I'm really not in the mood for door kicking today. It's been a shit night and I lost two people. So, how about you let me in?"

She strolls in on pipe cleaner legs, carrying body bags under her eyes.

"You gotta see the shrink," she says. "We agreed on that."

"You look like shit."

"Nice place. How long you think it's gonna hold?"

" 'Hold'?"

She helps herself to my couch, leans back, eyes wide open like they're propped open with toothpicks. "We've got three kinds of people out there that we've been seeing. Dead people. They're the biggest group. We're burning them now. It's for the best. Otherwise they stink and rot. We load them into the wagons and drive them to the public pool at the YMCA. The outdoor one. We drained it couple of months ago. Turns out it's the perfect place to burn corpses. Community bonfire."

She laughs.

At first I'm horrified: How can she be laughing at burning bodies piled into a community pool? How can she joke about that? It's a tragedy. Horror. There is no comedy in that scenario. Then I see it: the funny. The absurdity. And I laugh, too. The mental image of all those people, some in their designer suits, people who used to walk around like they were more important than the swarm; regular people I'd pass in the supermarket who minded their own business just like me; people from work; people living completely different lives, all of them heaped into that concrete shell and doused in—

"What do you use for accelerant?"

"Gasoline," she says between outbursts. "It's free now. We just take what we need."

—gasoline, going up in flames, is hilarious. *I thought you quit smoking.* *"I did, until the plague got me and I died. I figured I got nothing to lose now."* It's like July Fourth, with real baby-back ribs—and grown-up ribs, too. And I can't stop. The volcano is erupting and my laughter flows down its sides in great fiery rivers. Burning people. In the community pool.

We laugh until we're doubled over. And then something changes and the horror comes back and we start to cry.

"This is fucking bullshit," she says, "I'm a soldier. Soldiers don't cry, especially if they've got tits. It's hard enough as it is."

"The other two types?" When she squints, trying to figure out what I'm talking about, I remind her she said we were down to three types of people, and the dead ones were just the first.

"Two more types, right. You and me, the living. The ones who aren't sick. For whatever reason, we're the lucky ones who seem to be immune to this thing. Or unlucky, maybe. I haven't decided yet." She sits up straight, stares at the TV. The president is giving a press conference with what's left of the press. "And the others."

"'The others'?"

"Come on, you have to have seen them. The ones who got sick but didn't die. At least, not straightaway."

I think about Mike Schultz eating the mice. One day he was sick, the next he was supplementing his diet with test subjects. I think about my father and his Mr. Hyde routine. There's no way I can twist that to make it sound normal.

"I've seen some. How bad is it?"

She nods at the TV, reaches for the remote.

"Human beings are no longer compatible with life."

These words are heard around the nation. Heads turn like sunflowers to the sun. A split second after the gasping chorus sweeps the crowd, the president of the United States realizes his microphone is not turned off.

We watch his eyes widen, his mouth sag, as he takes in the truth, and now everybody left knows our leader has no faith in any of us.

He clutches his face. He is Edvard Munch's *Scream*.

Sergeant Morris buries her face in her hands—that's how bad it is. "I always thought I was a survivor, but now I'm not so sure that's a good thing. I wish I knew . . ."

"Knew what?"

"How this shit all went down. How it began. The war, the disease, everything. I wish I had a neck to crush. Maybe that'd make me feel better about all this. Barring that, I wish we had the things we need. First sign of trouble, everything got looted. Drugstores first."

"And electronics."

"I know, right? World turns to shit and people steal big-screen TVs. Like that's gonna save them."

The world is broken, its contents smithereens. Therapy won't change anything. I don't want to sit around and talk about how I feel about losing everyone. I don't want to shred my psyche to pulled pork, then pick through the strands looking for that moment when I began to fail everyone I loved. I don't want to lie here on this couch and wait for the end of all things. And it's coming, the end; the president knows it, the woman next to me knows it, and I know it. The end is coming. I don't know if this is Armageddon, because there's a distinct lack of religious people shaking their fists and yelling, "We were right! We told you so!" There's no leader stepping forward to pull us together and stamp bar codes on our foreheads. If there's a beast, we're it. My religious studies have fallen far from the wayside, but I'm sure that possibility wasn't accounted for: man as his own Antichrist.

A thin stream of air seeps from my lungs. "I'm not going to see your shrink."

"I can compel you." No conviction in her voice—just deep-boned weariness.

"You can try, but you're overtaxed. I'm not going to do it. If you make me, I'll just sit there and say nothing." I take a deep breath, try not to think about losing everyone. "That sounds like a bullshit reason for coming here, anyway."

"You're right," she says. "It's partly bullshit. Truth is we could use more uninfected heads and hands. You've got both."

I like that idea. I want to be more than a part of my couch. And I tell her so.

"I can get drugs," I say. "Medication."

"Legal?"

"More or less."

"Is it dangerous?"

"Maybe," I say. "But does it even matter anymore? I can't sit here and do nothing."

She shakes her head. "You're stubborn as hell. Nick's gonna love you."

My heart stops. "Nick?"

"Our therapist. Good guy. Delicious. Makes me wish I was interested."

Heart starts. "My best friend James was gay, too. I miss him like crazy."

She smiles, tight and small. "No, I'm not gay. My husband was one of the first casualties of this fucking war. And for what? We're all gonna die anyway. As much as I know it was his job, I think he died for nothing. He could have been here with me."

I reach across the couch, take her hand. We sit there like that, still, watching the struggling Secret Service men try to rush the president to safety. But their hearts aren't in it. The president is just a symbol of something that no longer exists, of dignity we no longer possess.

Pope Pharmaceuticals is a sterile tomb. My footsteps echo on the lobby floor before the high ceiling whisks them away.

The pharaoh greets me. *Pope Pharmaceuticals considers you part of the family.* It's the devil inside me that makes me flip him off on the way past as I hoist my knapsack higher. I'm here with a shopping list that begins with George P. Pope.

I ride the elevator to the top floor. When the doors part, I am in the ivory tower, staring into the face of the sanest madman I have ever seen. He sits behind his vast marble desk, hands flat on the blotter. To his left sits a fountain pen in an ebony holder. To his right is a cell phone that's as impotent as the men for which Pope Pharmaceuticals develops drugs. These are the tools of the modern villain in this new Wild West.

"We've got a problem," George P. Pope says.

He looks like he wants to tell me, so I wait.

"We're like the mice. All of us. People. Including you. What do you think? Why are you still alive?"

"Really?"

His nod is an almighty blessing. The great and terrible George P. Pope wants to hear my opinion. I can hardly contain myself.

"I know I should be grateful, but when everyone around you is dead or dying, it's hard to find comfort in being alive."

"I don't give a shit about your personal feelings. I asked for your thoughts. That means I want you to tell me why you think you're special. What's different about you?"

"I don't know," I say truthfully. "I don't even take a multivitamin."

"We could cut you up and find out. You're company property. And it's a new world. Laws are gone. Pope Pharmaceuticals owns you. *I* own you." His fingers slowly tap out a steady beat on the blotter. "I want to show you something." He gets up from behind the desk. There's an odd lurch to his steps, like a woman trying to walk in too-high heels. "Follow me."

Commanding.

Inside the elevator, he pokes the keypad with a trembling finger.

"Your family?"

"They're all dead. At least, I think so."

"You don't know?"

And it's the strangest thing, because suddenly I'm standing there, telling about the day we found out Mark died and the incident at my parents' house the last time I heard from them. I start talking and I can't shut up. He just stands there and listens, no polite noises, no grunts or nods in the socially appropriate places.

When I'm done, I take a long breath. We've stopped and the doors have opened down on what has to be a subterranean level. There's no illumination but that which comes from tubes of gas. A white, harsh light with no life in its glow.

Pope pushes past me. "I don't care about your family. I didn't ask for their life stories."

"What do you care about?"

He turns, sweeps me with his ice chips. "My business. The board. Shareholders. No one else ever mattered."

"What about your own family and your wife?"

"I don't have family. I no longer have a wife. I have—*had*—employees. You can only trust the person who relies on you to eat. Have you ever been fucked in the ass?"

"None of your business."

"That's what family does—and friends. But employees think about their next meal, their benefits, their professional reputations, so they keep their cocks in their pants."

After that, there's nothing else to say. We're in a long white hall broken periodically with doors. They have numbered plaques instead of names. The only other splash of color comes from the red of fire alarms and emergency axes. Orderly blood spatter on a maxi pad. Pope lurches left. With each step, the right side of his jacket swings as though there's a counterweight concealed in the pocket. I keep distance between us just in case—

He's a rat-eating monster.

—he stops in a hurry. But he doesn't show any signs of stopping until we reach a door labeled TC-12.

"TC? Torture chamber?"

"Yes."

I cannot read him. His face is a foreign language. The expression is there in his eyes, but I can't grasp the truth. A torture chamber—really? What is this, this company where I've worked for two years? What is George P. Pope that he needs such a place?

"Do you know what I am?"

It takes me a moment to formulate an answer that doesn't involve a stifled scream.

"A businessman?"

He nods slowly, as though his neck hurts. "A businessman, but also a scientist. I enjoy experiments. Throw a cat into a flock of pigeons and what happens? Don't answer—we both know what happens. I like large experiments with potentially extreme results. Not this small-scale . . . *stuff* where I inject a rat and wait to see if it's more or less likely to lose weight. My passion is the big stage."

He lifts his hands: God displaying His grand works. "Life. Sometimes the only way to test a drug is to put it out there and see what transpires. The mice only tell us what happens to a mouse. But I make medicine for people. To know what happens to people, you must use people."

"You're a monster."

"Don't look at me like that," he says. "For years, I have sought other ways. Our prison system, for one. All those forfeit lives could be put to use. Testing on real people—that's how you get real results, solid data. Good employees—that's what a businessman needs. Good employees—that's what visionaries need. Give an employee enough money and he will do anything you ask of him. Particularly if he can kill two birds with one shiny coin. Jorge was such an employee. He had no morals, enough debt to crush that truck of his, and a serious grudge against you for reasons he never shared with me."

Every muscle that makes up *me* tenses until I am as stone as he.

"He wanted my job for his cousin."

"Ah. A male minority pissed off because a middle-class white woman took a job he felt belonged to his blue collar. Yes, I can see that. Entitlement is just as powerful as jealousy, although not, perhaps, as all-encompassing as lust. Interesting. Although I don't care why he did it, only that he did. You were a wild card. I never expected that you'd hold on to the container as long as you did. And to be immune as well? A double curse. You were supposed to be exposed and spread my work like a good little incubator. Instead you sat on the thing and went to therapy." He waves a hand when my lip twitches. "Yes, I know about all that. One of my employees farts and I know about it. Pardon me: passes gas. But my creation found a way to leap into a host body. Perhaps Jorge didn't seal the container as tight as he should have in his eagerness to see your *employment* was terminated. Perhaps he touched it with contaminated fingers. Perhaps the virus grew legs and climbed out." His laugh is chillingly sane. "Survival of the fittest."

"You created a weapon."

"You say weapon, I say medicine. You may not believe this, and what you believe is unimportant to me, but we started with the best of intentions. Like everyone else, we sought to cure cancer. You wouldn't understand the science—I barely do—but sometimes it's possible to hit an On switch when you're aiming to turn it off. Did you ever walk into a room and flick the light switch the wrong way? That's what we did. And the result turned out to be potentially more profitable than our original idea. Although, of course, we continued to develop that, too. More product, more money. More money, more power."

"Is there a cure?" Hope creeps.

"No. I'm a businessman, not Jesus. I can't even bring myself back from the brink of extinction." He shoves his left jacket arm high. The skin underneath is a pincushion plucked of its metal quills. The injection sites are strawberry red with infection. "I am a dead man walking, a Dr. Frankenstein who has become his own monster."

He pushes the door to Room TC-12 wide: bold, confident befitting his status between these walls. "Good employees will do anything for a sum of money slightly larger than what they feel they're truly worth."

The white blinds me with its cleanliness. Willy Wonka's Wonkavision room.

"Get in."

I hesitate.

"That wasn't an invitation." He reaches into his pocket, pulls out a gun, points it at me like he means it.

"What's inside?"

"An old friend. Of yours, of course. I don't have friends."

I see it now, the blood. I've seen too much of it, but I don't think there's a quota these days. I scan through the mess until I find remnants of a face I knew. The splayed body still wears its puffy coat, the one I knew from the train.

"It was easy to lure him here. All I had to do was offer him a glimpse at his big story."

Not Jesse. No, no, no. He was just a kid trying to prove his worth.

"You're a fucking monster."

"I suppose I am."

"Why? Because he wanted to expose you for what you are?"

He grabs me by the throat, but though his heart might be in it, his fingers tell the tale of a body weak with disease.

"It's a new world. I'm not the man I was. If the tests are to be believed, then I'm not a man at all anymore. I'm some kind of animal. New species, new rules."

Then he turns the gun to his chest and fires.

Blood mist on the pristine wall. Pope slumps to the ground, a sack of potatoes in an ill-fitting suit. He grins up at me as his body leaks.

"Do something for me." Blood bubbles.

I don't look at Jesse. "No."

He laughs, gags. "I had your sister killed. What do you think about that?"

"Why?"

"She was supposed to be you."

My body heat circles the drain; I don't need a mirror to see that I'm as white as these walls. Pope is the thief of hope.

"Why me?"

"Villain's choice, you might say."

"Just die, you miserable shit."

With his last breath, he whispers his want. Then the great George P. Pope dies with the image of a horrified me burned into his retina—a portent of his journey.

DATE: NOW

"Coward," the Swiss spits. "For a man to take his own life tells me he knew he had no value." Something slides off his native tongue.

"Who gives a shit?" Imminent death has loosened my lips at both edges. Nobody's going to slap my hand for cursing. *My mother's dead . . .* "Why do you even care about George Pope?"

He rants on. Not English. Not even English enough for me to pick out words. Somewhere along the way, while I'm busy not listening, he switches back to English.

"His wife. I knew her. A foolish, foolish whore."

"She's a whore, I'm a whore, your mother's a whore. We're all whores." I am going to die and I don't care. I just want him to shut up. "You knew I worked for Pope Pharmaceuticals. Is that why you helped me save Lisa?"

"I had to see, America."

"See what?"

"I had to know how a nobody, a janitor, is the only Pope Pharmaceuticals survivor. When all others died, why did you live? You are nothing special."

My fingers feel around for the blade in my pocket. I hold it there like a blood-slickened talisman.

"You are not stupid. I thought you would be, you know. A janitor. A stupid janitor. Someone who cleans rat piss from the floors."

There's no pain now. Just warmth enveloping me in its fluffy pink blanket. I want to snuggle down and lose myself in its hold. Soon.

"You're the stupid one, assuming people are only one thing. We're an amalgamation of things we've collected along the way. I was never just a janitor."

"What else were you? A whore?"

"A daughter, a sister, a wife, a lover, a friend." I thought I was going to be a mother, but I'm not going to make it. I'm sorry, baby. *I'm unable to sustain life. Your incubator is broken.* "A killer."

"You? I do not think so."

Am I still bleeding? It's too wet to tell. "You don't know any-thing, you overgrown piece of cheese."

"I know everything. Things a creature like yourself could never imagine."

I laugh, because that's all I've got left. This is how I'm going to go, not kicking and screaming like some dying animal, but laughing. I'll die with a side stitch and tears streaming because the Swiss actually believes he knows it all.

"What is so funny?" he says.

"Because."

"You make no sense, America."

"George P. Pope was a coward. He couldn't stand to live another minute with his disease. He couldn't stand what it was doing to him—what it might do to him if he kept on sucking oxygen."

"I do not see the humor in this."

Saliva bubbles between my lips. "You wouldn't. You weren't there. It's so funny. It's so damn funny."

"Tell me."

I've never giggled, but now, at the end, I do. The Swiss shifts on his haunches; attack is imminent. His breath comes closer. I feel him. My bloody hand reaches out and touches the end of my world.

DATE: THEN

There is only one way to do what I do next: remove my emo-tions, place them in my pocket, keep them safe from the rest of me.

I look up at Jesse. *I'm sorry,* I want to say. *I thought I was doing the right thing by talking to you.* But I'm not sure if that's true or if it's just another story I'm telling myself to feel better about him being dead. But for the sake of coping, I try to believe it.

I want to be different-good, not different-bad.

Nothing. I feel nothing. My psyche has flatlined. That's a good thing. That makes it easy to heft the long-handled ax I wrenched off the white wall. It's little more than a feather in my hands. I pull it up high, behind my head, and let it fall. Gravity does my dirty work. Gravity hugs the blade close. Together they disconnect George P. Pope's head from its body.

I feel nothing.

I feel nothing.

I feel nothing.

Just a hole where my soul used to be.

DATE: NOW

I will not die with my eyes shut and my heart in my throat. Not this far have I come to die a coward. My hand is ready, the scalpel tucked away in my palm: my bloody ally.

In the dark the Swiss grabs my throat, shoves me so hard against the wall my jaws snap shut on my tongue. Blood fills my mouth. I spit it into his face and laugh.

Can't control the laughter. Merriment is helium in my balloon. My nitrous oxide.

"Why do you care? It won't do you any good. Nothing can help any of us now. Soon we'll be dead, too."

His fingers are a ring tightening around my throat. One good squeeze and my laughter dies, bottling up below the seal. I see stars. I see a light hurtling toward me, and voices whispering just beyond. I have seconds until the end, and I'm taking the Swiss with me on the ride.

"Pope just had to screw with me one last time. And you're wrong, you know."

"I am never wrong."

"This time you are."

There's a perverse pleasure in withholding what I know is true from this man in his final moments of life. So I do not speak of Pope's final request: it might bring the Swiss joy.

There's not enough room for a bold thrust, but the scalpel's edge is more deadly than a razor. The blade skates across his throat, shudders as I scrape up the last of my energy to drag it sideways. The Swiss gasps; his pupils widen enough that even I can see them in this dim space.

His hand tightens. This is it. The end. Lights out. Ladies and gentlemen, Zoe has left the building. But he slackens and slumps to the ground and his fingers slap against the concrete. I reach out, shove his face with my foot as hard as I can muster.

The voices are getting louder. The light is drawing near. This is it, my tunnel, my emergency exit. *Sorry,* I tell my baby. *Sorry I didn't get to be a good mother, or any kind of mother. I'm sorry I couldn't keep our tiny family safe.*

Then my world flashes yellow and I see maybe the world has a surprise left in her yet. There's no tunnel, and the voices belong to actual people.

Hopefully they will bury us far away from the Swiss.

SIXTEEN

DATE: THEN

Are you for real?" Sergeant Morris asks the question across her desk.

A slow nod through air soup.

She pulls the vials and packets from the bag and lines them up. Soldiers marching across paperwork mountains.

The ground undulates beneath my feet. Or maybe I'm the one swaying to and fro. One palm flat on the desk doesn't make a difference. My world is shifting sands.

"There's more where that came from. But if you want it, you'd better move fast. There's no security now, and the CEO is dead. It's just a matter of time until the place is gutted."

"I'll send some people over. It would help if you'd go with them. We need all the meds we can get."

"Okay." My words tilt. I slap my fist on the desk, next to my hand. It's heavy. The air is stew. No, I'm holding something. A white sack. Not a sack—a lab coat, the ends tied together to form a crude swag that would make Huckleberry Finn proud.

Sergeant Morris grimaces. "What's in the sack? Shit, girl, it's bleeding."

"It's nothing," I say. "Nothing at all."

"Nothing, my ass. Nothing doesn't look like Aunt Flo came to visit and wound up moving in her furniture." She tries to take it from me but it's my burden to carry.

I sit, trapping the swag between my knees. "It's nothing."

DATE: NOW

I don't die. At least, not then. And for a time I'm not sure if I'm sorry or glad. My baby still lives, though, and that is something. It dances inside me, celebrating our victory. We are still two.

The sun beams at me through a window. *See?* it says. But I don't. Not really. So I mirror its smile while I try to discern which of us is the village idiot.

The groan comes all the way from my toes when I sit, press a hand to my sutured wound so I won't pop open like a worn teddy bear. I am surrounded by women. They watch me with wary eyes and sullen faces.

"What is this place?"

No answer. They chatter amongst themselves with foreign tongues.

"What happened to the man?"

They stare at the oddity in their midst. I have nothing more than cobbled-together sign language—mostly obscenities.

"Jesus Christ."

The women cross themselves. Head to sternum. Shoulder to shoulder. Religious figures—those they understand. One of the squirrels breaks away from the pack. The rest of them stare at me as though I'm a spaceman. Maybe I am. I'm from another world, I know that much. We look at each other, all of us trying to find a way to bridge the language chasm. My language is, in part, descended from theirs, and yet the pieces that now belong to the English tongue are useless to me here.

I drag myself to my feet, one hand on my arm. Pain slices through me. I am white-knuckled, dizzy, displaced in this reality. Hands grab me, hold me steady. Mouths tsk.

"I'm okay, I'm okay. I have to keep going," I say.

"You are going nowhere today."

My head jerks up, because those are words I understand. Amongst the static they are clear and bright and shiny. They belong to a boy not yet old enough to scrape a blade down his skin.

"I went to the English school in Athens," he explains. "My name is Yanni. In English, I am John."

His hand dives into his pocket, retrieves a pouch filled with tobacco and a box of white papers. He crouches on the dirt floor, pushes the tobacco into a neat line on the paper using his leg as a table, seals the edge with his spit, and lights up. One of the women reaches out, flicks his ear. Screeches at him until his head sags. He offers me the hand-rolled cigarette, one end soggy with spit. "Would you like?"

Humanity has crumbled, yet here are people who would still instill good manners in their children.

"No, thank you." I watch as he shoves the damp end greedily into his mouth and sucks deep. He can't be more than eleven, maybe twelve.

"Where am I?"

He speaks with the women. Arms flap until they reach a noisy consensus.

"Not far from Athens. My people found you. They were look-ing for . . ." He puffs on the cigarette, drawing deep like he means it, flipping through his catalog of English words, looking for one that fits. "Supplies. Clothes and things we can maybe swap with other people."

"There are others?"

Again he consults the women.

"Some," he says. "And some . . ." He shrugs, tries to look cool as he flicks the cigarette ash. "My people do not talk to strangers."

"You're talking to me."

"You are sick. When you are well, you will go."

Sounds of children scooting a ball across the ground end the conversation. He drops the cigarette, grinds it into the dirt with a worn boot heel, his body humming with tension. Wants to run and join his friends.

"Wait."

He stops.

"The man—the one who was with me. What happened to him?"

More talking. Solemn words.

"Your husband lives. But for how long, who knows?"

He must be mistaken.

All this world is theirs to live in now, yet the Roma choose to stay here in their familiar nest of lean-tos and shacks with their suspicion of outsiders to keep them warm. But who can blame them? My clothes are brown with the blood of three. I wear blackface made of sweat and road dust.

They are wary; I am wary. Too many faces twist diabolically of late. My faith in my own kind has evaporated to mist. But when

I reach out, my bag is beside me untouched. That small gesture lends me some hope that I am among those still as human as me.

DATE: THEN

Cups of steaming tea come and go. Voices swim around me like I'm fish food. Faintly, faintly, I'm aware that my sanity is going walkabout, that I'm acting as though I've got one foot in an asylum and the other in a pool of blood. How much can a human mind take before it breaks?

Then he is there.

And here I am.

The desk groans as Nick clears an ass-shaped space and sits. I don't look, but I feel the air divide as he leans forward and fills what was empty. He's close enough for me to smell. No cologne, no aftershave. Just Nick. Made of sunshine.

"What's going on, Zoe?" His voice caresses my cheek.

"The sky is falling."

"Feels that way, doesn't it?"

"It's going to kill us all, one by one, one way or another." My hand that is not my hand rubs my face. "He started this. All of it. We were an experiment. My apartment was his Trinity Site."

"Where they conducted the first nuclear test?"

"He wanted to test his drug. No, not a drug: a weapon." I tell him the things George Pope related to me in the last few minutes of his rotten life. Nick listens with the attentiveness of his profession. When my words fade to ellipses, he remains taut, alert. And when I look up to him he is still wearing that old familiar mask, the one that stops me from knowing him. So many questions. Who are you? What happened to you on the battlefield? Do you cry for your brother? Did you think of me while you were gone? But the questions stick to my tongue like sun-warmed gum to a shoe sole.

"What's in the sack, Zoe? Can you show me?"

Penitent and afraid, I kneel before him, the bleeding sack a guilty offering. "Are you sure?"

"Show me."

His is a command wrapped in silk, but an order nonetheless. Somewhere deep in my soul a gong strikes; I have no choice but to obey.

Stiff fingers untie the knot binding the lab coat. The fabric is soaked with blood and sticks to the contents. Wet red cotton peels away from the cold flesh inside.

Meat. Just like beef or pork or lamb. The lie that dams the bile in my stomach. If I stop and think about where it came from, I will run screaming from this room.

Meat. Just like the supermarkets used to stock.

Nick inhales. I close my eyes and wait. He doesn't state the obvious, doesn't ask the stupid question. He can see the coat contains a severed head, so he doesn't need to underscore and bold.

"Okay," he says. "Okay. Whose is it? Does anyone need medical attention?"

I shake my head. Just meat, Zoe. Chicken and ham. "He was dead already. I was following instructions."

"Whose?"

"His." I nod at the just-meat-maybe-turkey. "George Pope."

He sits. Processes. Then he asks why. And I tell him how Pope was afraid that he'd rise in death.

"Do you believe he would have?"

"I have to." Otherwise I chopped off his head for nothing.

Nick pulls a notepad and pen from his shirt pocket. Without looking at me, he begins to scratch words onto the page.

I look at him. "You're making a shopping list."

"I'm making a list."

"A list."

For ten more beats of my heart—I tick them off—he scribbles, then pockets the pad.

"I'm going to help you. That's what I'm here for."

"I'm fine. I can deal alone."

He crouches in front of me, wraps the head so it's no longer staring up at us.

"We might all get our fill of alone. Take companionship while you can, Zoe. I'm reaching out my hand. Don't slap it away."

Nick and I are not done.

Jesse makes the front page that day—and the second. The *United States Times* has turned him into a different-bad person. A villain. A criminal who tried to pin the blame on a company committed to saving us from, not just this disease, but a whole host of ills.

That night a preacher from the South gives the disease a name that rolls easily off tongues and sticks inside heads.

"This disease is a white horse coming to claim the sinners. The end isn't nigh, it's *here*." He speaks to an audience of dying millions where his words find purchase and flourish.

White Horse. It gallops amongst us.

DATE: NOW

A week passes before I can walk more than a few steps without my vision fading to black. During that time I eat better than I have since before the war. These fringe people are smarter than the rest of us. Forced to exist on the periphery of society, they've developed skills suburbanized people allowed to devolve. They grow what they eat. Each member of their clan performs tasks to help the whole. While the rest of us were mourning junk food, they kept on doing what their people have done for generations. Cogs in a simple, elegant machine.

Another week passes before I seek out Yanni. I don't believe the Swiss survived. He can't have. Unless my mind fabricated his death so I'd go to my grave victorious.

"What does the man look like?" I ask the boy.

If he thinks my request is strange, he doesn't show it. Every word is a chance to show off his English skills.

"He is"—Yanni waves a hand over his head—"white. His hairs is white. Not like old man. Like a movie star."

It's the Swiss; it has to be. I don't know how he survived, what Gypsy magic they wove. I don't know how I failed.

"Blond," I say with a thick, numb tongue. "We call that color blond."

He tries the word on for size. "Blond."

"I want to see . . . my husband." A gallstone, bitter and bilious, rolling around my mouth.

Two women come, both clad in tie-dyed T-shirts and tiered skirts that hang like tired draperies. They talk to the boy, stare openly at me without social propriety. To them I am a curiosity, both a foreigner and an outsider.

"Is he alive?" I say. Please let him be dead. Although it goes against everything I believe, and makes me a little less human, I want that to be true. Can I still look myself in the eye?

"He is not good," the boy says.

"I need to see him."

"Okay, I will take you." His arm links through mine. Stronger than he looks. Wiry. We go slow.

A man cuts across our path wheeling a barrow heaped with watermelons. It's warm here. Feels like high summer. A caterpillar of sweat hunches across my upper lip. I can't help but wonder what the weather is like at home. Although it no longer exists, home stands still in my memory, a monument to what it was before the fall. My heart has been rubbed raw with steel wool. Words need to come out of my mouth, and soon; otherwise I'm going to lose it. I swallow. My throat stings with the big gulp of clean air.

"There are lots of people here."

"Yes. Many people."

"Did they get sick?"

A pause as he translates on the fly. "Some. Not as many as the city."

"I'm sorry."

"It is life. Many of my people die young."

Corrugated iron walls and roofs form makeshift mansions. Maybe fifty in all. Nothing that couldn't be broken down easily enough and hitched to the back of a donkey. The Roma have livestock. They congregate untethered at the edge of this shanty town, smart enough to stay close to food they don't have to gather themselves.

Yanni's boot-clad feet halt outside a shack slapped with white paint. "Your husband is in here." He tugs my sleeve as I stumble toward the door. "He is not good."

I'm a shit lying to this boy. But I make it right inside my head, tell myself they chose to believe this. They assumed the Swiss and I were together. A lie of omission. They were there, they saw him bleed. They could have gone the other way, seen the truth, that I cut him to save myself. To bring him to break bread with the Reaper.

The boy hangs back, lets me enter the building alone. It's a cracker box room with a thin curtain bisecting the space. The room stinks of blood and shit and piss and death.

Foot by laborious foot toward the curtain. He's back there, that Swiss bastard. His boots jut past the flimsy fabric. They do not move.

I hope he is dead, or at least close enough to tumble over that edge into the long sleep.

My fingers jerk back the curtain and there he is. I half expect him to leap up from that military cot and strangle me, but he doesn't. His eyeballs perform a vigorous ballet under the thin membranes. His chest rises and falls rapidly; his breathing is shallow. Parchment skin stretches across the planes of his face. He's a parody of himself carved in damp wax. Not so male now. Not so intimidating. All the bite leached from his bark. Across his throat a poultice sips the infection from his body, but the area is raw and red. The infection has taken hold. Death creeps. Too slow.

I've tried so hard to be good, to stay human enough to recognize myself in those quiet moments when it's just me and the voices inside my head. But the gods of this land are either testing me or telling me something, because they've placed a thin pillow covered in striped fabric just inches from my hand.

Do it, they're saying. *Snuff him. Take him outta the human race before he gets another shot at you.* My fingers twitch with want.

Ladies and gentlemen, the parade marches through my head. Theme: Thirty Years of Yearning. On the first float a pony stands, its saddle so polished that all my other desires reflect back at me: Cowgirl Barbie with Dallas the horse; just one more chocolate-frosted cupcake; red shoes, like Dorothy; impossibly high heels; a Trans Am; a Ferrari; Sam; a good education; and then Nick—only Nick. On the last float, the Swiss takes his final breath and exits the world stage left.

The pillow is in my hands, then it's not, then it is again. My hands keep changing the game. So easy to wipe him out. One firm, enduring press and there would be one less thing to worry about. A rectangle of salvation. All I have to do is act.

But . . . but . . .

Lay the pillow across his face and lean as I would on a ledge. Easy. Pretend the tin wall is a shop window filled with unbroken things. Mentally, I could tally the coins in my pocket and choose one thing as a treat for coming this far, while the Swiss finally climbs off the fence and chooses death.

Inside me, tectonic plates clash and collide, scraping at each other, wrestling for dominance. To kill or not to kill? That is my question, my imaginary friends. I push the pillow away from me, release it from my tight embrace, lower it onto the Swiss's sweat-slicked face. The stopwatch starts in my head. I need three minutes, maybe four.

Thirty seconds. His hands twitch at his sides as he tries to suck air and gets nothing but cotton for his effort.

One minute. A struggle. Jerking shoulders. Snapping knees.

Two minutes. The Reaper chews a breath mint, shoots his cuffs, primes himself for seduction.

Then my baby kicks, swift and hard, right where it counts.

The anger dies. A disappointed Reaper slinks away, toting his blue balls. I'm tired, I want to rest, I want to go home and find my family still alive and raise my child with Nick. I don't want to have to kill to survive.

The Swiss isn't coming back. There was no real fight in his movements, just the herky-jerky reactions of a brain stem with enough power left to simultaneously breathe and piss his pants. He's already dead, it's just that nobody's bothered to deliver the bad news.

"I don't know how the fuck you're still alive, you bastard. But if you don't die, I promise I will kill you."

Yanni is still waiting outside, cigarette dangling from his lip. A little kid playing at being a man. I want to snatch the cigarette from his mouth, tell him to be a child awhile longer, because being an adult isn't always fun. Hard choices have to be made. Battles need to be fought. Struggle is inevitable. Then I look around and see this is no place to be a kid. It's a hard world encapsulated in a brutal new world. Being an adult before his time might just save his life.

The boy rushes to steady me.

"He is not your husband. No?"

"No."

"I did not think this is true."

"Does anyone else know?"

"No. I hear everything and no one says nothing. They say he is a dead man."

"Good."

"Is he a bad man?"

"Worse."

He leads me back to my own bed. I don't look back. If I do, I might race to the building and finish what I started. I want to. I don't want to.

If he leaves that bed, I will kill him. Can I look myself in the eye if I do that?

I think I can.

DATE: THEN

Nick watches me for cracks. I watch him for pleasure when he's not looking. Life has changed him, scraped away any softness he once had, so that he's all hard edges. If we two were strangers passing in the street, I'd hold my purse a little tighter while checking him out.

"I'm not crazy."

"I know," he says.

"I'm not."

"I know."

"Is that your professional opinion?"

"Are you sleeping?"

His fingers are long and thick, even curled around a pen. Capable hands. Safe hands. I wonder how they'd feel cupping my ass, tearing off my clothes, holding my legs up over his broad shoulders. How would he look holding our children? Dangerous thoughts anytime, but now more than ever.

"Zoe?"

"Some."

"Do you dream?"

"No."

He knows. It's in the set of his jaw, the steel in his eyes. He knows when I lie.

"I dream about Pope. Fifty times a night I lift that ax and let it fall. His head bounces. Not like a ball. Have you ever dropped a melon?"

"Sure. Once or twice."

"It's like that."

"How do you feel when you wake up?"

My face burns. "Like shit. How do you think I feel?"

"It's okay," he says. "Feelings are healthy."

"I'm *not* crazy. But if I'm not crazy, why do I feel like I am?"

Sometime later, Morris says, "He wants you."

Steam rises from the two coffee cups between us.

"I'm not going to risk loving him."

"Who said anything about love?"

"What else is there?"

She laughs. "You want him, too."

I slurp my coffee, fill my mouth with piping hot liquid so I can't say, "I do."

Moving into the old boarding school is merely a formality. Nick and Morris help me carry the few things I can't live without. Clothing, important papers, the plain gold band Sam slid onto my finger on our wedding day. I almost never think of him now and it shames me. I could tell Nick, but I don't want him to see me naked. My soul is not a newspaper to be read.

I claim a room on the second floor as mine. A space that has never known the jar.

DATE: NOW

In a world full of death, things are still born: legends, myths, horror stories. The imaginations of men don't need to toil hard to create terror in these times.

The moon is a narrow slit once more. She waxes and wanes, oblivious to the planet beneath her. She is an absent guardian and a fickle friend, one who tugs the tides and denies she's made of green cheese.

At night, the Roma congregate around the campfires. Meat and vegetables bubble over the naked flames. A lone accordion holds the night's feral sounds at bay. After the meal, the music becomes infectious—

White Horse, coming right for us.

—flitting from body to body until most join in the song. When the song changes, voices drop out and others rise up to take their places. These are people who've never heard of karaoke or *American Idol*; they sing for love, for expression, to nourish their souls.

Afterward, the vocal cords change patterns and tongues tell stories not set to music. There's a rhythm to tales oft-told. A smoothness to the words. Polished stones that have witnessed a million high tides.

"I have to go soon," I tell Yanni.

"The women say you will have your baby here."

"I've been here too long already."

I shake my head, feel the whips of my hair.

"I have to keep going north." His head tilts. That is his tell, the one that signals that he hasn't understood. "North is up."

"On the road?"

"Yes."

"The way up is not safe."

"Nowhere is safe."

"No. Listen," he says, "to the story." He nods at the man who, by his sheer physical presence, manages to occupy the head seat at a round campfire. Not a large man, but he expands to fit the tiny crevices in the air around him and defends his space with broad hand gestures that supply punctuation and italics.

Yanni translates in hobbled English.

"He talks of Delphi. Do you know it?"

All I really know is Delphi's famous oracle, but my head nods regardless.

The boy listens for a moment before continuing. The Gypsy man has drawn his arms close to his body, hunched his shoulders, scrunched his neck. Taut vocal cords push out a voice drum-tight.

He talks of Medusa, the woman with snakes for hair and a gaze that turned all who looked upon her to stone. By Perseus's hand she was decapitated, and from her neck sprang Pegasus, the white winged horse, and his brother Chrysaor. Greek mythology involves many creatures born from un-holey body parts.

The mood shifts to something darker. There are rumors, he says, that Medusa is reborn, that she dwells in the woods near Delphi, petrifying anyone who dares meet her gaze. The woods are filled with statues that were once people with hopes and dreams and families. Anything she doesn't turn to stone she devours. The main road north along the coast was destroyed in a quake. Now the only way up is a perilous pass through Delphi, through the territory of this modern-day Medusa.

"You see? Is very dangerous."

A flesh-eating woman who turns people into columns of stone. A year ago I would have scoffed, but no more.

"Has anyone seen her?"

Yanni thinks. "Many people. My uncle. He sees her carrying the wood and he runs away fast. Do not go north. Is not good. Stay here."

I've lingered too long. I have to go soon. I have to find Nick before our child comes.

SEVENTEEN

DATE: THEN

Nick makes a list. He always does.

"You're assuming blame that doesn't belong to you," he says. "You're not responsible."

"I opened the jar."

"People were dying before that."

"I know."

"So taking the blame isn't logical. Pope was going to do this—with or without you."

"I know."

He makes his list. Of what, I don't know.

"Are you sleeping?"

"Yes."

He checks my face for lies. There are none to find.

"What do you write now?"

"Now?"

"It can't be a shopping list. There's no shopping to do."

"It's a list," he says, "of all the good things I've still got."

"Like what?"

"Like you."

"Why me?"

"I'll write you a list."

DATE: NOW

My body mends. My belly swells. My child treads viscous fluid, ignorant of the sins of men. She'll never know a whole world, just the fragments of what civilization used to be. To the absent God I say nothing. Instead, I direct my prayers to the ones who once ruled this land. I ask for a safe place to raise my child, a place with enough food to nourish a growing body, and healthy people to serve as teachers. I want my child to know what we once were, and how we fought to maintain our humanity.

I am a being with three pulses now: my own, my child's, and her father's. All three dance to a steady beat in my soul. If he were dead, I'd feel the Nick-sized hole in my heart.

I have to go.

DATE: THEN

The war doesn't so much end as it simply stops happening.

Our men and women come home to silence. At the docks and airports there's no one to greet them except a few reporters who ask questions in which they're not invested; they'd rather be at home, dying with what remains of their own families.

A bold one shoves his microphone in the face of a coughing corporal who doesn't look old enough to have hair around his cock.

"Are you glad to be back?"

The soldier stops. He's too thin, too tired, too war-weary for civility. "Glad?"

"To be back home."

"My whole fucking family is dead. How d'you think that feels?"

"How—"

"I just want a fucking cheeseburger."

"Do you think we won?"

The corporal lunges, his hands choking the reporter as they fall to the ground. "I . . . just . . . want . . . a . . . fucking . . . cheeseburger." He punctuates every word by bashing the man's skull on the concrete. Flecks of bone rain down in the creeping blood pool.

No one stops him. No one says anything. Someone mutters, "Did someone say *cheeseburger*? I'd kill for a cheeseburger." Another voice laughs nervously. "I think he just did."

We watch this on the news as Luke Skywalker's about to discover Darth Vader is his father. When regular television comes back, the movie is over and we're left blinking at the screen without so much as a crinkle of a protein bar wrapper. Twenty-something bodies, a whole bunch of muscles, and not one of us twitches.

The weather war is over, and we're down about three hundred million citizens. Maybe more. Maybe all, before White Horse is done. Despair folds us in her arms and squeezes us in her loveless arms.

Hope is a four-letter word rotting in antique dictionaries between *hop* and *hopeless*.

High upon the rooftops, Nick and I watch night arriving, a sky full of stars hitching a ride on its coattails. From up here the world looks almost normal. Only the curious absence of cars skidding through the icy streets makes the eye catch and the mind whisper: *The world is not okay.*

"You're really not afraid of heights, are you?" he asks.

"No. Heights don't bother me. I haven't fallen yet, so there's no precedent for fear."

He nods. "Good attitude. Heights scared a lot of my patients. Wide spaces, too. I see—saw—people all the time scared of life. Every day I wanted to shake them, tell them that this day is the only guarantee they've got."

"But?"

He gives me a tight, wry smile. "It's not in the psychologists' handbook. We're not supposed to freak the fuck out and shake the shit out of clients."

"Even if it's for the best?"

"My clients don't always want what's best. They're human. They like what's comfortable. Coming to therapy every week is comfortable, familiar. Even at a hundred-plus bucks a pop."

"Was I comfortable?"

He turns to face me, but I don't look at him. I keep staring at the city. That's what's comfortable, familiar, safe. Nick isn't safe.

"You could have just told me the truth. I was on your side."

"It sounded crazy."

"Hey, crazy is what I do every day. I see women who save their shit in plastic Baggies and weigh it so they can make sure what goes in comes back out. I see guys who spend their nights beating off to Internet porn when they've got beautiful wives in the next room. Real women don't turn them on anymore, they're so into the fantasy. I see kids who cut themselves to mask pain, kids who cut themselves because their friends do it and they want to fit in. You want crazy? I can tell you a million stories. But some jar showing up in your apartment? That's criminal, not crazy.

Crazy was lying about it to someone who was on your side—a person you were paying. You wasted your own money. That's crazy."

"I get it, I'm crazy. You're the expert, you should know. Do you want me to climb up on the cross or would you like to nail me up there yourself?"

"C'mon, Zoe . . ." He's big and broad this close, densely muscled enough to crush me if he chose. And maybe I'd like that.

"Kiss my ass."

I stalk toward the door, grab the handle, meet resistance. The building has two rooftop entrances—or exits, depending on how you look at things. One gets locked at night so we only have to guard the other. Morris doesn't like to keep both locked, in case of emergencies.

"Shit."

He groans. "It's the end of the world. Let's not fight."

His words deflate my anger. "You're right."

"Say it again."

"You're right."

"I'm always right."

"I wouldn't go that far."

"You will when you see I'm always right."

This is almost flirting, except neither of us are smiling. A million million miles away, a star hurls itself across the sky.

"I don't want to be Chicken Little," I say. "I don't always want the sky to be falling."

"It's going to be okay."

"Is it?"

"Truth?"

I nod.

"I don't know. I don't think so. Or if it is it won't be okay in the same way. We've lost too much."

There's a wall between us. I long for a sledgehammer.

"I'm sorry about your brother. I saw his name on the list."

He slouches to my side. I want to slip into his arms. He has the perfect place for me right below his chin, but I don't dare. Not without an invitation. Maybe not even then.

"I have to get to my parents if they're still alive."

"Are they in the city?"

"Greece. Every summer they head back to the motherland and talk about how great America is." He smiles. "When they're here, all they do is talk about how perfect Greece is."

"How the hell are you going to get to Greece?"

"There are still planes—if you can pay the price."

"Which is what?"

"Blood. Medicine. Food. Whatever they don't have enough of."

The city goes out. The night stays on.

Nick and I stare at each other through the darkness, three hundred million corpses stacked between us. In another life I could love him. In this life I could only lose him.

The lights flick back on in the morning. This brings us no comfort, because we know it can't last. The electricity will leave us forever; it's just a question of when. We hold our breath and wait.

DATE: NOW

The animals have a secret.

Birds are the first to leave, in one giant airlift, a dense cloud thousands thick, from the surrounding trees. The Roma begin to whisper amongst themselves. Something is happening, but I don't know what. Mass migration is never a good thing unless it's fall.

The lurchers are next. Those lanky Gypsy dogs pace ditches into the earth, their ears low, their tongues thick, red rubber lolling from their mouths.

Secret keepers, all of them.

DATE: THEN

One morning a thousand feet come, shambling along the weather-worn blacktop. They're a stew of ages and sexes, all of them exhausted, filthy, dull-eyed. They brought their bodies on their journey but forgot to pack their souls.

"Canadians," Nick says. "They're migrating south."

"Like the birds," Morris says.

The others trickle in behind her. Through the second-floor windows we watch the indigent parade trickle past.

"We should feed them." This from a big guy named Troy. He's barely out of high school. Now there's no college for kids like him. Everything he learns has to come from the streets.

"What, all of them?" Casey snaps. Former National Guard. A twig who used to hawk cosmetics.

Troy crosses his arms, increases his bulk. "They're starving."

Morris serves as peacekeeper. "We can't feed all those people from our supplies. They're gonna have to find their own food. There's still food out there—shelter, too. If they want it bad enough, they'll find a way. We can't do everyone's surviving for them. All we can do is watch and make sure there's no trouble."

The bickering fades to a cease-fire. Everyone knows why there's shelter. So many died that there's a surplus of everything except people and fresh food and optimism.

"We're being naturally selected," someone mumbles.

"No we're not," I say. "There's nothing natural about this."

Morris claps her hands, wrestles for control before we turn friends to enemies.

"Positions, people. Let's make sure there's no problems. I don't think there will be; they're too beaten down, but they're desperate, too. Desperate people don't always think right."

Everyone leaps into action. It's been days since we've had new scenery. The power comes and goes as it pleases, and the television and news along with it. New is new. New is different. New is shiny. New means there's still life.

A family comes, also from the north road, its members clinging to each other as though the least thing might sever their delicate ties. Their feet are soundless, but they do me a kindness and cough politely to warn me of their approach. I unfold myself from a crouch and shake the numbness from my legs. My hand rubs away the cola foam from my mouth's chapped edges.

Each man is a bookend keeping his three children upright. They stop on the sidewalk, their mouths full of questions.

"We've never been here," one says. "We always meant to but never did."

"And now here we are," says the other. "What's there to do here?"

Besides wait to die or fight to live? I don't say that, though, because I don't want to frighten the children. But the men know it; that hard truth is ground into their posture.

"Not much," I say. "We have a good library and a great museum."

I am a tour guide selling my dead city.

"Is there food here? Some place decent to stay?"

"If you'll tell us where to go, we'll go there."

I reel off directions, but they stare at me with blank eyes, because everything that is stale to me blinds them with its newness. So I offer to walk with them a short way and show them what sights still stand. Before we part ways, they press a paper envelope into my hands.

"It's all we have," they tell me. "Worthless at best. But maybe someday . . ."

Tickets to Disney World, the happiest place on earth.

"Be safe," I say before good-bye.

There is a long, dim hall inside the old school, and Nick stands at one end with bloodlust smeared the length of his face. At the opposite end, I wear a mask painted with indifference. In between, there's a doorway that leads to a room with coffee. We set out together: Nick taking long, murderous strides and me on a Monday stroll.

"I know why you're pissed," I say when we meet.

"Don't ever do that again."

"I'll do what I need to."

"Don't sacrifice yourself for other people."

I stare him down like he's the devil asking for one last dance.

"It was the right thing to do."

"Bullshit. You could have been raped, beaten, killed. Sold into slavery. A million things."

"I'm a lot of things, Nick, but stupid isn't one of them. They were good people. It was the human thing." I turn away from him and make a break for the coffee, but he uses my ponytail as a crude brake, then reels me in. His thumb strokes my collarbone. Heat radiates from that tiny spot until I am a bonfire on a dark night.

"I want you."

"Don't pull my hair like that again." My protest barely escapes the deafening lust haze.

"I might." His eyes make me a promise. "But next time you'll like it."

DATE: NOW

It's night when the quake punches its way through the ground. The earth seizes and shakes. Vomits rocks and dirt.

This is it: the secret the animals were keeping.

All the usual rules don't apply. There's no bathroom to hide in, no table for cover, no doorways with headers strong enough to hold up a roof, just makeshift shacks with the staying power of light-hold hairspray. Flimsy metal walls struggle to stay upright, but they have nothing with which to grab the earth and hold on for the ride.

I snatch up my backpack and run.

People zip around me, none of them paying attention as I stumble through the camp. Rocks roll from around the fire pits, creating open paths for the red coals to bounce free. The ground is dry enough for the leafy debris to spark, then burst into naked flame. Mother Nature's temper tantrum splits the ground, shooting each half into jagged inclines. The dilapidated pickup trucks are homicidal bowling pins, pinning bodies between them. The world becomes a tangle of bodies and metal and movement. Pained braying punctuates the cacophony as the donkeys realize they can't out-stubborn seismic activity and they rush to save themselves.

We're running, all of us, with nowhere to go. This can't be outrun.

When the ground grinds to a halt, the night holds its breath.

"Yanni?" I call out.

A woman is lying on the ground nearby. I help her up. She's hurt, her face bloodied, but I can't do anything for her right now. Another woman is a magician's trick gone wrong, her body severed by a sheet of corrugated iron. There's no cavalry coming for her, either.

Yanni is a puppet sprawled across the hood of a pickup truck. A tree pins him to the grill. Gone is the boy who would be a man. He's devolved, a child again, his jaw shuddering as the tears pour in sheets from his face.

I race to him. I can't help it. But there's nothing I can do to make his body right. There's no way to separate his ribs from the mangled chrome.

"Hi, baby boy." I try not to choke on my tears. "How are you doing?"

He doesn't even try to smile. "Cigarette?"

With shaking hands, I reach into his shirt pocket, roll the paper around a thin finger of tobacco like I've watched him do. And although it's no good for me or my baby, I suck on the stick until the end flares red before wedging it between his lips.

Smoke leaks from his mouth. Not enough lung capacity to draw a good breath and hold it fast, so he puffs at it quick, quick, slow, before letting it fall. A smoky serpent coils around my wrist as I lift it up again for him to take.

"Will I die?"

I don't want to lie, but the truth hurts too much to tell.

"No, baby. You're just sleepy."

He nods slowly. "I *will* die."

"We're all going to die one day."

"Today. Where is my mama?"

Saliva thickens in my throat. I can see his mother from here, burning and inert.

"With your brothers and sisters."

"Good."

There's no room between the tree and the truck for me to slide in alongside him, put my arm around him, give him comfort, so I reach across and fit his hand in mine. His fingertips are ice chips, but I cannot thaw them with my body heat.

"It's just a bad dream. When you wake up, this won't have happened."

I am a piece of shit, lying to a dying child.

"Do you know songs?"

"Yes."

"Sing. Please."

In a light place in my memories, I find the song my mother sang to me, of a maiden in a valley pleading to her love, begging him not to forsake and leave her. And as I sing to the boy, I cry.

Miles down, the plates slow dance again, grinding against each other in the dark. Fire spreads, climbing the tinder-dry trees with the ease of firemen scaling ladders. Up, up it goes, until the canopies are ablaze and night becomes artificial day. What buildings still stand are falling now, crushing their contents with no care for whether they hold people or possessions. Dark heads bob and blur as everyone tries to save themselves. Mothers cry out for their children, husbands for their wives. The land is on the move and she is merciless. My hand tightens on Yanni's arm. I keep singing.

Flames lick at a truck at the far side of the camp, kissing their way up the metal body like an attentive lover. Higher, higher, until the night explodes. The light stains my vision white as the fireball unfolds like a flower, its petals reaching out . . . out . . . out, until it races back to its moment of conception.

My face is dry and tight. The white spots are old celluloid melting until I'm left with a dim picture of the disaster zone. Bodies still and bodies moving.

At the edge of my vision something creeps. When I flick my head around to capture the form, it fades. My body turns cold, stiff. In my heart I know what it is, and if that muscle wasn't already in my boots, it would be sinking fast through my chest and organs. The Swiss is still alive. He survived all this and now he's getting away.

But it can't be. He's stretched out on a cot, fighting for his life. What I saw was a ghost.

The hand in mine falls slack. My fingers understand before I do.

Yanni's head sags to his shattered chest. All the singing in the world can't bring him back. A cold mist seeps into my body. Anger will come in time, but for now I need to remain calm, leave this place behind, keep pushing north.

But first I need to be sure.

Lisa's ghost follows me to the shack. My earlier vision was just the night and the trauma and my fear playing cruel tricks on my mind, because the Swiss is still here, dormant and benign in his illness. But something has changed. His wound is the neat, pale seam of a long-ago injury when it should be pink rope.

What was new has turned old too quickly. It's not *right*.

This time, when I pick up the pillow, I am resolute. All this death, all this destruction and loss, and still I can say the world is better without this one life in it.

His body tenses as it realizes there is no oxygen to be found in the pillow's fibers. His fingers curl up, dig into his palms. One moment he's struggling, then everything fades away. The last switch has been flipped on his life.

Lights out.

The end.

Beneath my boots, the earth gives another shake, rattle, roll. I have to go. There's no time to make extra-sure the Swiss is gone.

A stopped pulse is good enough; I don't have time for breath and mirrors.

I tell myself I did this for Lisa and the others, but beneath the lie the truth prevails: this wasn't revenge. This was insurance. The small black stain on my soul is the premium.

I killed a man. I killed a man and I don't care.

With calm purpose, I slip my arms through the backpack's straps and cut a path through the dead and the dying. There are enough hands still alive to help those in need. I'm not necessary here. My place is somewhere else.

I wipe the back of my hand across my eyes and try to convince myself it doesn't come away wet.

I killed a man and I don't care.

PART
THREE

EIGHTEEN

It's Morris's doing, I know it is, constantly pairing me with Nick. She's got this wild idea that love and romance can still flourish in a dying world, as though the dead are some kind of emotional compost. When I confront her about it, she denies everything.

"We all talk to him but he gets to talk to no one. Doesn't seem right, now, does it?"

I assume the indignant position: palms flat on her desk, leaning inward. It's behind this pose that I hide my feelings.

"So you've assigned me as his—what? Therapist? Jesus, I was a janitor."

"Domestic engineer."

"A janitor. And I don't know a thing about therapy."

She shrugs one-shouldered. It's a feminine movement inside a gender-neutral uniform.

"You went to therapy."

"I've flown in a plane, too, but that doesn't make me a pilot."

"Just listen to the guy. These are dark, dark times, my friend, and even cavemen need a shoulder to lean on."

DATE: NOW

I name the donkey Esmeralda for no good reason. It fits. I don't know why, but when I speak it, the name slips on the way a favorite sweater does on a chilly day.

She comes willingly, does Esmeralda, for all the quirks of her stubborn species. Maybe she knows where there's people there's food. Or maybe she likes the looks of me and wants some company. Or perhaps she just wants to feel like she has purpose.

So we take turns carrying the backpack. Just because history makes her a beast of burden doesn't mean I desire the same. I do my share. Either way, she plods along behind me at the end of her rope. When she stops, I do the same. Esmeralda is skilled in the art of finding water and food.

The Roma camp lies miles behind us now. I don't know how many. Two days' worth, however many that is. I'm on the path to Delphi. Yes, I remember what the Roma said about the monster woman who lives there. Medusa, they said, with her snake hairdo and petrifying gaze.

Another day slouches by, followed by the night, and on its heels another day. The road narrows the closer I get to Delphi. Or maybe it just seems that way, compressed and colored in ominous tones by the Roma stories.

My imagination doesn't conjure up the earth's split lip as we round the road's gentle curve. The chasm is real and it's separating me from where I need to go, so deep and so wide is the injury.

There's a flip-flopping in my belly, as though the little person growing in there senses my longing and finds me pathetic with need. Pressing a not entirely reassuring hand against the bump, I stop to figure my way through.

There is another road, though it is less traveled. Instead of asphalt, it's a flattened grass dogleg that jags north, then east, then north again until it fades from sight. It's not its disappearance that bothers me but the *where* it's disappearing to. While the road slices through towns and countryside, the lesser path *delves*. Into a bank of brush and olive trees it slithers, parting the greenery just enough to dip its tongue inside.

There should be a sign, one fashioned from weather-worn planks, staked into the ground. There should be a fading message in once-white paint, warning me to turn back or die. But there's nothing, not even a dent in the grass where a stake might have been shoved into the ground. The lack of a sign is a sign in itself: *Keep Out*.

Foreboding fills me until I'm bloated with dread. What would Nick say? If it was just we two sitting in his comfortable office, batting banter across the low table, what would he tell me about handling this situation? I suck in my breath, hold it until my chest stings, then let it out nice and easy because I know what he'd say.

He'd tell me to take a chance. To not be afraid to explore the unknown. It's only strange until we stare it in the face and say, *Hey, how are ya doing?*

"Hey, how are ya doing?" I mumble the words, don't inject any substance or volume. The last thing I want to do is tempt fate by announcing my arrival. So I stare down the unknown, hoping to dispel its air of doom.

Esmeralda snorts, her hooves suddenly stamping an agitated dance on the blacktop.

"Settle, girl. Easy." I whisper the words and listen. The sensation of someone—or something—else creeps over me like a smallpox blanket settling around my shoulders.

Out there, alien breath is held as fast as mine. It eases out in time with my own. Could be paranoia, but it's not paranoia if they're really out there. Isn't that how it goes? I've long tired of this world where I'm constantly stalked by things I can almost see, things that hide on the edges of plain sight. Once upon a time, just a few months ago, if you held your bag tight, stayed away from dark alleys, locked your doors and windows, you were relatively safe from harm.

My hand tightens on the rope that binds us. Judging from the defiant head toss and the challenging snort, she's not happy about me leading her off the path and into the olive grove. She doesn't have to be comfortable with it, she just has to follow and watch my back.

The bushes and undergrowth have become set in their ways and they're reluctant to part when my boots tamp them down and shove them apart. We come to an uneasy agreement where they spread enough to let us through, then spring up into their previous position. This way they retain their wild dignity and Esmeralda and I have more or less safe passage.

The wall of silvery green swallows us whole, presenting me with a double-edged blade I have no choice but to grasp. Along one honed edge, that presence dances with its copycat breath, while the unknown glides along the other. Choose the evil you haven't looked in the mouth and counted its iron fillings. Risk the other choice being your salvation.

Nonetheless, the choice is made and I press on with my ass on my ass. Laughter burbles up my throat. This is ridiculous. Nothing about any of this is sane. Each tragedy has stacked up on the last so that I'm left staring at a teetering tower of black blocks. And yet, the harder I stare at them, the less real they become.

"If I'm crazy, do I know I'm crazy or am I in denial?"

Esmeralda says nothing. She plods along behind me without expression. We walk quietly, although not silently, and I hope that the sounds of nature's takeover are enough to drown out the *us*.

"It's not just a river, eh?"

We walk and I watch for her, the wild snake-haired woman of the woods.

DATE: THEN

Nick laughs when I say, "If you need to talk, I'm here for you."

"Did Morris send you to do my job for me?"

"Yes."

"But you didn't want to."

"No."

"Why not?"

I look up at him and, despite myself, my lips twitch upwards. "Are you analyzing me now?"

He gives that half smile, the one that should be delivered over drinks in a dimly lit bar instead of this makeshift infirmary.

"Why not?"

I laugh, shake my head. "Don't even try it. I don't want to be picked apart like meat from a chicken bone."

"Why not?"

Why not, indeed? But I know why. I don't want him rooting around inside me, helping himself to the bits and pieces I stash away for safekeeping. Gadgets and walls, some of them hiding silly things like my attraction to him.

"Because . . . because it's easier to keep all this together, to keep the horror in perspective if I wrap it up in pretty paper and stash it in a box marked *Do Not Touch*. That's why. Giving it a poke won't lead to anything good." I expect him to laugh again but he doesn't. Instead, he nods. His booted feet swing up until they're resting on his desk. Mine mirror his. For a moment I think we're two people who look comfortable together, and maybe part of me is, but there are pieces of me that are anything but comfortable with Nick. Looking at him pokes and prods me in tender places I don't want to be touched.

Hands clasp behind his neck. He shifts in the chair, and as he does, his eyes slide from my neck to my navel and back up to meet my eyes. "So pick me apart. Analyze me. Do what Morris ordered."

I swallow slow, wishing I could rise from the chair and walk away, but I know if I do, the movement will be clunky and herky-jerky. And if there's one thing I don't want, it's to look anything less than cool and composed in front of him. I don't want him to see what's there. I don't want him to see what isn't there.

"I think you're like me."

"Go on."

His words embolden me; my thoughts begin to pick up steam, and along with them, my mouth.

"I think you're functioning on autopilot, doing what has to be done. Part of you died in that war because you're a doctor, not a killer, and being ordered to kill made you feel like shit, then you came back here, to hell, and all you found was another serving of death, only bigger and scarier and more personal, because it took everyone you loved. I think you want me because I'm from *before*, when things were normal and sane. I remind you of the way it used to be. It's not me you desire, it's the memories I evoke. I belong to that other world. And any 'us' there could have been belongs to that world, too."

On that note, my voice dies so I sit and wait and watch. At first there's nothing, but I can see him chewing on my words and I'm half afraid he'll tell me I'm right, that it's not *me*, really, he wants, but the past and me by default because I'm a relic from that time.

"You know what I want right now?"

A thousand things spring to mind, all involving twisted sheets and bodies slick with sweat. My eyebrow lifts, asking the question because my mouth can't be trusted.

When he smirks, I can't discern if he's inside my head without permission or if I'm wearing my lust on my face for him to see.

"Kentucky Fried Chicken."

"KFC?" Not what I expected to hear.

"No. Kentucky Fried Chicken. The way it used to be when we were kids. Crispy skin, gravy, coleslaw, the whole shebang."

"Back before fast food became too fast to be good."

"You're there," he says.

"I'd kill for pizza." The words pop out easily, and then in a flash I realize what I've said. I should feel bad and I do, but I can't help myself, I start to laugh.

Nick throws back his head and lets out a belly laugh.

"Shit. Could I be less sensitive?"

"Gallows humor, baby. It's good to get that out."

When, I wonder, did I go from *Zoe* to *baby*? "But—"

"Don't worry, it was funny." He pats his lap. "Come here."

"I'm your appointed therapist. It would be unprofessional."

"Where's the harm?"

"I could love you and then you'll be gone or you could love me and then White Horse gets me and I die. That's the harm. We've been hurt enough. All of us."

I look away because I've said too much. I intended to close a tiny window and wound up throwing open a door.

Nick doesn't speak. His boots fall from the desk; he rises from the chair and moves around the desk to my side of the barrier.

"You sound like Oprah."

"Dead. About a month ago." Morris bounces in through the open door and stops. "Am I interrupting?"

I look at Nick. He's watching me, waiting for my cue.

"Yes," I say slowly. "I kind of think you are."

"About time," she says.

He touches me then, and I am lost in him forever, though I do not speak the words.

We make love at the end of the world, but we don't pin a name to what we do. Lack of a label makes it no less true. The love is there in his hands as they clamp my hips hard against him. It's there on his tongue as he sets me ablaze with explicit descriptions of all the things he wants for us. His eyes shine with it when he understands I've let down all my walls for him and only him.

Love fills all the gaps in our souls.

"I have to go," Nick whispers in the dark one night.

"What?" I prop myself up on one elbow and try to look as serious as I can with bare breasts and hair styled with an egg beater. "You can't just leave."

"If there's even a chance my parents are alive, I'm gonna take it."

And what about me? *What about* us? I leave the words in my head, don't speak them, because they're soaked in selfishness.

"What if I want to come with you?" *Ask me to come. Please.*

His fingers stroke the curve of my hip.

"You'll be safer here. At least I'll know where you are."

"None of us are safe anywhere."

"I won't risk you."

"Look around, Nick, don't be naïve. We're all at risk."

He grabs my arms. His fingers press hard against my flesh.

"Do whatever you have to to survive, Zoe. You're the best thing in my world. Don't fuck it up by dying."

"I won't."

"Promise me."

"I promise."

His fingers unhook themselves from my skin. He buries one hand in my hair. Holds my face with the other. And this time when he's inside me he roars until he's empty and I am full.

In the quiet afterward, I stay close to him, half hoping our bodies will melt together so we'll be bound forever.

"Don't go where I can't follow," I whisper. "Please."

I will stay awake. I will. But sleep snatches me and drags me far from him. When I awake, it's in a warm bed with a stone-cold Nick-sized patch along the length of my body. The frost spreads until it holds my heart hostage in its crystalline grip. Nick has left, I can feel it.

I can't hate him for leaving me. How could I when all I'm capable of is loving him?

"What is it?"

I stare at the envelope in Morris's outstretched hand. She waves it at me like I'm supposed to do something clever with it.

"It's a letter."

"Is it a bill? Because the utilities haven't been all that reliable lately."

She flips it at me. "It's from lover man."

"Nick?"

"Unless you've got another one stashed away."

I snatch the envelope from her hands, pinch it between a finger and thumb. "He left."

"Why didn't you go with him?"

"I tried."

"And he said no?"

So I fill her in on our pillow talk and watch as she shakes her head increasingly fast until I'm sure her head will pop clean off her shoulders.

"Shit, girl. You're gonna follow him, aren't you?"

With fingers stiff from anger, I stuff the letter into my pocket. "When hell freezes over. *He* left *me*."

"You're gonna follow him," she says.

"Fuck him."

"Right now, that's just the anger talking."

My anger talks a lot once I get to my room and hermetically seal myself off from the compassionate world. Mostly it rants and raves about what a jerk Nick is for leaving, for not giving me a chance to go with him. He started this. He made the first move. He made me love him.

God, how I love him.

We'd been building up to this from the day I walked into his office with a head full of worry about that damn jar. I laugh bitterly because the jar started all this: the end of the world and me falling in love with Nick. With one smooth move, it destroyed, built, then devastated.

I fall to my knees, bury my face in my hands, and sob.

DATE: NOW

Delphi is more than ruins and remnants. There's a souvenir shop, its postcards long gone, having fluttered off in a stiff wind, or perhaps decomposed into a pile of colorful pulp before being rinsed away by a cleansing rain. The rack still sits outside the shop, rusted and ready for new stock. One firm push would force it to turn with a reluctant squeal. Branches and leaves blow through town, past stores with names that mean nothing to me. I can guess, though, what they used to contain. Through one window, a baker's peel is visible, long and leaning against the bakery wall. Four other walls hold up a roof from which meat hooks descend, brown with stale blood.

Esmeralda takes food where she can find it, and she finds it in abundance. But I don't have that luxury. These grasses and plants are mostly alien, and I have more than just myself to consider.

I should stay hidden.

I have to eat.

My child needs to eat.

It's no contest.

"See that?" I speak of a narrow building with a blue door pressed into the middle. "I'm going in. And you're coming with me."

My companion says nothing. Keeps on chewing something of interest low to the ground.

"No, no, you have to," I say. "Just in case."

A gentle snot rain sprinkles me as she lifts her head and snorts, but she follows me, leaving a polite distance between us.

The asphalt crust is hard beneath my boots. It's an old habit the way I stand at the road's edge and look both ways. Although it's not traffic I'm trying to dodge now, but trouble. But really, what can I do if it comes? I could fall back into the woods, or run forward and hide in a building. Slender options.

Pebbles crumble away from the blacktop as I work the leather toe against the hardened tar.

Think, Zoe. Think.

My pregnancy pokes holes into my brain matter, making the thoughts harder to congeal and solidify. In the untamed groves, I am weaponless. Stealth is my only real advantage. So I cross the road, make the baker's peel mine, lift a knife with a gleaming edge from the meat shop. And I rest easier because I am armed once more.

The blue door opens freely.

Silence pours into the street accompanied by the sweet stench of old milk and older cheese. There's an omnipresent gloom that reaches out and pulls us in. The door swings shut behind us; its click is a death knell.

Stop it, Zoe.

This is a grocery store of sorts. I hoped it would be. It's not like an American supermarket. The floor is a dark and violent concrete. Products are cramped on shelves that cut me off at the neck. A thick blanket of dust mutes all signs of color to a depressing dinge.

My breath catches; my lungs don't want the sour air. I force the spongy organs to draw oxygen. Right now I'm grateful I'm long past that first trimester, otherwise I'd be on my knees, painting the floor green. The shop's stock comes into focus: there's food on these here shelves, and it's processed and packed and likely still edible. Whoever said processed foods were bad hadn't vacationed at the end of the world.

The second best thing about being in a grocery store is that there's a ready supply of plastic bags. I rip open a box of oatmeal and pour it into a neat heap on the floor for Esmeralda before reaching for a fistful of sacks. And I apologize for the burden I'm about to bestow on her.

She doesn't seem to care.

It's the chocolate that catches my attention. I can almost taste the sweet, smooth confection before I peel away the packaging and cram it into my mouth. Flavor explodes and my taste buds shiver with orgasmic pleasure. Moments later, there's a rolling sensation in my belly as my baby somersaults. I laugh and unwrap another bar—some kind of wafer layers with chocolate pressed between. I scrape off the top wafer with my teeth and shamelessly lick the others clean. Soon my fingers are sticky and there's that feeling of insubstantial fullness that only comes from ingesting mass quantities of junk food. My body hums as I surf the sugar high; I'm Superwoman shoving boxed foods and luxuries like toilet paper into bags.

And then Esmeralda stops snuffling the ground and begins the soft-shoe shuffle of unease.

My entire body tenses. Even my baby holds still. The thought is fleeting: how sad it is that my child has to come into a world where there's no chance for normal, no pretense even of safety.

The word floats in on a malevolent draft from beneath the blue door: *Abomination*.

A taunt.

If not for the donkey's agitation, I could convince myself my mind had manufactured the word using my fears as tools.

Someone is out there. The cleaver takes on new weight, reminding me it's ready and waiting should the need arise.

The wall presses against my back as I take a measured step closer. Gravity works its magic and eases me to the ground. My bones creak in appreciation. From here I can see the front door and both windows. There's no other way in or out. I balance a candy bar on my belly and wait for dark to come.

Minutes tick by. They huddle together to form hours. I don't know how many, only that the sun shifts slowly in the sky.

The heat grows, but down here on the concrete floor I can feel the cool of the earth seeping into my skin. When Esmeralda dumps her oats, I try not to care about the smell.

Wait. Watch. Listen.

Eventually, the night strides in and forces the sun from her comfortable chair. As she's unseated, so am I. For hours there's been no noise beyond the usual sounds nature makes. No more whispered taunts, no breathing that doesn't belong. But I don't trust it so we have to leave under the cover of dark and hope that gives us enough of an advantage.

The truth is I could leave Esmeralda, cut my way through the land with just me to worry about, but I don't want to. Her company makes me feel less lonely. One by one, everyone I've cared about has been stripped from my life, and yet I can't stop feeling a bond with this beast. Please let me be able to keep her safe.

We ease out of the building, onto the barren road. Hugging the curb is a necessity because I can't see my way back into the bush without light. Risking a fall is not an option. Whoever is out there is likely watching anyway. For now, all I can do is make that task more difficult by hiding in the shadows, the baker's long-handled peel held in my hands like a magician's staff.

At first there's a gentle wind that stirs the leaves making a soft *wikka wikka* sound. This swallows our footsteps, so I welcome its presence, until a short way down the road it dies, leaving us exposed.

I stop. A half a beat later, there's the faint echo of another footfall. We're being followed or pursued. Is there even a difference? One implies a sense of urgency, while the other says, *Hmm, let's wait and see how this plays out.* Either way, I don't like it, nor does my central nervous system; it's shooting adrenaline like my body is a firing range.

On the heel of my boot, I turn and scan the pitch.

It's just a flicker in my peripheral vision, like the fluttering of a panicking insect when it realizes it's just flown into a spider's web and become entangled. That's all it is, nothing more substantial than that. *Look!* my senses scream. As my neck twists, I glimpse it: hair blond and neatly fitted to a smooth skull. Hair that belongs to a ghost.

The adrenaline seizes control. Propels me toward the twisted olive trees. I half run, half walk, deeper and deeper into the wild land. Esmeralda stays close without complaint, more surefooted than me. Guilt washes over me; she trusts me to keep her safe and I hope I can honor that.

Fate steps in, reaches out and places a hole where ground should be. My ankle twists. Pain shoots through my shin and I fall. The last thing I see is a woman emerging from the black, her face scarred, her hair that of a madwoman.

The Medusa of Delphi.

NINETEEN

The city has fallen into an endless hush. Silence is a sponge soaking us up. Shoes slap silently on the sidewalks. Coughs fade before they've left their irritated throats. The only noise comes from vehicles moving through the streets: occasionally passenger cars, sometimes buses with a handful of riders staring hopelessly ahead.

"Where are you going?" Morris asks one day. The bus is straddling the broken yellow line. The driver stares at us expectantly and shrugs. He thrusts a thumb at his fares.

"Wherever they want to go."

"Any place in particular real popular right now?"

He shrugs. "Airports, mostly."

"What's there?"

He looks at her like her brain just dribbled onto her khaki T-shirt.

"Birds. Big silver ones."

"They're still taking passengers?"

"Hell if I know. I just drive the bus. Nothing else to do except sit around and wait to die."

The bus doors sigh and hiss as he eases his foot off the brakes and keeps right on following the yellow line.

"Oz," I say.

Morris peers at me over the top of her aviators.

"*The Wizard of Oz*. Did you ever see that?"

"Sure I did. Those flying monkeys freaked me the hell out. What about it?"

"Have you heard any planes lately?"

Head shake. Expectant look.

"Exactly. They're all going to meet some wizard who doesn't exist, in search of brains, a heart, or whatever it is they need."

"Are you going somewhere with this?"

I turn and head back toward the old school. "Nope."

"You're losing it. You should go talk to—" She stops dead.

"Nick. Don't be too much of a sissy to say his name. I can. Nick, Nick, Nick." I hold up my hands. "See? I'm okay with it."

But I'm not okay with it. My heart's been bruised before, battered and bandied about by others. Boys at first, then Sam's death. And now Nick. But this is different. Bigger, like a bubble of grief that holds me within its thin walls. No matter how fast I run, the bubble moves with me. Hamster in a wheel.

I take to walking the streets on my own. I have a gun. I know how to use it; Morris taught me. There's a knife in my pocket and I know how to use that, too. Can I, though? I don't know. But I have it—my cold, hard, metal insurance.

Other things go into the pockets of my heavy coat: food, money, and my keys. I can't break that habit.

And Nick's unopened letter. All I have left of him.

DATE: NOW

Do you love me, Mommy?
  I do.
  Why?
  Because you're mine.
  Why?
  Because I'm lucky.
  Then why don't you look happy?
  Oh baby, I'm happy about you, but I'm sad, too.
  Why?
  Because I miss your father.
  Do you love him, too?
  I do, baby. I do.
  Then why isn't he here?
  We're going to him, baby. Soon.

DATE: THEN

There's treasure in this basement. Bars of gold wrapped in plastic, their crumbs packed tight around a chemical core. Their value is immeasurable. I open a box. Slip a precious bar into my pocket.

"You're actually going to eat that?" Morris says behind me. "I quit them years ago."

My body jerks with surprise, and the Twinkie falls to the ground with a shallow thump.

"Supplies," I say. "I was on my way out."

"Again? What do you do out there?"

"Walk. Window-shop. Go out for morning tea with the girls."

She steps into the pantry. It's a room the size of my apartment filled with food. Little Debbie's entire line of food is here; good eats at the end of the world. Morris plucks a golden cake from the box, unwraps the confection, crams it into her mouth. And a second. When she's done eating, she grins at me with cake-crumbed teeth.

"Damn, I forgot how good these are. Did you open Nick's letter yet?"

"No-o-o-pe."

"That's mature of you."

"Says the woman who just crammed a whole Twinkie into her mouth."

"Two."

"Ladies and gentlemen, Tara Morris, Twinkie-eating champion of what's left of the world."

We giggle like silly girls, carefree and alive, until reality begins to lap around the edges like a thirsty cat.

Morris turns grim. "Open the letter. Please."

"I can't."

She shakes her head at me, her eyes forgiving though her mouth is not. "You're scared, and for what? That fear buys you nothing except a whole lot of walking the streets with a pocket full of Twinkies, worrying yourself sick over him."

"It's just one Twinkie."

It's just one Twinkie *at first*. Then two. Four weeks after Nick left, I take my walk accompanied by three chemical cakes. I pretend he never existed. I believe he's dead. I pray he's alive and safe and with his family.

I'm in the library when it happens, the same one where my sister's dreams died before Pope slaughtered her on an empty street. There are no new lists. The old ones flap with excitement when I push the door open. Look! A person! Then they fall still. The librarian is gone, her haughtiness relegated to the history books as a once-cliché. She's no longer here to care whether or not I eat near the precious tomes.

I peel away the plastic wrapper.

Crumbs fall onto the pages of the atlas I've spread open. I press my finger to the page, then lick the yellow dots. The dry finger of my left hand traces an invisible line across the thick, rich paper, across the pale blue ocean—first the Atlantic, then the Mediterranean—from New York to Athens. From there I creep north, inch by colorful inch, across the splintered states that form the country of Greece.

The name, the name, what was the name? Nick told me the name of the village where his parents were raised, but standing here looking at this swath of unfamiliar places, I'm overwhelmed by their otherness. The names swim on the page until they're meaningless.

My stomach lurches. The atlas swirls. The bright mosaic tiles rush up to greet me.

Thank God, I miss the books. The librarian would never forgive me.

DATE: NOW

I am dead and this is hell. Fire licks my face, dances with the shadows, forces its partners into the darkness before taking others. Light plays across the faces of sightless marble men, twisting them into fiends. Soldiers whip their horses, *Faster! Faster!* as they gallop across plaster walls.

"Not hell." The words are not mine. They come from outside me; I'm awake enough to know that.

"Where?"

"Delphi." The voice quavers at the edges as though the vocal cords have been slackened by time. She pronounces the word *Thell-fee*, not *Dell-fie* like the corporation.

Moving my body hurts, but I manage to feign sitting. An outsider might see me as a sack of potatoes, and that's how I feel, my weight constantly shifting, my insides compressed yet lacking the structure a skeleton provides. My perspective shifts. The fire retreats to its pit, leaving the room awash in a preternatural mix of shadows and light. The woman lingers in the half-light.

Two stone men tower over me.

"Who are they?"

"Kleobis and Biton. Heroes rewarded by Hera with the gift of endless sleep." The words are hesitant.

"Not something you can regift."

"What is . . . regift?"

This is Greece, the woman is Greek, and though her words are English, I realize their slowness is a result of translating the words in her head before presenting them to me. I wish I could offer her the same courtesy.

With simple words I explain and she nods.

"Gods give freely . . . or not at all. Their mother sought a boon and was punished for her pride in her sons."

Their mother. My hands go to my stomach. "My baby—"

"Still lives inside you. He is strong."

"He?"

"Or she."

I close my eyes. The ache is too much—relief that Nick's child still lives, despair that he isn't here with me. "At least I have that."

From the shadows she comes, her face a tangled web of burns. "Snakes," she says as my gaze slips away from her right side. "A gift from the sickness."

I look at her and her face, and I know at once what she did. "You burned them off."

One nod. "Yes. I burn them off with the fire. It was"—she raises a hand to her face, then pulls away as if she dare not touch—"very painful."

"Like Medusa."

Another nod. "Of all the figures from mythology, this is the one my body chose. Me who is nobody, just a servant of the gods."

"The gods? Not the one God?"

"I find more comfort with ones who walked the same path as I. Their feet . . . mine . . ." Two fingers step through the air. Then she changes tack. "You know someone follows you."

For a moment, I'm confused. "Did the gods tell you that?"

"No. I hear. Now is time for rest."

I close my eyes but do not sleep.

Abomination. **That single word is** a malignancy that takes hold in my mind. Tendrils snake out and coil around the rational thoughts, squeezing them like they're there to be juiced dry of reason.

Abomination.

My child is fine. My child is—

An abomination.

—healthy.

My savior finds me on the low wall outside the museum. Her gaze fixates on the ground as she walks so that her hair falls forward, concealing the scars with a black waterfall threaded with silver. She's older than I first thought, skimming the edges of fifty. Only when she's seated beside me does she lift her head.

"Are you . . . sick?"

The snake woman's words tug at the elastic band binding those thoughts, but it does not snap; the bundle of doubt remains.

I shake my head. "Last night, you said someone was following me. Did you see them?"

"No. I just hear."

"You heard what, exactly?"

It takes her a moment to translate, formulate her reply, then translate again. "Shoes. Who?"

"I don't know. A ghost, maybe."

She turns to face me, a question in her eyes. Daylight is cruel and unforgiving: out here the scars are knotted and gnarled and red as though irritated.

"A dead man." I draw a line across my throat, wiggle my fingers in the air. "Ghost."

This time she nods. "The dead, they stay with us. But I do not hear your ghost. Maybe mine, eh?"

People used to flock here for this sunshine, this view, this experience. A cobblestone path stretches from the museum's steps all the way to the famed ruins, interrupted in places to accommodate sapling laurels. The museum is a geometric hillock rising from the path in a seamless transition of color and stone. Someone planned carefully, matching the colors of the new to the centuries old. I can't see what remains of ancient Delphi from this angle, but there's a quiet energy that hums through the trees. There are ghosts here, spirits of the dead who walk these paths like death was an inconvenient stepping-stone on their way back to right here, right now.

I'm not convinced and I'm sure she's not, either, by the uncomfortable way she raises her hand to her face and gingerly scrapes a nail across the mangled flesh.

"Does it hurt?"

She smiles with one side and shrugs with the same. "Eh, a little."

My hatred for Pope flares anew before fading to a dull contempt: what havoc he wreaked on the world because of his selfish desires.

"Do you have a family?"

"My family is here." She waves a hand toward the disappearing path.

"Children?"

"I am the child."

Grief shivs my heart, but it's dry of tears. "You're lucky."

"Perhaps."

The cryptic word accompanies an equally impossible-to-decipher half smile. Who is this woman? I ask her and so we swap names the way people in polite society do, then we go back to staring, both of us fixated on the same stretch of cobblestone, both of us seeing something completely different, neither of us having shared a thing about ourselves beyond an arbitrary title.

Abomination.

Aren't we all now?

DATE: THEN

Morris leaps from her seat. "Jesus Christ, what's wrong?"

My cold, clammy hand slips and slides against the door's slick painted jamb. "Don't come near me. I'm sick."

Fear blossoms in her dark eyes, shrinks as her face softens into concern, twists as anger rages in. She snatches up the clipboard on her desk, hurls it at the wall. Two broken pieces clatter on the floor.

"Fuck."

"It's okay," I reassure her, like she's the one who's sick. But it's always like this, isn't it? The terminally ill assuring their loved ones that everything will be just fine if everyone thinks positive and wears a smile. Nothing holds death at bay like a rainbow over the river Styx.

"It's not okay. It's so not okay. It's not even on the same planet as okay."

"I have to leave. I can't let it spread."

"No," she says. "You have to stay. Besides, if we haven't caught it by now, we're immune."

"We don't know that. We're just guessing. If we follow that logic, I shouldn't be sick."

"You're right. Shit. I can't think. Jesus, Zoe. You can't be sick. I—"

"Won't allow it?"

"Yeah." She picks up the clipboard pieces, tries to fit them back together, but they're not cooperating. "I can't lose any more people, Zoe. You, the others, you're my family now. I thought we were all safe from that fucking disease. I was relying on it."

"I'm sorry."

She stomps over to her second-floor window, shoves the glass pane high in the sash.

"Fuck you, George Pope!" she screams into the empty streets. "I'm glad you're fucking dead, you asshole. Burn in hell." In stoic silence, the other buildings stand, reserving their judgment yet unwilling to yield to her hard words.

"Tara," I say gently. "It really is okay. We all have to die somehow, right?"

"Wrong. We should be immortal."

"That's mature."

"So is you stomping out of here because you think you're sick."

"Look at me. I'm sick. I just puked all over the library floor. Soon God knows what's going to happen to me. This thing will flip my genes on and off and I'll turn into something that isn't me anymore. There's no telling what that will be. Maybe I'll survive as some kind of evolutionary freak, maybe I'll die. I'm going to pack."

"Don't," she says. "Please."

"I have to."

Morris sighs, hard and loud. She bends over, presses her elbows into her desk, bangs her head against the surface. After a few good thunks, she looks up at me.

"You're not going to change your mind, are you?"

"Not a chance."

"Fine. Do me a favor. Don't go too far. Set up in one of the buildings across the street where I can keep an eye on you."

I nod, turn away from my friend. What I don't tell her is that death isn't totally unwelcome. For the first time in my life, I'm flirting with The End and I don't care. Let it slide its tongue into my mouth, taste the metal and take control.

Anything to stop my heart from hemorrhaging.

TWENTY

E eny, meeny, miney, mo. The street is filled with choices, each as unappealing as the next. Oh, they're all fine to look at: office buildings and businesses and apartments hewn in bricks and rough stones. The thing is, I'd feel like an intruder living in someone else's home, even though they're long gone.

Dead. You helped burn them, remember? They didn't go on vacation.

Morris is a whippet bouncing at her office window. She's pointing directly across the street at what used to be a Kinko's. Technically it still is—they're just no longer printing copies. Directly above that is a small office space once filled by a small accounting firm. No beds, but they have a decent sofa in the waiting room, Morris told me. That's where she wants me.

My wave is limp and lacking, and hers is just as weak. I don't want to do this. I have to do this. No choice. I turn to take another long hard look at my new home. It's just me, the backpack digging into my shoulders, and this box in my arms. For a moment I balance the box on my knee and readjust the weight, and then let myself into the building. The previous tenants made it easy, or maybe Morris and her crew did; either way, the door opens freely. The door is made of both bars and glass. Anything coming through is going to make enough noise to wake the dying.

That would be me. I can't help but laugh a little. Who knew death could be amusing?

It's true, there's a sofa in the bland waiting room, along with two generic armchairs and a cheap desk. In places, the laminate is warped and stained with rings from hot, wet cups. My knees bend; I touch my backside to the very edge of the chair that doesn't have its back to the window and place the box between my feet.

What do I have?

A great view with a direct line of sight into Morris's office; all the clothes I can carry; toiletries, food, water, and bedding; an extra-bad attitude that starts somewhere behind my eyes and reaches out so far even my toes feel wracked with ill will. I want to hurt something, break it, control it until destruction is inevitable.

The wall yields easily beneath the toe of my boot. Only about twenty good kicks before it punches right through the Sheetrock. A pile of crumbles amasses on the synthetic beige pile, like Pop Rocks half pulverized by a brick. Guilt is a serial killer, stabbing me for losing control of my anger, then choking me for being foolish enough to think: *To whom do I send the check for the damage?*

Nausea washes over me, using me like I'm the shore of a long-abandoned beach. Once again I'm on my knees, praying to the gods of cheap carpeting.

Please let death be swift.

DATE: NOW

Shadows stretch across the cobbled path, from east to west. The sun is still new in the sky and hasn't yet gained her confidence. From room to room I wander without pausing to contemplate the relics of the dead. There's a stillness in the air that tickles my intuition, telling me I'm alone, so I put it to the test and establish that my instincts are sharp and true: Irini, the Medusa of Delphi, isn't here. There was a time when this wouldn't have bothered me, but that was before. I'm calm. Honest. The museum's expansive windows tell me so. The bouncing pulse in my throat is the lie. A fabrication concocted by my hormones and fears for the sole purpose of feeding my paranoia.

The steps are empty. So is the path as far as I can see. Only Esmeralda is there, and she's busying herself with grasses and the other things donkeys deem important. Her calm state presses a cool hand on my forehead and tells me to chill. My ears listen. My brain processes the message. My pulse continues to thump, regardless.

We walked up there yesterday, Irini and I, just far enough for her to point out the areas of interest: the stadium, Apollo's temple, the tholos—a circular structure with three of its original twenty Doric columns still standing—but we didn't move close enough to do more than admire the passage of time from a distance.

I'm trapped in a déjà vu loop. Only the scenery changes, but the dangers and the accompanying reactions are the same. Something is following me, someone disappears, and I chase after them, only to be too late to help. In truth, there's nothing to suggest Irini is in trouble. There are no signs of a struggle, and if she'd called out, I'd have heard her. But my intuition whispers its brand of poison, and I listen.

The ruins are tall and proud and blond in the morning glare. A noise trickles between the rocks and spills into the sunshine. At first I think it's Irini talking to herself, but it soon separates into two distinct voices: Irini's hesitant lilt and another, thicker, harsher, struggling against itself.

Go. Stay. Go. Stay. I do my own internal dance. Then the decision is made for me.

"Come. I know you are there," says the thickened tongue.

I move as if in a dream.

"Closer. I want to see you."

Around a corner. Along the Sacred Way until I see the Polygonal Wall. Then I stop, because there's a rock jutting up from the path and my mind is trying to make some kind of sense out of what it's seeing. Yes, it's a strange, pale rock, but with a human center. Arms and legs spring forth from the boulder's core, hang there like laundry in the sun. These useless limbs are topped by a woman's head, her hair piled high in a loose bun, her eyes keen as if she knows all. A vine creeps up to her middle, spreads itself around her like a thick green belt. She's older than Irini, but their eyes are the same shade of nut brown and their noses hold the same curve.

Jenny lying inert on the sidewalk, a red circle marring her forehead. The hole in my soul widens another inch.

"It is true," she says in hesitant English. "You are carrying a child."

My hands move to cover my belly. "Yes."

"Come here."

"No."

"You don't trust?"

"Almost never. Not now."

She nods. "Why did you come up here?"

"To find Irini."

"And what would you have done had she been in danger? Would you have risked your life and that of your unborn child to save her?"

"My child has been at risk since the beginning."

"Irini tells me you are looking for your husband."

I don't correct her. "Yes."

"You have traveled across the world, all the way from America, to find this man?"

"Yes."

"How many women would do such a thing? If our world was not dead, they would write poetry about you—long, gamboling stories filled with half-truths, all of them predicated on one solid fact: you are a hero."

"Heroes die."

"We all die. Heroes die gloriously, for things bigger than themselves." She glances at Irini. "Water, please."

Irini lifts a bottle to the woman's lips and tips slowly. They've done this before, perfected the art.

"What happened?" I ask. "Can we get you out of there? There have to be tools somewhere near."

Her laugh is more wheeze than mirth. "It is not rock. It is bone."

Shock steals my words. My cheeks pinken with embarrassment.

"I was sick before with a disease that was turning my body to stone, as they say. The tissues, the bones, all of them stiff and fused. But it was slow. Then the disease came and my own skeleton began to consume me." Another wheeze. "My sister became Medusa and I became part of the landscape."

"Why here? Why not stay closer to the shelter?"

"I like the view. It makes me believe I am free."

The whole world has become a house of horrors. Women made of snakes and bone, men with tails, primordial beings

who feed on human flesh. Those of us who survived are cling-
ing to the edge of the soup bowl, trying to find a spoon to ride
to safety.

"I have to keep moving," I tell them. "I have to find Nick if
he's still alive."

"He lives," says the rock woman.

"How—"

Irini bows her head. "My sister has the sight. She knows many
things. She is the sibyl, the oracle of Delphi where there hasn't
been such a thing for centuries."

"Hush, Sister. The gods have been cruel enough. Do not give
them reason to take more from you."

"What more can they take?" she asks simply.

"You still live, do you not?"

"This is not a life," Irini snaps. Immediately she dips her head
in contrition. "I'm sorry. I did not think."

The woman of the rock looks straight at me. "Take her with
you. I implore you."

Irini's head jerks up. "No."

"Go with her."

"I have to stay with you, Sister. Who will feed you, bring you
water?"

"My time is short. You will go with the American, deliver the
child into this broken world. Maybe some good will come of her
birth. Everyone needs a purpose. This is yours."

The screaming wakes me on the third morning. Holding my
belly, I race up to where Irini is standing, her face melted in
horror. My brain processes the scene like an investigator, in
explicit, full-color snapshots. The rock woman's head dangles
at an unnatural angle, her useless limbs hacked off and used

to form the letters *I* and *N* in one single word painted on the ground in scarlet letters.

ABOMINATION.

My mind flips through the searing photographs with gathering speed.

"We have to go. Now."

Irini doesn't argue. With methodical detachment, she gathers her things and stacks them neatly in a sleepover bag. It's high-quality leather, the kind that improves as it is passed down through the generations. Within minutes we're moving on with Esmeralda in tow.

There's a hole in my soul and it's filled with the dead.

"Not a ghost."

"No."

"Who, then?"

I know what she wants: some explanation so she can make sense of her sister's death. But all I have is an improbable story that sounds like a lie. I give her the bones, then the story's meat. My tongue lifts my mind's petticoat and skirts and displays my regret: that I didn't double-, triple-check that the Swiss was dead.

"Why?" she asks.

"Why what?"

"Why you?"

"I don't know."

"You must."

"I don't."

"Then why chase?"

Why do crazy people do anything? Why did I sprint across the world to find one man?

"I don't know."

DATE: THEN

I leave a note in the box, place it outside the front door. When Morris comes, she reads it moving her lips.

"Crackers and Twinkies?"

"Everything else makes me sick," I mouth through the glass door.

She shrugs, scratches her nose. "Okay." She disappears across the street with the box. We've been doing this for a week now: I leave the box out front, she returns with supplies within minutes.

Only, this time the minutes drag by slow enough that I have to run to the ground-floor bathroom twice to throw up. She comes back empty-handed.

"Where's my box?"

"C'mon. Doctor wants to see you."

"I'm in quarantine."

"He doesn't care."

"Fine."

"Fine."

Reluctantly, I open the door, step out onto the sidewalk, maintaining a distance between us. Our boots echo down the hall once we enter the old school. Hers clip along cheerfully while mine drag all my baggage behind them.

Joe is in the infirmary waiting on us, blowing into a latex glove. He holds it to his head and grins. "I'm a rooster. How long has Nick been gone?"

Morris glances at me. "Six weeks."

"Six weeks, two days, six hours. Give or take."

She raises an eyebrow, scratches her nose.

He pulls open a drawer, rifles around, tosses a box to me. I stare unblinking at the packaging.

"When was your last period?"

"I don't remember."

Morris scoffs. "All this stress, who bleeds anymore?"

"Did you use protection?"

My cheeks flush. "Mostly."

"Well, then it mostly worked," Joe says with a brightness that makes my retinas burn.

Although the box is light in my hands, the gravity of the situation elevates it to the weight of a brick. I can't be pregnant. I wanted children, yes, but not like this. Not now.

Joe ties a knot in the glove. "Go pee on the stick."

Morris steers me out of the room. Numb, I allow her to propel me to the bathrooms. I pee on the stick while she paces. Two pink lines slowly form in the white window.

"How many lines?" Morris asks.

"Two."

There's a hoot of laughter.

"I'm glad one of us finds this funny."

"I don't know nuthin' about birthin' babies," she screeches.

Joe grins when we walk in. "Looks like your death sentence has been reduced to life imprisonment." He throws me a bottle. The irony of the rattling container is not lost on me. "Prenatal vitamins."

Like all bad ideas, this one is born in the middle of a sleepless night when my mind has inevitably turned to a channel where I'm a child again. I've flipped through the other pages of my life already tonight: the regrets, the embarrassing moments that still manage to color a grown woman's cheeks; all those choices made and opportunities that languished while I wandered down life's side streets. Then I'm seven, six, five, four, three years old, dragging Feeney, my toy monkey, along behind me in a cherry-red cart. An invisible finger yanks one of my heartstrings and holds it taut until I'm aching to see the monkey again. The sensation of longing evolves in a painful fantasy where I'm holding Nick's hand, watching our child toddling ahead of us with Feeney tucked under his or her arm.

When I wake, my pillow is wet.

At breakfast I tell Morris about Feeney.

"I'm coming with you," she says.

"Huh?"

"You're planning on going back to your folks' place, right?" She knows me too well. "You got me."

"Coffee first. Then we'll rustle up some bicycles."

An hour later, we're peddling through the badlands. Out in the burbs, the grasses grow wild, concealing the curbs, defiantly shooting pollens into the crisp air. They seem to know they'll never see another lawn mower, never have their stems whacked ever again. There are signs everywhere that nature has seized control. Vines race up the brick veneers, competing for the highest gutters. They grab saplings in choke holds and wrestle them for precious sunlight. Our tires roll along parched blacktop that's become cracked and warped enough for green sprouts to poke their heads through. Nature is having her wild way with the land—a party to end all parties.

My mind plays a cruel game, stripping away these new adornments, giving me furtive glimpses of how it used to be. I used to ride these streets when they were cared for by people who had no idea how soon the end was coming. The lawns were once neatly manicured, the flower beds free of weeds, and the houses didn't peel. There's no longer the soft tsk-tsk-tsk of sprinklers accompanying the birds and bugs. Now my old neighborhood is a strange new world where the curtains twitch and things creep. I have my gun. I have bullets. Or rounds. Whatever they call them. I'm not a gun person. All I know—and need to know—is how to load and pull the trigger.

The last time I cruised these streets, I was driving Jenny's car. That was the last time I saw my parents alive. Maybe they still are. Hope fills me like helium and I pedal faster, hoping to get there before some big prick bursts the bubble.

It's like old times almost, me coasting to a stop, throwing my bicycle onto the lawn, but this time I don't run to the front door. Morris stops, butt on the seat, feet on the ground. She lets her bicycle down easy next to mine, draws her weapon.

I came prepared: I have keys.

The smell comes up and backhands me across the face. I stumble backwards into my friend.

"Jesus H. Christ," she says. "You never get used to that smell. You okay?"

I give her a look.

"Didn't think so." Her voice takes on a soft, gentle sheen. "We'll go slow, okay? Where's the monkey?"

I'm holding my nose, trying to not to breathe, trying not to think about how this smell is probably what's left of my parents. Morris pats me on the back.

"I'm okay. He'll be in the attic. They kept all our toys up there in boxes."

The air is stale and the silence deafening. Growing up with electricity, I never appreciated how much noise it made. Everything is the same. The den is neat, although the cabbage rose couch is cultivating a layer of dust. The kitchen is clean, the dishes put away, the sink empty. The beds are made and somehow the bathrooms are mildew-free. Mom cleaned before—

"Up there." I point at the trapdoor in the hall ceiling, its synthetic rope dangling low enough for me to grab. We climb deeper into the gloom. Sun leaks in through the tiny grimy windows. Dust flecks aimlessly ride the beams.

Morris coughs.

My whole childhood is up here, packed in boxes bearing labels in my mother's tidy hand. One side belongs to Jenny, the other to me. Easier to sort that way, Mom used to say, when we had our own children.

My eyes heat up. Tears make threats. So I fake a cough to chase them away.

"I wish I could take everything," I say.

Morris gives me a wry smile. "You'd need a moving truck."

She's right. These boxes are stacked in minor mountains.

"Maybe someday," she says.

"Maybe."

We get to work. I don't linger over old photos. I barely recognize the happy people depicted in the quilted albums. They belong to a time I'm not entirely convinced ever existed. Maybe the past is all a fairy tale we tell ourselves over and over until we believe it's true.

I find Feeney crammed into a box with other old toys and claim him for my child.

On the way out, I use the bathroom. Stare at the trapdoor in the floor.

It's locked.

I wonder which of the neighbors was left standing long enough to slide the bolt home.

Morris sneezes. "Allergies."

It's not allergies. Morris knows it and I know it. But neither of us wants to jump to the right conclusion. We're walking down the hall at the school when she paints the floor in two of three primary colors.

She pulls out her pistol, shoves the end into her mouth, and *bang!* Just like that. Her skull shatters. Brains splash. The wall is Morris-colored on institutional beige. And that damn jingle keeps dancing around my head: How many licks to the center of a Tootsie Pop? Cleanup in aisle five, Dr. Lecter. Don't forget to bring a nice Chianti and those fava beans. And a spoon. You're gonna need a spoon because this is one sloppy mess and a fork isn't going to cut it.

The voices are distant, miles away at the end of a long dark tunnel. But they're getting nearer. Closer. Closer. Closer. Until they're right in my face, shouting at me, trying to pull me away from Tara Morris. That's when I realize I'm kneeling, holding her in my arms, trying to scoop up her brains and shove them back into her head. A rerun of Jenny's murder.

"Don't touch me!" I scream, but their hands keep tugging until I'm forced to let her go. A sob blocks my throat, reducing my voice to an animalistic whimper. "No. No."

Then something inside me snaps into two pieces—maybe my mind compartmentalizing, stowing away the grief and horror in a steel vault until I can gain perspective and cope. Suddenly I'm looking down on the scene, not dispassionately, but through a cool veil. Separate. Other. Not part of this. Not part of this at all.

"Let's clean her up," I say.

Detached.

I stride down the hall in the direction of the broom closet. Bucket-and-mop time. Someone has to clean the Morris mess.

It's me who lights the match that burns my friend. I try to pretend I can't smell her body cook. When she's reduced to the contents of an ashtray in a dive bar on a Saturday night, I let myself into Nick's room and pull his letter from my pocket. The envelope's edges are worn now and the paper brittle from the cold. This room smells like him, like sunshine and citrus still, although there's nothing of his left in here. Not that any of us brought much. A person doesn't need a lot of stuff for survival in a temporary home.

That Nick smell intensifies as I lift my feet off the floor and sink into his bed. I close my eyes and rifle through my memories, searching for the perfect image.

I remember him. I remember us. The things we did. The things we talked of doing back when I had no idea how little time was left for us. A mixture of anger and lust builds inside me. How dare he go without giving me a choice? How could he make that decision for me? I don't want to be here. I don't want to be safe. I can't exist on some fucking pedestal like some precious *thing*. I picture him standing there, listening, riding out the tempest until I'm empty of rage-coated words.

My hand slides down the flat plane of my stomach, down, down between my legs, and I remember everything good until I'm biting my lip to stop from calling out to him.

Sometime between the storm and the calm that comes afterward, I slide Nick's letter back into my pocket, unopened still. And I know that I am leaving.

The librarian would understand: I tell myself that as I tear maps of Europe from her precious atlases. She would understand.

The week whittles away.
Monday creeps. Tuesday crawls. Wednesday stumbles by like a drunk searching for the perfect gutter to piss in. Christmas never took this long to arrive.

On Thursday I hear a familiar rumble. The bus sounds close, but it's still blocks away. Nonetheless, I pull on my boots, grab my backpack, and run, leaving my good-byes to float back over my shoulder. The well wishes fly at my back like arrows. They hit true: right at my heart. It's all I can do not to turn back and look at what's become my family. But I have to go. I have to find Nick, if he's still to be had for the finding.

The morning air takes a crisp bite out of me like I'm a chilled apple. I jiggle to stay warm.

The bus hisses to a stop. The doors whoosh open. Same guy behind the wheel.

"More questions?"

"I need a ride."

He chews on this a moment. "Where to?"

"The airport." I slide the backpack strap off my shoulder, offer him payment: a bag of Reese's Peanut Butter Cups. He snatches them from me, stashes them between his heavy legs.

"Where else?" he mutters.

Shocks whine as we take the first corner. The old school disappears from my view, probably forever. In the round mirror mounted high at the front of the bus, I see the driver peel the foil from the candy. He meets my eyes and something primal creeps across his expression as he chews furtively. *Don't you touch them, don't you dare. Mine.*

I slide my hand into the backpack's front pocket, finger Feeney's soft fabric, and hate that the world has become every man for himself.

TWENTY-ONE

The easiest distance between the two towns is a high-way. The shortest distance is whatever road our feet can make for themselves. My biggest problem with the former is that it's so visible. Our every move is out there for the Swiss to see.

I remember his too-healed wound and wonder if he used this same voodoo to overcome the death I gave him.

The battle rages in my head. Take the high road and hide, or take the highway and risk open warfare?

"You cannot walk the mountain," Irini says. I know she's right. Neither of us is as sure-footed as a goat.

I nod. There's nothing else to say. At least if we're in the open, our enemy is, too.

We are turrets with feet, so tightly are we concealing our respective pain, following Eleanor Roosevelt's advice, doing the things we think we cannot do. I lose myself in thoughts of Nick; he is alive there in perpetuity.

The numbers parade through my head. I divide the total distance into palatable chunks that we can safely chew in a day. One hundred and forty miles. It's nothing compared to the trek across Italy, but the funny thing about the past is the gloss with which it paints itself the further it is removed from the present. Those miles passed seem sweet and easy, walked with a calm and luxurious gait, while these are fraught with tension and peril. Maybe because the Swiss walked with us instead of chasing behind us, when he should be good and dead.

My feelings divide themselves in two teams: one berates me for not waiting until his body cooled on that cot bed. The other gleefully wipes the black smudge from my soul with a ragged sleeve edge. In the middle is my heart which stands up for what it believes: we would be safer with him deep in a hole in Greece's rocky earth.

The sun moves faster than we do, waving as she climbs overhead and sails by. By the time a small arrangement of stones shimmers on the horizon, my shoulders have crisped to bacon. My face stings. Thank whatever deities are listening that I don't possess a mirror. I don't think I could bear myself.

With her naturally olive skin, Irini fares better. Her hues deepen while mine fluoresce. She lifts her arm to point at the distant heap.

"Do you believe in God?"

"Right now, today, I believe if He exists, He's an asshole. If we survive, I reserve the right to change my mind."

Her head tilts so, using crude sign language, I explain. Her mouth attempts a smile, but I can see by the way she presses her fingers to her scars that it hurts. So I change the subject. I don't want this kind woman to feel pain. She's had enough.

"What is that?"

"Is a shrine to *Panagia*. You know her?"

I nod. "We call her the Virgin Mary."

"We will stop. I will pray to her for your child."

"Thank you." My belief system is broken, but hers is not, so perhaps that's enough.

We walk on, our steps making strange sounds on the blacktop. The heavy fall of my boots. The soft shuffle of Irini's rubbersoled espadrilles. Esmeralda's keratin-thick clops. The shrine slowly comes into focus, its blurred edges sharpening until it's crisp and real. Someone has taken care in building this monument, choosing stones carefully, pressing each layer into thick mortar, treating each to a slather of whitewash. Inside the arched hollow, a gilt-rich portrait of the Virgin Mary smiles as though she knows good fortune awaits. I wish I shared her optimism. I wish I did not think her a happy fool. Above her haloed head a brass bell dangles, and higher than that, on the shrine's roof, the white cross is an advertisement to travelers, should they lose sight and forget that Greece's old gods have been shunted into the backseat—at least for appearances' sake.

Irini crosses herself, moves to push the bell, shake it from its slumber, but I stay her. My silent warning feels foolish, because here we are out in the open, advertising our location to anyone with two eyes and decent vision; but for all we know, the ghost of the Swiss isn't the only danger that stalks us. The lazy peal of the shrine's bell could easily alert anything lurking in the hills that border this inland road.

We pray silently, lost in our own heads. I pray for my baby, for Nick, for Irini, for Esmeralda, for everyone I love, and for the dead. I don't pray for myself. When Irini asks why, while we eat crackers dipped in chocolate spread, I tell her that it feels like bad luck to offer that kind of temptation to the universe when it's already having such a laugh at humanity's expense.

Then Esmeralda surges forward, her cereal scattering and popping as her hooves stomp it to powder. She lets out a cry of pain. I leap up, try to soothe her.

Irini stoops, picks something off the ground. "Look."

There in the flat of her palm is a rock, brown with old blood. My head snaps up. One hand shielding my eyes, I scan the hills for a glimpse of our enemy.

Nothing.

Cracks form in my fragile temper until I cast aside my own good counsel.

"Fuck you!" I yell through cupped hands.

Laughter echoes through the hills.

We sleep in shifts, just like Lisa and I did. But unlike that poor dead girl, Irini is meticulous in her efforts. During the day we walk, until one day the scenery changes. The generous foliage bends over the road, concealing us from the sun, dipping us in a pool of cool shadows. My skin temperature plummets immediately. I sigh with the relief. Even Esmeralda perks. Temptation taunts us, urging us to walk faster, but the shade feels so good I want it to stretch on forever.

Just before the bend in the road, there's a sign shoved deep into the earth.

"'Lamia,'" Irini reads. "Half."

I know from the map she means we're halfway to our destination. Halfway to Nick.

"Have you been here before?"

"Yes. On the bus. There is . . ." She mimes eating.

Sure enough, there's a roadside restaurant up ahead, its entire front made up of glass panels, the grounds dotted with picnic tables and umbrellas that were once dyed bold colors. Now, with no one to secure them in bad weather, their tattered and faded fabric flaps freely in the breeze. Tour buses sit abandoned on the roadside, waiting on passengers who will never pay their fare. Their seats beckon to us, issue seductive invitations of comfort and rest.

So we do. There's a ready supply of springwater, restrooms that—thanks to some miraculous feat of engineering—still have flushable toilets.

"Tell me of him," Irini asks when we've settled down in the plush seats.

"Who?"

"Your husband."

"Nick's not my husband."

"Is okay."

I get up, double-check the door is secure, and give thanks that the glass is tinted a gray the sun can scarcely penetrate. Esmeralda is up the front, where she has room to move. I stroke my hand down her back, then let my tired hips sink back into the seats.

"There's nothing much to tell. He left. I followed."

"Why?"

"Because I love him. Have you ever loved a man before?"

"Once. Perhaps."

"Would you have followed him anywhere?"

"Perhaps yes, perhaps no. He was killed."

"I'm sorry."

"It was many years now."

"I'm still sorry."

There's a pause, then: "What will you do if he is dead?"

I think about the possibility, although it leaves me so empty each breathe is a knife wound.

"Mourn him forever."

"What's up here?" I point to the map beyond Lamia.

"More." She indicates the trees and the hills. "Then the water."

We walk on. I wonder where the Swiss is now.

"What will you name her?"

I look at her, surprised. "I don't know."

"You have time. In Greece, babies don't have names until . . ." She draws a cross on her forehead.

"Baptism?"

"Yes. Until then they are named *Baby*."

I try it on. "Baby."

"Does he know, the man?"

"About the baby?"

She nods.

"No."

"What will he do?"

"I don't know," I say honestly, because until now that thought never occurred to me.

"Do not worry."

Too late.

Towns shuffle by. They're ghosts now, dead and purposeless. They served the people, but now the people no longer keep them alive. They're purposeless shacks. Even the trees look tired from living. The heat drinks the life from the land. We stop and look for food, but the perishables have long passed their expiration dates, forming decaying sludge in their containers. Sometimes we find cookies and candies, and after we scoff those hungrily, we add what we can't eat to the stash.

There's salt on the breeze now. There's something else, too: the bright acidity of new pennies or copper piping. I know what it means; I've smelled it before. Irini has, too, but she says nothing.

"I smell blood."

"Yes," she says.

"I'm sorry about your sister. She was wrong, though: you should have stayed. It's not safe with me."

"I need a reason."

"For what?" I ask.

"To exist."

We see a trio of Roma women who do not look us in the eye as we pass each other in the street. Tense and alert, them and us. Their mismatched clothes hang from their bodies like shapeless sheets.

"Excuse me," I say after they've passed. The short one stops, turns, watches me under heavy lids. I hold out a handful of candy bars. She moves away.

They keep walking and so do we.

Irini glances at me.

"It costs nothing to be kind," I say.

There's a chair by the ocean and it's filled by an old man. The rising tide has its lips wrapped around his ankles. He minds not. On his lap is a puppet, the Edgar Bergen kind with a smart mouth and wooden composure. He and his companion turn their heads as one as our footsteps make themselves heard. He waves to us before turning back to the sea. The puppet continues to stare. As we draw abreast, I see the puppet is not made of trees but of flesh and bone and papery skin. Then she looks away and the two continue their tandem deathwatch.

Wind whips the seas into a rabid frenzy. Sheets of hot rain blow off the ocean, drenching us so thoroughly I can barely remember what it is to be dry. Shades of Italy.

Sanctuary appears in the form of a church, small and humble and dry. We bar the doors from inside and listen as they rattle on their ancient hinges. Jesus weeps for us from up high on His cross. Would that He had more to offer than painted tears. From window to brilliant window I move, peering through to the outside. Nothing is visible besides fat drops rolling along the glass. The length of the church passes under my feet several times while I contemplate our safety. Eventually, I abandon my task and do my thinking sitting in one of the few seats. Unlike American churches, the Greek Orthodox church is short on pews. Standing room, mostly.

So normal is discomfort by now that I don't notice I'm wincing until Irini kneels in front of me, her eyes wide and worried.

"Is it the baby?"

"No. I don't think so. It's my back."

"It's the baby."

"It's too soon."

"Yes, once. But now? Who knows?"

"It's not the baby."

It can't be. Not yet.

But in truth, I've lost track of time. Or maybe it lost me.

———————

The storm rants and rages, but we are safe in our wood and stone bubble. Our wet clothes are limp flags hanging over the altar. Like all Orthodox churches, this one has a generous supply of thin candles meant for prayer. They remain unlit. Why leave a porch light on for trouble? Instead, we bury the ends deep in the sea sand holder and offer our prayers in quiet desperation.

The first shift is mine. I use the altar as a seat so I can look Jesus in the eye.

I have a bone to pick with You.

Choose whichever most pleases you. I have many.

Your Father let everyone die.

No. You were all at the mercy of one man's free will.

What about the rest of us? What about our free will to live?

He chose for you all. For selfish reasons, but it was still a choice. My Father could have no more stayed His hand than He could stop Judas from betraying me.

So You're saying it had to be this way.

I'm saying it is *this way. It's what you do now that matters.*

Do You have plans to come back?

Who's left to notice?

I don't really believe in You.

His tears are frozen in paint. *I don't believe in Me, either.*

With my scarred guardian angel keeping watch, I am free to meet Nick. I feel like a teenager sneaking out the bedroom window; the waking hours are my prison while my real life comes in dream snippets.

My fingers draw lazy circles upon his smooth chest. He feels real and warm and not at all drawn by wanton parts of my brain.

"I had a dream," he says, "that you walked across the world to find me."

"Not true."

His dark eyes ask the question.

"I flew in a plane, rode a bicycle, and sailed one of the seas in a boat."

I love you, my fingers trace on his skin.

"I told you to stay."

"I couldn't. You're all I've got left. You and our baby. Morris died, did I tell you?"

He strokes my hair. "She told me."

"You spoke to her?"

"She's here."

"Where? She can't be. I watched her die."

"Nearby."

I wake with a sick feeling in my heart, like something I didn't even know I wanted has been snatched away before I had a chance to love it.

The dream paints my mood with a thick, foul substance that taints the day. To prevent myself from snapping at Irini for no good reason other than that she's available and my temper desires a release, I hunker down in the corner nearest the doors. The ache in my lower back has eased some, now that I'm not constantly pounding pavement.

The rain, the fucking rain, rains on until I'm sick of the sound. No crash of thunder to break the monotony. No ease from downpour to sprinkle. Just relentless rain.

My turn to watch comes and goes and then I sleep again. Nick and I sit across from each other in his old office, the one where I first spoke to him of the jar.

"Pandora's box," he says. "I told you to open it."

"This isn't your fault."

"No. But you being here is." He writes on his notepad. "You shouldn't be here."

"In the dream?"

"Greece. I should have told you. Why haven't you opened my letter?"

"I don't know."

"I'm your therapist, Zoe. Tell me."

"Because I'm scared."

"What scares you?"

"What's inside."

"What do you think is inside?"

"Something that takes away hope. I can't let that happen. I need to hope. I need to have hope."

He stands, pulls his T-shirt over his head, tosses it on the chair. When he reaches out to me, I take his hand and let him pull me close so that my back presses up against his hard planes. His fingers pinch my nipple, hard, so that I wince and moan at the same time. His breath is hot against my ear. It sets my blood to boil.

"I need you to wake up, baby."

"But I want you."

"Baby, wake up. Now."

Invisible fingers drag me from my dream. With a gasp, I go from there to here. Clean, bright light pours through the colored glass, wrapping everything in a rainbow. The rain has stopped.

"Hello, sunshine," I say.

Irini is at the doors, her ear pressed against the seam. The colors dance upon her shiny scars. Her forehead has that telltale crinkle. I go to her side, shucking off what's left of sleep.

"What?" I mouth.

Her eyes meet mine. "Someone is out there."

I'm not surprised. When he would come was my only question.

Irini watches me arm myself. Cleaver. Baker's peel. I'm a homeless ninja hopped up on pregnancy hormones.

"You can't."

"I am." Her lack of understanding doesn't stop me from explaining. "This way I control it. My terms. In the open."

Foolish. Furious. Forced into a corner. Fucking tired of it. All those things are me. I own them as I stomp into the blazing light. For a moment I'm blind and helpless. Slowly the burn fades. My pupils do their job, get real small, while the dot on the horizon swells.

"You're supposed to be dead," I tell him.

"And yet, America, I am here."

"I killed you. I watched you die."

"You watched me hold my breath until you scampered away like a coward. You are a failure in everything."

"Come on, asshole. You and me. Right here."

I must look a sight, ripe and round in the middle, bones jutting through my skin everywhere but there. Even a steady supply of chocolate hasn't fattened this calf. My baby is taking all I can ingest, but that's as it should be. Mothers go without so their children can *have*. Although I haven't read all the right books, I still know that.

The Swiss is as ragged as the rest of us, a scarecrow with an attitude. Not like Nick's confident, relaxed swagger, but more like he made it up one day after inspecting himself in the mirror. *Ah, yes. That's who I want to be.* There's nothing organic about the Swiss. I see that now.

He stares at me with an obscene fascination.

"I can't wait to cut you, neck to navel, America. Slice you open like a melon."

"Like you did to Lisa?"

We circle each other. Perpetual motion.

"No. You I will keep alive. At least long enough so that thing inside you can breathe on its own. Then I'll cut it, too, piece by wretched piece."

"There's something men never quite understand about women."

"What is that?"

"The most dangerous place in the world is between us and the things we love."

"Like shoes and jewelry and shallow pleasures?"

"Like people." My words are shrapnel right in his face. "Stuff doesn't matter. Only people."

"That thing which grows in your womb is not a person. It's an abomination—of God, of medicine, of science."

His words play me like a cheap violin. The notes are there but the melody is off, the tone hollow and thin.

"My child is fine."

"You don't know. Not for certain. Don't you lie awake and wonder, *Am I going to give birth to a monster?* You've seen them out there. We saw them together, did we not? Creatures of mutant flesh and bone, like that creature in Delphi. It was a kindness what I did to her."

"Who the hell are you that you can just walk in and dish out this . . . kindness?"

He reaches behind. Pulls out the gun he stole from the Italian soldier.

I fall to my knees. Hands on my head. See Irini framed in the doorway. She's holding a large can of something. I can't make it out. Run mental inventory searching for a match. Pineapple. I think it's pineapple. I know what she means to do: hit him over the head until his skull mashes to gray-pink pulp. I can't blame her: he killed her sister. But I can't let her do it. Her reach is too short. Too much time for him to shoot. She won't understand, but I have to protect what's mine. And right now she's part of what belongs to me. My world-battered family of refugees.

"Stop."

She doesn't listen. Maybe the English-to-Greek translator fails. Maybe it's just too slow. Or maybe she doesn't care, so much does she want him dead. She rushes. Enough time for the Swiss to turn and backhand her with the pistol. Across her scars. The taut, shiny skin splits, bleeds. She tumbles sideways, slumps to the ground clutching her broken face. Physics is no friend to the losers in battle. Momentum carries them where it will.

He circles around us, the winning dog in this round. Waves the gun at me.

"Get up. Walk."

TWENTY-TWO

The sound of two seething women is silence. Curious, because you'd think we'd be like silver kettles whistling as they reach a rolling boil. Esmeralda glues herself to my side and plods along, slowing when I slow, stopping when I stop—which isn't often enough.

"Keep walking," he says.

"We need water."

A pause. "Okay."

Greece's most precious treasure is never mentioned in the travelogues. Springwater flows from the mountains into faucets dotted over the landscape. They jut from ornate facades of marble and stone. Irini goes first. Then Esmeralda. The Swiss indicates I should fill a bottle for him so I do. Then I drink for my baby and myself. When we're hydrated, we continue the walk.

The Swiss took my map back at the church. The places Irini reads from the signs are different from what they should be. I know this from the furtive glances she gives me as she reels off the names. The sun still rises in the east, sets in the west. We are still going north, but on a coastal road that clings to the sea.

"Why are we taking this road?"

He doesn't answer.

I can guess why. He's worried we'll encounter Nick or maybe Nick and several someone elses on the way. An ambush. I'd told him so little of my plans, nothing beyond the basics, born of my need to withdraw from the world, pull my resources in to survive, focus on my plan. My intentional isolation has had an expected side effect of the pleasant kind: he is uncertain, so he's taking a risk calculated with arbitrary data.

"I thought the Swiss were neutral, not cowards."

"I am no coward, America."

"Tell me something."

"What do you wish to know?"

"Why take us north? Why not back to Athens?"

"I want to go home. To Switzerland."

"So, why are you here? Italy is closer to Switzerland."

"My affairs are not your concern."

"Bullshit. You've made them mine. If you're going to kill me, at least tell me what's going on."

"I have business here."

My raised eyebrows are wasted on him because he's behind me. "There's no business left anywhere."

"You know nothing, America." He reaches forward, nudges Irini's cheek with the gun. "What happened to her face?"

"Fire. A childhood accident."

"It looks new."

"Sunburn," I say.

I keep Irini's secret close and walk.

She gives thanks later when the Swiss stops to piss on a gas station wall. I squeeze her hand, sorry I brought her into this, yet selfishly glad I'm not alone.

Night arrives with all her baggage and none of the melodrama of day. She brings a hostess gift: a small hotel, a plain white vanilla cake hugging the road's curve. Behind a wrought-iron fence, the swimming pool masquerades as a swamp thing filled with rotting leaves and mold. Esmeralda waits as we traipse inside. The Swiss is at the back. Always at the back with the gun.

The dead are inside, sprawled out on once-snowy sheets, their final resting places so far from home—wherever home is. Even the breeze can't carry the smell of this much death out to sea.

"Take a mattress outside," the Swiss barks.

We choose a queen from an empty room. The bed is neatly made and we keep it so until it's in place where he wants it, butted up snug against the iron fence. I wait for him to demand another but he doesn't.

"Is this for us?" I ask.

"Yes."

"What about you?"

"Such comforts are for weaklings and women."

I almost gag on the words. "Thank you."

He laughs cruelly. "You'll need rest. Soon we'll be in Vólos."

What business do you have there, you bastard?

Irini and I share handcuffs and a bed: the Swiss takes no chances. Nick doesn't come to me that night. I'm too far gone, too wrapped up in crisp sheets with my head pressed into the softest pillow I've ever known. I hope he forgives me.

"Are you ladies in trouble?" the Russian asks. He's dressed in swimming trunks and introduces himself as "Me, I am Ivan." For a man in a dead society, he looks well. Healthy. Nourished, but still too lean.

The gun muzzle is hard against my spine.

I smile and hope it doesn't falter. "We're fine. Thank you for asking."

"Where you going?"

"To see family up past Vólos. Do you know it?"

He scratches his head. Glances over his shoulder. "Yes, is that way."

"How—"

My head explodes, eardrum stretches to its thin limits. Ivan doesn't have enough time to register surprise as the slug punches its way through his right eye. He slumps to the ground, perennially helpful and friendly. Forever Russian.

Hands over my ears, I yell at the shooter. "What the fuck is wrong with you? What? He was only trying to help. What's your malfunction?"

The Swiss steps around me, nudges Ivan with his boot.

"Walk."

"Vólos," Irini reads, although the first letter looks like a B. In the middle of the name someone has pitched a crude tent—an A without its supporting bar. There's no hallelujah chorus to herald the city's appearance or our arrival. It juts out above the dusty shimmer, a geometric concrete maze. *Take me as I am or leave me,* it says. *I care not.* Perhaps I'm painting the city with my own subjectivity, slopping gobs of doubt on the boxy apartment buildings with their abandoned balconies. My own fears make the city glower. The empty tavernas lining the promenade scoff as if to say, *People, they think they can endure? They who are so small?* The ships and boats sinking in the harbor are reruns of Piraeus. Here they sit a little lower in the water as though they're exhausted from fighting both gravity and salt. The *Argo* waits on its pillar for Argonauts who will never sail again.

It's a strange thing to claim kinship with objects crafted from steel, but there's a heaviness in my bones that's mirrored in their submission to the sea. Although, in essence, metals are born of the earth and our bodies become earth when we're finished with them, so perhaps there is some common ancestor. Some people are more resilient than others, some metals as pliable as flesh.

So lost am I in my thoughts that I hear the Swiss's words, but they don't register.

"What?"

He prods me with the gun. "I said we are stopping here."

For supplies, I assume, or maybe for respite. "Right here?"

"No. There."

My gaze travels the length of his gun all the way to the wasteland of marine vessels. Amidst the sinking ships and loose slips, some boats prevail. Small wooden fishing boats, mostly, painted cheerful colors like you'd see on a postcard. *Wish you were here. Glad you're not.*

"I don't understand."

He moves so he's standing right in front of us, lifts the weapon, shoots Irini. Blood flows. There's so much. I can't tell where it's coming from, only that she's a gushing fountain of brilliant scarlet. She falls into my arms and I sink to the ground with her, try to find the hole. There it is, buried an inch below her rib cage. It's a tiny thing, I think as I press my hand to the wound. So tiny I can't even shove my finger inside to plug the leak like the little Dutch boy did the dike.

Sounds of things scuttling away from where we are. Still human enough to be scared of the gun. Or animal enough to shy from loud noises.

My jaw is spring-loaded with tension. It's all I can do not to leap up and tear his throat open with my teeth like some crazed animal. But that's what he's done to me: pushed me to the desperate edge as though he wants to measure how much I can lose before my sanity snaps into jagged pieces.

"What more do you want?" It hurts to speak. My teeth ache from the tension. "What else?"

"Your baby."

Hate fills me until I'm radiating pure loathing. It's a wonder it doesn't take corporeal form and slay him.

"So many people caught White Horse. Why couldn't you have been one of them?"

He looks at me. "I did."

Surprise hits me like an automobile. "What did it do to you?"

"Nothing."

"Bullshit. It changes everyone who doesn't die from it. What did it do?"

"It made me stronger. Better. I can hold my breath longer. Heal faster."

If I had it in me, I'd laugh at the delicious irony. "Do you hate your own kind? Is that it? The abomination hates his own."

No more answers. He just curls those steel-cabled fingers around my forearm and pulls until Irini slips away.

"Go," she says.

"Come on," he says to me.

"Why? Why shoot her?"

"Fewer mouths to feed."

"I hate you."

"This is not school. Life is not a popularity contest. Power wins."

He drags me. My boots scrape across the concrete. I sag, make myself deadweight, flail. Anything to inconvenience him. He wants me alive. He needs me alive. That means there's still some luck left to push.

"I'm going to kill you. First chance I get," I say.

"I believe you. But you will not get a chance."

"We'll see."

He slaps me. Hot, angry tears fill my eyes. I don't want them to, but my body has other plans.

"Your friend will be dead soon. Look." He grabs my chin, makes me look at her. She's sitting in a crimson pool. Steam rises from the blood in serpentine curls. I have a crazy thought that if I could press that hot concrete to her wound, it would seal her shut.

"Don't you dare die," I tell her.

The Swiss laughs. "You cannot save anyone. Not England. Not this creature. Not yourself."

"Don't die," I say over and over, all the way up the gangplank onto an abandoned yacht. In a game of rock, paper, scissors, fiberglass beats metal. Man-made outliving earth-made once again.

One half of the handcuffs encircles my wrist, the other snaps around the rail. My captor unloads Esmeralda's cargo and stows it belowdecks.

"Where are we going?"

"I'm going home with my child. To build a new Switzerland."

But not me. He'll cast me overboard the moment I outlive my purpose. I wonder if he means to let me live long enough to be a wet nurse to my own baby?

Irini isn't visible from here, so I twist around until I can see her, ignoring the metal biting into my skin. *I'm with you,* I want to tell her. *I don't want you to die alone. I'm so sorry.*

My face is hot and wet; I can't tell where the sweat ends and the tears begin.

The Swiss leaves, taking Esmeralda with him. She tags along dutifully.

"Don't you hurt her." My lips are dry and cracked and it hurts to speak. The skin splits and bleeds the more animated I become. He says nothing, just keeps on leaving. I know he'll be back, because I have what he wants.

It's just me and Irini now, or maybe it's me and Irini's ghost. Is she still alive? I can't tell. The sun sears my retinas until I'm seeing in dot matrix. I bow my head, try to shield my face from the relentless rays. My sunburn has sunburn. If I'm not careful, I'll wind up with an infection. I almost laugh, because on a scale of one to catastrophe, bacteria rates somewhere in the negatives.

I don't realize I've been asleep until the Swiss's yelling jerks me awake. He's pacing the promenade, waving his gun, ranting in his own tongue. Using my hand as a shield, I start looking for the source of his anger.

Irini. She's gone. All that's left of her is a browning stain. The sun and the thirsty concrete have sucked away the moisture. But there's no evidence of the woman who bled so they could drink. My body shivers as I contemplate what might have happened. Did something drag her away? If so, how close did I come to being consumed in my sleep? Or did she escape? No, not possible: her injury was fatal. There's no way. There's just no way. But a little voice reminds me that the rules of biology are different now. Things exist now that didn't before.

The Swiss slides the gangplank into place. The boat shakes under his footfalls.

"Where is she?" His veins are like engorged worms under his pink skin.

"I don't know."

"Don't lie to me."

"I didn't see anything."

"How could you not? Were you not right here?" He jabs the air with his finger.

"I . . . was . . . asleep."

"Stupid bitch."

The boat shakes and heaves again. He returns dragging a bulging tarp. This he stashes down below with the other supplies.

"I'm going to find her," he says. "If she is not dead already, I am going to kill her properly."

TWENTY-THREE

He returns near sunset with more things. Baby things. Clothes and diapers and cream to prevent tiny cheeks from chafing. Things I haven't had time to think about because I was so focused on surviving.

He holds up a dress, yellow, sprinkled with white flowers. "What do you think?"

The words stick to the walls of my throat. All I can do is look away.

He brings food. Cold meat from cans, a combination of pigs' lips and assholes and whatever other remnants were lying around the processing plant. Cold vegetables, also from cans, with labels I can't read. Depicted on these slips of sticky paper are families smiling so cheerfully, they can't be real. Who smiles like that? Nobody I've known in this new life. I slurp down the juice after I'm done chewing the chunks. For dessert he has tiny chocolate cakes wrapped in plastic. I eat these greedily, licking the plastic clean when I'm done. I'm a shameless and wanton eater. I don't care what he thinks of my manners. When all that's left is the taste of chocolate in my mouth, I ask about Irini.

"Did you find her?"

"No."

"Good."

"She was probably eaten by animals. Or worse."

"Or she escaped."

"Unlikely. Not with a wound such as that," he says. "How is my baby?"

"My baby is fine."

"May I?" He holds out his hand as if to touch me. Suddenly polite.

"Touch us and I'll cut you." Cold. Calm. Truthful.

He laughs like I'm kidding.

"I thought for certain your womb was empty, like that stupid girl's."

"When are we leaving?"

"Soon," he says.

"What are you waiting for?"

"My baby."

I won't let him take my baby. I won't. Never. I'd die first, and that's what he wants. A plan. I need a plan. I have to get away now before it's too late and I'm dead and my child is his.

Where are you, Nick? Why won't you come and save us, you bastard? I came this far for you. Just come the rest of the way for us. Please.

The thought is unfair but I can't control it; Nick has no way of knowing we're here. The thing bobs around in my head like a speech balloon in a comic. It's not supposed to be this way—for any of us. But as people used to say in the old days, when there were enough of us to create and perpetuate slang: It is what it is. And that's what I have to work with.

He leaves just after dawn. Gone again to get things for a child that isn't his. This time he cuffs me to the single leg that holds up a tabletop in this tiny room below the deck. He empties my backpack onto the carpet, picking out anything I might use as a weapon. Good-bye, nail clippers, tweezers, and an old dress-maker's pin that's been rusting in a side pocket for maybe ten years. He locks the cabin's door. I know he's worried Irini isn't dead, despite his protests and his faux certainty. Nothing is certain anymore—not even tomorrow. I wouldn't even put money on the sun setting this evening.

I'm on the floor of a boat surrounded by everything I have in this world: old clothes, maps, and Nick's letter. What can I do?

The carpet peels away easily enough. I don't pull up much, just enough to figure out how the table's attached to the floor. Bolts. They're on as tight as tight can be.

What do I have? A big fat nothing.

Pain cuts across my back. I change positions, lie back, breathe deep. Junior rolls with me. I stare up at the underside of the table. It's crafted from cheap fiberboard that flakes when I scrape my fingernail over it. There's a lot number scrawled on there. Or maybe some secret code meant for someone long dead.

When I see it, I wonder how I didn't see it sooner. Whether it's pregnancy or malnutrition or exhaustion, my mind isn't as sharp as it once was. But I do see it now, I do, and hope unfurls her tiny wings. The tabletop is held in place by four shiny silver screws that run through a T-shaped bracket. Hope goes through its rapid life cycle, dies as quickly as it was born. There's no way the cuffs will fit over the bracket. It and the table leg are one solid piece.

I am doomed. The Swiss will take my child.

Why don't you come for us, Nick?

Now is all the time I have left. I can't die without reading Nick's letter.

I dreamed of the letter last night.

Again?

I nod.

The exact same letter?

Always the same.

Describe it for me, Zoe.

It's just paper. Dirty. Tattered edges.

How does it make you feel?

Terrified. And curious.

It's the jar all over again. I have no hammer so my fingers unwrap my fears.

> Baby,
>   I have to go. It's killing me to have to leave you when
> I've only just found you. It's more than my family: it's
> me. I'm sick. It feels like White Horse. I won't put you
> at risk. I love you, you know. I hope you feel the same
> way and I hope you don't. That would be easier. I'm
> going to Greece to find my family—or at least I'll go
> in that direction and see where it takes me. Live on.
> Please.
>   I love you more than anything in this world.
> Nick

Bang. Out of nowhere a train comes and knocks my heart and soul right out of my body, leaving a crater where *me* used to be. There's no way—Nick can't be dead.

No.

No.

I don't believe it. I can't believe it. I *won't* believe it.

There's not enough heart left in me to conjure up a tear storm. I'm an empty space on the verge of collapsing in on itself like some dead star. I'm a black hole.

Cold. Calm. A vacuum.

I fold the things the Swiss scattered on the floor and fit them neatly into my backpack. Nesting. When that chore's done, I sprawl out on the floor to relieve the ache in my back. The cabinets start to look interesting. I can reach them with my feet. If I slip off my boot, I can use my toes to flip the latches that keep the doors in place while sailing rocky seas, so that's what I do. The lower cabinets are stuffed with cans of baby formula and water in plastic bottles. My gaze snags on something I've seen before, although not in months.

Nick can't be gone. I won't let him. If I do these things, then he isn't really gone. I can hold death at bay by *doing*.

The pain in my back increases as I stretch further, reaching for that holy grail, the mystery of mysteries: a rectangular box made of metal and painted a slick black. The Swiss has carried it with him all this way. And now my curiosity is eating me alive. My toes dip under the handle. White-hot lightning shoots up my thigh. Cramp. I relax the position, wait for the pain to die, then slowly ease the box out of the cabinet until I can reach it with my hand. There's no lock. Just a silver latch. Strange that he'd be so cavalier about something that clearly holds meaning. It springs apart, almost promiscuous in its ardent action, as though it's been waiting for this moment and wants me to look inside. The box's wanting doesn't save me from the guilt. I don't like to snoop, but I make an exception for the Swiss. He'd afford me the same courtesy, after all.

The metal box is filled with photographs. Fading Polaroids, yellowing pictures with curling edges depicting people in fashions that might have swung back into favor again someday. The subjects differ, but they're all blond, Nordic, lean and fit people. The Swiss's family, I imagine, for who else could they be?

My fingers pick through the leaves of his family tree. It's the strangest thing: all of these photographs, and he's not in a single frame.

It made me better. Stronger.

Faster and faster, I flick through the pictures, searching for clues. What did White Horse do to him? How did he change? Then I'm looking at a grainy photograph from some newspaper or another and my face falls slack like somebody sucked out all the bones. I try to fit the pieces together in some way that makes sense in some universe where everything isn't wrong.

George P. Pope and a cool, sleek blonde woman. He's grinning at the camera, pompous and proud—even in freeze-frame—while she looks like she'd rather be anywhere but there. Oh, she's smiling, but it hurts. I know that face. I've seen it in the last hundred or so photographs. I've seen it in a lab. In an elevator. The pained expression is a repeat, too. Her brother wears it. Or maybe he's a cousin or a young uncle, but I'm betting he's a brother—otherwise, why carry all these memories across the world?

I want photos. I want my memories in print. I want Nick and our child and the children we haven't had a chance to make yet, and I want to be able to look back at pictures and laugh at the things we did. But that future is gone, snatched away by that egomaniacal prick in the photograph and that bastard who's coiled in the grass, a snake waiting to take the only thing I have left of the man I love.

I can't cry. The pain is so fresh, it's still steaming. All I can do is sit here like a soulless puppet and rip these photographs to shreds. Ruin them like the world is ruined. Steal the Swiss's memories like he's stealing mine.

And suddenly, even though my face is dry, I'm sitting in a lake my own body has created. I know what it means: my baby is coming.

Hard and fast, labor comes. Too fast, maybe. I can't gauge. I'm choking on sweat and tears, panting, try to get air and some relief from the pain. But with every sweet, sweet breath my body tears another inch.

Stay inside a little longer, I think.

But I'm ready.

It's not safe out here.

I want to see the world.

Oh, baby, there's no world left to see. Only death.

What's death?

I pray you never know.

I came for nothing. For a dead man. To deliver my child alone in a boat.

My daughter arrives in my darkest moment. We cry in tandem.

In the middle of my delirium, Nick comes.

She's perfect, he says.

Her tiny hand curls around my finger. All her pieces are where they belong. Nothing missing. No extras.

Not an abomination? I ask of him.

No. She's beautiful like her mother.

I look like hell.

He laughs. *Women. You carried our child; you've never been more beautiful to me.*

Are you sure she's perfect?

Yes.

He wants to take her.

You won't let him. I know you.

But I'm tired. So tired. Can I sleep now?

Not yet, baby. Soon.

I read your letter. I love you, too, you know.

This would all be easier if you didn't.

There's no such thing as easy anymore.

A kiss pressed on her forehead and on mine. His lips are warm. How can imaginary lips be warm?

This is love, he says. *This is all love should be.*

Ether. That's what woo-woo people call it. Nick fades from sight, and maybe he goes into that ether or maybe my brain's just flipped a gear, switching me back to sanity. Doesn't matter. Nick is gone and the Swiss is back and he's filling up the space that used to hold a locked door. Now I don't know which is worse, because he's looking at my baby—*my* baby—with a covetous expression on his hard-planed face. *Thou shalt not covet.* I want to kill him where he stands.

He inches toward me. Us.

"Give me my baby," he croons.

Visceral loathing. Hot, bubbling, seething. I'm a lioness primed to tear the pulse from his throat if he dares to touch what's mine.

"What the fuck are you?"

"Please be calm. You're crazy."

"Because you're trying to steal my baby," I spit.

"*My* baby."

Now he notices that something is different. I've redecorated while he was busy hunting and gathering. The things he held dear to him were used as confetti and ticker tape in my rage parade. His gaze travels from piece to piece to the empty box to the newspaper clipping I purposely placed just so on the small table.

"What did you do?"

"Why didn't you tell me you're related to George Pope's wife?"

"Those . . . are . . . my . . . things. What gives you the right?"

"What gives you the right to hold me hostage and steal my baby? What gave you the right to use Lisa like some sexual spittoon, to cut her open and murder her? She was just a girl. And the soldier. And the Russian. And Irini. Who died and made you God?"

"I *am* God!" he screams. "I am the only God you will ever know."

I'm too tired for this fight. "I don't believe in God anymore. Why should I?"

My baby lets out a thin cry. Poor girl. Just born and already she's in the middle of a primitive custody battle. But this one will be different. This one will be to the death.

"Just let us go," I say. Quiet. Calm. Alpha female protecting what's hers.

He crouches beside us. Holds out his hands. I recoil as much as the handcuffs will allow, but it's not nearly enough.

"Give me my baby."

"Why? I don't understand why you even care. Why us?"

His laugh chills me. "I want your child because it's born of two parents with immunity to the disease. Your child will survive untouched."

The puzzle pieces shift and turn. "You're looking for a cure."

"Don't be stupid: there is no cure." He bites each word, spits it in my face. "The dead are gone and they will stay that way. I engineered the disease to endure. I made it. I. Not George. I designed the changes so they would last. Nobody could guess which chromosomes would evolve and turn the host into something completely new. We are all of us abominations. We should be dead."

I want to beat him, pound him with my fists, but what strength I have left is all in my mind.

"You and Pope. You did this to all of us."

"You don't know anything, America. You are a stupid woman. You cleaned floors and the shit from mouse cages. I am a scientist. A doctor. I want a child. Me, who will never have my own. Me, who gave up my womanhood to the disease. I became a man *against my will*. George took everything from me. My work. My chance for children. He owes me this!"

The laughter explodes from my mouth, fire and ice in the same breath. Pain slices through me but I don't care. If this whole thing wasn't a tragedy, I'd wager I was in a soap opera. The mustache-twirling villain is a real girl. The Blue Fairy was a trickster.

"You're the woman in the photographs?"

It all makes sense now, what Lisa said about the Swiss not being like other men, his constant misogyny, the overtly masculine movements that often seemed rehearsed in front of a cheval mirror. Somehow the genetic lottery machine dug around in the barrel until it pulled out an X chromosome and gnawed off one of its legs.

"I was before I became sick. I was George Preston Pope's wife for fifteen years! He was a cold, cruel man, something I never fully comprehended until he made me sick against my will. We needed to test on humans, so he injected me. Not himself—me. I knew then he cared nothing for me—only business, money, his reputation as a great man. He owes me a child."

I laugh like this is the best joke ever told. Stand-up comedians would have killed for this kind of comedy black gold. I throw Nick's letter in his face like it's a brick. "Read it."

"Do not laugh at me. Give me my baby."

"Read it!" I scream, until my lungs ache from the word rush. "Read the letter."

He scans the page. A transformation happens. A devolution of rock to sagging flesh. A hopeless body sublimating. He sits for a time amidst the wreckage of his past and future.

"I do not understand."

Who's a stupid woman now? I want to say, but can't. I'm still human, still a person. I still have compassion, however misguided. No matter what happens, my humanity stands. Even if I don't live through the night. Kill him? Oh yes, I can, but I can't mock him—*her*—for what he's become.

"Nick died. He got sick with your disease and he died. So you see, she could still get White Horse, could still get sick, die, or turn into some awful thing. As you keep saying: an abomination."

"No." Disbelieving.

"Yes."

"No. This cannot be."

"It is."

Nothing.

"And now we both have to deal with it. You made this bed, you and your husband. Now we all have to sleep in it. Even you."

"Shut up," he says. "Listen."

But I've already heard it. Something approaches. Night has come while we were busy fighting, and along with it those that dwell in the city's secret places.

TWENTY-FOUR

Not the screaming. No. The vociferous noises of angry humans shoo away weak things. Yell, and a creature that believes itself to be weaker—either by size, constitution, or pecking order—will scurry away lest the brunt be turned on it. Even in concrete jungles, such laws of nature persist. It's why they haven't come sooner. They've been crouched behind doors and dumpsters, evaluating our weaknesses, trying to determine which rung on the evolutionary ladder we occupy.

The dynamic only changes when variables alter: when there are more of them than there are of us; when they believe we're wounded or weakened; when we have something that will ensure their survival.

No, two adults yelling has not awakened the shadow things and brought them here; it's the crying of my newborn.

"Silence the child." He locks the cabin door. Peers into the darkness. A scared thing. Now I see for myself what my mind glossed over before. All those weeks, I looked without seeing.

So plain to me now, the slightly feminine movements that are nigh on impossible to erase: a hip tilt; a hair tuck; the telltale sway in an unguarded moment.

I hold my girl to me, jiggle her in a way I hope is comforting, but she's only warming up for her debut performance. Even my breast cannot divert her from her song.

"I said silence."

"You'd make a lousy mother."

"Look at yourself. Are you a paragon of motherhood? You are handcuffed to a table after chasing a dead man across the world like some common slut. If he had wanted you, he would have brought you with him to care for him as he died."

The vicious retort is there, balanced on my tongue, just behind my teeth. One small flick is all it needs to nail its target. Shred him with my words. But one word stays my tongue.

"Zoe?"

The voice comes filtered through a door, but still I know it and my heart races.

"Irini?" I yell.

The Swiss explodes like a flare in the night. "Shut up. Shut up, you idiot."

"I told you she was alive."

"You know nothing. Look," he says. "She has betrayed you to her kind. Monsters uniting with other monsters."

"I don't believe it."

"You should see her, America, standing on the dock with the others. She means to kill us, and perhaps your child."

Your child. A shift. He no longer wants her now that he knows one of her parents is dead from the virus he created for Pope in Pope Pharmaceuticals' labs. What a fickle bastard. But that bothers me. It really does. Because now she's as useless to him as I am, which means my daughter's life is worth as much as a foam cup.

"How can I look if I'm cuffed to the floor?"

A dance ensues. Two choices wrestling for the lead. He wants to gloat, he wants to keep me subjugated, and the two are mutually exclusive in this time and place. His ego seizes control. My restraint falls to the floor. I am free as I can be while still imprisoned.

On gelatin legs, I amble to the door. See Irini for myself, her skin glowing under the moon's caress.

The Swiss is right: she is not alone. They swarm the dock's end. People who are not people. And yet, under this moon, they appear real and whole. I can't discern what is still human and what is other. Irini stands on the gangplank, apart from the others. It is from there that she calls to me while my daughter wails on. It is there the moonlight stops to admire itself in the blade she holds.

"Is a girl?" she calls out.

"Do not speak," the Swiss says.

But I do not take orders from him. "Yes."

"Is she well?"

"Yes."

"Come. I want to see you."

The Swiss's hand is an iron band around my arm. "You cannot go."

I stare him down in the dark. "How many rounds do you have left? One? Two? Enough for me and them? Or are you saving the last one for yourself?"

He reaches for my child.

"Touch her and you will die."

Then I step through the door. I choose the lesser of the evils.

———————

The gangplank bows and flexes under the weight of my broken heart. Bodies shift and shuffle to let us come ashore. What they are isn't clear in this light. They look like me, world-burned and weary. Maybe they *are* me, but with tongues that speak another language.

"Who are they?"

"People," Irini says.

"Are we safe?"

"Yes."

"You're still alive."

"Yes."

"How?"

"Maybe not only my face is changed. Maybe inside, too."

Irini lifts my child from my arms, cradles that fragile skull in her sunburned palm. Too close to the knife's fine edge.

"Please."

"I will not hurt her." She smiles down at that sweet, new face. "We want people to go on." Then she turns that smile on me. "We come for you. To save you. I prayed we were not late."

They surround us then, peer at my child, and she falls silent, done with her song.

"It's like they've never seen a baby before," I say.

One by one, they dry-spit on my child.

"To ward away the Evil Eye," Irini says. This comforts me, knowing they are all still human enough to cling to their superstitions.

"They will never have their own," the Swiss says from his fiberglass perch. "No abomination can breed."

I turn, stare at him, barely able to contain my disgust. "Is there anything you didn't take from them?"

"The disease stole from me, too."

"There's no excuse for the hurts you've caused," I say.

My rescuers move away now, a human tide peeling itself from the rocks. And when they return, they bring the Swiss with them and hold him fast.

He looks to me for help. "Will you let them take me?"

I shake my head. "I don't have any mercy left to give. You've used it all up." Gently, I take the knife from Irini's hand. "My hands are already stained with blood," I tell her.

A piece of my soul flakes away as the knife moves in an elegant arc. I wrap it in silk, encase it in an ice block, and stow it in a lead-lined trunk. Someday—if there are days left that belong to me—I may pick the lock and set that fragment in the sun to thaw. *Ah,* I will say when I look upon it again. I remember now. *I remember who I used to be. Just a girl with simple dreams and a crush on her therapist.*

How does it make you feel? Nick says from the past.

Terrified.

The blade skims the surface of his man-made Adam's apple, draws a thin red line upon the skin, a half inch above the scar I already made, allows gravity to pull it down into a neutral position at my side.

"You can't do it," he gloats.

"I *won't* do it," I say. "There's a difference. You poor bitch."

I reach out to Irini, the snake woman of Delphi, and take my daughter from her arms. Then we turn and go and leave the Swiss at the mercy of his own creations. He owes them.

My heart is still tender enough that I flinch at the sound of his screams.

I am still human, with all the frailties and strengths of my kind.

We walk in the half-light of a benevolent moon. North again. Always north, we four. We've taken what we can from the boat: things for us and Baby. Esmeralda hauls them without complaint. There's barely enough energy in my body to carry my daughter and myself.

"Why?"

"Forward is the only way. One foot in front of the other."

"We could go back to Delphi."

"Just a little further," I tell her. "Nick wanted to know if his parents were safe. Now"—my tongue thickens—"I have to do that for him. You're free to go wherever you choose, my friend."

She holds her head high now. Proud. As she should be.

"We are more. Family."

I wonder how a fractured heart, with all its ragged holes, can still hold so much love.

We stop so I can bathe in the ocean and drag dry, clean clothes over my purified skin. Then we move on.

Onwards. Past the gray stone church with its misspelled English graffiti. Alongside a gulf filled with diamonds. We move slowly, but that's okay, the bomb no longer ticks with the same urgency. The Swiss is dead—Nick, too—and my daughter is here.

Dawn comes. Morning slides into noon.

Greece is made of roads that curve and hug the landscape like a favorite pair of jeans. We skim her hip and find a cement factory hulking over the water. On the mountain behind the abandoned facility, terraces are tribal scars cut into the land by men with dynamite and hard hats. In the water, rust buckets with Cyrillic letters painted on the side await cargo that will never come. There are bones on the low-slung decks, sucked clean of the bodies that once held them. Cement dust clouds, stirred by a fledgling ocean breeze, smell of freshly poured pavement. I double-check that Baby's head is protected from both sun and smut.

Beneath the red, Irini's skin is pallid. When I touch her forehead, she smiles.

"I am okay. You?"

I don't believe her. She's dry when she should be steeped in sweat.

"Fine."

A falsehood. We both know it but we're too proud to admit to our lies lest we seem weak—not for ourselves but for each other. I'm losing blood and so is she. Only my baby has skin still pink and new and alive.

We don't speak as we walk. Conversation comes when we're resting. When we've cleared the cement factory, we break again under the protective cover of an olive tree. Its fruit is green and thick like a man's thumb, but the crop will rot without someone to pick the bounty at harvest time. We sip water from bottles refilled from a roadside faucet. Candy bars for the sugar rush that comes slower and slower each time. Baby pulls what she needs from my breasts faster than my body can replenish the source, so I stir formula on the side of the road to satisfy her. She's a good girl. Quiet. Alert. The road is all she knows, so the vibration from my footsteps must soothe her soul in ways it will never comfort me. I yearn for a home that's mine, on a piece of land that never shifts, in a place not teeming with death.

"What happened?" I ask Irini when we've filled our shrunken stomachs.

"I do not know. I . . . was dying. Then not."

"And in between?"

"The gods came for me and made me whole."

"You're still bleeding."

"Whole . . . a little . . . to help you and the baby."

Just enough. How do you thank someone who turns away from death to come back for you?

TWENTY-FIVE

The first sign of life is no sign of life: abandoned cars and motorcycles, rusted and rotting along the winding road. Conspicuously absent are corpses, which have become the most prevalent form of litter in urban streets. Bones and half-eaten carcasses are as omnipresent as burger wrappers and beer cans—but not here.

Irini shades her eyes, smiles as she delivers the news. "Agria. This is the place."

My everything sags with relief and I slump against a BMW with a chronic case of rust acne. We're here. We're really here. Some magical *how* happened and we are here.

"This is your ancestral home, baby girl." My daughter's hair is soft against my lips. She makes a small sucking noise. Then the fear comes for me, rolling, rolling on wooden wheels, a chariot carrying its terrible driver, his bullwhip held aloft waiting to strike me down.

"I can't do it."

"You must."

"What if they're dead?"

"Then they are dead and you have lost nothing."

"Just more hope."

"Hope is what you hold in your arms."

The truth of her words can't hold the gathering storm at bay. I sink my teeth into my lip, clamp the delicate flesh tightly until the physical pain reduces the emotional to a dull ache. I nod. This is reality. Nick was a beautiful, magnificent fantasy, but now he's dead and soon I might be, too. I look at my girl and I know in that instant that, if not for her, I would be fine knowing that today was the last day, the end cap of my life. I wish I was home. I wish I was in that place before all *this*. I choke on a sob, because I'm longing for something so dead, so cold, so gone, that I might as well wish for a rocket ship to Mars.

It takes a cluster of clanging bells to pull me from own head. I look to Irini in case it's a sign I've lost my mind and I'm doomed to spend all my days as a tragic hunchback in a bell tower that doesn't exist on any earthly plane.

"Goats," she says. "Sheep, maybe."

Bo Peep – less goats. They bleed between the cars and motor-cycles from someplace beyond the crook in the road, swarm around us, inspecting our belongings with slitted yellow gazes. Then, just as quickly, they mosey on down the cracked street in search of green pastures. Their dull bells jangle and fade into the past.

Each new step depletes me further. I see it in Irini, too. She's my mirror, and in her I watch myself wilt and weaken and drain myself dry. If this was a video game, we'd be out of extra lives.

"I can do this," I say. "I have to. Sit. If there's help, I'll send it."

"No. Together."

I take her hand in mine and we walk. The strangers are come to town.

Around the corner is a village that resembles the last, and the one before that, and all the others before those. This place is not unique. Tavernas line the streets. Fishing line still hangs outside so fishermen can display the day's catch. The gulf laps at the shore like a thirsty cat. Two chairs sit by the shore, between them a small table and two glasses filled with brown liquid and foam. Two people stand in the middle of the road, intent on a conversation. A man and woman dressed in Bermudas and tanks.

A vacation snapshot. The end of the world is someplace else.

Irini and I limp into the picture. We two bums and our donkey spoil the perfect scene with our broken bodies. Irini's stomach blooms with its carmine stain. She needs help, and soon.

I stand there in the same middle of the same street. "Hello?"

They turn. Echo. "Hello?"

Americans.

The woman is built like a good armchair: soft, sturdy, her skin sun-worn to a rich nut brown. Her companion is tall and lean, with eyes I've seen in another man's face.

"You're Nick's parents," I say. And then I cry.

They stare at me, at each other, at me again. The man speaks.

"The world's gone mad. We quit asking questions a long time ago, just accepted the strangeness as much as we could to survive. But now I have to ask: How the hell do you know our son?"

The woman slaps him, gentle, mocking, only a minor punishment for his lack of etiquette. A whole conversation in the space of a heartbeat the way only couples who are tightly cleaved can communicate.

"Don't you know?" she says. "It's Nick's Zoe. Who else could she be?" She looks to me for confirmation. "You are, aren't you?"

All the words I prepared have poured back into the soup of unspoken thoughts, broken down and formless once more. Nod; that's all I can do.

She comes to me, touches my face with a palm callused and cracked, and yet the touch is tender: a mother's touch.

"I miss my mom," I say.

"You always will." Her gaze falls. "Who is this?" Rises.

"Nick's daughter."

"Oh my God. What have you brought us?" Then she holds us both in her comfortable arms. Her husband comes next.

"I don't believe it," he says. "How can this be? How did you find us?" But he's crying, too, so I know he believes, even if his mouth can't yet form the words.

I look to Irini. Her scars are bathed in tears.

"You brought hope," she says.

But I didn't. The message I carry is a mixed blessing. I know how this will go. I am the messenger, the one who bears news both good and bad: *Here is your grandchild, but your son is dead.* Then the struggle will begin inside them: Should they love me for holding hope in one outstretched, sunburned palm, or hate me for performing the bait and switch of an inexpert con man? *Have this child, for yours is dead.*

"Nick." I swallow; his name hurts.

Miracles are tiny things, meaningless except to the person who seeks one. To that one person, a miracle is everything. One

happy event can change the course of a life. In the blackest
moments, they hide.

Wait . . .

Wait . . .

Ignoring prayers and pleading, miracles enjoy the element
of surprise. They love those who would step forward and meet
them halfway.

Nick's father moves slowly, a boulder being rolled aside. And
there it is: my miracle. My white knight does not ride a steed,
nor does he hide behind armor gleaming from the goodness of
his deeds and a polishing rag. He does not need those things.
He comes instead in shorts and a baseball cap pulled low over
his eyes, bare-chested and barefoot, a fishing rod in his hands
instead of a sword. Just Nick.

"Zoe!" he yells. And then we are one again. Me, Nick, and
our daughter.

This is my miracle. It is small to everyone but me.

Irini leaves us that night, slipping out alongside the sun. The
men bury her while I sob quietly for the woman who saved our
lives.

We name our daughter for her, Nick and I. Irini. Peace. As
the ground claims her for its own, I pray the snake woman of
Delphi has found her peace as I have found the beginnings of
mine. I thank her—for all days.

And when I lay my head upon his chest on those hot summer
nights, I try not to notice Nick's beating hearts.

Red Horse

by

Alex Adams

One City considers you part of the family.

PROLOGUE

The natives are restless, so they are killed, leaving behind a bloody calm. We watch from our boats as our saviors secure a disease-free future. Our morality is conditional. We bend it like plastic until it meets our needs.

There are no white horses here. There are no horses at all. We left them behind the wall with the rest of the animals. No more man's best friend—we're our own best friends now.

Safe, we go viral. Take over their buildings, their houses, their sea air. Take over their lives. In no time, we're walking over the bones of their civilization. Then we choose to forget. That way we don't have to ask . . . .

ONE

I t's winter in here, yet sweat floods my guest's pores. I pass him tissues, watch him wipe until his skin is a snow storm.

"I can't do this, Emma."

"Yes, you can. It won't hurt a bit, I promise. It's not like you haven't done an interview before."

Ben Stone smiles, but the edges are soggy. "That was different. I was relevant, then. Now I'm just some regular schmuck, hiding on an island."

So do what I do, I want to say. *Pretend you're playing the part of you.*

We're in a sealed glass box, wrapped inside a larger building that's seen other, better, truer days. Now the world crumbles around us, and we avert our gazes and hold our hands still in our laps, because we're the lucky ones: alive, unaffected by the disease we named white horse. We constantly maintain, but never improve the lot that has become our life.

I throw him a reassuring smile. Usually it comes back to me like a boomerang, but Ben pockets it and throws back a spring-loaded frown.

"Just be yourself," I say, as though any of us are our true and real selves.

Ben hooks a finger in his collar, tugs. "Right. Be myself." Now the smile comes. "I'll be myself. That's what I'm here for."

A bell rings. It's coming from inside my head—and out. There's more to his worry than stage fright, I feel it, but it's too late to try and pull answers from his mouth; the red light above the door is flashing, counting down the seconds until The Emma Frane Show goes live.

For all his worrying, Ben is a superb dance partner. We move easily through my script; I make my statements and he fills the lines with shade and light until a picture of him emerges. How real it is doesn't matter—good radio is what counts. The Emma Frane Show isn't about answers, it's about entertainment.

I relax—I do—as he weaves his rags to riches, to slightly better rags tale. The arid years of waiting tables, where the tips were larger than the opportunities, and the tips were little more than pennies. Those pennies multiplied into platinum credit cards and gold bathroom fixtures when chance sat at his table, saw something it liked, saw something from which it could profit. And profit it did, until people started getting sick. First in the United States, then across the globe.

"I loved your movies," I say truthfully. "The perfect popcorn flicks."

"Popcorn. And Coke . . ." His voice fades with longing. "I remember Coke. That first swallow made me gasp, every time."

"That fizz."

A sweat bead rolls down his cheek. "Yeah. The fizz." He leans forward then, past the microphone, looks at me like the rest of

City One doesn't have their dial set to 89.5 FM. "We should be fighting this. We wanted safety, but we've screwed up. City One is a prison sentence, not salvation."

My tongue is peanut butter, stuck to my mouth's roof. I don't know what to say. His words are an unwelcome mirror; in them I see my own private thoughts—the ones I don't dare share or I'll be killed.

Ben isn't finished. He pulls the mic to his mouth. "I'm doing this for the freedom of City One's citizens. You have a voice, too, so what are you going to do for our people, Emma Frane?"

For a moment I consider his words, until the question mark sinks in.

"No." A whisper. Then louder: "Stop."

He gives me a sad sort of smile. "What are you going to do, Emma Frane?"

My body doesn't know what to do first. It throws me across the desk, snatches the microphone from his mouth, while my other hand slaps at the buttons to kill the transmission. Anything to stop Ben Stone from committing suicide.

But it's too late: Ben's already falling forward, the microchip in his body responding to his question with its final answer.

I've witnessed this kind of death before, watched a man cook from the inside out, lost my everything.

We knew the risks, but we scratched our signatures on that dotted line, anyway.

Breathe deep, Emma. Don't think *about that smell.*

I wobble towards the break room on ankles that would betray me if my head showed the slightest sign of fixating on Ben Stone's burning skin. I want to let my joints collapse, allow my knees to fold at the seams until I'm on my hands and knees, digging a hole to hide in. But I will not show weakness. I've stomached worse and held myself together with bits of tape and glue until I could unleash my grief in private. Here is not where I will lose control.

People are looking at me as I navigate the hall—my people. Anger stains my cheeks with fire. He used me. That I can tolerate, I've been used before, but *they* didn't deserve this. The name on the show is mine, and I would use it to shield them all.

"It's going to be okay," I reassure them. "I'll take care of this." If they can see I'm at ease, then perhaps they will be, too. They're decent people; I hate that Ben used my turf to deliver his message, regardless of his noble intentions.

It's me who calls for help, throws a blanket over what's left of the once-famous Ben Stone, sends everyone home so they can begin to forget.

The studio door clicks shut behind them. I press my back to its cool surface and try to create my own jigsaw puzzle, made of logic rather than cardboard pieces. Ben knew the risks. He planned this. He'd held out his hand and offered it to Death. This was in no way like what happened to Clay.

I count backwards. Ten. Nine. Nine and a half. Eight. All the way to zero.

Ben was wrong, none of us has a voice. Least of all me.

I'm alone when the Law Keepers come for me, scrubbing the invisible stain from the radio station's floor. We ride in their car, the one with the triple ones painted on the trunk. Each front door panel wears City One's logo: a black question mark in a black circle, a scarlet slash bisecting the punctuation. Lest we forget.

I keep my head up. I am not a criminal. It wasn't me who

asked that question. And yet they left me no time to wipe the cold sweat from my skin, just bundled me into the car's back seat. *Debriefing* they call what's going to happen next. That means they'll ask questions and I'll answer, all the time feeling like my pants are pooling around my ankles, while a too-cool breeze bites my bare skin.

The Law Keep isn't far. Oh, there's about a half mile of rocky roads between the studio and one of the few new things we've built here. Everything else is crumbling. The streets are pocked and pitted, as though a plague has scarred their once-black faces. The Law Keep rises above all else, a cylinder crafted from stone and steel and glass. The same logo is etched into the revolving door that leads from the street, away from the people, and to my Questioner. It is he—or she—who'll throw me on the grill, ask me the questions that need asking. It's a privilege tied to law and medicine, though it's restricted to on-duty hours. Off the clock, they suffer the same fate as regular citizens if they slip.

Behind the reception desk is a map of the world with seven white seas, red continents, and on a small edge of what used to be North America, a single green island. This poster is omnipresent in government buildings. It serves to remind us that this is all we have left, and for that we should be grateful and not question what we do not have.

They take me to a small room with curved windows. From here, thirty-six degrees of the city are visible, although I do not look. Instead, I take the seat appointed to me on one side of a table the color of grubby snow.

The Questioner does not make me wait; I thought he would. He strolls in like this is Sunday and we're in a park. Without speaking, he stands at the window, compiles his questions. At no time does he look at me. To him I am just another panel of glass.

"They call me Okham," he says when he's gathered his

thoughts or perhaps when he thinks I've waited a sufficiently uncomfortable amount of time. They've sent no underling to speak with me; I know of Okham, he sits too comfortably on top of the heap. His posture is steel. His hair is salt and pepper, bitter and burn.

"Emma Frane."

"I know who you are. Were you previously aware that Mr. Stone would use your show to exercise his illegal views?"

My ponytail moves with my head as I shake it. "No."

"I don't believe you."

"That doesn't change my answer."

"Are you confident of your ignorance?" He doesn't wait for my reply, delivers his next probe. "Do you know why it's illegal to ask questions in City One?"

"Questions lead to disease and death. Our laws keep us safe."

He glances at me now, to gauge if my reply has a honed, sarcastic edge. He cannot tell; I am still wearing my Emma Fran mask.

"Did you know the Breaker before today?"

Breaker. The name we use for those who escape City One by suicide or covert means. It's meant as a slur to most. To a precious handful, it's a dream.

"He's been on my show before."

"Without incident?"

"Without incident."

He turns another corner in his interrogation. "Have you ever asked a question?"

"Not for seven years."

"Not even a small one?"

There are no small questions—not here. "I wouldn't be here if I had. I'd be dead—like Ben."

"But you're a . . . talk show host, are you not?" He speaks the words through a sour mouth, with lips dragged low by constant disapproval.

"I don't ask questions, I look for answers they want to give. It's not the same thing."

"Are you splitting hairs, Mrs. Frane?"

Without meaning to, I pause. "No."

"Do you want to know what's out there now, beyond the wall?" He doesn't look like he cares that I have no answer. "Sickness and death. Sickness and death and the monsters who resulted from the former."

He looks at me now in full and I shiver as he flicks frost in my face with the coldest gaze I have ever known.

"There will be others," he says, "who would use your program as a forum."

"Today will be a deterrent."

"You are a happy fool if you believe that. Some people seek only to make their perverted point, and they care nothing for consequences. For the hearts they break. For the havoc they wreck. For them, the public display is the entire point, because for one moment they are heard, and that makes them somebody. I cannot allow that to happen. I will not ask you if you understand. You're an intelligent woman. I see things going on behind your eyes. I will be watching you, Mrs. Frane."

Then you'll be bored, I want to say.

"You are wondering, no doubt, why we did not intercept the feed. The answer is that you're right: I hope it will be a deterrent for other dissidents. I do not believe it, but I hope. The function of the Law Keeper is to maintain the law. It's possible Mr. Stone believed his status as a celebrity would protect him. You of all people should know we do not discriminate. You're only twenty-eight. Too, too young to be a widow."

I would kill him where he stands, but my hands shake from

his truthful stab. I know. Oh yes, I do know how unforgiving the law is, how none of us is safe. With that one observation, he has unwrapped my grief and laid it bare to bleed anew.

"Are you . . . well, Ms. Frane?" An unkind emphasis on the Ms.

A nod. Well, but never fine.

"Are you? Good."

A alarm squeals from the timepiece on his wrist. He lifts it for inspection then lets it fall as though it has disappointed him—a disobedient child.

"It appears as though I can no longer question you."

He does not dismiss me. Instead, he exits the room so brusquely I wonder if he fears the room might leave him first should he linger too long, leaving him powerless.

Then I'm home free—as free can be in City One.

City One is a place of low-slung houses that have never known personal space. Many of the great diseases in history were born as a result of cramped living spaces, bodies bunched together like overripe fruit. And between them animals crept and cuddled and transmitted. Fresh air in ample doses discourages sickness and gives plague no comfortable foothold on which to climb man's ladder. So why this place was chosen will never make sense to me.

We do what we can with the land we've taken. What tiny lawns some have use the space were given and no more; roses do not ramble; vine does not creep along unwelcoming surfaces; everything has a place and in its place it stays unless invited to do otherwise.

We live like caretakers, borrowing land and time.

We'll take you home, the Law Keepers said when my interview was complete. *We insist.* But I told them I had other plans, so we do not take the arterial road toward the east, but the venal that lies to the west. Now their automobile rolls along stretch-marked streets, past silent houses in random formation.

My parents are waiting on their porch. The house is not sumptuous; my memories cling to the walls, to the carpet, to the rich, gleaming wood furniture of the home they used to own, to the place where my parents belong. Like most of the families who took the offered hand and gave up their fortunes for guaranteed safety, their possessions lie abandoned, collecting dust in a long, lost continent. But not all their luxuries were left behind: I have known all my life the silver knives my mother uses to cut paper thin slivers of meat from the bone. So that, at least, is still the same.

"Hello, hello, we are fine." The words come from my mother's mouth, but she speaks for them both. She is a good woman and she glows with it, although my lens is well-biased. My prejudice is equal for my father, a man with dancing lights in his hazelnut eyes. Together, they are joy.

My smile is genuine, as is the warmth we exchange as we clasp hands. "I'm fine, too."

Dad wastes no time. "Bad business on your show today."

"For shame," my mother says.

"It's fine," I say, though it's nothing like it.

We pass pleasantries like a child's ball between us, until the dinner table separates us into our respective corners. Then the same old conversation rewinds and plays anew.

"Your father and I, we think it's time you married again—"

"No."

"—while you are still young. You could have another family."

Fork tines scrape across my salad until the limp leaves tear. The resulting screech kills the conversation, and I am glad for once to live in a world where they cannot poke me and prod me with crooked sentences.

Logically I know my bones cannot rattle, that it's a nerves making the napkin rub my lips until they sting, but I feel as though I being shaken from my skeleton out.

"People aren't replacement parts." My voice crackles. "We can't slide new ones into old places when they go."

Metal touches china. "I know," my mother says. "I've lost people, too. And a son. But here I am."

I don't bite back. I know her brand of pain, and how much effort it takes to draw each next breath.

"Not today," my father says the words kindly. "Not after the incident."

So polite. A man's death reduced to happenstance with such casual affect: Oh look, a cloud is coming; the coffee's ready; the paint is dry; a man is dead.

My mother admits defeat—for now. The meal resumes and I try not to notice the three empty chairs or the silence that makes us a family divided.

Afterward, we squeeze hands, the turbulence for all appearances forgotten. But we know. It's a new splinter jutting from the family tree, and from it our frayed emotions hang like entrails. Would that I could stir them with a stick, divine the future, and see that all will be well.

"Stay safe," I say.

"Stay safe," they echo.

My heels strike hollow on the gray concrete ribbon that splits in two at their gate and races into the night in opposing directions. I turn at the newel to wave. They are there, heads bowed toward each other, but not touching. Together, but apart.

Theirs is a quiet affection. It chokes me with its simplicity.

I kick my shoes off first. Hang my dress on the floor. It's a blue gash on terracotta tile. I leave it there just long enough to feel the familiar pull of guilt; citizens of City One don't leave messes. Mess leads to filth. Filth leads to rats. Rats lead to cats, which lead to disease. And if there's one thing we don't have in this new, perfect world, it's tolerance for sickness.

Civic duties are not for the shirking.

Shoes lined up like soldiers. Dresses shapeless on wood shoulders. Everything in its place. And me in my robe, now: white cotton that wraps around me a time and half. It's too large for my small frame by far, but something about its generous expanse soothes me. Inside the smooth fabric, I can breathe deep and true. Unfettered. Now there's a word that strolls right off my tongue and dives into the evening air. I feel emancipated in this light, loose garment.

But when I turn, the world drops its weight on my shoulders once more.

To get to the dirty laundry basket I must pass by *that* door.

The tile smudges beneath my bare feet and I feel a flicker of anger at myself. It does not matter that they almost immediately fade; I know if I turn quickly, I will see my footsteps evaporating and I will have to acknowledge the door with its battered knob.

I do it. I turn. I cannot stop myself. And there are my steps framed in moisture. My attention slides toward the door and the black gap beneath. Thank small mercies it is night and the sun is nowhere in sight. For when light pours through that crack, it taunts me. *See*, it says. *All is well here. Come inside. Mara is here.* Some days temptation slams me. I reach for that knob, but I always look down before I twist. And there I see me as the camera and mirror never do—the real me, my head warped and large, bulging with the questions that fill it.

I believe there is a point where I will pop like a too-full balloon.

But tonight there is no light to tempt me. I stand and watch my steps fade, and then it is as if I never was outside that door, outside that room. I can turn on one heel and continue my journey to the laundry room, unimpeded by the past.

Into the basket, my undergarments fall. They are quite alone there, and I suppose we have that in common, for I am alone here in this house, the one I've lived in since before I traded Marshall for Frane, before I became *the* Emma Frane everyone in City One thinks they know. I could move to a different, better home. But then I fear I would not know if I was her or simply me.

I walk through the rest of my rooms: The kitchen with its bold tile counters and walls so bright they constantly clash with themselves. The bathroom. The dining room with its high-backed chairs and antique sideboard, salvaged from before. The living room, appropriately named because this is where I live when I'm home. On clear days, the sun tumbles through the windows for a chance to lie in this room. There it sprawls for all the morning, an oozing yolk on lightly-toasted bread.

All the ingredients for a safe life, yet I move about this nest of my own making in relative unease. I am alone, and still I cannot ask questions here.

But soon I will, and this false city will fall.

If you're listening, Ben Stone, that's what I can do for my people.